LOVE UNDERCOVER

LOVE UNDERCOVER

•

Jean C. Gordon

AVALON BOOKS
NEW YORK

PRINTED IN THE UNITED STATES OF AMERICA
ON ACID-FREE PAPER
BY HADDON CRAFTSMEN, BLOOMSBURG, PENNSYLVANIA

Many thanks to my critique partners,
Elaine Stock and Janice Simmons, and to my toughest critic
of all, my daughter Carrie Jean Gordon-Stacey,
who never hesitates to point out when something
sounds cheesy.

Chapter One

"Do I have a man for you."

Tina Cannon turned away from the spreadsheet on her computer screen.

"Not you, too, Uncle Jack," she said to the distinguished-looking man standing in the doorway of her office. "I thought Dad had already fixed me up with every eligible bachelor in the three-county area."

Jack chuckled. "The man I have in mind is a new client, Devon O'Neil. I think it's about time you started building your own client base."

About time? Beyond time in Tina's view. She'd spent the three months since she'd finished her Certified Financial Consultant course work at Uncle Jack's financial planning practice crunching num-

1

bers and researching investments for Jack's clients. Not exactly what she'd had in mind when she'd given up her part-time law practice in Albany to move back to Genesee.

"So, tell me about this Devon O'Neil."

A sly smile spread across Jack's tanned face. "Why don't you find out for yourself. He'll be here in a half hour for a consultation."

Late afternoon sunlight filtered through the etched glass window in the carved oak door, its prism of color reflected back by the chrome and steel décor of the reception area. Tina scanned the room. Whatever had possessed Uncle Jack to choose such stark furnishings? They were totally out of place in the rambling old Victorian house he had renovated into offices.

She settled into the receptionist's comfortable Aeron chair, opened a file folder, and leafed through the financial statements she had printed. Oh well, Jack's clients didn't seem to be put off by his lack of decorating acumen. Over the past year, he had almost doubled his clientele.

The sharp click of the doorknob turning caused her to straighten in her seat. She closed the folder and placed it on the gleaming glass-topped desk. The door opened and a casually dressed man walked in. He hesitated for a second, taking in the room, the sun glinting off his blue-black hair. Then, his mouth spread in a half-smile, softening the sharp slash of his cheek bones.

Tina stifled a laugh—so she wasn't the only one amused by Jack's decorating taste.

The man crossed the space from the door to the desk in three long strides. "Devon O'Neil, here to see Tina Cannon."

"Mr. O'Neil." Tina stood and offered her hand, receiving a firm shake in return. "I've been expecting you."

"Ms. Cannon?" He pursed his lips, as his gaze moved from her long honey-blond hair to the siren red nail polish adorning the hand she proffered in welcome. He shook her hand firmly. "I'm sorry, I thought you were the receptionist."

Tina winced, thinking of Crystal, the current receptionist, and the parade of other inexperienced community college students Jack had hired for—and fired from—the front office in the past three months. If only he'd given her more notice of this meeting with Devon O'Neil, she would have removed the gaudy polish her five-year-old daughter Amy had applied to her nails last night, worn her hair up, and dressed in something more formal than a cotton cardigan twin set and drawstring cargo pants. She pushed a strand of hair behind her ear. Too late to worry about appearances now.

She curved her lips into a smile. "You made a reasonable assumption, since I was sitting out here in the reception area."

"Ah, but I try not to make assumptions. I know appearances can be deceiving," he said, favoring her with a broad smile that brought a sparkle to his deep blue eyes. "For instance, what do you think I do for a living?"

Tina crossed her arms and rubbed her chin. He looked about her age, late twenties or early thirties. From his dress—a generic polo shirt and faded jeans—and his demeanor, she ruled out his being one of the frenetic young executives Uncle Jack catered his practice to.

"You're not from around here," she mused. "I'd recognize you if we'd gone to school together." She recalled the note of quiet authority in his deep, almost melodic voice. "That's it. You're a teacher, one of the instructors at the community college."

He grinned.

"Am I right?"

"Not by a long shot. I'm an unemployed millionaire."

Tina looked him over. "Seriously?"

"Seriously. And I'd like to stay one, which is why I'm here. A friend of mine from Rochester recommended Jack Kendall as the best financial planner in the area."

A tide of disappointment rushed through her. Devon's friend had recommended Jack Kendall, not

Kendall & Associates. Had she misunderstood Jack when he'd said it was time for her to start building her own client base, or had Devon misunderstood?

"If you'd rather work with Jack, I'm sure we can arrange something." Tina picked up the folder with the financial statements and joined Devon in front of the desk. "Since you're here, I can take down your preliminary information and you can contact Jack for a follow up appointment. My office is right down the hall."

As they walked side by side down the short hallway to her office, she noted with surprise that he was only a couple of inches taller than she—maybe five-eleven, six-feet, tops. He'd appeared taller.

"Make yourself comfortable." Tina motioned Devon to an overstuffed sofa and two matching chairs upholstered in a tapestry of muted reds and greens. The sofa and chairs circled an ornately carved coffee table. "Would you like coffee? A cold drink? I have iced tea."

"No, thanks, I'm fine." Devon chose one of the side chairs. He leaned forward slightly, his fingers curled around the polished wood of the chair's armrests.

Tina turned away to file a folder in her desk drawer. Devon watched her movements closely, wondering what was in the folder that she had hurried to put away, and trying to figure out her angle. He'd caught the flicker of disappointment in her eyes when he'd inferred his preference for working with Jack. What were she and Jack up to? Devon had checked, and Jack didn't have many other clients with the amount of money he'd said he had. Why would he pawn him off on his junior partner?

"We have a standard short questionnaire we like to have prospective clients complete." She sat in the matching chair, questionnaire in hand. "It's a simple form, but I'd like to go over it with you so we can get to know each other better before you decide to use our services."

She looked up from the papers. "Unless you'd prefer to take it home and have me—or Jack—go over it with you later."

Devon caught and held her gaze for a couple of seconds. Tina Cannon was completely transparent. Regardless of her neutral words, she obviously wanted him as her client. Or she was a very good actress, playing on his sympathy, so he'd choose to work with her rather than Jack. He ran his hand through his hair. What purpose would it serve Jack to have Tina in charge of his account?

"Mr. O'Neil?"

"Hmmm?" Devon shifted in his seat. Clearly she'd asked him a question.

"Would you like to complete the questionnaire now or take it with you?" she repeated.

"Now . . . now is fine."

Tina wrote down his general information: name, address, phone number. "Social security number?"

"Zero seven six—" Devon stopped himself. His social security number could give them too much information on him. He gave her what he hoped was a sheepish grin. "Can you believe I've forgotten it."

Skepticism clouded her expression. "No problem." She tapped the pen on the form. "Occupation? You said you're an unemployed millionaire. I'm intrigued."

I'll bet you are, Devon thought. *Especially about the millionaire part.* "I won the New York State Lotto. After taxes, my share is just over a million dollars."

"Congratulations!"

Devon weighed whether the gleam in her eyes came from sincere pleasure in his good fortune or greedy delight at the prospect of getting hold of a million dollars. Darn—he should have done his homework better. Jack Kendall was a known entity; Tina Cannon wasn't.

He nodded. "Thanks."

"Now, back to the unemployed part. You quit your job after you won?"

"Technically, I'm on a leave of absence. I'm a model maker. When I gave my boss my resignation, he wouldn't take it. He said I'd be back within six months, either to escape the boredom of not working—my boss has a high opinion of his operation—

or because I'd run through all the money. Proving him wrong on the second point is one of the reasons I'm here."

Tina scratched something on the form. "A model maker? You make models of what . . . buildings?"

"Nah, nothing that interesting. I made models of machine parts."

"And you don't plan to go back?"

"You tell me. Can you manage my money so I don't have to go back to the nine-to-five—or, in my case, seven-to-three—grind?" Devon waited for Tina to echo the boasts Jack had given him over the phone of how he'd doubled and tripled his clients' money.

She gave him an indulgent smile that accented her fine-boned classic features. "It's not quite that simple. If you decide to use our services, we'll need to get an overall picture of your financial situation and talk about your short- and long-term goals, and where you want to be in twenty years."

"Relaxing on a Caribbean beach without a care in the world," he quipped.

Tina laughed, a playful glint lighting her eyes. "It's tough work, but I suppose someone has to do it. Seriously, though, you'll need to think about your goals."

"I *am* serious." Devon leaned further forward and lowered his voice. "Can't you get me in on the bottom floor of one of those explosive deals that will double my money in six months?" He kept his eyes focused on hers.

The glint returned to Tina's eyes. Ah ha, now he was getting somewhere.

"Sorry," she said with forced levity. "To borrow a phrase, 'I make money the old fashioned way; I earn it'."

Devon waited for her to continue. Why didn't she just say what he wanted to hear and strike an agreement? Was this a ploy to gain his confidence?

"Maybe you have the wrong idea about our services, and what we can do for you."

But Devon knew what they could do for him, what Jack had done for his grandmother.

Tina shifted through the papers on the table and pulled out a glossy brochure. "This explains our practice, the services we offer and our philosophy on investment management. Would you like me to go over it with you?"

"Sure, why not." He leaned back in his seat. Even though he had a pretty good idea of what their investment philosophy was, Devon had to admit he enjoyed watching the animation with which Tina talked about her work.

Her cheeks flushed a soft pink that complemented her ivory complexion and the honey highlights in her hair. Her controlled gestures quickened. If he wasn't careful, her enthusiasm just might convince him.

Tina wrapped up her presentation. "Any questions?"

"Not now. I'll take the brochure and get back to you in a few days."

"That would be great. Take my card, too. And you might want to talk with some other planners before you make a decision. Compare our services."

"Yeah, sure." Devon stood and took the brochure and card from Tina. He was surprised at her confidence, that she'd suggest he talk to anyone else. Maybe she and Jack had agreed on a soft-sell approach. That it made sense. From what they knew, he was an ordinary Joe who'd probably respond better to a warm approach, rather than a pressured one. Most likely that's why Jack had Tina represent the firm.

No doubt about it, she was a beautiful woman. What red-blooded American male wouldn't enjoy spending time with her? Jack had taken a calculated risk that Devon wouldn't mind a woman telling him what to do with his money.

Tina walked Devon to the door. "Thanks for coming. I look forward to hearing from you."

"Yep, I have your card." He patted his shirt pocket. "Goodbye."

She watched him walk down the path to his sports utility vehicle before returning to her office.

So *that* was the man Uncle Jack had in mind for her. Tina pulled out a new file folder and wrote

Devon O'Neil across the tab in bold black marker. If she were in the market for a relationship, he certainly had a few features in his favor—those blue-black curls, a ready grin, and a sense of humor.

But her tastes ran more toward the brooding intellectual type. And Devon O'Neil was a potential client—albeit a rather confusing one—not a potential date. She put the file in the drawer and firmly closed it.

Devon pulled into the driveway of his grandmother's lakeside house—his house now. He parked by the back door, rather than in the small barn that had been converted into a garage, and took the stairs into the kitchen two at a time. Grabbing the telephone receiver, he punched in the numbers, tapping his foot on the old speckled linoleum while it rang.

His gaze traveled to the account statement on the kitchen table. His grandmother's last statement from Kendall & Associates had reported losses in investments he couldn't find listed on any major U.S. exchange, and transaction fees far higher than the account's monthly earnings.

The phone rang a fourth and fifth time. *Come on, pick up,* he urged silently.

"Hello."

"Cam, it's me."

"Devon! I wondered when you'd be calling."

"When, not if?"

"When, definitely."

"So, you're okay with what we talked about?"

"Yes, I'll front you the money. You gave me my son back, it's the least I could do."

"I'll put up the house as collateral." The thought of being beholden to anyone, even someone who owed him, like Cam, didn't sit well with Devon. "You wouldn't believe what this old place is worth, the way people from the city are buying up the old farms around the lake to subdivide and build summer homes."

"Mm-hmmm."

"Yeah, I guess you would believe it, real estate mogul that you are."

His benefactor chuckled at the other end of the line. "Well, if you're ever in the market to sell . . ."

Devon tightened his grip on the phone. "I just might be. Once this is over, I'm outta here for good."

Uncle Jack stuck his head in her office. "What did you think of Devon?"

"Interesting man. He won the lottery, you know."

Jack nodded. "He told me on the phone."

Tina cleared her throat. "I'm not certain I sold him on Kendall & Associates."

Jack frowned.

"He seemed to be looking for some quick and

easy way to make big bucks." She finished in a rush. "And, he may prefer to work with you."

Her uncle smiled knowingly. "I think he'll come around."

Chapter Two

Tina checked her watch. Four forty-five. Another day had passed without Devon O'Neil calling. After Uncle Jack's pep talk, she'd been convinced he would. She'd better get going. Amy's Daisies meeting would be over at five, and she needed to swing by school to pick her up. And, of course, Dad would have dinner on the table promptly at five-thirty.

Funny how some things never changed. Mom had always had dinner promptly at five-thirty, and she could remember Dad stopping by school on his way home from the post office to pick her up from scouts, sports, or band practice. That consistency was one of the reasons she'd left Albany and brought Amy to Genesee.

Her computer flashed its shutdown notice and

14

snapped off. She opened the desk drawer, grabbed her bag, and stood—face-to-face with Devon O'Neil. Tina took a sharp breath. "Devon!"

"Hi." He leaned his hip against the desk, effectively blocking her. "No one was out front, so I thought it would be okay to come back."

Tina shook her head in disgust. *Crystal was out again. Who knew what her excuse was today?* Uncle Jack claimed he just couldn't get better help, but this wasn't professional, and it wasn't the image they should be projecting to clients. Tina and her law partner in Albany hadn't had any problem finding reliable front office staff. Maybe she should hire someone this week while Jack was out of town at the Certified Financial Advisor national conference.

"It's not okay?"

"No, I mean, yes." Great, now he had her tongue-tied. "It's fine," she reassured him. "You just startled me."

"I was going to call you tomorrow, but I had to come by this way. I figured you'd be here since Jack is out of town, but when I didn't see your Lexus parked outside, I thought I'd missed you."

"The weather's so nice today, I walked." She hiked her bag up on her shoulder. *How does he know Jack is out of town and I drive a Lexus?* Tina measured the distance between her, Devon, and the door.

"I am on my way out." She took a step toward him. "I have to be at the elementary school by five to pick up my daughter."

Devon pushed off the desk. "I'll walk along with you. We can talk about my finances."

He grinned, deepening the creases bracketing his mouth.

Tina's heart leapt. So, he was going to hire her after all. Discussing the details while they walked through town wasn't exactly her style, though. "I'll be in the office all day tomorrow, why don't we set an appointment?"

"I don't mind walking with you."

"What about your truck?" she asked, trying another tact to put him off. "You'll have to walk back and pick it up."

"I have the time. I have all the time in the world."

That grin again. How could she resist?

He opened the front door. "After you."

They walked down the slate steps and out to the front sidewalk. This part of Main Street was all Victorian houses, some of which had been converted to offices, as Uncle Jack's had. Others were apartments or one-family homes. Genesee's storefront businesses were at the other end of Main, on Market Street.

Tina lifted a stray hair and patted it back into her chignon. The day was still unusually warm for late

September, and the citizens of Genesee seemed to be taking advantage of the nice weather en masse.

"We'll want to cross the street at the corner," she told Devon. "The elementary school is on Prospect Street."

"I know."

So Devon had familiarized himself with the village. A pleasant warmth settled inside her, matching the warmth outside. "I see you've done your homework, checked out the local landmarks."

"No."

Tina started at his crisp tone.

"When I was a kid, I used to ride my bike into town to shoot hoops at the school."

His answer confused her. If Devon O'Neil was from Genesee, why didn't she remember him from school? Devon didn't strike her as being from a private school background. Besides, most of the kids from Genesee who attended private schools in Rochester had gone to elementary school in town, and they belonged to local church or scout or sports groups. If she didn't know them personally, she knew of them.

"I thought you had moved here recently, after you won the lottery."

"Ah, didn't I tell you assumptions could be dangerous?"

"Yes, you did." She slowed her steps to cross the street and waited for him to elaborate.

"Tina!" A petite woman loading plastic produce crates into a dilapidated pickup truck shouted to her.

"Kate!" Tina called back. She checked traffic and hurried across the street, Devon following. The women hugged. "You must be keeping yourself busy down on the farm. We haven't gotten together in ages."

Kate stepped out of Tina's embrace and gave Devon a quick once-over. "Aha! Looks like your father is back at it. And, he's done a good job— this one could be a keeper."

Devon lifted an eyebrow.

"No, not this time." Tina laughed. "Kate Bauer, this is Devon O'Neil, a new client."

Or, at least I think he is. He hadn't really said that, though. He'd just mentioned talking about his finances while they walked. Which they hadn't.

"Kate is a long-time friend," Tina explained to Devon. "She has an organic fruit and vegetable farm a couple miles outside of town. Best produce in the area."

"Nice to meet you." Devon picked up the remaining crate and loaded it in the back of Kate's truck.

Kate thanked him, which evoked a smile that changed his face from merely attractive to devastatingly handsome. She shook her head at Tina. "You might want to reconsider. Like I said, this one could be a keeper."

A twinge of irritation pricked Tina. Kate didn't even know Devon. "Were you making a delivery to Mrs. Mann?" she asked.

"Yeah, I had some fall peas and broccoli I knew she'd like."

"How is she?"

"Madder than a wet hen that her rheumatism acted up this spring and she wasn't able to get a garden of her own in this year."

"That sounds about—"

Devon interrupted. "Mann? Are you talking about Evie Mann?"

Tina looked at Kate and they both shrugged. How did Devon know Mrs. Mann, their second grade teacher? He was turning out to be a man of many surprises.

In answer to their unspoken question, Devon said, "She was a good friend of my grandmother's. They taught together at the elementary school."

A grandmother who lived in Genesee. So that was the connection, how he knew so much about his new hometown.

"Who is your grandmother?" Kate beat Tina to the question. "Maybe we had her in school, too."

"My grandmother *was* Rose Sullivan. She taught—"

"Kindergarten," Tina and Kate chimed in unison.

"For years," he finished, softly.

"She was a really nice lady," Tina consoled him.

"I was so sorry when Dad told me she had died. He said everyone in town attended the services. But then, you'd know that."

His eyes glistened ever so slightly and his voice sounded strained. "No, I missed the services. I had to work."

No wonder Devon wanted to retire on his lottery winnings, if he worked in an industry where he couldn't even get time off for his grandmother's funeral.

"I'd like to meet Mrs. Mann sometime."

"I'll be making another delivery to her on Saturday. Want to come along?" Kate asked.

"Sure. Sounds good," Devon answered.

"It's a date, then."

A shot of resentment and competitiveness pierced Tina, reminiscent of seventh grade when Tina had had a violent crush on a classmate and Kate, her best friend, had accepted an invitation to go to a school football game with him. They hadn't spoken for weeks afterwards. But this wasn't seventh grade, and she most certainly didn't have a crush on Devon O'Neil. He was a client, a prospective client.

Kate reached for the door handle of her truck. "I've got to get going. Nice meeting you, Devon. Good to see you Tina. You and Amy should come out to the farm again and see how big the lambs have grown."

"Oh, my gosh, I forgot Amy. I'm supposed to be

at school to pick her up. Kate, I'll call you tomorrow." She glanced from Kate to Devon. They did make a cute couple, with his dark good looks contrasting with her auburn fairness. Why did it bother her? She didn't have the time to sort it out.

"Devon, are you coming?" She started up the walk without him, but he quickly caught up with her.

"So what happens if you get to the school a minute or two late? Does your daughter turn into a pumpkin?"

From his light tone, Tina knew he was teasing, probably trying to put her at ease about being late. But it irritated her just the same. She'd always tried to balance work and motherhood, with the scales weighted toward motherhood. It bothered her whenever she wasn't able to keep it all in place.

"The Daisies meeting will be over, and Amy is expecting me to be there." She hurried across the school parking lot, thankful she'd put sneakers on for the walk over.

Devon reached the door first and pulled it open. A miniature version of Tina peeked around the doorway of one of the rooms up the hall. The little girl's face broke into a wide smile that lit up her dark-fringed brown eyes. She raced up the corridor. So this was Amy.

"Amy!" a stern voice called from the room.

Amy didn't slow her pace a bit. "Mommy!" She grabbed Tina's hand. "We had the bestest meeting. We made birdfeeders. Papa can help me hang mine in the tree by my bedroom window and I can watch the birds." The words poured out. "And I could get a book with pictures of birds and know all the kinds."

"Sounds great, honey." Tina's gaze darted to the woman following Amy.

Amy spun around. "See, Mrs. Wells. Mommy didn't forget me."

She turned back to Tina. "Mrs. Wells had me call you at work because she thought you might have forgot today was Daisies. When you didn't answer, I told her you were coming; something 'portant must have made you late." Amy studied Devon with a quizzical gaze. "Is he the something 'portant?"

Devon could feel Tina's embarrassment, although the only outward sign was a slight stiffening in her posture.

"Ms. Cannon." The title came out awkward on the woman's lips. "We have a field trip next week, and Amy didn't have her signed permission slip with her today."

"Mrs. Wells," Tina said, "I apologize for—"

"Mommy, can I go get my bird feeder?" Amy interrupted.

Tina gave her a stern look.

"Sorry. But can I?" Amy begged, bouncing up and down, shaking Tina's hand in the process.

"All right." Tina nodded.

"But I need help with my backpack." Amy pointed to Devon. "Can he help?"

Indecision crossed Tina's face. *Okay, what could he do to Amy in the two minutes it should take to collect her things from the classroom?*

"Sure." She relented. "Go ahead. I want to talk with Mrs. Wells a minute."

Amy dropped her mother's hand and grabbed Devon's. "Come on." She tugged his hand. "What's your name? I'm Amy."

He didn't associate with kids much. Should he tell her Devon or Mr. O'Neil? Mr. O'Neil was too formal. "Devon."

"Are you Mommy's new friend?"

So, Mommy had *friends*.

Amy chattered on. "Our friend Brett, who lived next door before we moved in with Papa, had a little boy, Jake, who's five, just like me. Me and Mommy used to babysit him on the days Mommy wasn't being a lawyer in Albany. Mommy didn't used to work every day. But now that I'm big and in school, she does 'cause Uncle Jack needs her."

Devon couldn't help smiling at the little magpie, who was clearly echoing her mother's words.

"I don't think Mommy liked being a lawyer. She

used to get 'pressed about her cases. Everybody was always fighting with each other."

"I see." Amy was pretty perceptive for a little kid.

"Then the bank wouldn't give Mommy the money to buy our house, so we decided to move here."

So Tina had had money problems. That piece of information could be useful.

"Brett's married to Molly now, you know. Next summer they're all going to come and spend their vacation at the lake, so I can see Jake every day. Papa, my grandpa, is gonna take me."

"Is that right?" This Brett obviously wasn't that kind of friend—now, at least.

"In here," Amy directed.

Devon followed her into the classroom.

She picked up a suet bird feeder from the teacher's desk. "I made this. Isn't it cool?"

"Very cool," he answered.

"And that's my backpack." She pointed to a little blue pack next to the desk. "Can you carry it for me, please?"

"No problem." He picked the pack up.

"It's a Blue's Clues pack, you know. That's one of my favorite TV shows."

No, Devon didn't know. Were all small children so talkative?

Amy skipped out of the room ahead of him. Tina was alone in the hall, headed their way.

"Mommy, did Mrs. Wells go home? She has choir practice tonight, and has to get home to fix dinner," Amy said with the all-knowing authority of a five-year-old.

Tina winced. "We'd better get going, too. Papa will be looking for us." She reached for the backpack Devon held.

He handed it to her, their fingers touching for a moment before he shoved his hands in his pockets.

Tina squatted down to help Amy put the backpack on. The little girl held the bird feeder carefully in one hand, then the other, while her mother slipped the straps over her shoulders.

Devon studied the two blond heads bent together in concentration—one a mass of riotous curls held back with butterfly hair clips, the other pulled back neatly into a roll. He liked Tina's hair better the way she had worn it the first time they met, long and loose.

"There you go honey." She adjusted the straps and lifted her gaze from Amy to Devon. "We never did talk. Can we get together tomorrow, at the office?"

"Yeah, sure. I'll come by about nine-thirty, if that's okay."

"Can we make it in the afternoon? I'm volunteering at the school bookfair tomorrow morning." She stood and looked at him expectantly.

"Fine with me." It wasn't like he had anything

else to do. Getting to know Tina and her uncle was his number-one priority. "How's two?"

"Two o'clock is good."

He walked with Tina and Amy to the front sidewalk.

"I'll see you tomorrow, then," Tina said.

"Right." He nodded goodbye.

"Bye, Devon." Amy's singsong voice rang out, as he turned to walk back to his truck. "Thanks for carrying my pack for me."

"Any time." He reached down to ruffle her curls, then pulled away, not knowing if Tina would approve. What the hey; he ruffled her hair anyway. He liked the kid.

Devon left them and strode up the sidewalk toward Main Street. He slowed his pace and turned down a side street—one he had often used to bike from his grandmother's house to the school.

The Main Street business district had changed and grown a lot since the last summer he spent with his grandmother. But barring the encroachment of businesses like Kendall & Associates on upper Main Street, Genesee's residential areas had remained pretty much the same over the years.

Clapboard and shingled houses of varying ages, from turn-of-the-century to post-World War II, sat in neat rows shaded by the maple trees lining the streets. There had been new construction on the edge of town, but these streets were the essence of

Genesee, the kind of place he'd wanted to live as a child, rather than the series of small walk-up apartments he and his mother had shared in Rochester.

He understood now that she'd done the best she could on her waitress earnings, but he'd envied the kids with mothers who came on school field trips and to holiday parties. Mothers like Tina, who could take off work to help at school library sales without losing a day's wages.

Against his better judgment, he was starting to like Tina. She obviously put a high importance on parenting, and seemed genuinely concerned about Mrs. Mann. He kicked a stone out of his way. So she liked kids and old people; she probably liked dogs, too, but that didn't make her an honest person. Amy, on the other hand, was innocent and open. Getting closer to her through Tina could prove useful.

The sun moved behind a cloud and a chilly wind came up. Taking advantage of a child wasn't his style, but Jack had had no qualms about taking advantage of his grandmother.

Chapter Three

Nostalgia gripped Tina. She couldn't even begin to count the number of times she had walked the same route home from school. At one time, she had known everyone on the block. She still knew most of them, except for the few younger families that had moved in since she left for college twelve years ago. At eighteen, Genesee had seemed like a place to escape from; now, it was a good place to come home to.

When their house came into view, Amy pulled her hand from Tina's and skipped ahead. The Cape Cod style house stood at the end of the street on a double lot. The pumpkin hue wasn't a shade that Tina would have chosen herself, but the house had

28

been that color for as long as she could remember
and it meant home to her.

Amy flung open the aluminum screen door to the
breezeway and let it slam behind her. Tina opened
and closed it more carefully. She could already hear
Amy chattering to Dad. The rich aroma of roasting
meat enveloped her when she opened the wooden
door to the kitchen.

"Hi, Dad."

Kurt Kovsky stood by the stove admiring Amy's
birdfeeder, punctuating his words with gestures.
Tina was pleased to see him so animated, looking
more himself. Her mother's unexpected death last
year had hit him hard, making him appear older than
his sixty-two years.

He smiled a welcome. "Hi, honey. How was your
day?"

"Interesting."

"Good interesting or bad interesting?"

Tina thought for a moment. "Oh, good, I guess."

"Well, you can tell me about it over dinner." Kurt
took the roast from the oven, placed it on a platter,
and carried it to the kitchen table. "It's ready if you
are."

"Come on Amy." Tina put her hand on her
daughter's shoulder. "Let's put your birdfeeder on
the counter by the door and get washed up."

"Okay, Mommy." Amy handed the feeder to her

reluctantly. "Papa and me are gonna hang it up as soon as I finish my dinner."

"I don't know, sweetie. Did Papa say that? Today is Wednesday. Remember he has bowling league on Wednesday, the same day you have Daisies."

Tina glanced at her father for a confirmation. Dad didn't get out enough as it was—she didn't want him missing his one regular social outing for something he and Amy could do just as well tomorrow.

"Don't worry. I'm not skipping out on bowling." He winked at Amy. "Amy is such a good helper. I figure we'll have plenty of time to put up her bird-feeder before I have to go. That is, if I can get you two to sit down to dinner."

They washed their hands and returned to the table.

"Papa," Amy said, starting the dinner conversation, as usual, "Mommy has a new friend."

"Is that right?"

"Yep, his name is Devon, and he's very strong. He carried my backpack with one hand, just like you can."

"That strong, eh?" Kurt waved his fork at Tina. "Does this new friend have anything to do with your interesting day?"

"Yes, but Devon isn't a friend. He's that new client I was telling you about. The guy who won the lottery."

"Mm-hmm." Her father nodded knowingly. "And

how did this client get the pleasure of carrying Amy's book bag?"

"Dad. Let's not go there," Tina said with an exasperated sigh. "He is a client, or at least I think he is."

Her father's eyes twinkled and he winked at Amy again.

She giggled.

Tina ignored them. "Devon stopped by my office just as I was leaving to pick up Amy. He wanted to talk about his finances. I took that to mean he's going to hire us—me."

"That sounds good. Now tell me, did you introduce your law firm clients to Amy, too?"

His teasing put her on the defensive. "Some."

"I think your Mom is getting a little prickly." Kurt addressed Amy. "Maybe she likes this Devon fellow?"

"*I* like him," Amy proclaimed.

Once he started teasing, Dad was next to impossible to stop. Now he had Amy double-teaming her. "Anyway." She gave both of them a quelling look. "We planned to talk as we walked to the school. Then we ran into Kate."

"Kate. How is she?" Kurt interrupted.

"Kate's good," Tina answered, glad for the change of topic.

Kurt waved his fork. "She's a great gal. I'm really surprised no young man has snapped her up."

"Dad, I'm not sure Kate wants to be snapped up. She seems perfectly happy running her business."

"Still, she's not getting any younger."

Meaning I'm not getting any younger, either. Tina removed the napkin from her lap.

Kurt went on. "I'll tell you, though, it was a real surprise when her mother gave her the farm and up and moved to Arizona to marry that guy she met on her cruise. But I wish them the best."

Tina frowned. Had her father always been this much of a matchmaker, or was his lack of socialization getting to him? She thought back. He'd always regaled them with stories about the people on his rural mail route. She might as well reciprocate by telling him about her day—the interesting parts, at least—even if it meant bringing the conversation back to Devon. Whether she liked it or not, he'd been the subject foremost on her mind since they met.

"Kate was making a delivery to Mrs. Mann, which reminds me: Devon O'Neil is Mrs. Sullivan's grandson. Remember, she was my kindergarten teacher?"

"Rose Sullivan?" Kurt asked.

"Uh-huh," she answered between bites.

"Rose was on my mail route. She had a couple of grandsons, if I remember right." He looked to Tina for confirmation.

"I don't know. Devon mentioned his grandmother

when Kate said she'd made a delivery to Mrs. Mann."

"Hmmm," Kurt mused. "One of Rose's grandsons used to spend summers with her. A dark-haired little rascal who once put a cat in the mailbox. It leaped out of the box and into the car when I opened the mailbox door. The poor little thing. I had a devil of a time coaxing it out from under the seat. I caught Rose's grandson watching from behind a bush and marched him up to the house for his grandmother to deal with."

Dark-haired rascal. "That would be Devon," she said.

"If he's still that mischievous, he should be an interesting client."

"Interesting good or interesting bad?" Tina asked, mimicking her father's earlier words.

"Touché!" Her father laughed. "I'm pulling for interesting good. You need some fun."

"Dad," she reminded him, "he's a client."

"Papa, Papa." Amy bounced in her chair, unable to remain quiet any longer. "I'm done. Can we put up my birdfeeder?"

"Amy, give Papa time to finish eating. Put your plate in the dishwasher while you wait."

"Okay." The little girl hopped down and grabbed her plate and silverware.

"I'll be done in a minute," her grandfather called

after her. "Tina, have I told you lately how much I enjoy having Amy—and you—with me?"

Warmth infused her heart. He'd done so much more for her these past few months than she'd done for him, and without smothering her and Amy with the overprotectiveness that had been a conflict between them during her teen years and following her divorce. "Dad, Amy and I like being here, too."

"And, speaking of Amy," Kurt gathered his utensils and placed them on his empty plate. "Would you have any trouble covering my after-school duty for a few days?"

Tina halted mid-way out of her seat, the grip on her plate tightening. Dad had had a doctor's appointment earlier this week. Fear sparked by her mother's recent death gripped her. Was his diabetes out of control again? The last time, his doctor had hospitalized him for a couple of days to monitor it. Would he tell her if it was? He and Mom had been so private about Mom's health, not wanting to concern her.

"Sure," she said hesitantly. "I'll cut my hours back or ask Kate if she can watch her." Tina chewed her lower lip. "Why?"

"Don't look so worried." He assured her. "I'm fine. I saw Dr. Klein just the other day."

Relief set Tina's heart rate back to normal.

"The Park and Strides are going to walk the next section of the Appalachian Trail later in the month."

The Park and Strides were a group of retirees who got together regularly for a few days of camping and hiking.

He rearranged the utensils on his plate. "I thought I'd go, even though I missed the first two treks this year."

"Dad, that's great. You and Mom loved the hikes you took with them last year."

"Yeah." His eyes misted. "I've been sitting around the house too long. It's time I got out and worked myself back into shape."

Her father didn't have an ounce of extra fat on him anywhere; he never had. But maybe it wasn't physical flab he was talking about. "When is the hike?"

"Starts two weeks from Monday, near Fayetteville, Pennsylvania. I thought I'd drive the camper down the Saturday before."

"You're going by yourself?" Tina asked. It was a long drive alone.

"I'll check around first to see if anyone from this area is going."

Tina nodded. "I'd feel better if you had some company for the drive."

Kurt waved off her concern. "Who's the parent here?"

She laughed.

"So, you'll be able to get someone to watch Amy?"

"No problem." She placed her dishes back on the table and gave her father a big hug. "I'll make sure I have arrangements made for Amy."

He patted her arm. "If you don't mind doing the dishes alone, I have a little girl and a birdfeeder to attend to."

"Excuse me." Devon addressed the young woman at the reception desk, who was totally engrossed in a spy thriller.

She shrieked and dropped the book.

"You scared the wits out of me." The woman picked up the book, put it aside, and took a deep breath. "Can I help you?"

"I'm here to see Tina Cannon. She's expecting me at two."

"Hi, I'm Crystal." The young woman batted her mascara-encrusted eyelashes at him. "Let me see if Tina is here." The woman picked up the phone and punched a number in.

From first impressions, Devon was unsure whether Crystal was an improvement over no receptionist. It probably made sense from Jack's vantage point, to have an uninterested person at the front desk rather than a career-oriented one. Someone who didn't know better, and didn't care wouldn't be likely to question any of Jack's practices.

While the receptionist waited for Tina to answer

the phone, she gave Devon a thorough once-over—
and from her smile she was obviously pleased with
what she saw. Devon shifted his weight from one
foot to the other and resisted an urge to roll his eyes.
Where had Jack found her?

"Tina, someone's here to see you." The woman
spoke into the phone. "Who? I didn't ask his name.
Kinda cute, dark curly hair."

She paused, listing to Tina on the other end of
the line. "Are you Devon O'Neil?" she asked him.

He nodded.

"Yep, that's him." She hung up the receiver.
"Tina will be right out."

"Devon." Tina entered the reception area. "Right
on time, I see."

He took her hand in greeting, noting the contrast
between the firmness of her handshake and the softness of her skin.

"Did you get the message I left on your answering machine, asking you to bring your investment
records?" she asked.

"Right here." He patted the breast pocket of his
brown leather jacket. "What there are of them."

"Let's go to my office and get started, then."

As Devon entered Tina's office, he was once
again struck by how warm and inviting it was compared to the rest of the building.

"Did you decorate the office yourself?"

"Yes."

"Thought so. It's different, less, uh . . . more, um . . ." Devon struggled for a polite word.

"Less intergalactic?" More office-like?" Tina suggested.

Devon's laugh filled the room. "I was going to say more inviting, but I can't argue with your words."

"I know. Isn't it awful? Uncle Jack actually paid someone to decorate."

"You're kidding? A professional decorator?"

"Supposedly. Someone who came highly recommended to him. I'm tempted to represent Uncle Jack in a property damage suit."

Devon shrugged his jacket off with a quiet chuckle. "I'd say you'd have a good case."

"Hang your coat over here." She motioned to a wooden coat tree in the back corner of the room behind the sitting area.

He hung his coat and eased into one of the chairs, which had been rearranged to sit side by side. Tina joined him.

"Is it safe for me to assume that you've decided to use our services? You did caution me never to assume." While her face remained expressionless, her eyes twinkled with mirth.

"Smart woman."

A smile spread across Tina's face, transforming her classic features into true beauty.

She really was quite lovely for a crook. He placed the papers he had removed from his coat pocket on the table. "This time your assumption is safe. I'm ready for you to set me up."

" 'Set you up'?" Her brow creased in question.

Devon started. Did she suspect something? He pitched his voice to a light tone. "Yeah, set me up with a financial plan . . . to take care of me in style, for the rest of my life." He gauged her response.

She laughed. "You're not asking for much, are you?"

"Hey, I have the money; you have the financial know-how. The sky's the limit." That should give her the impression that he was willing to give her free rein with his money.

Tina's expression sobered. "Don't expect miracles. We need to take a look at your goals and how you can realistically accomplish them."

"I *am* serious. A million dollars is a lot of money. Can't I live off it?" Was he laying it on too thick? Nah, didn't most people think of a million dollars as a lot of money?

She whipped the cover off her calculator. "All right. How much a year would you like for living expenses?"

"A couple hundred thousand ought to do it."

"Two hundred thousand. You're thirty-two, right?"

"Yep." Pleasure filled Devon—she'd remembered his age without having to check the profile he'd filled out. But then, according to his research, he was her only client, so it wasn't *that* big a deal.

She bent over the calculator and punched the keys, her hair falling forward in a honey-colored waterfall.

Mmm-hmmm. He liked her hair a lot better down than pulled back as she'd worn it yesterday. Somehow, wearing her hair down made her seem more open and approachable—younger, almost innocent.

He wondered if she knew. Maybe that was her plan—to start off as the no-nonsense professional and gradually work into a more friendly relationship that would set him up for the kill.

"You're a little short."

Devon jerked his head up. "Pardon?"

"You're a little short on money."

"I have a *million dollars*," he said with feigned surprise. "How can I be short of money?"

"A million may not be as much as you think," she cautioned. "Figuring a life span of fifty more years or so, I just ran the numbers using a fairly aggressive investment approach and three percent inflation."

"And?" he prompted.

"You come up about eight-hundred thousand dollars short, if you want an annual income of two-hundred thousand dollars."

He leaned forward to see the number on her calculator. "You're kidding."

She held the calculator closer to him, the movement causing her hair to fall forward again, releasing an inviting herbal scent. He wondered if it were as soft as it looked.

"No, I'm not kidding." She broke his sensual concentration.

Now was the time to lay the real bait. "Couldn't you use some—how'd you phrase it—more *aggressive* investments?"

He stayed pitched forward, his elbows resting on his thighs and his face close to hers. "I've seen some mutual funds that had seventy- and eighty-percent returns last year. An eighty-percent return on a million dollars would be some kind of money."

"True, but the year before, some of those funds had negative returns, and people lost money."

"What about IPO's, then?" Investing his grandmother's money in initial public offerings of stock in what appeared to be fake companies had been how Jack had embezzled most of her money.

"IPO's? Oh, I see you've been boning up on investing. 'IPO's' isn't really a household word—in most households, that is."

Devon clasped his hands. She hadn't *immediately* struck down the idea of investing in IPO's . . . maybe he was getting somewhere.

"I normally wouldn't recommend IPO's to someone who's investing for current income." She tapped her pencil gently against her raspberry-tinted lips.

Devon checked her fingernails for a matching shade and was disappointed to find them natural. His vengeful side wanted her to be brash and flashy, a superficial person who was all show and no substance. He fidgeted, willing her to do something, anything unlikable. He didn't want to like her. Bringing down someone who appeared so nice— even if she wasn't—would be difficult. Not that he wouldn't do it to see justice done.

Tina continued, "If you wanted to set some money aside that you wouldn't mind losing, we could look into IPO's. You might even want to try some day trading for fun."

"Day trading?" He tapped his fingers on his knees, anxious to hear her view on day trading. "Could day trading earn me more money, faster?"

"You could earn a bundle or lose a bundle. Day traders buy and sell their positions—the stocks or commodity options they hold—daily. True day traders don't hold any securities overnight." Tina halted, apparently gauging Devon's interest.

"Yeah?"

"It can be kind of fun, done on a small scale. But it's very speculative."

"You've done it, then, day trading?"

Tina answered slowly. "Yes, a little."

"So, you can turn my million into *millions*?"

"Hold it—I didn't say *that*. I thought you might like to do the research and day trade yourself with a thousand or two. You seem interested." She reached for a flyer. "I can recommend a couple of good investment classes at the community college."

He stopped her, his hand covering hers.

She tilted her head toward him, her eyes filled with question. He reveled in the softness of her skin. Had she felt the current that had flowed through him from that simple touch?

Devon cleared his throat. "But I thought I was hiring *you* to handle my finances."

Tina stiffened at the sharpness of his voice. She pulled her hand from his, unsettled by the loss of warmth. Was the heating system acting up again? The room had taken on a definite chill.

She kept her voice carefully modulated. "Of course, that's part of the service." What did he want from her? It almost seemed like he *wanted* her to speculate his money away.

"But I won't recommend or use inappropriate investments." She reached for the client profile she'd placed on the table—anything to avoid Devon's intense stare. "I think we've drifted from our purpose. We were exploring your financial goals."

"Yeah," he said, his tone flat. "I want to live off my million."

Devon's apparent disappointment set her on edge. She took a deep breath to calm herself.

"Then you need to set your income expectations lower." She punched numbers into the calculator, hitting the wrong keys on the first try. "To, say, a hundred thousand a year. Do you have any other assets to invest? Any cash from an employer's retirement plan?"

"Nah, we didn't have a retirement plan at work."

A job that wouldn't let him take off for his grandmother's funeral and had no retirement benefits; Tina itched to ask him more about his work, why he'd chosen that field. But that wasn't relevant to their discussion. "How about other savings?"

"Not really. I have my grandmother's house and the acreage that used to be the farm."

"Out on Lake Road, right? How many acres?"

Tina knew the astronomical prices the land along the lake was going for. She'd done a closing for her friend Kate's mother when she sold a couple acres of her farm.

"Ninety."

Her fingers entered more numbers into the calculator. "If you're willing to sell some, you might get your income up to two-hundred thousand a year."

"I don't know . . . I like my privacy."

An odd relief flowed through Tina. At least he wasn't pushing her for some make-another-million real estate deal. She liked this side of Devon a lot better. While she certainly didn't need to be pals with her clients, she worked better with people for whom she felt a mutual respect.

"There's some stuff in the house and barn that might be valuable. Grandma called it 'old junk'. Some of it is really old, probably dating as far back as the mid-1800s. Know anything about old furniture and farm implements?"

"A little. I majored in American history in college. But an appraiser could tell you much more. I can arrange an appraisal."

"Okay." He eased back in the chair. "You'd be there too, right?"

His request was a little unusual, but so was Devon. "Yes, I could walk through the appraisal with you." Tina justified her agreement by telling herself that she'd get a first-hand impression of the value, along with the written report, which would help her evaluate any offer the appraiser might make—not that she wanted to see where he lived.

"Great. Set it up. I'm free the rest of this week and early next week." He glanced at his watch. "Except now. I've got to meet someone in Rochester in an hour."

A dinner date, maybe? Tina hadn't thought about Devon having a life outside of Genesee, nor did she understand why she was suddenly thinking about it now.

"I almost forgot." Devon pulled a check out of his shirt pocket and handed it to her with a folded sheet. "Here's your retainer and my signed contract."

Tina took the papers. *Good. At least they were making a little progress.* Devon was now officially her client. "I'll call you with the appraisal time and work up a couple of preliminary portfolios we can go over afterwards."

"Sure." He rose from the chair, briefly looming over her before she stood too. "Later." He turned and left.

"Was that Devon O'Neil I just saw leaving?"

"Uncle Jack." Tina jumped, nearly dropping the papers she was gathering from the table. "You startled me. When did you get back?"

"A little while ago."

"And you couldn't resist stopping by the office on the way home?" Tina teased, bothered by a niggling feeling that he was checking up on her.

"Work . . . home. It's pretty much the same for me." He sat in the chair across from her desk, leaned back and crossed his leg across his knee. "You didn't answer my question."

"Oh, yeah. That was Devon O'Neil. He's proving as interesting a client as you predicted—and challenging, too."

"Is that so?" Jack raised his eyebrows and smiled.

"I need to set up an appraisal of his house and its contents. He inherited substantial lakefront property from his grandmother, Rose Sullivan . . ."

Jack's smile faded. "Rose Sullivan?"

"Mmm-hmm, my kindergarten teacher." Tina scratched a note on her desk pad. "I thought I'd use Dunn Associates for the appraisal."

"Fine." Jack stood and paced to the door and back. "What did you say this O'Neil does for a living?"

"He's a model maker." Jack sure was wound tight today. Probably jet lag and information overload from the conference.

Jack paced again, and Tina rubbed her forehead, willing him to sit down. *Men!* Between Jack's edginess and Devon urging her to mismanage his money, she was developing a tension headache.

Jack stopped in front of her desk. "I heard Rose's grandson was a private investigator."

"Not this one," Tina assured him. *Private investigator* brought movie visions of Brad Pitt, police, gunfire and car chases. She recalled Devon with Amy, carrying her Blue's Clues backpack. The Brad Pitt part, a little—Devon had the same heart-melting grin. The rest of it? She shook her head.

"Nope, must be a different grandson."

Chapter Four

Pop! Rattle. Screech. Kate Bauer's truck sputtered to a halt in the parking lot behind the village square. Devon had volunteered his SUV when Kate invited him to join her at the farmers' market, with lunch afterwards at Mrs. Mann's. But Kate had said she could fit more produce in the pickup.

He jumped out to help her unload, hoping that this morning would prove fruitful to his investigation. While getting up at dawn to hawk vegetables wasn't exactly his idea of Saturday morning fun, he couldn't pass up an opportunity to find out more about Tina.

"Right here." Kate motioned to a stand prominently located at the entrance of the market. "See,

I told you getting here early would pay off with a good spot."

Devon lugged a crate of broccoli over, and set it down next to a bed of orange tiger lilies. He looked around for a coffee vendor. Kate's infectious enthusiasm was almost enough to wake him up, but not quite. "Any place to get a cup of coffee around here?" he asked.

"The Sugar Bowl across the street should be open."

"Would you mind getting me a large while I unload the rest of the truck?" He reached for his wallet.

She waved him off. "My treat for your help."

As Devon watched her walk away, he contrasted Kate's bouncy step and effervescent personality with Tina's more regal and reticent manner. Yep, he preferred his women with a little mystery. He removed the last crate and slammed the truck's tailgate. *His women?* What was getting into him? Tina was a *case*, nothing more.

"Here you are." Kate handed him his coffee. "Can you give me a hand?"

She unfurled a banner reading *Lakeside Organic Farm.*

He put the coffee down and helped her attach the banner to the front of the stand.

She stepped back to survey their work. "All right! Now we should have a few minutes to talk before the crowd arrives." They took their seats behind the display. "I assume the topic of choice is Tina."

Devon ran his hand through his hair. He *was* losing his professional detachment if Kate had picked up on his interest that easily.

"So, what would you like to know?" Kate hunched over a head of cauliflower like a fortune teller with a crystal ball. "Madame Bauer tells all."

She continued to wave her hands over the cauliflower. "Make that *almost* all—a woman needs to keep a secret or two."

Yeah? Well, he just might need to crack one or two of Tina's secrets to prove his suspicions.

Devon and Kate talked between serving customers, his frustration growing as nothing even remotely helpful to his case came up. Despite Kate's offer to tell all, she seemed more bent on playing matchmaker, expounding on Tina's good qualities and relating humorous childhood escapades. He had considered wooing Tina; it wouldn't be a hardship for him to give it a try. But that degree of deception left a bad taste in his mouth. He'd be stooping to Jack's level.

"I'm glad you signed on with Tina. She needs the diversion." Kate stopped to wait on a customer. "She's hasn't had an easy time of things this past year, you know."

"How's that?"

"Her mom's death was a real shock. It happened so suddenly that Tina couldn't get here from Albany before her mother passed on."

His chest tightened. Devon could relate. He'd been under such deep cover on a case that he hadn't learned of his grandmother's death until after the funeral.

"Sorry, I'm all out of broccoli until next week," Kate told another customer, her words bringing him out of his introspection.

"Where was I?" she asked. "Oh, yeah. On top of her mother's death, Tina's ex stopped sending Amy's child support."

Ah, money again. Devon tucked that piece of information away for later consideration. "Tina is divorced?"

"Yeah. She and her ex met in law school and married at the beginning of their last year. He left when Tina was about six months pregnant with Amy."

"That was pretty rotten of him." *What kind of man would desert his pregnant wife?*

"I agree, but Tina took it pretty much in stride."

"Really?" That seemed a little strange, too. "They couldn't have had much of a marriage."

"I think Tina was more in love with the places his family connections could take them than with him. They'd made plans to go to work for his father's firm, one of the big ones in New York City.

I can't remember the name, but you'd know it if I said it."

So, she married for greed.

Kate seemed to read his thought. "Growing up in Genesee in the eighties didn't exactly prepare you for the big wide world." Kate picked a piece of lint off her jeans, her mouth tightening in a grimace. "Believe me."

Kate had a point. The Genesee he remembered from his childhood summers was pretty insular. Still, marrying for money revealed an ugly side of Tina. But wasn't ugly what he was looking for?

"Tina didn't *have* to have the baby." He carefully monitored Kate's reaction.

"Oh, I don't think Tina ever considered that an option. Once she got used to the idea of being pregnant, she got pretty into it and realized that she didn't want to raise a child in New York—or rather, have a nanny raise their child while she and her husband pursued high-power law careers."

That jived more with the profile of Tina he'd gathered. Still, Kate had shown him another facet of Tina.

"Tina has full custody of Amy, then?"

"Yeah. Amy's father has never even seen her. But he always sent her child support, up until about a year and a half ago, when his son was born."

"Tina didn't press the issue?"

"No, she said it was only money, and a clean

break was best, even if it meant having to work full-time. She was able to hold off until Amy was ready to start kindergarten."

"That's when she came to work with Jack?"

"Mm-hmm. This past summer." Kate waved to someone in the crowd. "Speak of the devil."

Devon scanned the crowd expecting to see Jack, but with the bright morning sun in his eyes, he couldn't make out any faces.

"Mommy, Mommy, there's Aunt Kate. Can I?"

Amy had already dropped Tina's hand before she could answer.

"Wait." Tina scanned the stands for Kate, and saw her waving beneath the Lakeside Organic Farm banner. She waved back. "Okay, go ahead. But *walk*, so you don't bump into anyone." The small greenspace was virtually packed with people. She heard her father chuckle.

"Looks like Kate has a friend with her this morning," he said.

"Oh yeah?" Tina asked with interest, picking up her father's emphasis on 'friend'. She had been so intent on watching Amy's progress through the crowd that she hadn't noticed anyone with Kate. Now, the people ahead of them obscured her view. "Anyone we know?"

"Don't recognize him. May be that new physician's assistant at the medical center that Dr. Klein was telling me about."

Hmmm. Kate hadn't mentioned to her that she was seeing anyone. "Let's go see." Tina and her father made their way toward the stand. Her heart dropped. Kate's 'friend' was Devon.

Tina chided herself. Why should she care if he was here with Kate? It wasn't as if Kate was going to steal her client—and that's all Devon was, after all, a client. She tried to summon back the earlier delight she'd taken in the warm weather and spending time with her family. Seeing Amy happily seated on Devon's lap didn't help. Her daughter's attraction to Devon triggered maternal concern— she thought moving in with her father would satisfy Amy's need for a father figure.

"Are you coming?" her father asked above the buzz of the other shoppers.

"I'm with you, Dad." Tina hadn't realized that she'd fallen behind. She quickened her pace so that they reached the stand together.

"Hi, Kate, how's business?" Kurt took a paper bag from the pile on the stand and began examining the display of brussel sprouts.

Tina smiled in greeting to Kate and Devon.

"Pretty good, Mr. K," Kate answered.

"And everything else?" He nodded toward Devon.

Kate burst out laughing. "You never give up, do you?"

"I need *something* to do with my spare time.

What better than seeing that my favorite girls are happy?" Kurt looked from Kate to Devon to Tina and raised his eyebrows.

Tina shifted her weight from one foot to the other and picked up a tomato, absently rubbing her thumb across the smooth skin. *What was Dad up to now?* Out of the corner of her eye, she watched Devon lift Amy from his lap with ease before rising to greet Kurt.

"Mr. Kovsky," Kate said. "This is Devon O'Neil, a friend of mine—and Tina's," she added. "Devon, Kurt Kovsky, Tina's father."

"And my Papa." Amy skipped around the stand to her grandfather, not wanting to miss out on any attention.

Kurt adjusted his glasses and studied Devon. "This is Mr. Lottery?"

Now it was Devon's turn to chuckle. "Good to meet you, sir." The men shook hands across the display.

"My daughter has told me a lot about you."

"Is that right?" Devon cocked his head, his eyes sparkling with amusement before focusing on Tina with dark intensity.

Tina placed the tomato back in the crate and lifted her heavy hair off the back of her neck. She would have worn it up, if she'd known it would turn so warm. Must be the combination of bright morning sun and the crowd.

"Sounds like you and Tina are getting along well." Kurt's gaze moved from Devon to Tina, and then to Kate. "What's a well-heeled young man like you doing farm-hand work?"

Tina shook her head. If she could have found a hole to crawl into she would have. She loved her father dearly, but too often he had trouble seeing the fine line between friendliness and nosiness. "Uh, Dad. What do we need besides brussel sprouts?"

"Pick out anything you and Amy want." Kurt waved his free hand over the display before returning his attention to Devon.

"Gotta keep busy," Devon answered.

"Know what you mean. I'm retired, too. Wish I could have done it years ago, like you, when I had more energy." Kurt gave the trio his perusal again.

Tina wondered if she could discreetly hide under the display stand.

"And I'm not really working for Kate. Just helping out today in exchange for an invitation to lunch with Evie Mann. She was a friend of my grandmother's."

"That's right—Rose Sullivan was your grandmother. She was on my mail route. Heard from Tina that you used to spend your summer here in Genesee. Know anything about a cat getting stuck in a mailbox?"

Tina caught Kate's quizzical expression. "It's a long story."

Devon cleared his throat, a faint tinge of pink showing through the gray of the stubble that shaded the hollows of his cheeks. "I might." He grinned.

"Thought you might. Your grandmother had her hands full with you, but I think she enjoyed every minute of it. Rose was always up for a challenge."

"Thanks, I guess."

"So, what do you think of the new Genesee?" Kurt asked.

"I don't find it all that different than when I was a kid."

"You may if you stick around. Jack says Genesee is starting to be *the* place to live."

"Oh, yeah?"

"So he says. And the way lakefront property has been selling off, he just may be on to something. You could find yourself surrounded by new neighbors."

Devon leaned back in his chair. "I'm not sure I'd like that. I'm enjoying the privacy. Speaking of which . . ." He turned his attention to Tina. "Are we on for Tuesday?"

Tina ignored her father's raised eyebrows. "Yes. Jason Dunn will be over at ten. He seemed especially interested in the barn and the old farm equipment."

"I hope he's not disappointed. Gram and Grandpa always called it 'that old junk in the barn'."

"Jason says a lot of people are using old farm

antiques in their new homes. Barn wood, too, if you have any interest in dismantling the barn and selling the planks."

A pained look sharpened Devon's features. "I'd have to think about that. For now, I want to keep the place pretty much as it is."

Tina nodded sympathetically. "I understand." She and her father had had a difficult time going through her mother's things, deciding what to keep and what to give away. Although he kept talking about it, Dad still hadn't sold Mom's car.

"Mommy." Amy danced around her. "Are you and Papa almost done? We still have to get a present for the birthday party."

"Almost." Tina selected a few more tomatoes.

"A birthday party? What fun," Kate said.

"Yep. For my bestest friend from school. I'm getting her a paint set 'cause we like to paint."

"Sounds good."

Amy ran back around the stand.

"You know," she said in a loud whisper. "Mommy's birthday is next week."

"I know," Kate said.

"Maybe we should have a surprise party for Mommy."

Tina mouthed "no" to Kate.

"Papa and I could bake a cake and you and Devon could come."

Tina shook her head no emphatically, in case Kate had missed her earlier message.

"You guys are her bestest friends, right?"

"Your Mommy and I have been best friends since we were in kindergarten, just like you."

Amy tapped Devon's knee. "Aunt Kate is Mommy's old friend and you're Mommy's new friend. Papa," Amy called across the stand. "Let's give Mommy a birthday party. You and me."

Tina groaned audibly. Turning thirty was enough in itself, without dragging people over to celebrate the occasion.

"I think a birthday party is a great idea," Kurt answered.

"Dad!" Tina pleaded.

"Wednesday night, dinner and cake. Okay with you two?"

"That's good for me," Kate said.

I'll get you for this. Tina twisted the top of the tomato bag shut, tightly. *Just wait until your birthday comes around next month.*

"Devon?"

The corner of his mouth quirked up. "I'm free Wednesday night."

"Great! Amy and I will get started on the party planning tomorrow." Kurt winked at his granddaughter.

"And Kate, feel free to bring a date."

"Mr. K!" Exasperation colored Kate's tone.

"Or, if you'd like, I could invite that nice new physician's assistant that Dr. Klein hired."

"And I'll invite Mrs. Henley from church," Kate quipped.

"Gotcha there, Dad." Tina gave her father a playful punch in the shoulder. Anne Henley, a three-time divorcée, had been openly pursuing her father for months.

"All right. We'll see you all Wednesday. How much do I owe you?"

As Tina and her family walked back to the car, she asked, "Dad, why did you have to do that? I said I didn't want any fuss about my birthday."

"I know." He placed his arm around her shoulder. "But I think my little girl needs a little fuss in her life."

Chapter Five

"Not bad . . . not bad at all." Devon stepped back to admire his work. He'd spent the past two days cleaning the house from top to bottom, mowing the lawn, even weeding out the dead blooms in his grandmother's flower beds. He could have had cleaning and lawn services come in, but the physical work relieved some of his frustration. His investigation had turned up nothing but dead ends so far. Devon couldn't believe his grandmother was the only person Jack Kendall had scammed.

His gaze traveled to the breakfast nook and the antique rolltop desk set under the bay window. Now that his computer equipment had arrived from his office in Rochester, and his Internet connection was up and running, maybe he could make some progress.

The front door knocker sounded, and Devon checked the kitchen clock. Nine forty-five. Must be either Tina or the appraiser. Well, the place was ready for inspection—and for Tina. Devon couldn't deny that he wanted her to be favorably impressed—for investigative reasons, of course.

He walked through the house, giving the dining and living rooms a self-satisfied perusal. The front hall made him frown. He rarely used the front door, and hadn't noticed the peeling wallpaper. The knocker sounded again. Devon opened the door.

"Hi." Tina stood on the porch in full professional mode, her boxy wool pantsuit a sharp contrast to the fitted jeans and sweater she'd worn to the farmer's market on Saturday.

"Come on in."

Tina stepped into the hall. "Jason Dunn isn't here yet?" She repositioned her purse strap on her shoulder and fingered the clasp absently. "I didn't see his car outside."

So she was nervous . . . about her involvement in Jack's schemes? Devon was beginning to think she might be an unwilling participant. Or was it being alone in the house with him that was making her jittery? "No, he's not here yet. You're a little early."

"Punctuality is one of my virtues—or vices." Her smile erased some of the wariness in her eyes.

He checked his watch. "Jason should be here any minute. Do you want the short tour while we wait?"

Devon couldn't resist the strong compulsion to set her at ease. "Or we could sit in the living room. I have some coffee on."

"Oh," Tina answered quickly. "I'll take the short tour."

Okay, so she wasn't afraid of him. Maybe she was just nervous because he was her biggest client. "Right this way, then," he said with an exaggerated flourish.

Tina welcomed the warmth the house offered. After last week's summer-like temperatures, the weather had turned decidedly crisp today.

"This is the living room," Devon explained. "Originally it was the front parlor."

The room appeared exactly as Tina imagined an 85-year-old retired teacher's living room would look. Floor-to-ceiling bookshelves flanked the picture window. They held leather-bound classics, such as *Jane Austin, David Copperfield*, and *War and Peace*, along with a liberal mix of recent bestseller thrillers, and several books by Tina's favorite romance author.

Colorful throw pillows on the overstuffed sofa and matching chairs were invitation to settle down for a cozy read. Knickknacks adorned almost every open space on the bookshelves and end tables, with more housed behind the glass doors of a carved mahogany hutch.

"What lovely figurines." Tina reached for one on the table beside her. "May I?"

"Sure, as long as you're careful," Devon replied in a faintly schoolmarmish tone that made Tina think he must have heard those words—often—from his grandmother.

She lifted the figure of a rosy-cheeked little girl and inspected it closely. Just as she'd thought. "You're right in telling me to take care. This is a Hummel. Are they all?"

"A Hummel?" Devon asked, his bland expression a contrast to his questioning voice.

"H. I. Hummel." Tina searched his face for some name recognition. "Many of the older Hummel figurines are collector pieces."

"So they're valuable?"

Devon seemed to have slipped back into that irritating let's-make-big-money attitude of the other day. She walked to the hutch without replying. Didn't he see the beauty and craftsmanship in the figurines?

"Some of them might be," she finally answered. "Depends on when they were created and how many were made."

She scanned the hutch with interest. "Your grandmother had quite a collection."

"Grandpa bought her one for each year of their

marriage. There must be fifty-five of them, or more if he replaced the couple my cousins and I broke as kids."

"Wow!"

"Any idea what they're worth?"

His expression once again didn't match the eagerness of his questions. She rubbed her leather purse strap between her thumb and forefinger. Why would Devon hide his emotions, as if his heart wasn't in the questions he was asking? Tina shook her head and turned to find Devon's gaze fixed on her.

"Does that mean you don't know?"

"No. I have some idea," she admitted.

"And?"

Tina hesitated. "The little girl in the apple tree I looked at first could be worth almost twenty-five thousand dollars."

He whistled.

Tina checked his eyes for the glimmer of greed she expected to see. His gaze met hers, clear and strong. She blinked. A woman could lose herself in those deep blue depths.

He broke the silence. "Is that an accurate figure or a ballpark guess?"

"Pretty accurate. Jason Dunn can tell you for sure when he gets here."

"You seem to know a lot about these Hummels. You collect them, too?"

"Uh-huh. They're a bit beyond my means, especially with my little whirlwind Amy around. They wouldn't be safe. Mom had a pair of Christmas ones that Dad gave me."

"And you sold them." His words were more a statement than a question.

Tina frowned. "Heavens, no." It would have been like selling a part of her childhood. Did Devon feel like that about his grandmother's things? He almost seemed to be pretending not to. Maybe it was his way of dealing with the loss.

"Dad had the figurines appraised when we rewrote his will after Mom died. I got to talking with Jason about the figurines, and he told me about a pair he had sold for forty-nine thousand dollars at an estate auction—a matching boy and girl seated in apple trees." Before he could ask, she added, "Mine are worth about a hundred and fifty dollars each. Still, I keep them packed safely away, except for the holiday season."

Devon avoided her eye contact. "I'm being a jerk, aren't I?"

"You could say that."

"Sorry." He scuffed his athletic shoe on the rug. "Guess it's the idea of having people come in to auction off Grandma and Grandpa's things."

Tina could tell how difficult that admission had been. "Apology accepted. You know, you don't have to have the auction."

"Yes, I do," he said. "It's been more than a year since Grandma died, and I have no use for most of the stuff. Want to get back to the house tour?"

"I'd like that."

He opened his arms expansively. "The living room and bedrooms upstairs were part of the original 1814 house. The kitchen, dining room, and downstairs bedroom were added later. When Grandma was growing up, the living room was divided into two rooms, the front parlor and the family parlor."

"So the farm belonged to your grandmother's family?"

"Yep. Grandma's great-great-grandparents bought it in the 1850s."

The doorknocker sounded. "That must be the appraiser. Excuse me." Devon left to answer the door.

Tina couldn't resist testing one of the chairs, finding it as comfy as she'd expected. She hadn't realized that Devon had such deep roots in Genesee. Devon's mother must have gone to high school with her parents. She made a mental note to ask Dad. It was kind of surprising that his mother hadn't returned to Genesee. Many of her parents' generation had, after testing their wings elsewhere.

She looked up when Devon and Jason Dunn entered the living room. Walking side by side, they were a study in contrasts: Jason tall and blond, his hair neatly styled and casual business clothes impeccably tailored; Devon in jeans and a gray T-shirt that emphasized his wiry and less imposing physique. His blue-black hair fell in unruly curls on his forehead.

Jason greeted Tina. "Good to see you again. It's been a while."

Tina twisted the birthstone ring she wore on her right hand. She and Jason had gone out a few times when she first moved back to Genesee. They were old friends from high school, and she liked him in a friendly way, but he'd clearly wanted more, so she'd been avoiding him lately.

"It has been a while. I've been pretty busy with work." Tina hoped that didn't sound as lame to Jason as it did to her. "How about you? I'll bet the real estate boom is keeping you hopping."

"Busy enough. I try to make some time for fun, though. You know, all work and no play . . ."

Tina turned to Devon to avoid Jason's gaze and found him glaring at her and Jason as if he'd keyed directly into the undercurrents of their exchange and didn't like what he heard.

She crossed and uncrossed her legs, uncomfortable with the intensity of his scrutiny. Was it sympathy for Jason's unsuccessful pursuit of her, or did she detect a note of jealousy? Tina couldn't deny that the idea of having two men interested in her was flattering, particularly when the men were as attractive as Devon and Jason.

Her father's matchmaking attempts must be getting to her. Here she was in the middle of a business meeting, sizing up the qualities of her business associate and client. Tina slammed her palms against the padded arms of the chair. The loud thump drew Devon and Jason's attention. She scratched at an invisible spot on her pant leg and brushed it off.

"I was giving Tina an historical tour of the house," Devon told Jason, giving her a surreptitious wink.

Her heart warmed at Devon's attempt to help her cover her embarrassment. "Yes, Devon had just told me that the house has been in his family since the 1850s. Do you want to finish the tour with us or get right to the inspection?"

"Let's do a short walk around together," Jason answered, "so I can ask any general questions. Then, if you have anything outdoors you want me to look at, I should get started. The wind has picked up and storm clouds are moving in."

Devon nodded. "I'd like to auction the stuff in the barn, if it's worth anything. Since the roof isn't in too great a shape, you probably should start there."

Devon finished the tour and they walked across the side yard to the main barn. The structure leaned precariously to one side. When had it fallen into such disrepair? After his grandfather had died, he guessed.

The building moaned as he slid the door open. His gut tightened. He should have been here more for Grandma. The barn was a real hazard. If he stayed, he might have to take it down.

"There you go." Devon motioned Jason inside. A hand sickle and other smaller equipment hung precariously from hooks lining the side walls. Rotting canvas covered mysterious mounds in the center of the large structure. "I don't think anything in here has been touched in ten years," he added apologetically.

Jason flipped a sheet on his clipboard and removed a silver-toned pen from his jacket pocket. "Whether or not the equipment is in working condition will affect the value," he cautioned.

"I figured that," Devon said.

"I'll meet you at the house when I'm done," Jason said, dismissing Devon and Tina with a curt nod.

"Guess we're on our own." Devon turned to Tina. "Want to wait up at the house or take a walk around the property?"

"Let's walk around."

Devon eyed her shoes, little black leather slip-ons. "The ground is pretty wet from the heavy rains we've been having," he warned.

"I'll let you know if I want to go back."

"All right. We can walk the property boundaries. I've mowed a path."

He motioned across the backyard to a cut in the brown field grass behind. "We'll come out at the lake and . . ."

"Is the purple stork still there?"

"You know about Grandpa's stork?"

"Sure. Mrs. Sullivan brought our kindergarten class here for a year-end picnic. What five-year-old would forget a big purple stork? Amy would be wild to see it."

Devon shook his head, his mood turning as dark as the thunder cloud moving in above them. His grandmother had been wild about the stork, too. Grandpa had carved it himself and placed it on the end of the dock to signal to his family across the lake that Devon's mother—their first child—had been born. He flew a hot pink flag for his mother's and his aunt's births, and a blue flag when his uncle was born. Grandma and Grandpa had had a whole collection of other flags they flew for various holidays.

"Oh." Disappointment colored Tina's voice. "What happened to it?"

"A spring storm washed it away a few years ago. The base had rotted." Devon clenched his fists, imagining the sadness his grandmother must have felt the day she'd come out and found the stork gone. It was his fault. He was the only family left in the area. If only he'd come by more often to check on things . . .

"That's too bad. It wasn't something you could easily replace."

"Not with Grandpa gone."

"He made it?"

"Yep." Devon bent to pick up a small tree branch that blocked the path. He hurled it to the side with more force than necessary.

Tina looked at him with raised eyebrows.

"The path is getting kind of mucky. You sure you don't want to go back to the house?"

"No, I'm fine." Tina glanced from the path to the clouds above, as if judging the wisdom of her words. "I'd like to walk the beach before we go back."

"Okay," he agreed, trying to judge whether the moisture he felt on his face was mist from the cool air on the lake or fine raindrops.

Tina hurried ahead, seemingly oblivious to the mist and the muddy path. She reached the lakefront first.

"What a great view. Look," she pointed. "It's almost like one of those Arthurian tales. The Lady in the Lake."

Devon looked down from the slight rise above the beachfront. He followed the line of her outstretched arm to the mist rising from the lake. It *was* almost magical. Tina stepped closer to the lake, deeper into the mist, until her slim form was just an outline on the horizon. His nerves twinged with an urgency to stop her before she disappeared completely.

He closed the distance from the rise to the beach in a few long strides, oblivious to the softly pelting rain. "Tina."

She turned to face him. He reached over and brushed a wet strand of hair from her face. Her eyes widened and lips parted slightly in surprise.

He bent his head and brushed her lips with his. He pulled back a fraction of an inch, just far enough to look into Tina's misty brown eyes.

She took a short, sharp breath. What was he doing? He ran a finger down her jawline and lifted her chin. He didn't care. The herbal scent of her hair and the clean rain invited him back, compelling him to make sure she was real and not some image ready to disappear into the mist.

Devon brushed his lips against hers again, wrapping his arms around her waist. Tina shivered, whether from the wet or the closeness, she didn't know. He deepened the pressure until she curved her arms around his neck and returned the kiss. He drew her closer.

Crack. A bolt of lightning crashed across the lake, breaking the spell. The sky opened up with sheets of cold rain. Tina pulled away.

He grabbed her hand. "The gazebo." He pulled her across the beach, the soft sand impeding their progress.

"My shoe." Tina stopped and bent down to pick it up. The heavy rain and jarring motion of their mad run for shelter had pulled her hair down to surround her in a molten gold cape.

"Take them off."

She slid the other shoe off and held them both in one hand, reaching for Devon's with the other.

"Come on." They dashed to the gazebo.

Tina plopped down on the bench that encircled the inside parameter of the gazebo, her heart pounding from the run through the rain. Or was it from Devon's kiss?

"Guess we should have expected that."

Expected the kiss? No, it had come totally unexpectedly.

"The downpour," he clarified.

Heavens, she must appear as bemused as she felt. And Devon's nearness wasn't helping. He seemed larger standing over her, his soaked T-shirt defining his muscular build. Raindrops glistened on his thick dark lashes, intensifying the deep blue of his eyes.

"Yeah," she agreed, gathering her wits. Tina pushed her hair back and pulled it to one side, twisting the length to wring the water from it.

He sat beside her. "Guess we'd better wait until it lets up a bit before we head back to the house."

Tina studied her muddied feet and wrung the last of the water from her hair. "Good idea."

She stood and walked to the gazebo door, knowing Devon was watching her every movement. So what—she hadn't done anything to invite his attention, his kiss. It was him. She stuck one foot out the doorway, then the other, to let the softening rain wash them clean. If he was attracted to her, it was his problem. He'd just have to get over it. Tina turned back.

"About what happened out by the lake," she started.

"Forget it. Sorry."

Forget it? Sorry? The kiss hadn't moved him at all?

"You're a client." She stammered. "You know we can't . . . I'm not . . ."

Liar, a voice screamed in her head. Of course she was attracted to him. She'd have to be dead not to be. He was an attractive man. But Tina knew better than to be taken in by good looks and money. She'd been there before, with her ex-husband. How much did she even know about Devon O'Neil?

"Of course not." He spread his fingers and examined them. "The mist, the memories. I forgot myself. I proposed to Jenn here."

Jenn? Devon was engaged? She could have drowned in the flood of unexpected disappointment that washed over her. She sure *didn't* know much about him. Why should she care? *For professional reasons, of course. An impending marriage should be figured into his financial plan.* That's right. So why hadn't he mentioned it?

"You're engaged?" Did her question sound as inane to Devon as it did to her? Hadn't he just said so?

"Not anymore."

"Oh."

He looked so vulnerable sitting there, head bowed. Tina wanted to throw her arms around him and give him a hug—as she would any friend. But he was a client, not a friend. And the kiss stood between them.

Devon lifted his head. "Hey. Don't look so concerned. We parted as friends. She moved to California and married a software engineer. They have twin boys. She sent me photos last Christmas. Cute kids."

Tina couldn't tell if his casual attitude was real or feigned. Even a friendly breakup had to involve some hurt. By the time she and her ex-husband split, she knew she didn't love him and never had, but the break hurt anyway.

She turned her face to the gazebo door to test the rain and let it wash away the compassion Devon didn't seem to want from her.

"The rain is letting up," she said. "Do you want to go back to the house?"

"No." He waved her away. "You go ahead. See if Jason is done in the barn. I'll be up soon."

"All right."

Halfway up to the house, Tina looked back to check on Devon. She caught sight of him racing into the mist. From what? Memories, or her?

Chapter Six

"**W**as that Devon O'Neil?" Tina asked the receptionist.

Crystal looked up from filing her nails. "Yeah. He stopped by to pick up that appraisal stuff you had for him."

Tina frowned. She had left him a message that she had received the appraisal from Jason, and had a report with her comments and recommendations ready.

"Why didn't you let me know he was here?"

"Oh, your door was closed when I walked by earlier, so I figured you were busy."

Tina clenched and unclenched her hands. "How did you get the report to give to Mr. O'Neil?"

"From the computer network," she answered

proudly. "I'm taking that computer course at college. I thought it would be a real drag since it's not related to my major."

Tina shuddered to speculate what the girl's major might be that computers weren't relevant. Dating? Marriage?

The girl continued. "I had some trouble with the client code thing, but I got out the information sheet Jack gave me for the special project I'm working on for him, and Devon and I figured it out."

"*Devon* helped you?" Tina clenched her hands again against the uneasiness that waved through her. Crystal shouldn't be sharing client codes with Devon. More than that, why did Crystal even *have* the codes? What kind of special project would Jack have given her? The fact that it involved client records bothered Tina. She was going to have to have a word with Jack. What could he have been thinking?

"Think he's too old for me?" Crystal asked.

"What?"

"You know, too old for me to date."

"Jack?" Tina asked.

"Nooo," Crystal answered slowly, as if giving that idea some thought. "Devon. He's so cute."

What world does this girl live in?

"I can't say if Mr. O'Neil is too old for you or not. But we do have a policy here of not socializing with clients."

"What about you, then?" she pouted. "*Devon* said to tell you he'd see you tonight at your birthday party."

"That's my father at work. I have no control over him and Amy inviting Devon to our home."

"You mean, your parents still try to control your life—at *your* age?"

That question struck a blow—thirty wasn't exactly doddering.

"Sometimes," Tina conceded. "But we were talking about the computer. You shouldn't give clients or anyone else access to our office network."

"I needed a little help getting that report for Devon," the girl responded belligerently.

"I'm sure you did no harm this time," Tina reassured her. "You were only accessing his files. But we do have a lot of confidential information stored in the system—information our clients might not want made public. In the future, don't let anyone on our computer network."

Tina's better judgment wondered whether Crystal should even have access to the network herself.

"Are you going to report me to Jack?" The girl crossed her arms. "If you are, don't be sure he'll agree with you just because you're family. This *is* a business, you know."

Tina's point exactly: the practice was a business and should be operated that way. "As I said, no harm done this time, but I will have to tell Jack. He may want to change the access codes as a precaution. And he may talk to you about importance of maintaining file security."

"All right!" The girl huffed. "I won't do it again. You should know, though, that Jack told me yesterday what a great job I'm doing handling client relations. He even brought me this as a thank you." Crystal pointed a glitter-polished finger to a single rosebud in a crystal vase on the corner of her desk. "That's all I was doing with Devon—client relations."

It wasn't worth arguing about, as long as Crystal understood the importance of keeping their client records secure. And Tina thought she did—hoped she did—now.

"Make a wish and blow out the candles, Mommy."

Tina smiled fondly at her daughter, took a deep breath and blew, wishing the party would be over soon. Dinner had been indeterminately long, with her father blatantly playing matchmaker between her and Devon. She peeked at Devon. He winked at her, obviously enjoying himself, or at least giving a good impression of it. If Dad liked Devon so much, he could be pals with him. She needed to keep a professional distance.

The candles on the ornately decorated birthday cake flickered and died out.

"Yeah!" Amy clapped.

Tina pasted a smile on her face, taking in all the work Amy and Dad had put into her birthday party. A red and silver *Happy Birthday* banner spanned the dining room. Balloons hung from the ceiling and the walls. Dad had cooked all her favorite foods. And the cake. The cake was a labor of love, a two-layer, double fudge creation, with *Happy Birthday, Mommy!* written painstakingly across the top in pink frosting.

Amy hopped from her chair and gave Tina a kiss on the cheek. "There's a kiss to grow on."

"A kiss to grow on?" Devon raised an eyebrow.

Tina felt a flush of embarrassment start to color her face.

"That's right." Kurt interjected. "Margery, Tina's mother, came from a large family. When her older brothers and sisters got a little carried away with the old 'pinch to grow an inch,' her mother changed it to 'kiss to grow an inch.' It doesn't rhyme, but it avoids bruises."

"And everyone is supposed to give the birthday girl a kiss to grow on?" Devon's eyes sparkled.

Amy and Kurt nodded enthusiastically, with him adding, "Most definitely."

Devon pushed his chair away from the table.

Dread filled Tina. He wouldn't kiss her in front of Amy and her father, would he? What did it matter anyway. It was only a silly birthday tradition.

Tina looked directly into Devon's eyes.

He grinned, as if reading her thoughts.

On second thought, maybe she'd better put a stop to this right now. He *was* a client, after all.

"Who's ready for cake?" she asked, surveying the table for the cake server. Dad had forgotten to put it out. Good—she could escape to the kitchen for a minute. Tina stood and took a step toward the kitchen.

"Hold on."

The command in Devon's voice startled her to a stop.

"Don't we all have to do the kiss thing before cake?"

He placed his hands on her shoulders and lowered his head slowly.

Time went on interminably. He wouldn't kiss her, here, would he? Tina shivered imperceptibly, and he increased the pressure of his fingertips on her shoulders. She closed her eyes in anticipation.

Smack. He kissed her cheek with exaggerated loudness, causing Amy to clap with delight.

"There's your kiss to grow on." He beamed at her, as if to say, *got you.*

What an idiot she was, standing there anticipating—no, more than that—*wanting* him to kiss her. Right there in front of her father and Amy. She felt her face flush and heard her father laugh. She had to admit to herself that it was a little funny. All that build-up.

"Good one, Devon." Kurt chuckled again. "I think you really had my little girl going there."

Devon shot Kurt a look of male triumph.

Irritation replaced Tina's embarrassment. They were grown men, not schoolboys—although you'd never know it.

She glared at them both. "I'll go get the cake server."

"I'll come, too." Kate pushed her chair away from the table and trailed behind Tina to the kitchen.

"What was that?" Kate asked.

Tina waited until the kitchen door swung closed.

"Don't ask me." She pulled open a drawer and started rummaging.

"Hey, this is me, Kate. Your best friend and confidant." She reached over Tina's arm and lifted the cake server from the drawer. "Want to tell me what's going on?"

"Nothing." Tina closed the drawer with more force than necessary. "Everything."

She wanted to talk with Kate, but now wasn't the time. Not with the others waiting in the dining room. Besides, what would she say? *I have a crush on my biggest client.* She was thirty years old, after all. Maybe that was it: turning the big three-oh was getting to her.

"Well?" Kate pressed.

Tina sighed. "It's Devon. I'm attracted to him."

"What's wrong with that?"

"Not now." Tina nodded toward the closed door. "They're waiting for us."

Kate shrugged. "If you need to talk, you know where I am."

"Later," Tina promised. "I have to sort out some things first."

She couldn't deny that she liked the idea of a romantic relationship. It wasn't as if her failed marriage had soured her on men. She liked men; her best friend in Albany had been a man. But Devon O'Neil wasn't the man for her. She could come up with a hundred reasons why, not least of which was the fact that he had spoiled her birthday party—a party she hadn't wanted in the first place. Besides, if she pursued her attraction, she'd be breaking the bar association's ethics clause and risking disbarment.

"Here," Kate handed her the cake server.

Tina pushed open the door to the dining room.

"About time." Kurt greeted her. "I thought I was going to have to come in and get you two."

He waved them to their seats. "I know, I know. Girl talk. Now, sit down and I'll serve the cake. Birthday girl first."

Tina sat, watching Devon out of the corner of her eye. His face was expressionless, like it had been at his house when he was hiding his emotions about his grandmother. *Good*, she thought spitefully. *Hopefully his actions had put him in as much of a turmoil as it had me.*

She accepted a slice of cake from her father, and mechanically took a bite.

"Is it good, Mommy? Can you taste the fudge swirls? Papa let me do the fudge swirls."

Tina's heart softened. She couldn't let Devon spoil the party for Amy, too.

"Yes," she answered with forced enthusiasm, "The fudge swirls are delicious. They make the cake."

Amy beamed and attacked her own piece of cake.

Tina played with her dessert while the others chattered around her.

"I'm done Mommy. May I be excused?" Amy asked with uncharacteristic formality.

Tina smiled at her daughter. Was she on her best behavior for company, or had she sensed her mother's tension? "Sure, honey."

Amy removed her party hat. "Aunt Kate, can you read me a story?"

"I sure can," Kate answered. "Let's go pick one out."

They headed into Amy's adjoining toy room.

Tina pushed her half-eaten cake away. *Guess the party is over.*

"I should be going, too," Devon said. He slid his

chair away from the table. "Thanks for a delicious dinner, Mr. Kovsky."

"Kurt." Her father corrected him. "And you're welcome. We enjoyed having you."

Tina stood to gather the dishes.

"Tina will show you out. I put his jacket in the front hall closet," Kurt added helpfully.

And why couldn't he see Devon out? After all, he was the one who invited him.

She shot her father a questioning glare.

In response, Kurt added, "I want to check with Kate to see if we're on for next week."

Like Kate wouldn't be here for the rest of the evening. She stalled, glancing from her father to Devon, who sat with a bemused look on his face.

"What's next week?" she asked with false innocence. As if she didn't know.

"The Appalachian hike," he reminded her. "You said you'd ask Kate to watch Amy after school."

Which she had, and Dad knew it. Maybe she should have asked Kate to invite Mrs. Henley, the merry widow, to the party and given Dad a taste of his own matchmaking medicine.

Tina set the stack of plates down with a clunk. Walking Devon to the door wasn't worth fighting about.

Devon rose from his seat. Nothing like being an unwanted guest. "Hey, I can let myself out. No problem."

A walk-through by himself would give him a chance to check the living room for any signs that the Cannon/Kovsky family was living beyond its reasonable means. Although he had looked around briefly when Kurt had given him a tour of the house, it never hurt to examine a place a second or third time for more details.

He waited for Tina's next move, fully expecting her to agree. It was pretty obvious she was put out with him and her father. Probably because of the birthday kiss thing. Geez, he was just having a little fun, getting in the party spirit. Kurt had approved—and little Amy. Even Kate had cracked a smile before rushing to her friend's aid in the kitchen. *What was it with women anyway, always rushing off to dissect a man's every little action or comment?*

"Are you coming?" Tina half-smiled in his direction and started toward the living room. At least she wasn't glaring at him as she had at her father.

Devon followed her through the living room quickly. No time to check out anything except her stiff demeanor—not that watching her was a difficult task.

She opened the closet and reached for his leather jacket. He stepped to the other side of the open closet between her and the outside door, and saw the jacket fold open to reveal a New York designer label. Not exactly what you'd expect a tradesman to be wearing. Did she notice? He could kick himself for being so sloppy. Just because Genesee was a small town didn't mean he could let his guard down.

"Here you go." Tina turned and the leather whipped his shoulder softly. "I thought you were on the other side of the door."

Devon took the jacket, enjoying her surprise at his closeness.

"Thanks." He smiled to himself as she tried to close the closet door behind her without moving any closer to him.

Frustration hardened Tina's features.

He tightened his grip on the soft leather. What was with him? Here he was getting a rise out of Tina's discomfort. Devon could hear his grandmother's voice lecturing him sternly on not teasing little girls. But teasing girls had been fun. He thought about his recent bout with Jack's ditzy receptionist. But there was teasing, and there was teasing.

He stepped back as he pulled his coat on. "You know, I didn't mean to embarrass you at the party."

She pulled her mouth into a thin straight line.

"It was all in fun. The 'kiss to grow an inch' story your father told."

"Forget it." She took a deep breath and released it, as if clearing herself of her frustration. Or of him?

Dunce! Was his perception completely shot? Her

peeved attitude wasn't about the party kiss at all. And he prided himself on being able to read people.

"Does this have anything to do with the other day at the lake?" he asked.

"Of course not." She stared at him as if he'd grown a second head. "I'm a big girl. I know it was nothing."

Nothing? He wouldn't exactly call it nothing, although he had at the time.

"The mist. You were thinking of your fiancée."

He closed the space between them again and placed his hands on the closet door, one to each side of her.

Her eyes widened.

He'd probably regret it, but he couldn't resist.

"The light is good and bright here." He lowered his head until his lips captured hers in a soft, sweet kiss that ended before Tina could react.

Devon pushed away from the closet door.

"See you," he called over his shoulder as he slipped away from Tina's inviting warmth into the chilly night. He whistled his way to his Xterra.

Chapter Seven

Devon glanced furtively up and down the street to make sure no one else was out. The last thing he needed was Genesee's finest discovering him slinking along Main Street in all black, with a backpack full of tools. After one more fleeting look, he slipped between the two houses. The crescent moon appeared from behind a bank of clouds, offering just enough light for him to make his way around the Kendall & Associates building.

A dog barked. He halted. It barked again. Devon waited in the darkness until the sound drifted away in the quiet of the night. He moved to the back window of Jack's office and quickly scanned the yard. Fortunately, a stockade fence ran across the back property line, blocking the Victorian from the homes behind it. The apartment houses to either side were quiet and dark.

Devon checked the window. No screen or storm window—good. He pulled latex gloves, a butter knife, screw driver, and hammer from the pack. After slipping on the gloves, he tested the window. Locked. He slid the knife between the top and bottom panels of the old double-hung window and deftly unlocked it. Now, as long as the window wasn't painted shut, he was as good as in.

He positioned the screwdriver on the top frame of the lower pane and gave it a couple of light taps with the hammer. The window inched up enough for him to get his fingers underneath and lift it. Devon propped it open with the hammer. He reached into the pack again, pulled out his handy roll-up chain ladder, and hung it over the windowsill.

In seconds, he was up and through the window. Devon drew up the ladder, shaking his head as he closed the window. It had been all too easy. Maybe he should talk with Tina about installing some sort of security system. She seemed to be the last one at the office a lot of the time. Someone could come in from the back and she'd never even hear them.

Right. And what would he say to Tina? *When I was breaking in the building the other night, I noticed your complete lack of security, and from my totally unrelated work experience as a model maker,*

I advise you to install an alarm system on all the windows and doors. Yeah, right.

He flicked on the small flashlight he'd brought. Three steps brought him to Jack's computer. The machine seemed to take an inordinately long time to boot. Finally, a box appeared asking Devon for a password to login. Just as he'd expected. He typed in *golf.* He knew Jack was a golf fanatic, had traveled on the tour years ago, and owned an interest in the local golf course. "Access denied." He tried *golfer.* "Access denied."

Darn. He'd thought he had it with the golf tie-in. His mind went over the information he'd dug up on Jack. *P-r-o*, the keys clicked beneath his fingers. He punched enter. This had better do it. He didn't want to still be here at daybreak. The system whirred and clunked as it connected to the computer network. Bingo! *Pro.* He should have known right off—it fit Jack's ego.

He slid a floppy diskette into the disk drive, thankful that the old machine didn't take the larger five-and-a-quarter diskettes. For someone who wanted to appear on the cutting edge, Jack sure didn't seem to know much about computer systems.

Armed with the client file names he had jotted down from Crystal's list the other day, Devon went to work. With a click of the mouse he accessed the main network directory and easily found files for all of Kendall & Associates' clients. After copying those files to the diskette, he clicked on Jack's home directory—a directory accessible only from Jack's computer with Jack's password.

Interesting. Numerous client files were repeated, with an "X" prefacing each file name. *So Jack had his own little stash of X-files.* Devon copied those files, too, before shutting down the computer.

Next on the agenda—Tina's files. As Devon left Jack's office, he noted on his way out that Jack had his door set to open only from the inside. He changed the lock setting and stepped across the hall to Tina's office. She hadn't locked her door. Relief coursed through him.

Devon walked across the office and closed the blinds before switching on Tina's computer. In sharp contrast to Jack's, her computer system flashed on in a snap. Obviously, her hand in outfitting her office had extended to office equipment as well as furniture.

Devon settled in her chair and breathed deeply, catching a hint of Tina's familiar scent. He glanced back to dispel the feeling that she was peering over his shoulder, watching him pry into her private space. He hadn't felt this guilty in years, not since his grandmother had caught him sorting through her jewelry box to satisfy his six-year-old curiosity.

The login box blinked on and off the screen. Tina must have set her computer to automatically remember her network password. He wanted to take that as a sign that she had nothing to hide.

Calling up her home directory, he found only what looked like a series of client letters. He copied them to the diskette, then examined the shared office directory again for any other files that could be useful. A subdirectory caught his interest. *Confidential.*

Devon frowned. Files on the main drive would be accessible from any computer on the network—not exactly an ideal place for confidential information. He opened the subdirectory and a file popped to his immediate attention: *DONeil.doc.* Now his interest was really piqued.

He clicked on the name and checked the file statistics. Crystal had created the file and accessed it the last time he was in the office. Was Jack—or Tina—having Crystal keep tabs on him? Several other files seemed to refer to other clients. Devon copied them all. He started to shut down the computer, but couldn't resist opening the *DONeil* file first.

His laughter reverberated in the empty room. It was a diary all right—of his meetings with the receptionist. But the information recorded wasn't anything Jack would be interested in. *Devon O'Neil is a real hunk,* the entries began. *I think he likes me better than he likes Tina.* So, this was a concern? That he might like Tina? Was Tina concerned, too?

He read on. *I think Tina does like him. She always dresses up in one of her "I am a professional" suits when he has an appointment.*

Just as he'd thought—Tina wasn't as uninterested as she tried to appear. But he knew that. Her over-reaction to his kiss said so. It didn't hurt his ego, though, to have someone else see it too.

He couldn't encourage Crystal too much. While she could be helpful, he definitely didn't want to travel that road. She seemed all of eighteen going on twelve. Tina, of course, was a different story. He had to admit he could go there easily—once he'd cleared her of collusion with Jack.

Devon stood and carefully repositioned Tina's chair. When had he decided Tina wasn't involved? He hadn't; his logic said she had to be. But some-where along the way he'd started *hoping* she was innocent. And that hope seemed to be blotting out his logic.

He returned to Jack's office, locking the door be-hind him. A sweep of the room with his flashlight satisfied Devon that nothing was disturbed, that he hadn't left any of his tools behind—a real possibil-ity given the slipshod way he'd been conducting the investigation so far. Pack in hand, he left the way he'd come.

Tina stuck her head in Jack's office. "You busy?"

"Kind of. Why?" He continued to make notes on a yellow legal pad.

She stepped in and closed the door behind her. "I think someone has been using my computer."

Jack's head jerked up.

"Why?" he demanded. "What did you see?" That certainly got his attention.

"I noticed three files on my home drive that aren't mine."

"Oh." Jack laid down his pen. "I transferred them from my home drive on Saturday. I thought I'd put them on your hard drive."

"You can transfer files directly from your computer to mine?" She was no Bill Gates, but that didn't sound right.

"Sure." Jack smirked. "I can if I'm working at your computer and I've uploaded the files from my hard drive to the network drive."

Tina twisted a strand of hair. She hadn't seen any reason not to make her password automatic—until now. Not that she had anything secret on her home drive, but she felt her privacy had been violated.

"I see. Care to clue me in as to why you transferred the files?"

Jack must have caught the peevishness in her voice. "Don't get all bent out of shape. It's work. I'm letting you take over the accounts."

"Sorry. But the idea of my computer files being open to anyone who sits down in my chair creeps me out."

"Relax. Who's going to be in your office using

your computer except me?" He raised his eyebrows Groucho Marx style. "And you don't have anything to hide from ol' Uncle Jack, do you?"

Tina laughed. "Of course not."

"If you're concerned about other people in the office, make your password private."

"Yeah, I will."

"Just make sure you let me know what it is, in case you're out of the office and I need to check one of your files."

Since she kept all her work files on the network drive, she didn't see why Uncle Jack needed her password. Yes, she did—to be in control. While that bothered her, it didn't bother her as much as someone unknown using her computer.

"Sure," she agreed.

"Okay. Now sit down and let me tell you about your new accounts."

Back in her office, she looked at the account files she had pulled from the cabinet. Nothing very challenging. All three were elderly clients with large portfolios conservatively invested to produce income. The reasons Jack gave for transferring the accounts to her made sense: the clients needed estate planning more than they needed investment management, and estate planning was one of Tina's legal specialties. In addition, as an attorney, she was well qualified to act as executor of their estates—or to help a family member serve as executor.

It irritated her, though, that Jack didn't seem to trust her to handle any real business. And he hadn't given her much of an explanation when she'd asked him about Crystal's little project, either. Just something about time-shares in the Caribbean he was looking into. He thought some of his clients might be interested. Crystal was contacting the clients for him and keeping records of any that were interested. Tina still wasn't clear why Crystal needed access to all of the client computer files for the project.

She tossed the file she was reading onto the pile with the other two. Maybe she had made a mistake moving back to Genesee. Instead of the exciting financial planning opportunities Uncle Jack had offered, her clientele consisted of three octogenarians who were liable to kick off at any time, and Devon O'Neil—who was in a category all his own.

The man just plain confused her. She didn't know what he wanted from her. He caught her off-guard every time they got together. And, after all of their meetings, she still hadn't been able to put together his financial plan, or pin him down on his investment goals. That reminded her—she should call him back. He'd left her a voicemail message asking her to research some hot investment tip.

Tina dialed Devon's number, her pulse quickening with each ring. When the answering machine picked up, she wasn't sure if she felt relief or disappointment. She left a message telling him she'd find out what she could about his hot tip. Actually, the research might be interesting. At least it was something different to do.

Lightning cracked outside, shaking the window panes.

"Better shut down the computers, girls." Jack shouted down the hall so she and the receptionist could hear.

Girls! Uncle Jack lumping her in with Crystal reignited her irritation—with him, with Devon, with everything. If that was how he felt about her, what was she doing here? Another bolt of lightning flashed and concern for her Dad and his hiking group replaced her annoyance. They'd started their trek yesterday. Hopefully, southern Pennsylvania was escaping this storm. She watched the raindrops hit the windowpane while she waited for the computer to shut down.

Devon leaned his hip against the desk, listening to Crystal chatter on, exceeding his limit for small talk. She paused to breathe. Finally, a break.

"Uh, could you let Tina know I'm here?"

She wrinkled her nose at him and picked up the phone.

"Tina. Devon is here."

His name came out on a sigh, her displeasure with him short-lived.

"Okay." She hung up. "Tina's available."

She stood and smoothed her short skirt. "Shall I walk you down?"

"No, thanks." He smiled to cover the impatience that had crept into his voice. "I can find my way."

Devon reached Tina's office in record time.

"Hey."

She looked up, a bright ray against the gloom of the storm outside her window.

"Hey, yourself."

Tina's relaxed yet professional demeanor was a welcome change after Crystal's little show.

"Sorry I didn't call you back yesterday." He eased into the chair in front of her desk. "I was out of town until late last night."

"Forget it. I just wanted a little more information on that stock you asked me to research for you."

The stock—yes. That stock was his key to snagging Jack and Tina, unless she could satisfy him that she wasn't part and parcel of its very shady offering. The room darkened momentarily as the electric lights dimmed and then returned to full brightness.

"It happens all the time," she explained. "Uncle Jack had plenty of money to decorate the offices, but none to have the electricity updated. The main circuits date back to the 1930s."

Devon whistled. "Didn't he have to bring the system up to code when he renovated?"

"Guess not, or else no one pushed it. Uncle Jack started his insurance business here about the time Fallon Industries moved out. The local economy was in a near depression. Any business was good business. It wouldn't surprise me if Uncle Jack said he couldn't afford the required update, and the code inspector looked the other way. He can be very persuasive when he wants."

Devon couldn't argue with that.

"And, to give Uncle Jack credit, he probably has helped make Genesee attractive to people who wouldn't have considered moving out here a few years ago."

"The ends justify the means?"

"I can't say I totally agree, but basically, yes. Uncle Jack has helped a lot of people."

Right. Helped them out of all that nasty money they'd earned and saved. Devon itched to share what he'd discovered in the purloined computer files with Tina. And he would, as soon as he knew she was one-hundred-percent in the clear.

"Faulty wiring can be dangerous. Want me to take a look at it sometime?"

There were those protective feelings for Tina that kept cropping up.

"Could you? I mean, you're qualified?"

So much for playing the knight in shining armor.

Tina appeared to feel safer with the flickering lights than with him fixing them.

"I'm not a licensed electrician, but, yeah, I know something about wiring. The machines I model have to be powered by something—internal combustion or electric motors."

Tina blushed. As she should . . . questioning his offer.

"I sounded kind of snotty, didn't I?"

Devon agreed. "But you're forgiven if you have some information for me on Zeltek."

"I don't." Her blush deepened. "With the thunderstorms yesterday afternoon, we had to shut the computers down or risk frying them. So I couldn't go online."

"You don't have a Zeltek prospectus in your files? None of your clients have invested in it?"

"No, not that I know of."

"I'm surprised. It is hot, hot, hot."

Tina gave him that frown he'd come to expect whenever he tried to steer her toward recommending an unusual investment. He wondered what she'd do if he leaned over the desk and kissed the frown away.

"Where did you hear about Zeltek? I couldn't find it listed in yesterday's or today's *Investment Journal*."

"All the investment chat rooms are buzzing about it."

"I see." The frown reappeared.

Devon waited for her to say more.

She toyed with the edge of her desk calendar. "I know you're trying to learn more about investing, but chat rooms probably aren't your most reliable source."

"What about E-Brokers? It's number three on the E-Brokers buy list today."

Tina raised her eyebrows in surprise. "E-Brokers *is* reputable . . . maybe the stock is too new to be regularly listed in *The Journal*."

If Tina knew anything about Zeltek, she was doing an excellent job of hiding it.

"If you have some time, let me show you what I've found." Without waiting for her answer, Devon moved his chair around the desk and positioned it so he could see Tina's darkened computer screen.

Tina inched her chair back to put some distance between them. "How can I refuse?"

She reached across him to turn on the computer, treating him to her hair's herbal scent, the scent that had assailed him during his Friday night office visit.

The login box blinked on. He watched Tina type her initials and four numbers into the password box and hit enter.

So, she'd set up a private password since Friday. He wondered why. A current of alarm ran through him. Had she or Jack discovered some sign of his break-in?

"What was that?"

"What was what?"

"That message box. I don't get that on my computer."

He hoped he didn't sound straight out of *Computers for Dummies*. She had seen his computer set-up, and it wasn't exactly a basic system. But then, lots of people owned more computer than they needed. Hey, he was a millionaire. Why shouldn't he go overboard on his computer?

"Password login," she answered.

The operating system screen appeared.

He hated to continue playing the dunce, but . . . "Your computer won't come on unless you type the right password?"

"The computer comes on, but I can't access the office network files without my password. You can password-protect the regular computer hard drive, too, if you want."

He leaned back in the chair and assumed what he hoped looked like an impressed expression.

"Cool. Can you show me how?" Devon nodded toward the keyboard and moved his chair minutely to the left, so Tina could reach over him to use the mouse.

She hesitated, then took the mouse and clicked on one of the program menus. Devon enjoyed her nearness as she walked him through the steps.

The phone rang, cutting her short.

"Excuse me." Tina spun her chair away from Devon, her relief at the interruption so obvious it made him smile to himself.

She picked up the phone. "Good afternoon, this is Tina Cannon."

Devon pulled up a game of solitaire to mask his interest in Tina and her conversation.

"Mr. Mossman." Her voice rose in surprise. "Since when?"

The sharpness in her tone stopped him mid-click.

"Oh." Tina chewed her lower lip as she listened to Mr. Mossman. "No, I'll drive down today."

She picked up a pen and starting jotting information on her desk pad. "Yes, I'm sure. All right. I'll see you later."

Tina hung up the phone and turned to Devon, her eyes bright with tears. "It's Dad. A flash flood."

Devon's heart clenched. He knew how close Tina was to her family. He took her hands in his, waiting, not wanting to ask more.

"He's missing. Cut off from the rest of the group." Her voice trembled. "He and another member, a woman."

He squeezed her hands.

"They were delayed because the woman's stupid little dog ran off and Dad had to play the hero." She spat the words out, avoiding his gaze. "They should have reached the midpoint layover post last night."

Devon gently lifted her chin with his finger. "He'll be all right."

"I don't know . . . the rains. A flash flood washed out the trail between where the group left them and the layover lodge."

She tugged her hand from his and stood abruptly. "I've got to go. It's a seven-and-a-half hour drive down."

"We'll take my truck, in case the roads are bad." Devon stood and placed his arm around her shoulder.

She tried to shake it away. "We?"

"Yes, we. You're in no condition to make the drive yourself. Can Kate watch Amy?"

"Amy! I forgot about Amy." Tina slumped against him. "If Kate's home, I'm sure she'll take her."

"We can call her from your house."

Tina tilted her head in question.

He ran his gaze down her tailored suit to her brown leather pumps.

She blinked slowly, as if warding off a momentary pain. "The house—right. I'll need to change and grab a few things. I don't know how long we'll be." Her voice caught. "What if . . ."

Devon rubbed her shoulder. "Everything will be all right," he said, hoping the Fates wouldn't make a liar of him.

Chapter Eight

Tina studied Devon's profile as he maneuvered the Xterra around another bend on the dark mountain highway. His face was sharper from the side, or maybe his intent expression simply emphasized the planes and shadows.

Thunder sounded ominously in the distance, breaking the monotonous sound of rolling tires. She looked out the rain-washed windshield. A sign for a motel three miles ahead appeared on the right.

"Are you sure you don't want to stop?" Devon asked.

"No. I need to be there. Is that alright?"

He nodded, remembering the emotional toll the search and rescue of Cameron's son had taken on Cam and the rest of his family.

"If you're tired, I can drive for a while." She squinted at the map on her lap, barely making out the lines. "It can't be more than another hour or so."

"I'm fine. But you look wiped out."

She pulled the slipping band from her ponytail, smoothed her hair, and tied it back again.

"Better?" she asked, attempting a smile.

"At least a nine." He lifted his hand from the steering wheel as if to stroke her cheek, then jerked it back as a gust of wind caught the vehicle.

Tina clutched the armrest while Devon wrestled the truck back under control. She viewed herself in the mirror and grimaced. "Yeah, right."

"Like I said, a nine."

"Thanks," she replied softly, gaining a small inner peace from Devon's compliment that gave her something to hold onto in the sea of uncertainty that swept around her.

"Want to put on some music? The radio is pretty useless up here, but there are some CD's under your seat."

Tina reached under and pulled out a box. Green Day, Red Hot Chili Peppers, Matchbox 20. She sorted through the selection of popular alternative rock groups.

"I have couple of classical CD's that might be more relaxing."

She glanced over at him. The alternative rock she

expected, but classical, too? Another bit of surprise information about Mr. O'Neil.

He grinned. "They are probably at the bottom. I don't play them a lot."

Tina dug deeper in the box and found a selection to put in the CD player. She leaned back on the headrest, closed her eyes, and let the music flow over her.

Devon was right—she was wiped out, and she hadn't even done anything. He'd taken over from the moment she'd hung up the phone, and had done everything but pack her overnight bag. That didn't surprise her. What *did* was that she had let him.

Since Amy's birth, she'd worked so hard to be self-sufficient, to prove to her parents—to herself— that she didn't need them to take care of her and Amy. She couldn't remember the last time she had stepped out of her caregiver role and let someone else look after her. It felt good. She needed all of her strength to face whatever might be waiting for them in Pennsylvania.

Panic seized her. What if Dad was . . . was gone? She didn't know if she could take that, not so soon after Mom. Nothing was going as she'd hoped it would when she moved Amy from Albany to Genesee. Especially not work. Her job was about as challenging as mixing oatmeal . . . except for Devon.

She stole a sideways glance at him. His shirtsleeves were rolled up to his forearms, accenting the play of muscles as he steered the Xterra through the storm. She longed to surrender to that strength and control, but her swirling thoughts wouldn't let her.

What about Amy? Was Genesee the bucolic place she dreamed of for her daughter? Dad was a large part of that dream. Tina squeezed her eyes more tightly closed against the thoughts of her and Amy's lives without Dad. *Don't think about it. Listen to the music,* she chanted to herself.

Tina awoke abruptly to discover the Xterra stopped, her head resting on Devon's shoulder, his arm draped gently around her shoulder.

"Hi, sleepyhead." He greeted her softly.

She blinked at the bright red motel sign flashing in her eyes, struggling to orient herself. Devon's features came into focus.

"Are we . . . where are we?" she fumbled for words, disoriented as much by his nearness now as by the flashing lights.

When had she fallen asleep? The last thing she remembered was checking out the map. How had she ended up snuggled against Devon? Tina sat up and pulled the map from the floor where it had fallen. She smoothed it over her lap, almost like a protective coat. Protection against what? Fear for her father, or the closeness she'd felt snuggled up against Devon?

"We're in Fayetteville?" she asked.

"Yeah, just outside. I thought we'd get rooms and—"

"I need to call Mr. Mossman." She pulled a cell phone from her bag.

Devon placed his hand on the phone, over hers. "Tina, it's well after midnight."

"But, I need . . ." She stared at his hand on hers for a moment, then looked into his eyes. The concern she saw overwhelmed her. She wiped the corner of her eye with her other knuckle to stop the tear that pooled there, threatening to become a deluge.

He rubbed her captive hand gently with his thumb.

An errant tear slid down her cheek. "Mr. Mossman has my cell phone number. He would have called if he had any news."

"Mm-hmm." Devon agreed gently, continuing to stroke her fingers. "If you're okay, I'll check us in and get your room key."

She took a deep breath and let it out slowly. "I'm okay."

With a glance that said he didn't believe her, he released her hand, stepped from the truck and walked toward the low square building.

She wasn't okay—not at all. She hated not knowing. And as much as she appreciated Devon's concern and help, being dependent on him rubbed her the wrong way. She needed something to do. Being busy was better than being alone with her worries.

Tina followed Devon's steps to the office door, unconsciously drawing on the physical strength he exuded, even in the simplest of actions. What would she have done without him? She would have driven down herself. She could have; she didn't *need* Devon. But having him take charge was a welcome relief.

Sometimes the weight of being a single parent, of being the sole person in charge for her and Amy—and often for Dad, too, since Mom's death—was a heavy burden. A burden Devon had taken on today without a thought to himself. Why? Part of her wanted to believe it was because he shared the growing feelings she had for him. She rubbed her face. Now wasn't the time to analyze his motives. She wasn't thinking, or feeling clearly. All that mattered was that he was here.

Tina awoke the next morning with the sun barely above the jagged mountain horizon. The damp musty smell of the motel room and the weight of the extra blankets she'd pulled on last night threatened to smother her.

She threw off the covers and reached for the phone. The neon numbers on the bedside clock stopped her. Mr. Mossman wouldn't be up yet.

Tina watched the sun rise from behind the mountains, streaks of red and orange contrasting with the brown-green peaks. At least Dad wasn't hiking the peaks. That should make finding him easier.

Tina rose and headed for the shower. There was no way she could go back to sleep, and according to the bright blue and red card on top of the television, the motel café should be open in half an hour for Early Bird Breakfast.

After her shower, she put on a pair of heavy canvas cargo pants and a long sleeved T-shirt, and placed her bulky knit sweater at the end of the bed. As she reached for the television remote to turn on the morning news for a weather report, Tina noticed the blinking red message light on the phone.

Her heart leapt to her throat. News about Dad? She grabbed the receiver and fumbled with the phone instruction card. Taking a deep breath, she slowly punched in her room's voice mail code and waited. A cheerful recording announced that she had one message waiting, a call made minutes before. Were the searchers out this early? Had Dad made it to the lodge late last night? Her heart raced as she pushed the key to hear the message.

Devon's voice greeted her, filling Tina with both disappointment and relief.

"Hey," Devon's deep voice said. "I saw the light on in your room when I came back from my morning run and thought you might want to join me for breakfast. I'm down at the café."

Tina grabbed her sweater, locked up, and walked down the plank sidewalk to the café. The smell of greasy bacon and eggs hit her the second she opened the café door. Her stomach churned. Coffee. All she needed was coffee.

"Morning." Devon greeted her. He was standing just inside the entryway paying the cashier.

"Hi."

"I knew you'd want to get an early start." He pointed to two brown paper bags. "So I got us breakfast to go."

Her stomach rolled at the thought of what might be in those bags. It was nice of him to get her something, but she doubted she could keep anything down.

"Thanks. I assume you have some coffee there?"

"Two large ones, hot and black. Couldn't start the morning without it."

Tina didn't want to sound ungrateful, but she couldn't get her coffee down without some cream. She smiled at Devon and the cashier. "Could you put in a couple of creamers for one of those coffees?"

Devon picked up the bags. "And here I'd had you pegged as someone who wouldn't adulterate her coffee with cream."

"Adulterate!" Tina retorted with mock outrage, playing along with his tease. "All civilized people take cream in their coffee."

"Ah, another assumption. You're assuming I'm a civilized person," he said as he opened the café door for her.

"Not at all," she said, laughing.

His dark hair had curled wildly from his run, and black stubble shaded his cheeks. That combination, along with his worn wool plaid shirt, fitted jeans, and beat-up workboots, made him appear more like a mountain man than anything civilized.

They walked out to the truck, and Devon handed Tina the breakfast bags once she was seated.

"I hope you don't think me ungrateful, but I'm not really very hungry," she apologized.

Concern colored his expression. "I know this is difficult, but you need to eat something. You, we . . ." He paused as if searching for words. His brow wrinkled and his mouth drew into a thin line. "You have a tough day ahead," he finished frankly.

Tina clutched the bags tightly. He was right. She needed strength to get through today, and Devon's presence wouldn't be enough. Some of that strength had to come from her. She'd be of little help to the search if she were both tired and hungry.

Tina removed the two coffees from the bag and placed them in the dashboard drink holder. "I'll try one of the muffins."

"Good." He patted her knee. "Would you hand me one of the egg sandwiches?"

Devon finished the two sandwiches and the hash

browns on the short drive to the hiking lodge, while Tina sipped her coffee and made an effort to finish one muffin.

"This must be it," Devon said, maneuvering the Xterra down a sharp incline. The rustic log building was surrounded by cars topped with red and blue lights—police and fire vehicles. An emergency vehicle was parked off to one side.

Devon glanced at Tina to gauge her reaction to the scene. She sat stiffly, finishing the last of her coffee. His heart went out to her. Today was going to be tough, even if it had a good resolution, which grew less likely with every passing minute.

Devon parked the Xterra at the end of the parking lot opposite the emergency vehicle. "Ready?"

"As ready as I'll every be." Her voice wavered.

Hand in hand, they headed toward a small group of people gathered at the lodge entry.

Devon went directly to a sheriff department deputy, who seemed to be organizing the group. "Excuse me."

The deputy frowned at the interruption.

Devon ignored his irritation. "I'm Devon O'Neil, and this is Tina Cannon, Kurt Kovsky's daughter."

The officer looked from Devon to Tina, uncomprehending.

"Kurt Kovsky," Devon repeated.

"Oh," the officer responded, "the missing guy."

Devon squeezed Tina's hand. Obviously, the sheriff's department wasn't much on sensitivity training if this deputy was any example.

"Yes." Tina gripped Devon's hand more tightly. "Do you have any news?"

"Yeah, his backpack washed up last night a couple miles from where he was last seen. It had his ID—and hypodermic needles," the officer added with disgust. "Could be a good reason why he got lost."

"Oh, my God," Tina shouted at the officer, her voice rising with every word.

Devon could have decked him, if he wasn't so concerned about Tina.

"He's a little old diabetic man," she shouted. "I can't believe no one from the hiking group told you. He's in real danger, and you're making snide remarks?"

Devon released Tina's hand and wrapped his arm around her, pulling her tight to his side.

"Insulin, you say." The deputy's stony expression softened. "That would explain the needles, and put a greater urgency on the search."

"Sure would." Devon agreed, biting his tongue not to add, *as if two people over age sixty missing in a flash flood wasn't enough to put a little urgency into a search.*

The deputy looked at Tina huddled against

Devon. "I suppose you want to help with the search," he said with resignation.

Tina pulled away from Devon and addressed the deputy eye-to-eye. "You bet we do."

That's my girl, Devon said silently.

"I'm assigning teams for the day. You two can go with Haloran." The deputy pointed to an officer standing at the edge of the parking lot next to a split rail fence.

"All right." Devon answered for both of them.

"First," the deputy took Tina gently by the arm, "you'd better go tell the standby emergency team that your father's diabetic. So they'll be prepared."

Tina nodded. "You think they're okay, then? We'll find them today?"

"I like to think positive." He turned back to the group.

Good attitude. The deputy was probably an okay guy, just on edge. Devon knew the pressure and tension of missing person searches. In the case of Cam's son, even the hardened FBI agent Devon had worked with had almost lost his cool.

"You okay?" He wrapped his arm around Tina again.

"As okay as I can be."

He squeezed her shoulder. "Can you talk to the emergency squad technicians by yourself? I want a word with our team leader."

"Secret men stuff?"

"Something like that." Guilt pricked him. What he wanted to tell the deputy *was* secret—from Tina, at least.

Tina flashed him a mocking smile. "I'm a big girl. I think I can talk with the emergency squad people without a big strong man beside me."

He grinned. Being a bit put out with him might be exactly what Tina needed to get through the day.

"I'll make sure we don't leave without you."

"Do that." She spun around and headed toward the emergency vehicle.

Devon approached their team leader, a middle-aged man. "Deputy Haloran?"

"Yes?" the man responded.

"I'm Devon O'Neil." He reached out to shake hands with the deputy, and start out on the right foot this time. "I'm here with Tina Cannon, Kurt Kovsky's, the missing man's, daughter. We've been assigned to your team."

The deputy sized him up. "Do you have any search experience? It's no picnic, you know."

"Yes, I've been in on a couple of missing person searches." He reached in his pocket and pulled out his private investigator ID to show the deputy.

"I see," Haloran said shortly. "That's the way it is. The daughter has brought in her own people."

"No." He should have been ready for this. Local law enforcement agencies were often territorial, and sometimes downright hostile, to private investigators.

"I'm here strictly as a friend." Devon assured him. "In fact, she doesn't even know I'm a PI."

Haloran looked skeptical. "I'm certainly not going to turn down help, especially experienced help. I have one question, though. You and the daughter good friends?"

What business was that of the deputy's? "Good enough," Devon hedged.

The deputy's eyes narrowed. "It's been almost thirty-six hours since the other hikers last saw her father and the missing woman. She's going to need a real friend over the next couple of days."

"I know. I . . ." Devon stopped at the sound of approaching footsteps crunching on the gravel parking lot.

Tina stepped next to him and he draped his arm possessively around her waist.

"We'll be starting the foot search in a few minutes," the deputy explained. "The helicopters have already gone out for the morning."

"Have you been working on the search all along?" Tina asked.

"Been on it since yesterday morning, when the other hikers reported them missing."

"I see." Tina stepped toward Haloran as if physically pressing him for more information.

He scuffed his boot in the gravel, waiting for her to say more.

When she didn't, Devon filled in the conversation gap. "Where will we be searching?"

Relief flickered over the deputy's face, making Devon suspect the man was afraid Tina wasn't up to the search. She was a little pale this morning, and her bulky sweater made her appear delicate, almost waif-like. He tightened his embrace to reassure her—and him—that she was up to the task.

"We're going to take the Blazer down to where the trail bridge washed out." The Deputy motioned to a sheriff department vehicle to his left. "Go ahead and get in while I round up the rest of the team."

"All right." Devon answered for them.

They walked in silence to the vehicle. "Front seat or back?" he asked.

"Back's fine."

Devon opened the back door for her, and she climbed in. He followed, resting his arm protectively on the seat behind her.

Moments later, the deputy and two volunteers joined them. One of the men loaded a cooler and some other items in the back.

"Lunch," he explained. "It could be a long day . . . a real long day. Usually if we don't find 'em the first day . . ."

Devon felt Tina stiffen beside him and glared at the man.

"What?" the man's expression asked the deputy.

"This is the missing man's daughter," Haloran said.

"Sorry, miss. All I meant—"

"Forget it." Tina interrupted sharply. "I'm well aware of what we may or may not find."

Devon massaged her shoulder. "I'm sure your dad is fine," he said with a conviction none of them seemed to feel.

Tina pulled away. "I don't need you to pretend with me."

He deserved that. She had a right to the truth. Tina might look delicate, but Devon was finding a core of steel beneath her blond beauty.

She tempered her voice. "Let's just start out with a little optimism. That's all I ask."

Chapter Nine

Tina sat on the creek bank, knees up, head resting on folded hands, her sweater beneath her protecting her from the damp ground. She watched the water bubble by, carrying branches and debris from the havoc it had wreaked days before. It was hard to imagine that the now-shallow creek had caused the devastation around her—uprooted trees, bank erosion, the washed-out bridge. And everyone kept talking about how fast the water rose.

Where had Dad and the other hiker been when it all happened? What kind of match would they have been for rushing water that had torn down 100-year-old trees? She tossed a stone in the water. Her team had walked almost the entire trail back to where he had last been seen by the other hikers.

124

She tossed another stone, harder, and waited for the plunk as it hit the water. *Stupid man. Just because he'd been a Boy Scout a hundred years ago didn't mean he had to play the hero. And for a woman he didn't even really know?* Tina winged another stone. *Stupid dog. It was all the dog's fault.* A tear slid from one eye.

"Did you get it?"

"What?"

Devon sat beside her. "Whatever it was in the water that you were attacking with such a vengeance."

"Demons." She tried a smile and felt the wetness of the tear streaking down her cheek.

Devon wiped the damp path with his fingertip, leaned over, and gently kissed her lips.

She wrapped her arms around his neck, longing to lose herself in his embrace, to let him kiss away the demons that the stones hadn't vanquished.

Devon lifted his head. She answered the question in his darkened eyes by pulling him back until their lips touched again, this time more urgently.

"Devon, Tina," someone shouted from above. They pulled away like teenagers caught by a parent.

"Here," Devon called back, his voice a little hoarse. He stood and offered Tina a hand up. She retrieved her sweater and concentrated on shaking off the grass and twigs to avoid eye contact with Devon, until she felt her blush dim a bit.

Cripes. They were adults, and the kiss had made her feel better. There was nothing wrong with that. So why was she blushing like a schoolgirl? It had been a tough day. She deserved some tenderness. Dad always said she didn't have to take care of the whole world by herself, that every so often she could relax and let someone else take care of her needs for a change.

Dad! Maybe the others had found something. Tina hastily tied the sweater around her waist and turned to Devon. He took her hand firmly in his and helped her up the bank.

Deputy Haloran met them at the trail. He looked from their entwined hands to Devon, his eyes conveying some message Tina couldn't read. Devon rubbed her hand with his thumb.

She felt a flush creeping up her neck. Enough already. She'd probably blushed more in the few weeks since Devon stepped into her life than she had in the past ten years.

"Are we heading back?" she asked the deputy, not allowing herself to hope he had news.

"Yes. The others are already in the vehicle."

Her heart dropped. "Oh."

Devon tightened his grip on her hand.

"Yep. One of the chopper teams think they may have found your father."

"Really?" Tina tried unsuccessfully to stop the

tears from forming in her eyes. The deputy hadn't said they'd actually *found* Dad.

"We hope so. One of the team members spotted a message that looked like 'on something' written in stones alongside a campfire not far from the trail. No idea what the message means, but the man tending the fire waved the chopper down."

Tina's breath caught. "It's Dad!"

She dropped Devon's hand and flung her arms around him.

"I hope so honey." He whispered in her ear. "I sure hope so."

Tina pulled away. "It is!" she insisted.

Devon and the deputy exchanged a sympathetic look.

"Now, miss," the deputy cautioned, "we don't know for sure."

"Maybe you don't, but I do."

"Tina," Devon said softly.

She faced them, arms akimbo. "On-a-Scotia is our family code."

They stared at her blankly.

"When I was a kid, in case of an emergency, if someone other than Mom or Dad had to pick me up, they had to give the code, or I wasn't to go with them. I use it with Amy, too."

"On-a-Scotia?" Devon still looked confused. "Does it mean something?"

"Nova Scotia. As a toddler, I constantly asked

Mom and Dad where they were going. Mom started telling me Nova Scotia, which I called On-a-Scotia. Later, when I was a little older, I used to tell Mom I was running away to On-a-Scotia when I was mad at her."

"All right, then." Devon gripped her hand tightly. "We'd better get back to meet that helicopter."

A tremor of anticipation ran through Tina as they pulled into the lodge parking lot to the whirl of the helicopter making its landing. *'On something' had to be On-a-Scotia. Dad had to be the man who flagged down the chopper.*

She grabbed for the door handle. Devon reached over and stopped her before she could open the door. He gently pulled her hand from the latch and held it in her lap.

"Why don't you wait until we stop before you jump out?" he asked. "I'm sure your Dad would rather have you greet him all in one piece."

"It *is* him." She searched his blue eyes for confirmation. "Isn't it?"

He leaned closer and lightly kissed her temple. "Let's go see."

Devon released her hand and pushed open the door. Tina shielded her eyes from the low afternoon sun and squinted to focus on the people departing from the helicopter. Two men in uniform hopped down, followed by a medical stretcher. Fear squeezed her heart. *No, the person on the stretcher wasn't Dad. He . . . she was too small, and had a full head of riotous red hair. Definitely not Dad. But, it was a woman. A woman had been with Dad. The one with the dog he had to save.* A second uniformed figured jumped from the helicopter, and helped a third man down. The officer reached back and took a long-haired little dog from a figure in the chopper.

"Dad!" Tina screamed, immediately grabbing Devon's hand and pulling him at a full run toward the helicopter. The deputy in charge stopped them before they reached the helicopter.

"It's my father," Tina protested.

The deputy smiled sympathetically. "Can't let you any closer."

Devon nodded toward the still-spinning propeller. "Your dad will be a lot happier to see you with your head still attached."

"They'll be taking them over to the emergency medical team?" Devon asked the deputy.

"Yeah, go right over."

The deputy turned to Tina. "Glad they found him for you, miss."

"Thanks. Me, too," she added softly.

Devon and Tina were waiting at the emergency vehicle when the helicopter team arrived.

Tina's face shone with relief and love as her father came into view. A yearning to have a fraction of that love shine his way tugged at Devon's heart. She was a beautiful woman, even with her hair a mess and her clothes wrinkled and covered with grime. Maybe even more so. Devon had the distinct feeling that this tenacious, fiercely protective woman was the real Tina, the person she was with her family and friends. The cool, practical professional was her public façade.

"Dad!" Tina rushed forward and embraced her father. "Are you all right? The searchers found your pack, your insulin. I was so scared."

The words poured out as her father hugged her back and then held her out at arm's length.

"I'm fine. A little hungry."

A look of alarm passed over her face.

"Hey, you know me," Kurt reassured her. "I'm used to uh, adjusting my insulin to meet the circumstances."

Of course she knew. She and Mom had lectured him often about adjusting his dose so he could eat more of certain foods.

"Since I didn't have any insulin, I didn't eat for the first ten or twelve hours. After that, I found some collards left growing in the garden at the cabin where we took shelter from the storm. I ate those and a couple green apples." He shrugged as if it were nothing. "So, like I said, I'm hungry."

One of the emergency technicians interrupted.

"Mr. Kovsky, we'd like to take you and Mrs. Henley to the medical center."

"Mrs. Henley?" Tina's expression changed from concern to pure astonishment. *"Mrs. Henley* was the hiker you stayed to help?"

Devon would have sworn Kurt blushed. Obviously, Tina knew the woman and, if he read her tone correctly, didn't quite approve for some reason.

"Anne rode down with me in the RV. Didn't make sense for both of us to drive," he mumbled.

"Since when did Mrs. Henley start hiking?" Tina demanded. "I knew she was into chasing; didn't know she *hiked*, too," she continued with a cattiness that surprised Devon.

He looked from daughter to father. Definitely some conflict here.

"You know, your mother and I had such a good time last year, that she was talking it up to everyone who would listen. Guess I must have mentioned to Anne that I was going again this year. Besides, it's really not any of your business."

Tina reeled slightly as if her father's last words had physically struck her.

"Sorry, Dad." She gave her father a look that apologized a thousand times more than her spoken apology. "Like the man said, we'd better get you to the medical center and have you checked out."

"I need to find about Precious first."

"Precious?" Tina asked.

"Anne's dog," Kurt explained.

Devon stifled a chuckle. A dog named *Precious* was the cause of this debacle?

"Anne will want to know where they're taking Precious; where I can pick her up."

"Don't worry, Mr. Kovsky," the emergency technician assured him. "They'll take the pup to the local vet. She'll be fine. I'll write the address and directions down for you."

He helped Kurt into the vehicle. "You want to ride along, miss?"

Tina nodded and took a seat across from her father. Anne Henley rested with her eyes closed on a stretcher between them.

"You coming, too?" the technician asked.

"No," Devon answered. That was a ride Devon was glad he wasn't taking. "Meet you at the medical center."

Tina turned her head at the sound of his voice, as if she'd forgotten he was still there. "You don't have to. You've done enough already. Why don't you go back to the motel?"

"No, I'll meet you at the medical center."

Tina relaxed. "Thanks."

"Hey, I want to make sure Kurt is okay, too." He smiled at Tina's father, who looked at his daughter and shook his head.

The medical technician closed the vehicle doors. "The medical center is right up the highway about

seven miles. You can follow us. What are you driving?"

Devon pointed to his Xterra.

The technician nodded. "I'll make sure you're behind me before I pull out of the parking lot."

Devon followed the emergency vehicle onto the
highway. He really didn't have to go to the medical
center. Kurt seemed to be fine. But sitting in a hospital waiting room was never a good time, and he
wanted to be with Tina, whether she thought she
wanted him there or not. She might be tough, but
she still needed someone with her.

And he didn't care what she thought. He liked
the vulnerable Tina. Heck, he liked her cool, self-
composed professional side, too, and her maternal
side. He just plain liked the woman, and was going
to have to do something about it.

Tina tried to control the elation she felt when she
saw Devon sitting in the waiting room flipping
through a magazine. While she didn't want to become dependent on Devon, it was nice to have him
with her through all of this.

Despite the decidedly non-institutional décor of
the medical center—bright Aztec tile floors with
matching orange, red, and yellow trim and furniture—the medical center *was* a hospital. For Tina,
no amount of cheery colors could mask the antisep-

tic smell and underlying urgency that belied any real cheerfulness.

A pang of guilt slowed her step. She pictured her father waiting all alone in a similar room at Genesee Memorial after her mother had been stricken. No matter how hard she tried, she couldn't rid herself of the self-blame that she should have been with him—and Mom. She would have come sooner, but Dad had downplayed the seriousness of her mother's condition. They hadn't wanted to burden her unnecessarily. That was one regret Tina had about her relationship with her mother. She wished Mom had been more open, and hadn't kept things from her, ostensibly for her own good.

"Hi." She couldn't keep the catch out of her voice.

"Hi, yourself." He patted the seat beside him. "What's going on?"

Tina perched on the edge of the chair. "They're going to admit Dad for observation. Someone is supposed to let me know as soon as he's settled in a room."

Concern flickered across Devon's face. Warmth spread through Tina. He genuinely seemed to care.

"Dad really seems to be fine." Saying the words made her feel more confident that he *was* okay. "I'm sure the doctor just wants to monitor his sugar and insulin levels. Nothing new for Dad."

"Good. How's his friend? The woman who was with him?"

"Oh, you mean Mrs. Henley." The idea of Mrs. Henley and Dad as friends sent a shudder through Tina. The woman was a man-hunter. And Dad wasn't the most sophisticated man when it came to women.

"I checked with the ER when they were admitting her, and they thought it looked like she'd either broken her leg or fractured her ankle. I guess the swelling was pretty severe." Her previous uncharitable thoughts haunted her. Mrs. Henley was a childless divorcée with no one to check up on her.

"Ouch." Devon made a face. "I fractured my ankle a couple of years ago. It was painful, and seemed like I was laid up forever."

Tina surmised that Devon's 'forever' was probably a week or two. She couldn't imagine anything—even a fractured ankle—getting in his way for long.

"Mrs. Henley was pretty out of it on the ride here." Tina remembered the woman's white face and the way she had gripped Dad's hand more tightly with each curve or rough spot in the road. At the time, Tina had been peeved that Dad was holding the woman's hand. Now, she realized Dad was just being a friend, as Devon was for her. And if it were more . . . it really wasn't her business.

"Hope she's okay. Your dad seemed pretty concerned. Maybe the matchmaker has met his match?"

While Tina wasn't totally comfortable with the idea, she had to concede Devon might be right. "He's a little obvious, isn't he? About the match-making, I mean."

"A little obvious?" Devon laughed. "He seems pretty successful, though."

What was that supposed to mean? Before Tina could ask, a candy-striper volunteer approached them.

"Ms. Kovsky?"

"Cannon," Tina automatically corrected.

"The doctor asked me to come let you know that she's admitted your father."

Tina's alarm must have shown on her face.

"Just for observation," the girl said. "He's in room 2032. The elevator is down the hall and to the right."

"Thanks."

"I'll come with you," Devon said.

"You don't need to."

"I know." He grinned. "But I am anyway."

His consideration shot a jolt of warmth through her.

Devon pushed open the hospital room door for Tina. Kurt was sitting in the visitor's chair next to the bed, his arm hooked to an IV.

Tina walked in, followed by Devon.

"The doctor is keeping me here overnight," he complained, skipping any greeting.

"I know, Dad. To make sure your blood sugar is level. I'm not surprised. You were without insulin or food for almost two days."

"Yeah, yeah. Nothing new. But in the initial test my blood sugar was within range," he said impatiently. "Don't know why they won't let me leave."

Tina heard a chuckle from behind her.

"I know what you mean. I fractured my ankle a couple of years ago and had to stay in the hospital overnight, even though I was perfectly fine."

Kurt nodded. "A fractured ankle. How'd you do that?"

"I was on a ca—out running," Devon corrected himself. "I stepped in a hole and twisted it wrong."

Tina swore Devon was going to say *case*. She looked at her dad. From his placid expression, he hadn't seemed to notice. But a model maker would work on a job or a project; a case didn't seem to fit.

"Anyway," Kurt said. "I'm stuck here until tomorrow. Then I guess I'll just come on home. It will be too late to rejoin the others on the trail."

"I'll stay over and drive back with you," Tina offered. She didn't like the idea of him making the trip in the RV alone.

"What about Amy?"

"She's with Kate, probably having a blast. You

know how Kate is about letting her have her own way."

Kurt fiddled with his hospital gown. "I might not be coming back for a few days."

"I thought the doctor was only keeping you overnight?"

"That's right, but Anne may have to stay longer, and she and little Precious will need a way back to Genesee."

Anne? What was going on between Dad and Mrs. Henley, anyway? And little Precious? Dad had never been a dog person. Mrs. Henley would probably be more comfortable flying back, rather than spending seven hours bouncing over mountain roads in an RV.

"Dad!" she said in a tone she usually reserved for Amy when she was misbehaving.

Kurt's expression darkened to one Tina knew well. He looked past her to Devon. "Would you excuse us for a minute?"

A lecture. Her father was going to give her a lecture. She turned to Devon and willed him to stay. After her grueling day, she didn't need an argument with her father.

"Sure thing," Devon answered, the corner of his mouth quirking up. "I'll go get a drink from the cafeteria. Anyone else want something?"

That rat, abandoning her.

"Nothing for me," Kurt said. "They're monitoring everything I eat and drink."

"Me, either," replied Tina sharply, hoping to convey her irritation at his leaving.

"Okay." The door closed with a swoosh behind him.

"Now, Teenie."

Tina flinched at the baby nickname her father had given her.

"I'm going to stay a few more days until Anne is well enough to ride back with me."

"But Dad—"

"I'm not done talking, young lady."

She clamped her mouth shut, knowing when she'd gone too far.

Her father's voice softened. "Honey, I realize this—me and Anne—is a shock to you." He laughed. "Caught me by surprise, too, especially since I've spent the last six months trying to avoid her. Once I was forced into her company, I found I like her. I really like her. You will, too."

"Oh, Dad." She hugged him, her eyes filling with tears. "I'm so sorry. I was being selfish, wanting you to myself." Her voice caught. "Thinking of Mom."

"You know how much I loved your mother." Her father's voice grew thick. "Anne isn't replacing her. I'm just moving ahead, to a new part of my life."

He held her at arm's length. "I think Margary

would approve. You know, she always said that if anything happened to her I'd better find someone to match my clothes for me, so I wouldn't embarrass her memory by going out in clashing plaids and stripes."

Tears streamed down Tina's face. Dad's fashion sense—or, rather, lack of it—was a long-standing family joke. Her mother had matched his clothes for him when they were going out anywhere.

"You have a point." She sniffled. "And Mrs. Henley does always look pretty sharp."

Her father pulled her close for another hug. "Now, about you."

"Me?"

"Yes, you. Don't you think it's time you moved on? Gave some thought to yourself, and maybe, to giving Amy a daddy? I think I know her first choice."

"Dad!" Tina started to protest, but stopped herself. She thought about how Devon had been here for her these past few days, and the closeness they had shared.

"You may be right."

"Of course, I'm right." Kurt's eyes twinkled. "Father knows best."

Chapter Ten

"Watch out!"

Devon braked hard to miss a deer that darted across the road in front of them. So Tina could still talk. He didn't know what Kurt had said to her yesterday, but she had been quiet ever since. They'd been driving most of the morning without a word between them.

Tina picked at a cuticle. "Devon, I've been thinking of asking Jack to take over your account."

He gripped the steering wheel tightly. This sounded like a kiss-off to him. What did it matter, anyway? He did want to get closer to Jack. But it *did* matter.

"Had enough of me, eh?" He couldn't keep the edge out of his voice.

"No, it's not that." She clasped her hands in her lap. "It's just that . . . I . . ."

Devon's pulse raced in anticipation of her next words.

She threw her hands up in surrender. "I'd like to see you—not professionally," she said decisively. "And I can't do that if you're my client."

He couldn't stop the grin that spread across his face. "Is that so?"

She punched him in the shoulder playfully. "Or maybe not." She gave him an exaggerated look of exasperation.

Devon took a deep breath. Tina was going out on a limb here—in more ways than one. It was borderline unethical for her to see him socially, even if she no longer represented him.

"I'd like that," he said softly, "very much."

She laid her hand gently on his thigh. Geez, she was beautiful, with her long honey hair cascading around her delicate face, her eyes wide, pupils dilated. He fought the urge to pull the Xterra over to the side of the road and kiss her silly. They *were* in the middle of nowhere.

The bright midday sun disappeared behind the hill ahead. He had to tell her.

"Tina," he said gravely.

"What? Getting cold feet already?" She bestowed another smile on him. "I was suggesting we try dating, not lifetime devotion."

That was the problem—Devon *could* see spending a lifetime with her. His heart constricted. Might as well get it over with and suffer the fallout.

"I'm not who you think I am."

"Are any of us?" she teased back.

"No, seriously, I'm not a model maker who won the lottery." He avoided looking at her. "I'm a private investigator."

"You're a private investigator who won the lottery?"

Devon glanced at her out of the corner of his eye. Confusion wreathed her lovely face.

"Why did you say you were a model maker? I know PI's don't have the most favorable reputation, but neither do lawyers." She turned and leaned toward him imperceptibly. "Did you think we wouldn't take you on as a client if we knew you were a private investigator?"

Something like that. Especially if you knew it was you I was investigating.

He cleared his throat. Might as well get it all out. "I didn't win the lottery, either."

"But all that money. You have hundreds of thousands to invest." Her voice crescendoed. "I saw it. I have your bank statements."

"I mortgaged Grandma's house and borrowed the rest from a former client."

"So that's why you've been so slow to invest. It's not your money."

Oddly enough, a look of relief spread across Tina's face. Maybe he still had a chance.

"I thought you had reservations about me handling your money, and I was getting a little ticked off."

"No, if I had money, you'd be the first person I'd call for help."

"Even though I discouraged most of the investments you came up with?"

A premonition of doom enveloped him. Tina was getting into dangerous territory now. Devon tried to laugh it off. "Even though you shot down every suggestion I made."

"So just what *are* you investigating in little old Genesee?" She grimaced in disgust. "Not some messy divorce, I hope?"

He swallowed hard. *No, something much more messy than a divorce.*

"I hate to think of you as someone who goes around peeking in people's windows."

Not peeking in. Climbing in.

She sat face turned up to him, inviting an answer. He swallowed the hard lump that had returned to his throat.

"I'm investigating financial fraud."

"In Genesee?" she asked in surprise. "It's not what you'd call a financial center, in any sense of the word."

"No." He had to agree.

"The lottery rouse, was it to ingratiate you with me and Jack so that we'd help you? I wish you'd come right out and asked."

Devon had to get it out. "Tina, I'm investigating Kendall & Associates."

"What!" She pulled her hand from his leg as if scalded. "I don't believe this. Just what do you think Jack and I have done?"

"Jack, not you."

"Ridiculous. Just what do you think Jack's done?"

"He swindled my grandmother out of most of her money by churning her investments, and he's involved in a fraudulent IPO of Zeltek."

"That stock you were asking about?"

"Yes." He nodded.

"All those other risky investments, wanting to make money fast." She clasped her hands as if keeping them still would help her maintain her control. "You were feeling me out."

He winced as if she had physically stabbed him with the truth. "Yes."

"Would you just stop calmly agreeing?" Her face contorted with an emotion he couldn't read.

Fury or regret? Knowing Tina, he'd go with fury. Devon avoided eye contact and concentrated on his driving. He saw a green roadside information sign indicating a scenic overlook a mile ahead. Devon considered stopping and pulling her into his arms, telling her everything was all right. But it wasn't. He was tearing her life apart.

"I know now that you couldn't be involved."

"Now?" She asked, visibly restraining her anger. "Meaning that you thought I was before?"

"Not for long." His answer sounded evasive, even to him. But at least he wasn't just saying yes again.

"You thought I was a crook?" she pressed. "So you . . ." Her voice caught. "You decided to get friendlier with me."

"No." His answer resounded in the truck cab. He'd thought about that in the beginning, but that's not how it was. He could see from Tina's expression that she wouldn't buy any explanation he might give.

"Then why didn't you come clean with me earlier? I could have shown you that Uncle Jack isn't involved in whatever you think he's involved in."

"But he is, and it's ugly. I didn't want to tell you anything until I was sure. The stock market yesterday confirmed it."

"So you were protecting me from the big ugly truth." Her words dripped with sarcasm. "People have done that all my life. It doesn't work. Besides, I don't believe you. Uncle Jack would never hurt your grandmother, or anyone else that way."

"Maybe your parents protected you too much." He gauged her reaction. "You see only the good in people."

Tina sat very still, her mouth drawn in a thin line.

Devon didn't want to hurt her more. But he could see that no matter what he said or how he said it, she'd be hurt. "Jack *is* guilty. I didn't have enough to go to the authorities before, but I do now."

"You're wrong, and I'll prove it."

Her voice wavered on the last word, making Devon wonder if Tina didn't have some doubts about her uncle herself. Maybe they still had a chance. Her expression didn't soften, though, and if her eyes could have shot daggers, he'd be dead. Devon decided to wait and see how things played out. After all, he'd learned as a kid that batting 50/50 on things he wanted wasn't so bad. He'd at least make Jack pay for what he'd done. So where was the satisfaction he ought to be feeling?

Tina rubbed the back of her neck as she reached for the phone to call Kate. The second half of the drive had been excruciatingly long and silent, and now her head throbbed. She dialed the familiar number and laid back on the bed while it rang through.

"Hello?"

"Hi, Kate."

"Tina. You're back. How is your Dad?"

"He's well. The doctors kept him in the hospital overnight, but then released him yesterday morning."

"Oh, good."

Tina could hear the relief in Kate's voice. No surprise there; Dad had been like a second father to her. "So how's my baby?"

"Amy's fine. Anxious to see you and her Papa, to make sure herself that he's all right. She's over playing with Lindsay right now. Lindsay's mother is bringing her back at dinner time."

"She hasn't been too upset?" Tina had hated leaving her to go to Pennsylvania, knowing how concerned Amy would be about her Papa. Amy and Dad had grown so close since they'd moved back.

"No," Kate answered. "Really, she's been fine. She's just anxious to see you guys. Did your dad come back with you?"

"No, he wanted to stay and come back with Mrs. Henley. She's the other hiker who was stranded with him. She fractured her ankle, so Dad wanted to wait a few days until she's more comfortable before they drive back."

"Not that—I mean Mr. K and Mrs. Henley? What's with that?"

"He likes her," Tina said simply.

"That's it? Mrs. Henley, the man-stalking divorcée, and all you have to say is 'he likes her'?"

"Not now, Kate." The phone receiver was feeling heavy, and even chatting with Kate was an effort.

"Okay, then. How about a different subject? Fifteen hours alone with Devon O'Neil. You did say at the birthday party that you'd fill me in later about him."

Tina leaned against the wall and tilted her head back. "Oh, Kate. I can't believe what an idiot I was. The first man I've felt anything for in years doesn't really exist."

"I'm not following you. He isn't Devon O'Neil?"

"Oh, no, he's Devon O'Neil, all right. Devon O'Neil, hotshot private investigator, not plain old Devon O'Neil, model maker, lottery winner."

"Private investigator or model maker, there's nothing plain about Devon," Kate insisted.

"Yeah, except he's just a plain liar. All this time, he's been using me to investigate Uncle Jack on some kind of trumped-up securities fraud. Devon actually believes Jack scammed his grandmother out of most of her money. Have you ever heard anything so ridiculous?"

There was a pause on the other end of the line. "Tina, there *was* some talk around town about Jack, when Mrs. Sullivan's estate was probated. You know he doesn't have many local clients."

"So, the locals aren't where the money is." Tina massaged her temple. Jack was avaricious. But that didn't mean he was crooked.

"Does Devon have any proof?"

"He says he does. But what proof could he have? I work with Jack every day. I would have noticed any improprieties."

"I don't know. You've been complaining about Jack keeping all the clients to himself. Couldn't he be hiding something?"

"No!" The force of her words hurt her head. Actually, Jack *could* be keeping things from her. But he wouldn't. Jack was family. Tina refused to believe he'd do anything illegal. Maybe something a little shady if it meant more money, but nothing illegal. He didn't have it in him.

"All right. You don't have to bite my head off."

"Sorry. I didn't mean to take it out on you. I have a doozy of a headache and I'm not thinking straight."

"Are you okay?" Concern crept into Kate's voice. "Do you want me to bring Amy over? Maybe you shouldn't drive."

"Oh, Kate. I'm probably the world's worst mother, but I don't think I can cope with Amy right now. I just want to take a couple of pain tablets and curl up and go to sleep."

"You are *not* a bad mother. You've been through a lot in the past couple of days."

That was an understatement. Flashes of Devon's confession and deception throbbed through Tina's head. Maybe she wasn't a bad mother, but she certainly was a bad judge of men. First, her ex. Now Devon, the only man she'd had any strong feelings for since her marriage.

"Are you still there?" Kate asked.

"Yeah."

"Do you want me to come over? I could call and see if Amy can stay at Lindsay's a little longer."

"No, thanks. I'll be okay once I get some sleep and knock out this headache."

"If you're sure."

"I'm sure."

"I'll tell Amy you called and that you'll be there to pick her up from her Daisy meeting tomorrow afternoon."

It wasn't exactly a lie. But it wasn't exactly the truth, either. Tina ran her hand over her closed eyes and pushed her hair back from her forehead. Was she being a hypocrite? No. Devon's lies were much bigger. She wasn't lying to Amy—not really. "Yeah, that'll be fine."

"Okay. And don't worry about Amy. Just take care of yourself. I'll talk to you tomorrow."

" 'Bye." Tina placed the receiver back in the phone cradle and debated whether she had the energy to walk to the bathroom for headache medicine. A sharp pain made the decision for her. She pushed herself off the bed and plodded to the bathroom.

Blue-shadowed eyes stared at her from her reflection in the medicine cabinet door. Her hair framed her pale face in tangled disarray. She opened the door, took out the tablets, and slammed the door shut, sending another pain shooting through her head. She wouldn't let him get to her like this. After swallowing the tablets, Tina splashed cold water on her face and ran a comb through her hair. She'd take a nap and then, if she felt well enough, pick up Amy from Kate's. Tomorrow she'd deal with Devon O'Neil and his ridiculous accusations.

Chapter Eleven

Tina stared at the blank computer screen, half-wondering why she'd bothered to rush over to the office after dropping Amy at school.

No one was here. She wasn't surprised at Crystal's absence—after all, it was only nine-thirty. Pretty early for Crystal, who rarely made an appearance before ten, even though she was supposed to be in at eight-thirty. Why Jack let her get away with it was beyond Tina's comprehension.

What puzzled her was Uncle Jack's absence. He was always in the office by eight. She tapped a pencil on the desk while the office-scheduling program loaded. Maybe Jack had a breakfast meeting at the club this morning. No, the schedule didn't show a meeting. Something wasn't right. She'd called Uncle Jack at home last night and left him a voice message saying she needed to talk with him first thing this morning. He would have called back if he wasn't going to be in.

The sound of the front door closing blocked the wave of uneasiness that had started to flow through her. Jack must have had a big night to be coming in so late. She rose and walked to the reception area.

"About time you showed . . ." Tina began. But her tease was cut short. Rather than Uncle Jack, Nick LaBelle, the Chief of the Genesee Police Department, and several men in dark suits filled the reception area.

"Tina." Nick, a former classmate, greeted her. "Is Jack in?"

"No, not yet," she answered cautiously. Devon sure hadn't wasted any time.

"Do you know where Jack is?"

"I assume he's at home." Tina weighed whether or not to say more. She didn't want to sound like she was covering for Jack—*not,* she quickly added to herself, *that there was anything to cover.*

She took a deep breath to dispel her growing panic. What did she have to panic about? She hadn't done anything illegal, and neither had Uncle Jack . . . had he? *Of course not,* she chided herself.

"I checked Jack's schedule when I came in and he doesn't have anything booked for this morning."

Chief LaBelle turned and spoke briefly to a man

beside him, who quickly left the building. *Must be headed to Uncle Jack's house,* Tina assumed.

A pained expression crossed the chief's face. "I'm sorry, but we've had a complaint filed. I have a warrant to search the building and impound all the business records and computers."

"I see. Devon O'Neil has been in to talk with you."

Chief LaBelle looked startled.

"I know all about Mr. O'Neil's accusations."

The chief shifted his weight from one foot to the other. "Tina, we need to ask you some questions. If you would come with me to the station where we can have some privacy."

The men with Chief LaBelle had already fanned out through the offices to collect their records.

"Sure." *Where was Uncle Jack? Of all days for him to come in late.*

"Could I call our receptionist first? I wouldn't want her to come in and see this." Tina waved toward the team of dark-suited men moving through the offices.

"Certainly. I'll need her name and address, too. We'll want to talk with her later."

"Oh, Crystal is just a kid we hired part-time from the community college. Believe me, she doesn't know anything about the business."

"Regardless, we need to talk with her."

Tina stepped over to the receptionist's desk and picked up the phone. She dialed Crystal's number.

"Hello," one of Crystal's roommates said breathlessly into the phone.

"May I speak with Crystal, please?"

"She's not here."

Darn, she must be on her way in. "This is Tina Cannon, from work. Do you know if she's on her way here?"

"Oh, no. Didn't she tell you? She's on vacation in Costa Rica."

"No," Tina answered, trying not to take her irritation with Crystal and Uncle Jack out on Crystal's roommate, "I didn't know. Well, thanks. Goodbye."

Wasn't that just like Crystal to take off for a week without telling anyone? And right in the middle of a semester. Or maybe she'd told Jack. Tina decided to give her the benefit of the doubt. But whether Crystal had told Jack or not, she was going to give her a good talk on business practices once the girl returned.

"Did you get a hold of her?" the chief asked.

Like he hadn't heard the whole conversation. "No. It seems she's on vacation in Costa Rica this week."

"And you didn't know?"

Tina could almost hear him thinking, *What a shoddy way to run a business.*

"I've been out of town. Crystal must have told Jack," she added lamely.

"If you're ready, then." The chief motioned toward the door.

"Just let me get my purse and briefcase." Tina turned to go to her office.

"Wait. I'll send someone in to see whether the men are done searching them. Richards, can you check on Ms. Cannon's things?"

The man who was packing the receptionist's computer left and came back. "The bag's clean," he said. "You can pick it up on the way out. But we're confiscating the briefcase."

Tina felt violated that strange men had pawed through her purse. As for her briefcase, it wouldn't provide much excitement for them—all they'd find was a new will she'd drawn up for one of her clients. She followed Chief LaBelle out the door.

"You can drive yourself, if you want."

Gee, and miss out on everyone in town seeing her carted down to the police station like some kind of common criminal? Wouldn't that be great for business. Tina glanced around. People were at their windows staring at the police cars, anyway. There would already be talk. No need to make it worse. Pulling her keys from her purse, she answered the chief. "Yes, I'll drive myself."

* * *

"Mommy!" Amy exclaimed. "You put chocolate sauce on my cereal, 'stead of milk."

"Oh, no. How silly of me. I wasn't thinking."

Rather, she *was* thinking—about yesterday, and the police questioning. It had all centered on that Zeltek IPO she'd tried to research for Devon. Tina had left the station with the distinct feeling that no one believed that she didn't know more about Zeltek than she did.

She'd phoned Uncle Jack's house again, but he hadn't returned her call. Something wasn't right. *Could* he be involved in securities fraud? Maybe coerced into it? And perhaps someone had done something to keep him quiet? Now she was letting her imagination run away with her. This was Genesee, after all.

"Mommy! What are we going to do about my cereal?"

Tina surveyed the gloppy mess. "We could throw it out . . . or add milk and see if it tastes like chocolate puffs."

"Let's add milk. I like chocolate puffs and you never let me get them."

"Yep, I'm a mean, mean Mommy who doesn't let her little girl have enough junk food. *Grrrr!*" Tina growled until Amy almost fell off her chair in giggles.

A knock at the front door stopped their play. Tina wasn't expecting anyone, and people they knew usually used the kitchen door. Must be a delivery person. "You go ahead and pour your milk—carefully—while I see who's at the door."

Tina swung the door open. The police chief and one of the black-suited men from yesterday's office search stood on the porch. "Yes?" she asked, dread flowing through her like molten lead.

"May we come in?" the chief asked formally.

"Certainly."

The men stepped in. Tina looked over her shoulder. Good, Amy was still in the kitchen. She didn't want to have to explain to Amy why policemen were in their living room.

Nick dropped his formality. "Aw, Tina. I hate to do this."

"What's the problem? Has something happened to Uncle Jack?"

The chief scuffed the rug with his toe. "No, Jack is fine, as far as we know. He was yesterday, when we had him in for questioning."

"Jack's here, in town? I've left him two phone messages he never returned." Tina's uneasiness grew. Why hadn't he called her back?

"Protecting his back," the man in the black suit muttered.

"What?"

"Let's get this over with," the man said to the chief. He flipped open an FBI ID. "Tina Cannon, you're under arrest for securities fraud. You have the right to remain silent . . ."

"Hey, Mommy!" Amy came bounding into the room and stopped short.

Tina wished she could disappear into the floor. This was all Devon's fault. Much as she hated to acknowledge the thought, he must have set her up after he couldn't prove her uncle guilty. Two days ago, she wouldn't have believed it. She thought they had something special going. But obviously he'd been using her to get at Uncle Jack. She clenched her fists. Just went to show, once again, how little she knew about him.

Amy's eyes grew wide. "Chief LaBelle. What are you doing here?"

Tina swallowed hard.

"Mommy. Is Papa okay?" Her voice quivered. "When Lindsay's daddy was in a bad car accident, she said the police came to tell her mommy and take her to the hospital."

Tina bent and hugged her daughter fiercely.

Amy pulled away, her eyes still round with question.

"Papa is fine. The officers just want me to come with them to answer some questions." She stood and looked directly at the FBI agent, daring him to contradict her.

"Like you're helping them with a case, just like on TV?"

"Something like that," Chief LaBelle answered for her.

Tina thanked him with a small smile. "How'd you like to stay with Aunt Kate for a while?"

"Can't I come with you? I want to help, too. It would be so cool. I could tell everyone at school about it."

"No," Tina said sharply. *Everyone would know everything soon enough. And it would be far from 'cool.'*

Amy's smile faded. "Okay. But remember—you said you'd take me to the playground this afternoon."

Tina took a deep breath. "Maybe Kate can take you, if I can't."

"All right," Amy agreed, her pouting lower lip telling Tina it wasn't. Remorse threatened to overwhelm her. She had spent so little time with Amy in the past few days.

"Nick," she turned to the chief. "I need to call Kate Bauer to see if she can take Amy."

He nodded.

"Amy, honey, come into the kitchen with Mommy and finish your cereal."

The FBI agent followed them into the kitchen and paced while she made the call. Geez, did he think she and Amy were going to make a fast getaway? Tina made the arrangements and hung up the phone.

She brushed by the agent to return to the living room.

"Kate will be here in a few minutes," she told the chief. "We might as well sit down and wait."

She and Nick sat in silence on opposite ends of the couch, while the FBI agent paced, checking his watch every four minutes. After what seemed like an eternity, Tina heard the screen door slam. The FBI agent stopped mid-pace.

"Tina," Kate called from the kitchen before rushing into the living room.

Tina rose. Kate embraced her. "You'll get this straightened out. Do you want me to call Devon?"

Tina stepped back. "Why on earth would you do that? He's the one behind this mess."

"You can't believe that."

"I most certainly can." Couldn't Kate see that Devon had used her—had taken advantage of her strong feelings for him? "He couldn't prove Uncle Jack swindled his grandmother, so he's trumped up this charge to take his frustration out on me."

And, she added silently, *I made it easy for him by believing he cared for me.*

Tina caught the FBI agent rolling his eyes at Chief LaBelle. "Ms. Cannon. Let's get going."

The agent looked past her to the doorway, where Amy stood peeking around the corner. "Unless you want me to finish reading you your rights here."

"No. I'm ready. Amy, come give Mommy a kiss."

Amy ran over. Tina didn't want to let her go. What had she been thinking, uprooting Amy and bringing her here, trying to duplicate her childhood for her daughter? Ha—she might just get that. Amy growing up in Genesee with Tina's father, while she sat in prison somewhere.

"I'll see you later, sweetie. Be good for Aunt Kate."

"Okay, Mommy." The little girl snuggled up against Kate's leg. "Bye."

Tina tried what she hoped would pass for a reassuring smile and waved goodbye. She wouldn't break down. Not now. Not in front of Amy.

Tina sat in a small dreary room off the police station's booking area, reading the charges against her under the watchful eye of an FBI agent. The charges were ludicrous. She was no criminal lawyer, but the proof seemed awfully flimsy to her. Why, she'd have the charges knocked out of court in a millisecond. Of course, there was Uncle Jack's statement saying that all of the doctored accounts belonged to *her* clients. She'd never even heard of some of the people named.

Tears blurred her vision, threatening to spill onto the pages in front of her. How could he? Why would he write all these lies about her? Jack was family.

The doorknob clicked, and in a second, the FBI agent had placed himself between her and the door. Like she would rush whoever was entering and escape. To where? As a teen, she'd felt trapped in Genesee. Now she really was.

Chief LaBelle poked his head in the door. "Tina, you're free to go."

"The charges have been dropped?" She knew they wouldn't hold water.

"Uh, no. Your bail has been posted. Stop by the desk and sign the papers agreeing to your court appearance, and then you're free to go."

Bail. It wasn't as good as having the charges dropped, but it was better than a jail cell. The room seemed to brighten with the light from the open door. Dad must be home. Who else would have posted her bail? At least one family member cared. Dad would know what to do. He always did.

Tina picked up her copy of the charges and stepped into the hall, ready to fall into her father's arms. To let someone else be the strong one for a change.

"Hey." Devon greeted her with a slow smile he hoped would melt the icy glare she was giving him.

"You!" she managed to spit out. "What are you doing here? Presenting more fabricated 'evidence' against me? Haven't you done enough?"

Done enough? Tina didn't know it, but he'd just given the FBI an alibi and proof that the evidence her uncle had presented against her was bogus.

"Is that any way to thank me for posting your bail?" He tried another smile, to no avail.

You'd think she'd be a little grateful he'd sprung her, rather than letting her spend the night in jail while the FBI reviewed his investigative report. The minute he'd hung up from Kate's frantic call, Devon had called the lead FBI agent about the report the Genesee police had obviously chosen to disregard. Who knew how her case might have played out if he hadn't worked with this agent before on the rescue of Cam's—his benefactor's—kidnapped son?

"Kate called you, didn't she?" Tina demanded. "I told her not to."

"Yeah, she did. But if I'd known, I would have come anyway, whether Kate called me or not. I figure I kind of owe you."

Tina bristled, then relaxed as if some of the fight had gone out of her. "Thanks. Let's get this over with."

They walked over to the desk where an officer was shuffling through papers. "I have the paperwork right here—somewhere."

Devon was less than impressed with the local police, and kicking himself for assuming that they'd take the information he'd given them seriously. If they had, they wouldn't have arrested Tina. His report clearly showed Tina wasn't involved in the fraud the FBI was investigating, or anything else illegal.

He glanced at her out of the corner of his eye. She stood statue still, cool, untouchable. He speculated what she would do if he stepped over and took her in his arms. Considering the welcome she'd given him, probably have him arrested for assault. And he'd already risked arrest for her once today when he directed the FBI agent to his investigative report.

Much of the report was based on information in the purloined files from his midnight visit to Kendall & Associates. If the FBI knew, they'd book him on charges of breaking and entering, and larceny. Fortunately, he'd been able to substantiate a good part of the information in the files by interviewing some of Jack's former clients—mostly friends or former students of his grandmother's who were very willing to talk about Jack and their investments.

"Here we are." The officer scanned the pages. "Everything looks in order."

Tina stood expressionless while the clerk read the requirements of her bail bond. Devon wondered what she was thinking. Usually, she was so easy for him to read.

"Sign here, Ms. Cannon." The clerk pointed to an X-ed line. "And, here, Mr. O'Neil."

She signed the paper and handed the pen to Devon, her hand brushing his. Her fingers were ice cold. He quickly scrawled his name.

"Here's your bag." The officer pulled her purse from behind the desk and read her a list of contents. "Check the bag and sign here that you received all of your belongings back."

Tina signed the list. The officer handed her and Devon copies of the paperwork.

"You're free to go now," the officer said.

Tina nodded and walked out of the station with grace, her head held high in dignity. She stopped at the sidewalk in front of the building, and her shoulders slumped, belying her bravado. Devon's heart constricted. He hadn't wanted to put her through anything like this.

She straightened as he descended the stairs. "Guess I'm all yours," she said expansively, opening her arms wide.

Didn't he wish?

"Until the charges are dropped and you get your money back." She started down the sidewalk.

"Tina." He touched her elbow. "I didn't know the FBI was already investigating Jack and Kendall & Associates. I never thought they'd arrest you. Jack must have executed the orders to dump the Zeltek stock Kendall & Associates held from your computer, with you as the seller."

She stopped and faced him. "Jack did make a

point of learning my computer password. I didn't see any harm in giving it to him. I never dreamed he'd . . ."

Her voice caught and she took a deep breath. She looked so tired. Again, he wanted to fold her in his arms and assure her everything would be fine—that it didn't matter what Jack had done. But he couldn't. He wouldn't lie to her again. Chances were good that a number of people would hold Tina guilty by association.

He placed his arm around her shoulders. "Let me drive you home."

"No, I need to walk."

"Okay. Let me walk you home."

"Whatever."

Not really the answer he wanted, but it was better than "no."

"I don't think Jack meant to get you involved. He just got caught up in something bigger than him."

She looked up at him in confusion.

"Jack was working with a consortium on the Zeltek stock dump—a group with some pretty shady backers."

"Is Jack in danger?"

Devon marveled that she could be concerned about her uncle after what he'd done to her. But Jack *was* family to her. Besides, who was he to talk? He'd compromised a promising relationship with a woman he loved by not being honest with her. To avenge the wrong done to his grandmother, because *she* was family. A humorless laugh escaped his lips.

"So, it's funny that gangsters could be after Uncle Jack?" Indignation contorted her face.

She was beautiful, even with her features twisted in anger. "No. The only real danger Jack's facing is a jail sentence for securities fraud."

"He and I both."

Devon ignored her sarcasm. "From what I uncovered, the consortium approached numerous brokers and planners who have less-than-pristine records."

Tina bristled.

"You didn't know, then, that Jack had been censored by the Certified Financial Consultant Association last year?"

"No, I didn't know," she answered sharply.

"Anyway, the consortium approached Jack and the others and offered them a lucrative deal. They were to buy stock in Zeltek, an obscure Internet technology stock, for their clients' accounts and for themselves. The idea was that the purchases for their client accounts would drive up the stock's price. When the stock got high enough last Tuesday, the consortium gave the brokers and planners the signal to sell. They all sold and made a killing, which drove Zeltek's price back to its true value—almost nothing."

"Tuesday? When we were in Pennsylvania? Jack

was framing me while I was searching for Dad, his lifelong friend, who could have been dead for all Jack knew? And whom was he setting up with Zeltek? More of his friends?" Resignation replaced the irritation in her voice. "I'll have to make restitution."

Devon squeezed her close to his side, a glimmer of hope flaring when she didn't pull away. He tempered the feeling when he looked into her dull, heavy-lidded eyes. She hadn't pulled away because she was exhausted, drained. *Or was she leaning on me for strength? Nah, it had nothing to do with me, them. There was no them, never had been.* They were no more than a fleeting possibility that had never materialized. He kicked a stone out of his way. Geez, he was getting maudlin.

"The police will take care of that. And Jack is the one who'll have to make restitution."

"Jack, the practice, me. It's all the same. I won't feel right if I don't make it up to the people he cheated." She hung her head. "I knew he had a greedy streak, but I never thought he'd take advantage of friends, people he knew."

"I'm sorry."

"Why? You got what you wanted."

"Not really." He studied her profile, stopping at her pursed lips, remembering their softness. No, not by a long shot.

"So, you didn't expose Jack for swindling your

grandmother. If the police have the information you gave me, you have him nailed on security fraud." She stopped walking. "They do have the information?"

"They do now," he said absently, distracted by the way the breeze brushed her hair across his hand resting on her shoulder.

"Now!" She jerked away and stepped in the middle of the sidewalk, blocking his way. "You held back information that might have stopped them from arresting me?"

He rubbed her arms from shoulder to elbow. She was as rigid as tempered steel.

"No," he said so softly that she swayed closer to catch his words. "I'd never do anything to deliberately hurt you."

"Then why did they arrest me?"

He dropped his hands and they resumed walking. "The local police jumped the gun. They hadn't looked at all of the evidence. I talked with the FBI just before I posted your bail and straightened it out. I'm sure your charges will be dropped tomorrow."

"And you'll have what you wanted," she repeated. "All the police need to do is go pick Jack up. They'll have him on perjury, too. The statement he gave the police yesterday is a complete fabrication."

"Yes. I'll be glad when they arrest Jack. Is that

what you want to hear?" He wished he could erase the gruffness from his words.

"Yeah." She sighed. "You get what you wanted, and I'm left with nothing."

He wanted to say she had *him*, but he knew better. Not now. Not when she was silently screaming at him that he was as much at fault for her circumstances as her Uncle Jack.

"Here's my street."

He started to turn down the street with her, but she dismissed him.

"No need for you to walk me to the house."

"I don't mind."

"I do."

He stood on the corner and watched her figure grow smaller as she headed to the end of the street.

Chapter Twelve

Tina's heart lightened when she saw her father's RV in the driveway. He must have arrived home after Kate had called Devon. She rushed inside.

"Dad!" She fell into his welcoming arms.

"Honey, it's all right."

"Daddy. It's not. Even when—if—the charges are dropped, I won't have any practice left. Who'll hire a financial planner who's been arrested for securities fraud?" She battled to stop a sob and lost. "I brought Amy here to shield her from some of the ugliness of the city. Instead, I've brought the ugliness to her."

Kurt held her and rubbed her back as he would with Amy, as he had with Tina when she was a little girl.

173

But somehow the comfort didn't flow to her as strongly as she expected, as much as it had when Devon had placed his arm around her shoulder on the walk home. The revelation startled her. How could she still be so drawn to him? She buried her head in her father's shoulder.

"I'll talk with people. They'll come 'round, you'll see. Before you know it, you'll have more business than you can handle. People here know you. They'll trust you."

"Dad, I know you mean well, but you can't just sweep this all away and make things better. I was arrested for securities fraud."

"You're my little girl. I want to protect you."

She gave him a big hug and stepped back. "But I'm not a little girl anymore. You can't shield me from the unpleasantries of the world."

"I'd like to."

"I know you would. I try to do the same with Amy. I think that's a big part of the reason I moved back here." Tina looked around, expecting her daughter to bound in at any time. "Where is Amy?"

"Kate took her for ice cream. They should be back soon."

Good old Kate.

Kurt's expression sobered. "Are you're sorry you came back to Genesee?"

"No." She collapsed in a kitchen chair. "I just wish I'd taken off my rose-colored glasses before I came. You know, Uncle Jack really was cheating his clients."

"I'm not surprised."

"You're not? He's been your friend for years, even before you and Mom married."

"Yeah, and he's always had a bit of a greedy streak. The past few years it's become worse. With Genesee starting to suburbanize, he saw an opportunity to make more money fast. Maybe not fast enough."

She buried her head in her hands and shook her head. "I'm still finding it hard to believe. He made a statement to the police that made it look like I was responsible."

"That son of a gun."

"Who's a son of a gun?"

Tina and Kurt turned to see Amy bouncing into the kitchen, liberally decorated in chocolate ice cream.

"Papa and I were just talking, honey."

Her father gave a sheepish nod.

Amy climbed into her lap and put a sticky hand on her arm. "Are you done helping the police, Mommy?"

Tina's throat went so dry that her words came out with a squeak. "Something like that." She hugged her daughter hard, ignoring the ice cream dribbled down the front of Amy's T-shirt. She couldn't imagine what life would be like not seeing her daughter every day.

Amy resettled herself on Tina's lap. "We saw Devon on our walk home."

"Did you?" They must have run into him after he'd left her at the corner.

"I think he's sad."

"You do?"

"Yep. He was in a fight or something."

The kitchen chair suddenly felt uncomfortably hard. She and Devon hadn't fought, not really. But she hadn't given him a real chance to explain himself, nor had she been exactly gracious about him bailing her out.

"What makes you think that?"

"He said something about winning a battle but losing—" Amy looked at Kate for help.

"The war," Kate filled in, giving Tina a pointed look.

Had Devon said more to Kate? Not that what he had said didn't speak volumes. Tina looked over at her father, needing to escape Kate's knowing gaze. He lifted an eyebrow in question.

Now they were double-teaming her, as before. They both liked Devon. She liked—no, more than liked—him, too. But he'd hurt her. Maybe not on purpose, but he'd hurt her just the same by not bringing her into his investigation sooner. He could have prevented the humiliation of her being arrested and her reputation being torn to shreds. Would she have believed his claims against Uncle Jack? He'd said he'd had evidence. He could have shared it.

Tina felt Kate and Kurt's continued scrutiny. She had to get away, do something mundane that would absorb her attention and not require thinking.

"Come on, sweetie," she said to Amy. "Let's give you a bath."

"Mommy, Mommy! The police are here again. Papa just let them in. Devon, too."

Tina pushed her breakfast away and rose with trepidation. *What now?* She entered the living room and found Chief LaBelle and the FBI agent seated in the side chairs and Devon on the couch. She couldn't read anything from their expressions.

"Hey." Devon greeted her softly, patting the cushion beside him.

"Hi." Tina nodded to the two other men before joining Devon. She rested her forearms on her knees and clasped her hands.

"Amy, let's go check the mail," Kurt said.

Great—Dad was deserting her in her time of need. As if he'd read her thought, Devon put his arm around her shoulder and eased her back against the couch cushion.

"Do I have to?" Amy looked at Tina expectantly.

"That new bird-watching book we ordered might be here," Kurt said.

"Oh, okay. Let's check."

Her father gave her a smile of encouragement before he and Amy left.

The chief cleared his throat. "We wanted to come in person to tell you that all charges against you have been dropped."

The FBI agent nodded curtly.

"And, ah, apologize," the chief added. "Charges never should have been lodged in the first place." He drummed his fingers on the arm of the chair. "I'm probably risking your suing the department for false arrest by telling you this, but my guys jumped the gun when they discovered that Kendall & Associate's Zeltek sell orders had been placed from your computer. Then, there was that statement your Uncle Jack made."

The FBI agent shot Chief LaBelle a look that clearly said he thought the chief was hanging himself.

And he was, if Tina wanted to press the issue. But, as upset as she was, she couldn't bring herself to lay all the blame on the police. They had just been anxious to solve the case quickly for the FBI. Maybe they hadn't done the best job of it, but the Genesee Police Department didn't have a lot of investigative experience beyond criminal mischief and petty larceny. They weren't any more to blame than she was for letting Uncle Jack set her up.

"Thanks for being so candid, Nick. Apology accepted."

"You shouldn't be thanking me. You should be thanking Devon."

Tina turned her head toward Devon. He shrugged and avoided eye contact. He was embarrassed! A flicker of warmth sparked inside her.

"If we'd made better use of his investigation, we wouldn't have put you through this," Chief LaBelle continued. "Devon's report refuted every point Jack had twisted to implicate you. That's what I'd call a true friend. A real gentleman, protecting his lady."

Tina could have burst out laughing at Nick's stilted language. But she could tell he was being sincere. She looked at Devon again. *His lady?* He'd removed his arm from the back of the couch and was studying his nails. *What had he said to Nick to make him think we were a couple? Or was the chief just speculating?*

"I was just doing my job." Devon crossed his arms as if to challenge anyone to say differently.

Tina always liked a challenge.

"No, it sounds like you did more. While I still think you should have told me what you were doing sooner—whether I would have believed you or not—thank you for trying to protect me."

Devon finally looked at her, his gaze seeming to search her face for something. What? Sincerity? Tina didn't know what more to say. That she was used to handling her and Amy's life herself? That she'd finally grown up enough to appreciate someone stepping in to support and protect her? The warmth she'd felt earlier grew.

"Ah, hem." Chief LaBelle cleared his throat. Tina jerked her gaze away from Devon. How long had they been sitting there staring at each other?

"So, did you pick up Uncle Jack?" she asked to cover her embarrassment.

"No," the chief replied, clearly disappointed. "He seems to have disappeared right after we took his statement yesterday."

"You wouldn't happen to know where he's gone?" the FBI agent asked in a tone that said he suspected she did.

"I'm sure she doesn't," Devon broke in, glaring at the agent.

"I can answer for myself." Tina closed her eyes and took a deep breath. Why was she snapping at Devon? It was the FBI agent who'd irritated her.

She touched his elbow. "Sorry."

His smile said he understood.

"I have no idea where Jack may be. As you may have surmised from your and Devon's investigation, there are a lot of things I don't know about my uncle. Feel free to search the house if you'd like." She raised her hands in surrender.

Devon uncrossed his arms and laid one across the

cushion behind her as if enclosing her in a circle of support.

The agent ignored her offer. "What about your father?"

"I doubt Dad knows any more than I do, or he would have told Nick. And I'd appreciate you not harassing him about it. He's been through a lot these past few days and his health isn't that good." Tina stopped short. She was trying to protect her father like her parents had always tried to protect her, as Devon had in his investigation. Protect him because she loved him. *Could that have been what Devon had been doing for her?*

"What's this about your father not knowing something? Does this mean you no longer think I'm infallible?"

Lost in thought, Tina hadn't heard Kurt and Amy come back inside.

"Dad, don't you get enough hero worship from Amy?" Tina laughed, then sobered. "Uncle Jack seems to have flown the coop, without a trace. The FBI agent seems to think we might know where he went. I assured him we don't."

"Actually, I might."

"Really?" Tina hoped her father hadn't been withholding information.

"Not for certain. Amy, show your mother what she received in the mail today."

Amy waved a postcard. Tina took the card from

her. It was from Crystal. *Greetings from Costa Rica.* Tina didn't get the connection; she knew *Crystal* was in Costa Rica.

"It's from Jack and Tina's receptionist, Crystal," Kurt explained. "She sent Tina her resignation on a postcard from Costa Rica."

Tina watched Devon's eyes brighten. Were he and Dad thinking Crystal and Uncle Jack were together? She supposed stranger things had happened. But she never would have guessed Jack had that kind of interest in Crystal from his contact with her in the office, nor that Crystal returned the interest, considering her blatant flirting with every attractive man who walked in. But, there seemed to be a lot of things about Uncle Jack she wouldn't have guessed, and who knew what went on in Crystal's head?

"Costa Rica would make sense," the FBI agent mused. "Getting government cooperation there on extradition for financial fraud can be difficult."

"Can't say Jack's there for sure. But a couple of years ago, he was trying to get me to invest in some timeshares he'd bought at a resort there. I've got some literature upstairs in my file cabinet if you'd like me to get it."

Timeshares in Costa Rica? Obviously, there was more to Crystal's special project than Jack had shared with her. Tina couldn't believe how clueless she'd been.

"We'd appreciate it, Mr. Kovsky," the chief said.
"No problem."

Devon stood as Kurt started up the stairs. "Looks like I'm done here, so I'll be heading out. You'll keep me posted if you catch up with Jack?"

"Sure thing," Chief LaBelle said.

"You have my Rochester number. It's on the card I gave you."

Rochester? Devon was leaving Genesee? So, his move to his grandmother's house had been part of his façade, too. Devon was good, very good. The day they'd spent at the house, Tina had gotten the distinct feeling he had a real attachment to the place. She couldn't picture him selling it. Maybe he planned to hang on to it as summer place? Heavens, she had it bad. She was grasping at anything to keep him here, even sporadically. He'd said he was done.

He turned to her. "Walk me out?"

Hope sparked. If they had a chance to talk . . .

"Sure." She rose and walked across the living room with him to the front hall.

"Can we get together later today?" Devon asked.

The spark grew. "Certainly."

"I'd like to settle up. You *did* provide me with financial-planning services. I want to pay you whatever I owe beyond the retainer I gave you. Square up."

Tina worked at not showing her dismay. *Square up.* Obviously, she was just another business expense. "Certainly. I plan on going into the office for a while today to notify clients of the situation, wrap up a few things myself. Why don't you stop by about three?

"I'll be there."

Tina stood in the hallway for a few minutes after he'd left, gathering her emotions before she returned to the others. She had to admit one positive lesson learned over the past few days: she could still have strong feelings for a man, the right man. Devon had laid to rest her fears that her marriage and years of working in family law had killed that ability. Now, she had to do something about it.

Tina hung up the phone and checked her watch for the hundredth time. Two-fifty. She stopped herself from chipping the nail polish off her thumbnail. She'd already pretty much destroyed the polish on her fingernails.

Concentrate on work. She looked with satisfaction at the pile of file folders in front of her. Dad had been right. Most of the clients didn't hold her responsible for Jack's perfidy. And, to her surprise, many of the local ones—all of whom had heard one version or another of the story already—wanted to continue their accounts with her. That went a long way in restoring her belief that she'd made the right choice in bringing Amy to Genesee.

Tina heard the front door open and close. She

held her breath as she listened to the familiar foot-steps coming down the hall to her office.

"Hey." Devon stepped through the open door.

Her heart started racing at the sound of his voice. "Come on in. Make yourself comfortable." Déjà vu hit Tina as she motioned toward the overstuffed sofa. Their first meeting. The timber of his voice had affected her even then, before she knew him.

Her apprehension grew as she watched him slip off his jacket, hang it on the coat rack, and sit on the couch. He looked over at her, his face devoid of expression. She swallowed hard. It was now or never, and Tina didn't like the sound of never.

"I have your statement all ready." She picked up a folder, walked over, and sat next to him. Her hand shook as she handed the folder to him.

He opened it. A smile tugged at the corner of his mouth, and Tina released a breath she hadn't realized she was holding.

"All I see is a page that says 'stay'."

"That's right. That's my charge."

"But I assumed you'd want me to go, so you and Amy could get on without reminders."

"Seems to me I remember someone telling me never to assume anything."

"Is that right?" He favored her with a knee-weakening grin. "Then, I shouldn't assume you'd consider marrying me?"

Tina mustered all the control she had to stop herself from letting out a joyous whoop. "Au contraire. You could make that assumption. In fact, you could even assume I'd say yes. I love you, Devon O'Neil."

"And I love you, too, Tina Cannon."

Devon pulled Tina into his arms and kissed her, a kiss that promised a lifetime of love—and much, much more.

From the Liberian Minister Association

[signature] Howard

Author

10/31/2011

TURNING YOUR MESS INTO A MESSAGE

Dr. Josef A. Howard

authorHOUSE®

AuthorHouse™
1663 Liberty Drive
Bloomington, IN 47403
www.authorhouse.com
Phone: 1-800-839-8640

First published by AuthorHouse   1/31/2011

ISBN: 978-1-4520-7889-2 (sc)
ISBN: 978-1-4520-7890-8 (hc)
ISBN: 978-1-4520-7888-5 (e)

Library of Congress Control Number: 2010913821

Printed in the United States of America

This book is printed on acid-free paper.

ENDORSEMENTS

Dr. Howard is a man with great humility, compassion, integrity, and a true servant of the Lord. I am blessed to be a member of his congregation who has listened to many of his powerful sermons.

We have all experienced difficulties in our lives and didn't know what caused it and how to handle it. This book represents a message of hope and redemption. It will be a blessing to you as it was to me when I read it.

Dr. Howard's use of great illustrations and examples gives the reader an in-depth understanding of God's ability and power to transform any difficult situation that you are experiencing in life. You can't afford not to read this book in its entirety.

Del Bahtuoh, BA
Retirement Service Representative
Wells Fargo Institutional Retirement and Trust, MN

Life as a whole can sometimes become very difficult and challenging in spite of who you are. In some instances, the challenges we face in life degenerate from worse to ridiculous simply because of the bad decisions we make. Some of these unfortunate circumstances put us in an up-hill battle position and sometimes the devil makes us feel there is no way out.

My encounter with Dr. Howard was a life-touching and life-transforming experience. He enlightened me as he meticulously and emotionally shared some of the challenges he had encountered earlier on in life and how the Lord helped him triumph over them. His life certainly has and continues to be an inspiration to me, my family and many others who have gotten to know him.

As my husband and I got better acquainted with Dr. Howard, we became even more astonished as we observed the mature attitude with which he conducted himself, and his sound biblical teaching of the Word of God. Dr. Howard's vast biblical knowledge and experience are fully demonstrated in the subject matter of this book which brings fresh perspectives to readers about how God can help them turn their messes in life into powerful messages.

Maybe you feel that all is lost as a result of bad choices you have made in the past. Maybe you have not made bad choices but life simply has "dealt you a bad hand." You need to know that there is hope for you in this book! This book, I believe, was inspired by God and written by a man of God who has devoted his life to teaching God's people how they can triumph over any situation. His own life is a testimonial of how he faced his giants and impossibilities and overcame them by God's grace.

Dr. Howard uses vignettes from the Old and New Testaments of individuals who were at the verge of giving up in life but God miraculously turned their messy situations into incredible messages. These classical biblical and personal experiences provide attitude choices and divine perspectives that readers can apply to whatever situation they face in life. They also give you an "aha moment" of understanding that will allow the Spirit of God to arise in you, thus empowering you to victoriously overcome defeatist attitudes.

Don't let circumstances that are against you snatch away your hope! God has a message for you and the people around you. If you were to allow God to use this book as a tool in your life, He will guide you out of your mess and transform it into a message that will bring glory to His name, I guarantee it!

Pam Bragg
Break Forth Bible Church
Wibaux, MT

Dr. Josef Howard has done an excellent job in providing helpful biblical, experiential, insightful, practical and theological suggestions on how people who find themselves in "messy" situations may regain focus and turn their lives around for the better. He provides his suggestions through six mirrors (outstanding stories from the Bible), which resonate with a lot of us in this day and age. People from both religious and secular worlds will find this book very helpful. I highly recommend it to all pastors, leaders, and CEOs to read and have copies handy for their staff, members, clients, etc.

Rev. Dr. Francis O.S. Tabla
Pastor, Ebenezer Community Church
Brooklyn Park, MN

I met Dr. Josef Howard through the Liberian Ministers Association, a ministerial fellowship for Liberian pastors and churches in Minneapolis/St. Paul, Minnesota. Dr. Howard serves as the president of the organization. I was impressed with his vision and commitment to the immigrant community and became an associate member of the organization. Dr. Howard is the resident pastor of the Bethel World Outreach Church in Robbinsdale, Minnesota, and serves in the leadership of the international movement by the same name. He is highly respected, loved, and appreciated as a pastor and leader in the Christian community. We have developed a close personal relationship and friendship.

Turning Your Mess into a Message is a must read. Solomon says in Ecclesiastes 12:12, "Of making many books there is no end." Today, more books are published than ever before. Thus of necessity we have become selective in what we read. *Turning Your Mess into a Message* will resonate in the hearts of all who read the book. Every believer and every non-believer has experienced a mess in his or her life. Life is messy to say the least. A wise pastor once remarked, "You will have three kinds of problems in life: your own problems, other people's problems, and the problems other people make for you." Mess is a part of life; sometimes of our own making and sometimes of other people's making. Regardless, everyone deals with mess in their lives.

In his writing, Dr. Howard crafts a careful and balanced blend of Bible exposition, theology, real-life illustrations from his vast ministerial experience, and practical applications to those who yearn for their lives to be transformed from a messy situation to a message that honors and glorifies God. How often we ask, "Why has this happened, where is God, why didn't God do something, why am I like this, and how can I change?"

Each chapter expounds the miraculous way God used an unlikely individual with a messy life and turned his or her life into a positive message. The woman at the well, Zacchaeus, Jabez, Ruth, the thief on the cross, and Jephthah all faced challenging circumstances. Sin, genetics, the unexpected death of a spouse, rebellion, and poor family heritage placed these Bible characters in the "most likely not to succeed" category. All had three strikes against them.

God, in His infinite mercy and grace, had a plan for each of these lives. God turned their mess into a positive message. Regardless of what mess you find your life to be in, Dr. Howard will lead you to Jesus, the source of life, hope, and transformation. Everyone faces trials and difficulties in life. Dr. Howard likens the trials and difficulties of life to "potholes." Potholes appear out of nowhere – unexpectedly – and can be destructive and hurtful and take away our joy and sense of well-being. Dr. Howard says, "Being a Christian does not mean that we will not be faced with trials and tribulations, which are like potholes in our lives (some are big while others are small)."

Regardless of how messy your life is or how many potholes are causing you concern, *Turning Your Mess into a Message* will give you hope and lead you to the Savior, who alone can turn your life around. He did it for the six Bible characters expounded upon in the book and He continues to change and transform messy lives into a message today.

Never before has life been as complex and difficult as it is today. Modern conveniences, technology, and scientific advances cannot bring peace and hope to the human heart. Only Jesus can do that. *Turning Your Mess into a Message* will bring hope and encouragement to all who read it. You will be glad you read it. After all, who among us has never dealt with a messy life?

Rev. Paul V. Canfield
Former Missionary to Mexico and El Salvador
Director of International Ministries, Open Bible Churches (retired)
Missionary to Minneapolis and the immigrant community

CONTENTS

FOREWORD

People are precious; human lives immensely valuable. God has a plan for each one. I know.

As the Presiding Prelate of Bethel World Outreach Ministries International, I am blessed to travel extensively. During my trips, I meet people, different types of people; people of various ethnic and cultural backgrounds. And it is enormously gratifying to know that each one I meet, no matter their personal history or individual circumstances, has been endowed with amazing gifts and abilities by their Creator. Sadly, however, many don't see themselves as God sees them. Life has left them blind.

This is why I am so glad for this book. It will give light to those in darkness. It will open blind eyes.

In each chapter, Dr. Howard focuses on a Biblical character who, with God's help, rises above the "messy" circumstances of their life to live a life of meaning and significance. The "mess" they find themselves in varies from person to person. Some of their problems are self-inflicted, as in the case of the thief on the cross; others are brought upon them by circumstances outside their control, as in the case of Ruth. Sometimes the mess is spiritual; other times it is natural. But though the mess varies, the common denominator in each person's story is the ability of God to help them and to turn their "mess into a message."

Just the other day, I met a young man whose story could have come right out of the pages of the Bible and would have fit well into Dr. Howard's book. He was initiated into witchcraft as a very young boy. He became a witch himself. He personally presided over the murder of many children whom he offered as human sacrifices. He regularly ate human flesh as part of a cannibalistic ritual. Then, he had an encounter with Jesus. Today, he is no longer a witch or a murderer. His encounter with Jesus transformed him forever. He is now an evangelist and travels widely to proclaim the Good News of God's love and forgiveness. His life is a modern day attestation to the truth this book so loudly proclaims. Through his experiences, others are coming to know the God who can transform what Satan has deformed. Indeed, God can turn your mess into a message.

Dr. Howard writes with the skill of a learned theologian and with the practical aptitude of someone who knows from experience what he is writing about. This lends authenticity to his words. As he successfully intertwines sound biblical exegesis with creative imagination, the story comes alive and the reader can feel himself being drawn into the narrative. The result is that the reader is informed and inspired; touched and transformed.

Dr. Howard is a man at war. The war is on behalf of all of God's people. The enemy is hopelessness. The book you hold in your hand is his weapon.

Bishop Darlingston G. Johnson, D.Min., D.D.
Presiding Prelate, BWOMI

ACKNOWLEDGMENTS

Words are inadequate to express my thanks to God, who by His Spirit, gave the revelations, wisdom and skill needed to write this book. I am not sure why He loves me so dearly but heaven knows that I am glad that He does. I have been fearfully and wonderfully made by Him. He decided to make me the "apple of His eye" from the day I was conceived in my mother's womb. When I take a retrospective look at my life, I just can't help but fall on my face before the Lord in deep gratitude for what He has done and continues to do in my life. The song says, "See Where He Took me From." Who am I that He has been so mindful of me!

God, in demonstrating His love for me, did not stop at giving His Son, Jesus Christ, to die for me. He also gave me a woman who would love, honor, and stand by me. When I look at her, I call her God's mercy and grace. To my dear wife, Lees, I say thank you for being who you are to me. Without your support, I wouldn't have been able to write this book.

I would like to bless the Lord for those who helped me by reading the manuscript for theological, ethical, grammatical, and structural corrections. To Mr. and Mrs. Joe and Pam Bragg, Mr. and Mrs. Jim and Sheryl Freeman, Bishop Dr. Darlington Johnson, Rev. Paul Canfield, Pastor Rebecca Hanson, Mr. Delawoe Bahtuoh, Mrs. Williametta Saydee Tarr, and Mr. Otis Johnson, I say, thanks a lot for your help. May God Almighty be good to you and may His blessings be your portion.

Beloved, one of the ways to know that you are in the center of God's will is when He sends people into your life to help you accomplish a task or carry a burden that is weighing you down. During the final stage of this book, I encountered some serious challenges. God sent Bro. Nelson and Sis. Naomi Hard to rescue me. Without their help, this book would not have been one of the best books that I have written. They encouraged me, did the final editing, and made the publication of this book possible. I am truly grateful to God for you and will always remember the role you played in getting this book into the hands of those God has destined to read it.

In a special way, I would like to acknowledge my friend and brother, Rev. Dr. Francis Tabla, who is the Senior Pastor of Ebenezer Community Church in Brooklyn Park and Assistant Executive Director of the Liberian Ministers Association in Minnesota. Dr. Tabla not only read the entire manuscript, he encouraged me in the process and helped me in meeting the deadlines we established. Dr. Tabla is a childhood friend whose life has been a source of inspiration. As a peer, he has been an example for me in godliness, steadfastness, commitment, love, holiness, and dedication to God and his family. Doc, we can't afford to disappoint God and His people. Heaven is watching us and there is too much at stake. Keep up the good work.

I would like to acknowledge my senior pastor and his darling wife, Reverend Natt and Sis. Margaret Friday, and the entire Bethel World Outreach Church family of Minnesota. You have been a blessing to me and my family over the years. You continue to believe in me and God's call upon my life. You have trusted me in helping to shepherd your souls. What a privilege and an honor! May I continue to follow the footsteps of Christ as I try to make Him known to all who enter through the doors of our beloved church. Thanks.

Last but certainly not the least, I give God praise for the Liberian Ministers Association in Minnesota, a non-profit religious organization of beautiful, anointed and outstanding men and women who have been called as missionaries to the United States from our nation of birth, Liberia. You have had a tremendous impact on my life in the last three years since I took over the leadership of the organization. You are the finest group of ministers that God has anointed and set apart to fulfill His plans in the lives of people. Remember that there is a host of heavenly witnesses watching us; the Liberian community in Minnesota believes in us and is counting on us for spiritual and moral leadership; our American friends are watching our zeal, enthusiasm, and love for God; the Christian community in America is looking up to us to rekindle the fire of God in the Church and help them return to their first love; and our individual churches are looking up to us to be "Christ" in their lives. Please don't let them down. I hope that this book will help you in remaining faithful as we labor together in the vineyard of Christ our Lord and Master. While serving the Lord and His people, my prayer is that if you do find yourself in a messy situation, He would turn it into a message.

DEDICATION

This book is dedicated to Christ, the author and finisher of my faith, who by His death and resurrection made it possible for my mess to be turned into a message.

INTRODUCTION

There are few things that I can point to in my life that I know unequivocally happened because of the direct intervention of God. This book is one of those things for which I cannot take the praise or credit. In Isaiah 42:8 we read, "I am the LORD; that is my name! I will not give my glory to another or my praise to idols." This book was written because God intervened and made it happen. Of course you might be wondering why I am making such a claim or what were some of circumstances that led to this book being penned and published that made me think that God intervened directly. Allow me to share a few with you.

First, I did not intend to write this book at the time I did and the way I did. As a matter of fact, I had planned to publish my PhD dissertation on "Challenges Non-Westerners Face in Establishing a Multicultural Church," as my second book after I wrote my first book five years ago entitled, *Ushers, God's Frontline Commanders*. Little did I know that God had another plan. King Solomon understood the workings of God far more than I. It was for this reason that he wrote, "In his heart a man plans his course, but the LORD determines his steps" (Proverbs 16:9).

Second, when I decided to obey the "voice of the Lord" (a strong impression that I could not ignore) and started writing, I had a serious challenge with the title that kept coming to my mind, especially since the title included the word *Mess*. This word in my culture of origin is not used in a positive way. It is one of those words that is avoided and even considered by some individuals to be a "swear word" even though we know that it simply expresses a state or condition that is untidy, disorderly, offensive, or maybe unpleasant. A comparison could be made with the word "bloody" which could be used in a non-offensive way in the United

States to simply describe a terrible accident, one in which a lot of blood was shed. The same word "bloody" may not be used in the United Kingdom to describe the same accident because it might be considered offensive.

Similarly, in my culture of origin, telling a friend or a relative that he or she is "fat" is actually a compliment because what you are saying is that the person is living a stress-free life and is enjoying the best of meals which is resulting in him or her gaining a few pounds. Using the same expression here in the United States is a recipe for disaster and a "good way" to make long-lasting enemies. I learned my lesson the hard way when I offended another student (a female) while studying cross-culture ministry at Bethany College of Missions in Bloomington, Minnesota. Our friend had come from a foreign missions trip and we went to the airport to get her. Everyone was saying good things about how she looked beautiful, refreshed, etc. I thought that she had added a few pounds which made her look really good. I then said, "Wow, you look really good. See how fat you are!" You can imagine what happened after that. Unfortunately, it was a rude awakening for me to the fact that there are certain expressions one just cannot use in some cultures (even if your intentions are good).

Hence, in trying to be true to my conscience not to offend anyone by using the word "mess" in this book, I researched and talked to scholars, pastors, and some members of my congregation from both my culture of origin and the American culture in an effort to find another word that would express what I believe the Lord had placed in my spirit. I regret to report that we did not find any other word that would best describe or explain what I wanted to express. Interestingly, the more I wrote and wrestled with the use of the word "mess," the more it became apparent that I just couldn't change the title of this book. That is what God wants to convey to His people and I couldn't change the plan of God because of my uneasiness or cultural bias. I therefore sincerely apologize if the use of the word "mess" in the title, *Turning Your Mess into a Message* is offensive to you.

Thirdly, the idea of using six stories (three from the Old Testament and three from the New Testament) was not originally mine. In fact, my initial thought was not to write a book. I started penning my thoughts on one of the stories shared in this book with the intent to use it as a sermon. When I started writing, the Lord kept bringing one story after another to my mind and it finally dawned on me that the Lord was actually leading me to write a book and not a sermon. I prayed, submitted my thoughts to the control of the Holy Spirit, and obeyed His leading. When I was done, I realized what had happened, and I was ecstatic to know that I had written about six mesmerizing stories in the Bible. I was also fascinated when I became conscious of the fact that I knew very little about the characters in the stories that I wrote about before I actually started writing. I do not recall preaching a sermon or teaching on any of the characters in this book. Therefore, I have to humbly and honestly admit that God somehow opened my eyes to some of the revelations shared in this book and led me to write the way I have written.

Finally, if you are reading this book, then God has answered my prayer for a financial miracle. Currently as I write this introduction, I don't have the finances to publish this book. Publishing a book is very expensive, especially if it is a high quality book. I have committed the manuscript into the hands of God and have asked Him to provide the resources if He desires to have it published. I have prayed as well that the Lord would grant His people the tenacity to read the book and be blessed. I honestly cried before the Lord and told Him that I did not want to write a book that would be one of the many unread books on the shelf. If you are reading this book, then I can't help but join my voice to that of the Prophet Jeremiah who wrote in Lamentations 3:22-24, "Because of the Lord's great love we are not consumed, for His compassions never fail. They are new every morning; great is your faithfulness. I say to myself, 'The Lord is my portion; therefore I will wait for him.'"

As a result of some of the reasons mentioned above, you will notice as you read this book, that I have used different writing styles, namely: creative, expository, descriptive, narrative, and analytical to unearth, in a unique, interesting, easy-to-read, enjoyable, and yet thought-provoking manner how God turned the mess of each character into a message of a second chance, enlarged territory, honesty, trust, restitution, redemption, kinsman-redeemer, abiding presence, and ultimately, heroes of faith.

Chapter one is about the Samaritan woman who met Jesus at the well (John 4:1-42). It explores, in a very classical and literary way, the origin of the Jewish and Samaritan conflicts; the probable reason why the Samaritan woman went to the well at noon to fetch water (not at the time when everyone else was at the well); and her social, biblical, moral, cultural, and philosophical values. It highlights her internal struggles with doubt, self esteem, shame, disgrace, lack of acceptance, and sexual sin. This chapter reveals some deep theological truths as it unravels the complex questions the Samaritan woman asked Jesus and how He graciously opened her eyes in order for her to see in the final analysis that He was the Messiah (Hebrew: *Mashiach* מָשִׁיחַ).

Chapter two entitled, "Jabez: God Turns a Mess of Pain into a Message of an Enlarged Territory," is found in 1 Chronicles 4:9-10. Jabez, an Old Testament character, whose name means "pain," has become well known through a little book authored by Bruce Wilkerson entitled, "The Prayer of Jabez: Breaking Through to the Blessed Life." Being cognizant of Wilkerson's book and the attention that the prayer of Jabez has received over the past decade, this chapter was written in a creative way to draw attention to Jabez's life before he was born, the agonizing circumstances surrounding his birth, the logic and significance of his name and names in the Old Testament, and how he became a man who was most honorable in the eyes of God. It points out how Jabez realized that there were "destiny vultures" in his life and he had to deal with them head on (with the help of God Almighty) in order to change his future. The chapter is intended to help readers understand how God not only has the ability, but is also willing and ready to turn our life of pain, frustration and disappointments into a message of an enlarged territory.

Chapter three, "Zacchaeus: God Turns a Messy Life of Corruption into a Message of Honesty, Trust, Restitution and Redemption," is found in Luke 19:1-10. The main character is Zacchaeus, a short man. Have you ever thought about how physical disability can lead to spiritual disability? Better still, have you thought about how physical disability could influence and sometimes define social, political, moral, and ethical values? This chapter is an eye opener to "Zacchaeus' world," a world that many of us have never and probably would never experience. It touches core societal and contemporary issues such as bullying, trust, betrayal, and the quest to find justice, fame, and inner peace, even if it is at the expense of others.

Chapter four, taken from Ruth 1:1-4:22, is entitled, "Ruth: God Turns a Messy Situation of Death and Hopelessness into a Message of God's kinsman-redeemer." In life, all of us experience challenges. Being a Christian does not mean that we will not be faced with trials and tribulations which are like potholes in our lives (some are big while others are small). For some of us, the idiomatic expression, "When it rains, it pours," is indeed true. Our potholes just keep getting larger and no amount of patch seems good enough to stop the holes from getting larger. Ruth had her share of life's challenges. Beginning with the death of her father-in-law, brother-in-law, and husband and also the possibility of returning to her people and a god she once abandoned, this woman had to make a hard decision. What were some of the factors that influenced her decision? Why and how did God send a kinsman-redeemer into her life? Who is your kinsman-redeemer and how can you get your kinsman-redeemer to fulfill God's plan and purpose in your life? These are a few of the questions to which you will find answers that will change the course of your life forever.

Chapter five entitled, "The Thief on the Cross: God Turns a Messy Situation of Eternal Separation into a Message of Abiding Presence," is examined from Luke's account of the events that took place when Jesus was on the cross (Luke 23:39-43). This chapter deals with some serious theological issues such as deathbed conversion, participation in the sacraments of the church, Christ's view on offering forgiveness without prior repentance, different types of sins, etc. It is a solid biblical teaching on how anyone (especially those who have had an encounter with the Risen Christ) can change course even at the last moment of life when all hope is lost and all of hell is rejoicing because one more soul is about to be condemned for eternity. In the story, the thief recognizes his condition, confesses his sins, and commits himself to the King of Glory even after having been condemned to die a humiliating death on the cross. This chapter gives hope to those who feel that God will not accept them because of their past. It is about grace, the free unmerited favor that God has shown to us through the sacrificial death of Jesus, His One and only begotten Son. If you would like to understand the intricate details about grace, this is the chapter that will provide the theological foundation of Christ's work on Calvary.

Chapter Six entitled, "Jephthah: God Turns a Messy Life of Being an Outcast into a Message of Being a Hero but…" is found in Judges 11:1-40. Jephthah is best known by many because of the unnecessary vow he made to God in which he promised to sacrifice the "first thing" that greeted him if he returned home victorious from the battle against the Ammonites. Unfortunately as we know, the "first thing" that greeted him when he returned was his daughter (his only child). There were a lot of things that happened before that vow was made. Jephthah, the son of a prostitute who was unwanted, disgraced, and cast out of the house by his siblings while the elders of Israel stood by and watched, became a hooligan, ruffian, warlord, and head of a gang of outcasts. Later, he became the judge of Israel and head of the army. How did it happen? How did Israel go from being a nation that was very rebellious towards God to becoming a nation that wanted to make things right and make amends? How did the elders engage

Jephthah, ask for his forgiveness after having wronged him all those years while still keeping their dignity intact? How did Jephthah, an illegitimate son of Gilead, a child of shame, and a man with an improper pedigree, insufficient judicial and military preparation become the hope of Israel? Finally, when his dream was realized, what prompted him to choose that particular vow, and did he carry out the vow by killing his only child? In a thought-provoking, theologically accurate, and soul searching manner, this chapter deals with all of the questions mentioned above and many more. It cautions readers to be mindful of the fact that God can turn our mess into a message, but we have to guide that message so that it doesn't become a mess again! Read the chapter to find out how you could protect your message from becoming a mess again.

Finally, this book would not have been a complete literary genre without a concluding chapter. Whenever I preach a sermon, I try to end with the question, "and so what?" The question is intended to make the sermon applicable, personal, and contemporary. The same is true for the concluding chapter of this book. Its intent is to help readers understand that if God did it for others, He can do it for them. He is the same God yesterday, today, and forever. Based on the revelation that the Psalmist David received in Psalm 8:1-9, this chapter explains three basic facts that are applicable to you and all those who are children of God. It points out how you have been marvelously created by God, how He cares so much about you, and how He is ready to crown you with all of His glory. If you have any doubt in your mind that the outcome of the stories shared in this book could ever happen to you, open your spirit to the voice of God as you read the concluding chapter of this book. I can guarantee that God is ready to reveal His master plan for your life as you read this concluding chapter. Your life will never be the same! Sit back, relax, read, and let God do a new thing in you.

Chapter I: The Woman at the Well (John 4:1-42) God Turns a Messy Life of Sexual Sin into a Message of a Second Chance

When I take a retrospective look at my life, I find it quite embarrassing that I have made some very poor decisions of which I am not proud. Some of these decisions were made when I was under pressure to impress others, live up to someone's expectation of who I ought to be, or simply being naïve. The fact that I did not know who I was, Whose I was, and what I stood for, made others feel they had the right to redirect, realign, reconstruct, remodel, or reprogram me into the person that would suit their taste. This led people to begin to tell me what to do and who to become. They also felt it was their God-given right to tell me how to walk and with whom to walk; how to talk and to whom to talk; how to laugh and with whom to laugh; and how to befriend others and with whom I could become friends. I thank God from the depth of my heart that He helped me to break that level of control others had over my life, and I was able to develop an independent spirit under the leading and direction of the Holy Spirit.

Quite honestly, it would be very easy and self gratifying for me to blame others (family members and friends) for all of the bad decisions that I have made, but I know that I would be doing you and myself a disservice and I would be lying. Indeed there have been many individuals in my life who have helped me make some very positive decisions that turned

1

my life around. Without those individuals and obviously the leading of God's Spirit, I am not sure where I would be today. It means that most of the decisions I have made, both negative and positive, have either been influenced by others or by my own doing.

I have not conducted a scientific study to know what percentage of the bad decisions can be attributed to others or myself. However, I do know that I have immensely contributed to both the good and bad decisions I have made in life, and I take full responsibility even if others influenced my behavior in the past. What is interesting is the fact that almost every time I made a bad decision, I always sought to undo what had already been done. Of course, it was not always possible to undo it, but that did not stop me from thinking about having a second chance in order to redeem myself.

Have you ever had a strong desire to be given the opportunity to start afresh in life after making some bad decisions that resulted in devastating consequences? I am sure you have. Or perhaps for you, it is like receiving a fresh start in life especially after a bad day, week, month, or year.

It is quite common to hear people make resolutions at the end of the year that the coming year will be different: bad habits will be broken, weight will be lost, better jobs will be found, or that he or she will become a better husband/wife or Christian. The problem, however, is that while our intentions are good, our will and our ability are not, and we too often fall back into the same habits, the same actions, and the same pattern that brought us to where we were in the first place. Like Jesus said to His disciples in the Garden of Gethsemane, "The spirit is willing but the flesh is weak" (Matthew 26:41-42). When failure occurs enough times in our lives, we are tempted to believe and feel that our situation has become hopeless and that we will never succeed or make good decisions in life. It is at this point in our lives that God desires to step in. When the enemy has whispered lies about our ability to make a good decision and stick to it, and we begin to believe him and succumb to his lies, then it's time to call upon the name of Jesus. The Bible declares in John 8:44 "You belong to your father, the devil, and you want to carry out your father's desire. He was a murderer from the beginning, not holding to the truth, for there is no truth in him. When he lies, he speaks his native language, for he is a liar and the father of lies."

If indeed you do not belong to the devil, then you should not allow his lies to penetrate your spirit and take residence there. You need to refuse or reject his lies (in Jesus' name), then hold onto the truths found in the Word of God and declare them over your life. This is a fact that needs to sink into your spirit man. Even if what the enemy is accusing you of is true, you can still reject it if you have confessed your sins to God. The Bible describes the devil as the accuser of the brethren (Revelation 12:10). He will accuse you even after you have confessed your sin before the Lord, asked for His forgiveness, and abandoned the confessed sin. Thank God that we have the ability to overcome the accusation of the devil. In the same verse, the Bible says that we can overcome the accusing words of the devil by the blood of the Lamb and the word of our testimony. Let's examine what it means.

Our successes and victories in our Christian walk depend on a clear understanding and application of the power of the blood of Jesus in our lives. I am convinced that a Christian will never enjoy the full benefits of being a child of God until he or she gives the blood of Jesus its rightful place in his or her walk with the Lord. In Hebrews 9:22, we read, "And almost all things are by the law purged with blood; and without the shedding of blood there is no remission of sin."

This means that because of the blood of Jesus, I have been forgiven of my sin. If I have confessed Jesus as my Lord and Savior, and believe in my heart that God raised Him from the dead, I am a child of God (Christian). It is not based on my righteousness, holiness, or past life. It is not based on my affiliation with a particular local church or my financial contribution to a given local church or a charitable organization. It is simply based on the fact that Jesus paid the price with the blood He shed on Calvary's cross. Consequently, my life has been redeemed and my sins have been forgiven. All I have to do is accept that fact and become an overcomer! There are several blessings that I could, therefore, enjoy as a Christian who has been washed by the blood of the Lamb. Because of the blood of Christ:

1. I could experience atonement for my soul (Romans 5:11)
2. I could experience remission of my sins (Hebrews 9:22)
3. I could experience life and peace (Colossians 1:20)
4. I could experience redemption (Ephesians 1:7)
5. I could experience justification (Romans 5:9)
6. I could be brought near to God (Ephesians 2:13)
7. I could experience a pure conscience (Hebrews 9:14)
8. I could experience cleansing from sin (1 John 1:7)
9. I could experience sanctification (Hebrews 10:10-14)
10. I could become a part of a new and better covenant (Matthew 26:28)
11. I could experience a new birth (1 Peter 1:18-23)

12. I could have overcoming power (Revelation 12:11)
13. I could experience deliverance (Zachariah 9:11)
14. I could experience healing (Isaiah 53:4-5; 1 Peter 2:24)
15. I belong to the body of Christ - the Church (Acts 20:28)
16. I receive salvation (Hebrews 9:15)

The second way we can overcome the accusation of the devil is by the word of our testimony. Everyone has a testimony. Yours may not be as drastic as mine, but it is your testimony. Don't despise yours! It is critical that we understand that each test God brings us through is another testimony to His power and work in our lives. What God has done for you should serve as a constant reminder of His goodness as well as a faith builder for what He can do in your current situation. Isn't it true that one of the major reasons why many of us are overburdened by life's difficulties is because we forget what God has done and can do for us? Psalm 78:9-11 and verses 40-43 remind us that the generation of Israelites who had seen God's power displayed time and again was guilty of forgetting God and how He had worked so powerfully on their behalf. As a result, they angered the Most High God and didn't receive their inheritance. Basically, it is safe to say that an overcomer is a believer who sees his or her current test as an opportunity for God's power to produce another testimony. Hence, he or she stands on God's word and is not moved by the situation simply because God is in control. Consequently, that person (the overcomer) experiences the peace of God that surpasses human understanding and he or she can sleep peacefully in the midst of a stormy situation. In Proverbs 3:24, we are told that as servants of the Lord who obey Him and His word, when we lie down, we will not be afraid and our sleep will be sweet.

Given all of the above, when the devil comes to remind you of a sin that has been forgiven, you should say to him, "Satan, I have been washed by the blood of the Lamb, and I am no longer guilty of the sins I committed. Jesus paid the price for those sins and I have been cleansed by His blood. God remembers my sin no more and therefore, I am free in Jesus' name." When we get into the habit of leaving our sins at the altar and reminding the devil that we know of our covenant rights in the Lord, we will then begin to live victorious lives in the Lord.

There are primarily two ways in which the devil accuses us. The first is through our conscience and the second is through others. In the story found in John 4:1-42, we see that the woman is being accused by others. Analyzing this story from the woman's point of view might help us to see how it was the plan of the devil to destroy her. Fully understanding some of the cultural manners and customs that were prevalent at the time will assist us in understanding why Jesus reacted the way He did and why He decided to turn this woman's mess of sexual sin into a message of a second chance.

Here are a few things that need to be mentioned initially about the story. John states that Jesus "had to" go through Samaria. It is noteworthy that He could have gone around Samaria, because that is what most Jews did, but John says that He "had to" go through Samaria. The primary reason given by John (if we want to be true to Scripture) is because Jesus wanted to avoid being arrested before His time. John notes in 4:1, that the Pharisees had heard that Jesus was gaining and baptizing more disciples than John. There was a sense of antagonism against Christ and He decided to withdraw immediately from Judea and go back to Galilee. However, in order to get to Galilee, John states, He "had to" go through Samaria, the shortest route that unfortunately was a semi-hostile territory whose inhabitants, the Samaritans, had a strained relationship with the Jews because they were believed to be outside the covenanted mercies of Israel.

As a result of the strained relationship between the Jews and the Samaritans, it was expected that Jesus, a Jewish teacher, Rabbi, and religious leader, would avoid going through Samaria on His way to Galilee even though it would have meant taking the longer route. Thus, it is only wise and exegetically accurate to admit that Jesus went through Samaria because it was the shortest route and He was not going to conform to the petty quarrel that existed between the Jews and Samaritans. But, the other reason (not stated by John and the writers of the other synoptic gospels), and I believe that it is the most important, is that Jesus had to go through Samaria because He had a mission to accomplish. There was a woman and an entire village that needed to hear the gospel of salvation; there was a Messiah that needed to be revealed to those who had been waiting in anticipation of His coming.

As John begins to tell the story of Jesus' encounter with the Samaritan woman, he states that it was about the 6th hour. That would make it around noon time. I come from a society where women and children go to the "river" or "well" to fetch water for the family. This is done early in the morning between the hours of 6:00 a.m.-8:00 a.m. There are a couple of reasons why that time is ideal. Allow me to name a few.

The first is the fact that going early in the morning allows the women to fetch water before the family leaves for the farm. Customarily, in such a society where there is communal farming or cattle-rearing, members of the family leave early to work the earth or take their cattle into the field. When they return in the evening, they immediately begin preparing the meal for the day. Since water would be needed, it is only expedient to have it already at home.

Second, the water is at its best in terms of quality and quantity during the early morning hours. If an entire village is using a given well, the residue, mud or sand at the bottom of the well mixes with the water after several individuals have drawn from it. That is why it is better to fetch your share of the water as early as possible.

Third, when the water supply is scarce or the well is running low because of the "dry season" and there is insufficient rain to provide the necessary quantity of water everyone needs, families try to get their water supply early in the morning before it runs out.

Fourth, in a village like the one in which the Samaritan woman lived and some of those that are in my country of origin, when women went to the well in the morning, it was also an opportunity or avenue for communication and fellowship. It was during those long walks to the "river" or "well" when the latest news in the village was shared. It was the forum for gossip, encouragement, and discussion of women's issues. It was like listening to and participating in the *CBS Early Show* or *TMZ* (Celebrity gossip and entertainment news). What also happened at the "well" or "river" was a coordinated effort among women to help each other in loading the "bucket" or "pan" on each other's head in order to carry it home. The bucket or pan used to fetch water was usually too large for a woman to place on her own head; therefore, it was prudent that she went to the well when someone was around to help her place it on her head. It also meant that if a woman was arrogant, selfish, and rude or living a life that was a disgrace in the community, the other women would use this time to give her pieces of advice, encouragement, or even chastise and rebuke her if what she had done or was doing was outside of the village's norms and customs. If she refuses to listen, they would refuse to help her load her pan or bucket on her head. She would be forced to return home without water and her husband would then become aware of her behavior and she would be in big trouble (given the fact that it was a male dominant culture and the rules were different).

Fifth, the distance to the well or river where water is fetched is sometimes far and dangerous for a single woman to travel alone. Hence, women would usually go in a group to provide protection for each other.

Finally, during the morning hours or early evening hours, it is cooler and the sun is not as hot as midday. That is why it is difficult to understand and mind-boggling to read that this woman chose to go to the well at a time when the sun was extraordinarily hot or at its peak.

Given all of the reasons mentioned above, it is therefore strange, for those who know about village life, to read that the Samaritan woman went to the well at midday, a time when women usually would not go to fetch water in a village.

Obviously, the question is: Why did this woman decide to go to fetch water at the worst time of the day? Allow me to paint a picture in your mind about what may have happened. I want you to think about what she may have been feeling and experiencing as she went to get some water.

It probably started when she was in her room and she realized that she needed some water. Interestingly, she knew from the moment she awoke that morning that she had to get water, but she deliberately waited until midday, she picked up her clay jar (pan), opened the door and not surprisingly, the heat of the day hit her in the face. Taken aback for a moment, she exited and looked up and down the dusty street. It was relatively quiet. It was not really a good time to fetch water. In fact, it was not a good time to be outside. The sun was at its peak and it was beating down on her. She could have gone earlier, when it was cooler, but that would have meant facing the other women there. Also, chances were that if she had decided to wait until early evening when it was also cooler, she would have had to encounter other women. That's why she was going now. She didn't want to face the other women at the well.

She was the town's "bad girl." She was sleeping with a guy to whom she was not married and, as Jesus pointed out, she had already been married five times and none of those relationships worked out. She had tried for a fresh start before by trying to change her circumstances, but each time something was not right; something went wrong. Each of those five times she entered into a relationship, it was with the hope of having a different life, making a vow that things would be different and that life would be better. Each time, things turned out to be the same. It was never different. Her expectations were always cut short. Her energy was wasted, and her hopes dashed not just once, but on five different occasions. She had probably given up on marriage, living a decent and normal village life, and being one of the "good" or "normal girls" in the society within which she lived. She was simply existing from day to day and living the life of a shadow. That is the description that David gives when he spoke of a life without hope. In 1 Chronicles 29:15 we read, "We are aliens and strangers in your sight, as were all our forefathers. Our days on earth are like a shadow, without hope." Our shadows exist, but they don't live. They can be seen, but they lack importance and significance. They can be ignored, stepped on, disregarded, or erased depending on the location of the sun or the reflection of the light that makes our shadow visible.

Are you living your life on earth like a shadow? Are you living life without hope, and are you only existing because you have breath in your body? It doesn't have to be that way, you know. For the most part, many of us live a life of a shadow because of our past errors and our lack of hope for the future. Over the years, maybe you have made some terrible decisions that are haunting you to this day. Maybe you started smoking cigarettes, drinking alcohol, or even taking drugs and now you are addicted. Maybe you followed the wrong crowd, listened to the wrong advice and got some girl pregnant or you became pregnant and had a child when you were not ready. Perhaps it happened when you were still a child yourself. Maybe you refused to go to college because you thought college was a waste of time and you could earn enough money by doing "odd jobs." Maybe you got divorced when you knew in your heart that you could work out your problem with your spouse but you saw that everyone else was getting divorced, so you escaped from the unpleasant life with your spouse.

Now, you sit and wonder …. why, why, why? If you could undo the past, you would be glad to do a little bit of time traveling but logically, you know that it is not possible. As if the past errors that are dragging you down are not enough, you seem to have little or no hope for the future. That is the saddest, most pathetic, and most frustrating thing about what the enemy does to a believer who has experienced defeat upon defeat and has become disillusioned about life. Life becomes a routine. You get up and work another day, fetch another bucket of water to cook another meal or do another load of laundry. That is what this woman was doing. Life seemed to have no meaning. She was disconnected from life in the village and disconnected from relatives and friends. It meant that she was simply existing but not living. Isn't it sad that the enemy can put us in such bondage when we have made mistakes in life?

But thank God for Jesus. The story says that when this woman got to the well, in the midst of her distress, disgrace, dissatisfaction, and refusal to face her situation, she saw that someone was at the well. She probably stopped, hid quickly behind a tree in order to get a clearer view of the person. She may have said to herself, "Something is wrong. No one should be here at this time! Who could it be?" To her greatest surprise, it was not a woman, but a man. "What? A man!" What is a man doing at the well? Men should be on the farm at this time. "This doesn't make sense," she said to herself.

She decided to look again from her hiding place, and this time, she was even more surprised. It appeared like the person sitting at the well was a foreigner. Even though she did not have a good relationship with the people of the village, she knew everyone and they all knew her. That is what happens when you live in a village. It is a communal lifestyle and everyone and everything is known. At this point, the Samaritan woman was probably confused. She was not sure if she should turn around and go home or go closer in order to fetch the water that she needed. Could He be dangerous? Would she be putting herself in danger by approaching the well? Unsure, she looked again, and this time, noticed that the man was dressed as a Jew. She quickly remembered the history and strained relationship between the Samaritans and the Jews. He wouldn't dare try to hurt her because the people in the village (the Samaritans) would come to her rescue even though they didn't like her and disapproved of her lifestyle. However, the fact that He was a Jew, they would have, without any hesitation, come to her defense, and it would have become a scandal and a social and religious dilemma. This fact emboldened her and she decided to leave her hiding place in order to fetch the water she needed from the well. As she approached the well to get her water, she surprisingly noticed that she is very relaxed and not afraid at all. Surprised at her emotion, she reassured herself with the thought that this man, being a Jew, won't speak to her, since men were not accustomed to speaking to women openly. Additionally, Jews were not on speaking terms with Samaritans, so there was no way she would have any problem with him.

While she reasoned to herself, a delightful thought quickly crossed her mind: "Since He is not from this village, chances are that He doesn't know my story, and therefore He can't hurt me mentally or psychologically."

It soon dawned on her that she was wasting her time trying to be so cautious because nobody ever spoke to her anymore (not even from the village). She knew that they spoke about her and sometimes they even talked "at" her, usually calling her names, but they really never spoke "to" her. Her sins and her lifestyle had made her an outcast. She was a home-breaker, a marriage destroyer, a man chaser, and a married woman's worst nightmare. The only people who spoke to her were guys who wanted something from her. Sadly, she reminded herself that she had sunk as low as she could go in that town and therefore, there was nothing more of which to be afraid.

Armed with those thoughts, she left her hiding place and cautiously proceeded to the well to get her water. As she drew her water, without speaking or looking at the man who sat by the well, she was stunned to hear the stranger ask her for a drink. What may have surprised her most was the way in which He asked her for a drink, "May I have a drink please?"

His voice was pleasant and He had an air of authority that hovered over Him. He was not like the other men she had known. The way in which He asked the question did not appear to her like it was an icebreaker with a hidden agenda (to get her into a relationship). She was pleasantly surprised for a second and started to daydream; thinking that there may be hope after all; that she did not look that bad; that her news had not spread too far; that a man could still see her and admire her; that she still looked beautiful; that she might be able to have a decent conversation with a gentleman after all; that hope for a different life, a better future and a fresh start may not have totally eluded her. Oh my God….is it possible? It was like the high school girl who is an emotional wreck being noticed by the "hottest" and best basketball player in her school.

Suddenly, reality struck her and she stopped herself. She couldn't afford to hope again. She couldn't afford for her heart to be broken again. She couldn't afford to make another mistake. She couldn't afford to be laughed at once more. She couldn't afford hurting someone and being hurt again by another man. By the way, who is this man? Why is He asking her for water? Why is He being so pleasant to her? Can't He see who she is and who He is? He shouldn't even be talking to her or asking for a drink. This is not customary. Or, maybe….No, she reminded herself. It was not possible for them to have a relationship.

In verse 9, she asked a question that reflected her thoughts. "You are a Jew and I am a Samaritan woman. How can you ask me for a drink?

In verse 10, Jesus answered her, "If you knew the gift of God and who it is that asks you for a drink, you would have asked Him and He would have given you living water."

Jesus' choice of words is worth examining. He said, "If you knew." Basically, He was saying, "if only you understood or had the ability to perceive or recognize WHO it is that is speaking to you and WHAT it is that He offers, you would rush to give Him that water." This woman, in her "woundedness," saw Jesus as another Jew who was willing to reject her, or another man who had a selfish motive. Jesus basically said, "If you knew who I am, you would have asked me for the balm that quenches your thirst, heals your hurts, and binds your wounds." He was saying to the woman, "You don't have the slightest clue who I am!" Oh, if only we understood who Jesus is and what He offers, our lives would never be the same! The Bible declares in 1 Corinthians 2:9, "...No eye has seen, no ear has heard, no mind has conceived what God has prepared for those who love Him."[1]

Is it that this woman did not want to know or that she never had the opportunity of knowing about Jesus? I think that the latter is true. She had heard about the Messiah but had not encountered Him. In the same way, some of us have merely heard about Jesus, but have not encountered Him. We simply know about Him but do not really know Him. In other words, we have acquired a certain level of knowledge about Jesus but not enough to make a personal, heartfelt decision that would lead to salvation. Let me explain this further.

There are four basic levels and ways by which knowledge can be acquired, namely: knowledge obtained by transfer, knowledge obtained by acquaintance, knowledge obtained by participation, and knowledge obtained by discovery. Knowledge that is transferred is one that is learned or acquired through a formal or informal setting. Knowledge by acquaintance is one that is acquired by having some form of contact or connection with an individual, event, or a thing, whether physically, emotionally, psychologically, or even spiritually. These two levels of knowledge (transfer and acquaintance) are the types of knowledge generally considered to be "head or intellectual knowledge." They can be transmitted readily from one individual to another formally, informally, and systematically. Some intellectuals may refer to them as explicit knowledge which can be expressed in words and numbers. This kind of knowledge can be shared in the form of data, scientific formula, manuals, universal principles, and so forth. Knowledge by participation, which is the third level or way by which knowledge is also acquired, is known as "hands-on experience." This kind of knowledge acquisition allows the participants to fully examine the pros and cons of a given situation and even participate to a certain degree

---

1   The cross reference is Isaiah 64:4 "Since ancient times no one has heard, no ear has perceived, no eye has seen any God besides you, who acts on behalf of those who wait for Him."

in determining the outcome. It allows the participants to freely reach their own conclusion without external pressure based on the facts presented to them and what they believe to be true. Finally, there is the knowledge that can be acquired by discovery. This type of knowledge cannot be taught, or shown. It is the kind of knowledge that no level of education can buy. Both the knowledge acquired by participation and by discovery can be referred to as tacit knowledge (a kind of knowledge that is not easily visible, expressible, and transmittable).

These types of knowledge are deeply rooted in an individual's action and experience, as well as in the ideals, values, emotions, and faith practices he or she embraces. Hence, when Jesus said to the woman at the well, "If only you knew…," He was referring to the tacit type of knowledge (participation and discovery). This woman knew about Jesus through the knowledge acquired from the teaching of Scripture, and written or oral stories (transferred knowledge). She had probably read about Him and His coming and may have even been acquainted with some of the Jewish rituals surrounding His eminent birth (knowledge by acquaintance), but she did not *know Him* (a deeper knowledge that is only acquired by participation and discovery). Basically, she knew about Jesus but did not know Jesus.

Thank God that He took the initiative, made the provision, and made the offer for her and for us to know Jesus and not just know about Jesus. When we get to know Jesus, we quickly discover how lost we are without Him and how tragic the consequences are for the sins we commit each day. When we get to know Jesus, we instantly start to love and appreciate God's concern for us and the length to which He went to rescue us from the bondage of sin and slavery. When we get to know Jesus, we immediately stop searching. We stop feeling insecure, lonely, discouraged, indifferent, afraid, perplexed, disenchanted, and disillusioned about ourselves in particular and life in general. The Bible declares that the people who do know their God shall be strong and do exploits.[2] When we get to know Jesus and who He really is, we quickly realize that He is ready to turn our mess into a message. Additionally, we come to a godly and supernatural understanding of certain indisputable facts that have the ability to change the course of our lives forever. These secrets hidden in God's Word could have changed the course of events for some people during the days of Jesus but, unfortunately, they did not fully realize who He was. For example:

- If Judas knew Jesus, (knowledge gained by participation and discovery and not by mere transfer and acquaintance), he wouldn't have betrayed Him and then gone and hung himself. He would have realized that there was forgiveness at the cross even after the betrayal and that there is no amount of sin that Christ would not forgive. Christ's blood has the ability to wash away the worst of sin.

- If the Pharisees knew Jesus, (knowledge gained by participation and discovery and not by mere transfer and acquaintance), they wouldn't have accused Him of blasphemy and plotted against Him. They would have realized that He was the "I AM."

- If the inhabitants of Nazareth knew who He was, they wouldn't have cast Him out of their town and operated in unbelief and doubt. They would have known that they were precious in the eyes of God and that He had chosen that town to be a beacon of hope for the rest of humanity.

- If Pilate had known who Jesus was, he wouldn't have washed his hands to indicate that he was going to have nothing to do with Jesus' death. On the contrary, he would have stood his ground that Jesus was innocent and did not deserve to be killed, or he could have asked the Lord to forgive him of his sins before He was crucified, just like the thief on the cross did.

- If only the disciples on the road to Emmaus (Luke 24:31) knew Jesus, they would not have been so discouraged by the events of Calvary. They would have known, remembered, and stood upon the fact that He had said to them that on the third day, "I will rise again!" Additionally, they would have known who it was walking beside them. They would have known that they were in the presence of the Almighty God, the One whom the grave could not hold captive! If only they knew, they could have been jumping and leaping with joy as Paul and Silas did while in prison (Acts 16:25-34).

- If only Thomas knew (John 20:24-29) who Jesus was, and what He was capable of doing, he would have believed, and awaited the Lord's reappearance after he missed the first appearance of Jesus among His disciples when He arose from the grave on the third day.

- If only the disciples knew Jesus, when they gathered in the Upper Room (John 20:19-21) they would have been filled with joy and expectation instead of fear and trepidation. They would have known that in the midst of their anxiety and uncertainty, Jesus was standing right there to assure them that He meant what He said in John 14:18 "I will not leave you as orphans."

- If you only knew Jesus, you would stop playing around in your walk with God and realize that eternity is hanging in the balance and that God has made, called, anointed, and ordained you for a purpose. That destiny awaits the manifestation of the glory of God. Since the day you gave your life over to the Lord, He has been ready to use you as a vessel of honor to His glory and praise.

I pray that the eyes of your understanding will be enlightened so that you can understand WHO it is that is calling you or has called you into His service. That is the same prayer that the Apostle Paul prayed for the church in Ephesus in Ephesians 3:19: "And to know this love that surpasses knowledge – that you may be filled to the measure of all the fullness of God." Jesus' conversation with the woman at the well tells us that when we understand WHO it is we are talking to or dealing with, then we will ask Him for "living water."

There are a few things that must be said about the "living water" to which Jesus was referring. The first is that living water symbolizes eternal life through the intercession of the Holy Spirit (John 7:38-39). Jesus was offering salvation to this woman and through her to the Samaritans and others outside of the Jewish race. Second, He was offering this living water as a free gift of God, in accordance with Romans 6:23 and Ephesians 2:8-9. And finally, Jesus was giving an open-ended invitation to all who are thirsty; they could come and drink of this living water (John 7:37) simply because He is the source.

Unfortunately, this woman did not understand what Jesus meant and she retorted, "You have nothing to draw with and the well is deep. Where can you get this living water" (verse 11)? Let me say, my brothers and sisters, when the "living water" is flowing through us, we don't need a bucket! Yes, the well may be deep, but Jesus is deeper. Yes, the well may be deep, but Jesus knows how to get the water out. Yes, the well may be deep, but we do not depend on our strength and ingenuity to get to the water. If we could only know Him and what He is capable of doing, the water would be ours for the asking. The Samaritan woman at the well did not understand! She was thinking only in terms of one kind of water; the water that quenches our physical thirst. But Jesus was speaking of the water we need when we come struggling and straining up the "rough side" of the mountain; when we come crying and wailing because someone we loved and trusted has failed us; when we come depressed and disappointed because we have committed the same sin again after making numerous resolutions not to repeat it. This is the water that can only be given by the One who has the ability to forgive our sins. It is He who is the Prince of Peace, the Mighty One, the Great Mediator and Intercessor, the Counselor, and the Keeper of our Soul!

The Samaritan woman continued her interrogation by what could be interpreted as a genuine quest to find a logical answer because there seemed to have been a disconnection between what she knew (head knowledge) and what He was saying (heart knowledge). Yet, at the same time, her question could be construed as being sarcastic. She said, "Are you greater than our father Jacob, who gave us the well and drank from it himself, as did also his sons and his flocks and herds" (verse 12)?

Jesus answered in the next two verses, "Everyone who drinks this water will be thirsty again, but whoever drinks the water I give him will never thirst. Indeed, the water I give him will become in him a spring of water welling up to eternal life" (verses 13-14).

"WOW! Eternal life? I would like to have any life because as it stands, I don't have any!" she almost said aloud. "What is in this water that He is referring to? How can I get it? My life is a mess! I need a breakthrough."

Think about what is going on in this woman's head! Hope! It may not be too late after all. "If only I could get this water, I won't have to come to this well in the middle of the day to avoid shame, disgrace, and humiliation," she thought to herself. "Men won't have to use me again for their satisfaction. The villagers won't have to make fun of me again when I pass by. I NEED TO HAVE THIS WATER! I need it desperately!" Hope began to surface again. Her heart began to beat faster, her face lit up, her smile returned, her countenance brightened, her voice became stronger, and her expectation increased. "There may be light at the end of the tunnel," she thought to herself.

We need to understand that in order for God to change our mess into a message, we need to be desperate for a change. We need to be desperate for a miracle. Say, "Lord, I NEED A MIRACLE!"

This reminds me of the story of the woman who had been dealing with the issue of blood for 12 years and needed a physical miracle.[3] She could not afford to take "no" for an answer. She was not only desperate, but she was honest and ready to break the social taboo (as an "unclean" woman she was unwelcome in society and was hence socially isolated).[4] She needed a miracle desperately because she couldn't go on living like that. She couldn't afford to let the crowd stop her from touching Jesus. She couldn't afford to let Him pass by without touching Him. Though she did not say it, I know that everything within her was screaming: "JESUS, I NEED A MIRACLE!" That is how we need to come to God in desperation and full expectation that He is able to grant us that miracle (eternal life).

The Samaritan woman realized she was desperate for a new direction in life. She became conscious of the fact that life without a purpose is meaningless. She may have tried gossiping, stealing other women's men, running wild, parties, clothes, make-up, latest designs in clothes, and the list could go on, only to realize later that these things only give limited satisfaction. She became conscious, like King Solomon, that life is meaningless without God. We read in Ecclesiastes 1:2, "'Meaningless! Meaningless!' says the Teacher. 'Utterly meaningless! Everything is meaningless.'" The Samaritan woman was coming to the same conclusion like King Solomon did at the end of his life when he wrote the book of Ecclesiastes. He discovered that:

- **Life without God is meaningless because, in and of itself, it is transitory.** "Generations come and generations go but the earth remains forever" (Ecclesiastes 1:4). "The length of our days is seventy years or eighty, if we have the strength; yet their span is but trouble and sorrow, for they quickly pass, and we fly away" (Psalm 90:10).
- **Life without God is meaningless because head knowledge does not give lasting peace and satisfaction.** Solomon wrote: "I thought to myself, 'Look, I have grown and increased in wisdom more than anyone who has ruled over Jerusalem before me; I have experienced much of wisdom and knowledge. Then I applied myself to the understanding of wisdom, and also of madness and folly, but I learned that this, too, is chasing after the wind" (Ecclesiastes 1:16-17).

---

3   The story can be found in Matthew 9:20-22; Mark 5:25-34; and Luke 8:43-47

4   Read Leviticus 15:19-30

- **Life without God is empty because pleasure and wealth do not give lasting satisfaction.** Solomon had 700 wives, 300 concubines, a palace, and all the luxuries of life. He was the richest man in his generation, yet, he wrote: "'I thought in my heart, 'Come now, I will test you with pleasure to find out what is good.' But that also proved to be meaningless'" (Ecclesiastes 2:1). The Bible tells us in Hebrews 11:25 that Moses chose to be mistreated along with the people of God rather than to enjoy the pleasures of sin for a short time.
- **Life without God is meaningless because of the consequences of sin.** That is why King Solomon wrote: "Remember your Creator in the days of your youth, before the days of trouble come and the years approach when you will say, 'I find no pleasure in them'" (Ecclesiastes 12:1).

It is not surprising, therefore, that Solomon concluded at the end of his life, "Now all has been heard; here is the conclusion of the matter: Fear God and keep His commandments, for this is the whole duty of man" (Ecclesiastes 12:13).

The Samaritan woman was very smart. It took her only a few minutes of conversation with the Master to reach the same conclusion King Solomon reached after a lifetime. That is why she said in John 4:15, "Sir, give me this water so that I won't get thirsty and have to keep coming here to draw water." To her credit, she appeared to be an honest woman who was not intimidated by anyone. Culturally, it was not right for a Samaritan woman to ask for a favor from a Jewish man, but I am glad this woman knew what she wanted and knew how to get it. She realized that if she was to get this living water, she had to ask. Many women would silently desire this water but dare not ask a stranger for such a favor. Some would think that asking for this living water would be rude, impolite, uncultured, and uncivilized. It is true that in some cultures her action could be misinterpreted, but the fact of the matter is that when one is desperate for an answer or a miracle, respecting cultural norms is the last thing that comes to mind. Sometimes, when you need something from the Lord, you have to put aside some of those cultural values or norms and boldly approach God's throne of grace where you can find mercy and favor. Not that you become rude or forget your cultural values and norms, but sometimes out of desperation you have to cry out, leap, push, slam, kick, blow, wink, or wave in order to get what God has in store for you!

When blind Bartimaeus needed help from Jesus (Luke 18:35-43), he cried out to Jesus saying, "Son of David, have mercy on me." Many people told him to be quiet. They told him not to bother Jesus. They probably told him that Jesus would not do anything for him, but he just wouldn't keep quiet until he got what he needed. He was determined that no man on earth was going to stop him, no demon in hell was going to stand in his way, and no disciple (whether they were being led by the Spirit or not) was going to hinder him from talking to Jesus. That was the day for his miracle! His life was going to change and he was determined to ensure that no one robbed him of what heaven had destined for him. He realized that a desperate situation required a desperate measure. That is what the Bible means when it says, "….the violent takes it by force."[5] For this blind man, "no" was not an option. When you become desperate for a miracle, "no" will not be an option. That is the kind of faith that the Lord looks for on the earth when He is ready to bless His people – a faith that says, "God, you have to turn my mess into a message because I just can't keep living like this."

When you are tired of your situation and circumstances, you won't allow the strongest devil in hell to keep you from calling on Jesus. When you want your mess to be turned into a message, there is no demon in hell that can keep you from telling the Lord what you want.

I find it fascinating that Jesus asked Bartimaeus what he wanted. You might think that it was obvious because the man was blind, but Jesus still asked. Bartimaeus replied, "Lord, I want to see." The word translated "see" (in the New International Version) or "receive my sight" (King James Version) is the Greek word, *anablepo*, "to gain sight, whether for the first time or again." The blind beggar was very clear what he wanted: to regain his sight! He could have said, "Lord, I need some money to pay some bills." But, He said, "Lord, I need my sight." Regaining his sight was very important to him. What is it that you want from the Lord? Are you clear about your needs?

The Samaritan woman is clear as to what she wants: living water! If you know exactly what you want from the Lord then the Bible says, "Ask, and it will be given to you; seek, and you will find; knock, and it will be opened to you; for everyone who asks receives; and he who seeks finds; and to him who knocks, it will be opened" (Matthew 7:7-8). How can we accuse God of not changing our situation when we have not asked Him to change it? How can we accuse God of not changing our mess into a message when we don't even know that we are in a messy situation that

---

5   Matthew 11:12

needs to be changed? In order for my situation to be changed, I have to desire, request, and believe God for the change. However, if I am content in my situation, God is a gentleman and will do all He can not to disrupt my lifestyle, though His heart may be grieving on my behalf.

Jesus' reply to the woman at the well appears to be a little odd. He told her, "Go, call your husband and come back." Upon hearing His reply, she was probably taken aback and her hopes were dashed once again. He appeared to have been so gentle and kind. How could He say this to her? How dare He remind her of her sinful lifestyle? Can't He see that she is an independent woman? Why did He have to remind her that she was living in a male dominated society?

She was probably saying, "I can speak for myself, thank you very much." Or, "Do you see any man here with me? What's this husband business all about?" "You men, why can't you see that women have their own identities?" "Does it always have to be about the male dominating sex?" Sadly though, in spite of all that was probably going on in her head, His remark brought her back to the reality of her situation. She doesn't have a husband and she is sleeping with a man who is not her husband.

We can scream, yell, fuss, and even become angry when we are confronted about sin, but it does not change the fact that it needs to be addressed. You can't continue to hide from your sin as though it doesn't exist. Getting mad at someone or the pastor who confronts you concerning your sinful behavior will not solve the problem. Leaving one church and going to another because you don't want to be told to stop living in sin is not the solution. Wherever you go, if the Word of God is preached holistically, you will hear about sin. Even if you don't, God will confront you through His Spirit that lives inside of you. Therefore, stop running and fighting! Yield to the Holy Spirit and allow him to bring conviction where needed and confess your sins in order to receive forgiveness and healing.

The woman at the well had to decide how she would respond to Jesus' probing about a husband. Since it was likely she had earned the reputation as "a woman who takes no mess from a man," her first option could have been to say, "Thank you very much but the conversation is over. Keep your water." With that, she could have taken her bucket, jar, or pan and left the well. This is how Naaman, the commander of the army of the king of Aram reacted when he was told by Elisha to go and wash himself in the Jordan River in order for his leprosy to be cured. He became furious and was ready to return to his homeland had his servant not begged him to obey the simple instruction of the prophet.[6] Pride sometimes makes us not want to submit to very simple instructions – even if they are intended to help, heal, and restore us. That is why the writer of Proverb 16:18 says, "Pride goes before destruction, a haughty spirit before a fall."

The woman at the well could have asked another question in the form of a rebuke to Jesus. She could have said, "Do I need a man or a husband in order to receive this living water. If so, why? Don't you think that you Jewish are too egocentric and patriarchal?"

One can only speculate what Jesus would have said had the Samaritan woman asked the questions mentioned above. Since she didn't ask, it is quite safe to say that even though she had those two options at her disposal, she chose the third option, that of honesty.

She replied, "I have no husband."

Hearing her answer and seeing her honesty, Jesus said to her, "You are right when you say you have no husband. The fact is, you have had five husbands, and the man you now have is not your husband. What you have just said is quite true."

What a revelation! "This can't be true! My ears are playing tricks on me," she thought. "I can't believe it! He also knows my secret and did not say anything all this time." Instantly, tons of questions started flooding her mind: "How did He know? Who told Him? Why can't people mind their own business? Why should they always be talking about me? What have I done so bad that they can't just stop talking about me even to a stranger? Is this a guy that I have met before? Am I losing my mind? God help me!" Even though a few moments ago, she was beginning to hope, the pain of the woman's choices and her sins started to smack her in the face. She had begun to hope for a change in her messy lifestyle but that hope was becoming an illusion. It was showing its ugly self again in her life. She hoped in the first, second, third, fourth, and fifth relationship only to be disappointed. She was tired, scared, disappointed, and apprehensive. Why should this be happening to her? It dawned on her that living life with hope can be scary. She had been down this path before, only this time she thought it would be different. She was afraid each time she ventured down the path of hope, simply because she knew that if she placed her hope in someone or something and it turned out that she was wrong, she would have to live through all of that hurt and emotional turmoil once again. Does that sound familiar? Has your life been like that? Have you

---

6   The story in found in 2 Kings 5:1-15

been frustrated time and time again by others and nothing seems to be working relationally for you?

So many times we are disappointed in life. We are disappointed by ourselves, people, and circumstances. As a result, we are afraid of being disappointed again and therefore, we erect a wall of defense to protect ourselves from others. Thank God that He can see through our walls and reach into our hearts to remove the pain and suffering that we have endured over the years as a result of disappointments.

Whew! This conversation is getting scary. Should she continue talking to Him? What else did He know about her? As she frantically searched her mind for some answers, she realized that it was impossible for Him to have heard about her from someone else. She also realized that she had not met Him before. So, how did He know? "Who is this man?" she quizzed herself. Suddenly there was an unexplainable thought. She tried to dismiss it but then she looked at His outfit and said to herself, "Could He be who I think He is? He seems to know an awful lot about me and about the Scriptures. He is calm, polite, intelligent, and has an appearance of godliness." The Samaritan woman continued to soliloquize: "Yes, I got it! He must be a prophet. He can't be anyone else. Obviously, He is not like the other men that I have met over the years. He doesn't seem to want anything personal from me. He has to be...a prophet."

Her logical mind in its analytical mode said, "I must be right. Let's see...if He is, then I can't allow Him to continue to expose me. I have to change this topic. What do I say? What do I say? Bingo! I've got it. I will talk about religious issues. It is time to be spiritual, since he is a spiritual man."

"Sir," the woman said, "I can see that you are a prophet. Our fathers worshiped on this mountain, but you Jews claim that the place where we must worship is in Jerusalem" (John 4:19-20).

You have probably noticed by now that the statement about the place of worship is odd. The previous statement of the conversation being conducted had nothing to do with worship. It doesn't take a rocket scientist to see that she was trying to change the subject because she was becoming uncomfortable and did not want the spotlight to be on her. Engaging in a religious conversation was the safest thing to do now that she knew that He was a religious man. It is like meeting a stranger in an elevator. The safest thing to talk about is the weather. It is a topic that is comfortable, non-personal, non-confrontational, informational, and neutral. Jesus could have responded to the woman by saying, "Lady, look, no one is talking about where to worship here." Or, He could have said, "When was the last time you became interested in the place of worship? Do you even go to the temple or are you talking about this because you want to change the subject?" Isn't it good that Jesus is such a gentleman? He does not embarrass, belittle, or insult us even when we deserve it. He gives us room to grow and to realize our mistakes. His Spirit convicts us in a gentle and non-threatening manner. Even though the Samaritan woman tried to change the topic, Jesus is incredibly smarter than she is and, therefore, she could not set the terms for the conversation and its outcome. He used her question to open her mind in order to help her understand deeper spiritual truths. In verses 21-24 we read:

Jesus declared, "Believe me, woman, a time is coming when you will worship the Father neither on this mountain nor in Jerusalem. You Samaritans worship what you do not know; we worship what we do know, for salvation is from the Jews. Yet a time is coming and has now come when the true worshipers will worship the Father in spirit and truth, for they are the kind of worshipers the Father seeks. God is Spirit, and His worshipers must worship in spirit and in truth."

The Samaritan woman must have been thinking.…. "Hold on, I didn't mean for you to go that far. You are confusing me with all this worship stuff. Who is a true worshiper? When and how is a true worshiper going to be able to worship the Father in spirit and truth? What do you mean by worshiping in spirit and in truth? Man, you are confusing me! Why should life be so complicated? I just asked a simple question to get you off my back and now you are talking about things that only the Messiah should be talking about. Could it be that you are more than a prophet?" She may have even thought to herself, "Look, it is not your place to try to teach me these complicated theological truths. Let's leave it at that. Okay?" No wonder she voiced what she was thinking in her head. She couldn't help but say, "I know that the Messiah is coming and when He comes, He will explain everything to us" (verse 25).

This woman had acquired "head or intellectual knowledge" about worship but did not have tacit knowledge that comes through participation and discovery. She seemed to be waiting anxiously for the Messiah to come in order to bring this matter about worship to rest. She and many others were also waiting for Him to come and bring clarity to some of the spiritual struggles and confusion that they had been experiencing in light of their relationship with the Jews. Are you waiting for clarity regarding some issues in your life? Are you waiting for God to show up and speak into your situation? He may be doing that right now but you are not listening, seeing, or comprehending (Mark 8:18). The One who she had been waiting for was standing right there in front of her and she did not know Him. Head or intellectual knowledge can take you only to a certain point in your Christian life. You have to rely on your inner man or spirit to take you further. It is only the Spirit of God within you that has the ability to reveal Christ to you. You cannot love, obey, submit, or worship God based only on head or intellectual knowledge. It must be done in spirit and in truth. That is why Jesus was trying to help her understand some key spiritual truths about worship. Allow me to mention a few that may be of interest to you.

First, the word, "spirit," that Jesus uses does not have the definite article in the original language, so it does not refer to the Holy Spirit. Rather it is referring to our own inner life, emotions, will, our heart. In other words, to worship God in spirit is to connect with God (person to person). It is offering up ourselves to Him in a non-restrictive way, form or method. What we feel about God must be expressed. However, what is expressed must be felt first. Formality without feeling does not please God. Jesus was trying to teach the Samaritan woman at the well that to worship in spirit means that one has to go beyond the acquisition of intellectual knowledge about God and strive to acquire a tacit knowledge based on participation and discovery. She had acquired head knowledge about the Messiah, now it was time for her to experience, and discover Him.

Second, Jesus was trying to make her understand that worship does not take place only in a building or on a mountain. The issue at stake was not about the place where worship is conducted because true worship occurs in the heart and can take place anywhere. What is required in order to have an authentic and meaningful worship experience is a humble spirit that is longing to encounter the Lord. So, the question that the lady and all of us need to answer is: Do we have a humble and seeking heart? Do we long to have an encounter with the living Christ so that He can change our mess into a message?

Third, worship is truth. It has two components: accuracy and authenticity. For worship to be truth, it must first be accurate about who is being worshiped. This is where the Samaritans got it wrong (see vs. 22). They were sincere about their worship, but they had inaccurate information about God. Sincerity alone does not make for acceptable worship. It must be mixed with truth about the One being worshiped. Someone can be sincere in expressing what they believe to be true but they can be sincerely wrong.

Jesus was cognizant of the fact that it was time to reveal His true identity to the Samaritan woman, and declared in verse 26, "I who speak to you am He." Think for a moment the explosive thought that went through this woman's head. She probably said to herself, "I can't believe it! "What! That can't be true! Oh, my gosh, I should have known! Yes, yes, yes, you are the Messiah because no one else could have known those things about me. No one else would have spoken to me the way you did. No one else could have pierced through me with those incredible and loving eyes the way you did. No one else could have treated me as a woman like you have. Yes, you are the Messiah! Oh my God," she wanted to say out loud. "I have seen the Messiah....and oh no...no one else in the village knows about this. We have been waiting all this time for the Messiah when He is right here with us. I have to tell them. Oh yeah, I have to let them know that He is here. But, I have a problem! Will they believe me? But, I have to tell them. This is too good to be true. I know that they don't like me. I know that they despise me. I don't know if they would think that I am lying, but I have to tell them. I can't keep this to myself!"

In verses 27 and 28, John interrupts the Samaritan woman's thought process by stating: "Just then his disciples returned and were surprised to find Him talking with a woman. But no one asked, 'What do you want?' or 'Why are you talking with her?' Then, leaving her water jar, the woman went back to the town."

While running back to the town, all those thoughts kept rushing through her head. She must tell someone before He leaves. Someone has to know that the Messiah came by. Someone has to hear that there is no need to keep waiting and teaching that the Messiah is coming when He has already come. Being a Samaritan, she believed that the first five books of the Bible were the Word of God. In the second of those five books, she may have remembered that God had once said to Moses in Exodus 3:14, "I AM WHO I AM. This is what you are to say to the Israelites: 'I AM has sent me to you.'" Did she just hear this man at the well say those same words regarding himself? Wow, if He is the Messiah, then He is God in the flesh! Her blood was coursing through her body now. She felt her heart beating.

Her palms were sweaty and not from the heat. She was scared and excited. As she continued running, she realized that she felt different. "What is happening to me?" she asked herself. "Why do I feel different?

This is not an ordinary feeling. I have never felt this way before. It is like I am walking on the clouds. This feels good and I love it! I feel alive once more. Oh, I see, this is the Messiah. This is God! And oh no....God is willing to speak to me, a sinner. I have to tell someone that God is different. He can change their mess into a message. I know that I am not the best person in the village but I sure know of others who have lived worse or the same kind of life that I have lived over the years. Yes, I remember Ashera, Carmela, Liat, and Nitzan. They are like me and have made some bad choices also. They need to know that the Messiah is around. They have been living life as a shadow like me. We have been merely existing but not living. Now is their chance and they need to know!"

As she continued to run towards the village, hope kept coming alive in her. She was beginning to experience it already. Paul tells us in Romans 5:5 "And hope does not disappoint us, because God has poured out his love into our hearts by the Holy Spirit, whom He has given us." She found herself saying aloud, "This is what life is about, knowing the Messiah and making Him known." It did not take her long to realize that she had been placing her hope in the wrong things. That is why she had been disappointed on numerous occasions. It dawned on her that she had been placing her hope in others for a long time and that is why they continued to let her down over the years. It now seemed apparent to her that she had been placing her hope in her village, but the people in the village had been letting her down miserably. But this time, it would be different. This time, she was putting her hope in the Living God who loved her so dearly. It was for this very reason that He sent His Son, the Messiah, seated at the well to die for her and to give her a second chance in life. She would never be disappointed again and yes, from this point, she would begin to live a full life to His glory and praise in accordance with John 10:10, "I have come that they may have life, and have it to the full."

Before she realized it, she was already in the village. Oh no! What has she done? She can't talk to these people. They won't even listen and if they do, they might think that she is lying. As the thought of being rejected by the villagers swiftly crossed her mind, she realized that she did not really care if they snubbed her or not. She was no longer afraid of rejection. The main person who should have rejected her didn't. She now had a renewed self-confidence, self-esteem and boldness that made her brush off this petty fear of rejection. John writes in the fourth gospel, "For if the Son sets you free, you are free indeed" (John 8:36). The Samaritan woman had been set free and she loved her newfound freedom!

It also suddenly occurred to her that she was no longer mad at the people of this town who for so long had treated her as an outcast. She had received hope even though her future was uncertain given her history of having had five different men as husbands. She had this unexplainable joy and peace that she could only attribute to her encounter with the Living God who met her at the point of her need and at the time when she needed Him the most.

As if being awakened from a day dream and facing reality, the Samaritan looked and saw people staring at her. They hadn't seen her for a while. She was now in the heart of the village. The villagers looked puzzled as they stared at her. Simultaneously, they all started questioning each other: "Why is she sweating and breathing so hard? Doesn't she know that people don't run when the sun is so hot? What has gone wrong with her? Have the gods of the village met her in the bush and tried to punish her for her mischievousness and she miraculously escaped? Has she come to apologize for breaking the hearts of the men in the village?" They did not know what to think and did not have answers to all of their questions. Finally, someone shouted from the crowd, "Tell us woman, what is wrong with you?"

Unfortunately, she didn't know! "Oh, I hope I knew," she said. "Believe me, I have been asking myself the same question. I don't know. You have to believe me."

Someone else shouted, "But tell us, what happened to you? Don't be afraid." Did you see a ghost?"

"No," she said, trying frantically to find the right words and to catch her breath. "Just, just, just, come with me, please," she stammered. "Come, and see a man who told me everything I've ever done. Could this be the Christ?"

Have you read John 4:39? It states that many of the Samaritans from the village believed in Him because of the woman's testimony, "He told me everything I ever did." Now notice that it was before they met him. Many believed because of her testimony! Think for a moment with me? Did she say more than, "He told me everything I ever did?" Did she recount every detail of her visit with Christ? Obviously, we don't know the answers to those questions. However, we can safely say that God had given her a message just as He has given you a message. The Bible declares that those He calls, He equips.

A servant of God once said, "For every new assignment, there is a new anointing." These were the same people who probably despised her and considered her to be a man-grabber, home-breaker, deception-master, and a disgrace to decency and family values. But, when God turns your mess into a message, He changes your stained testimony for His glory and praise. Most interestingly, He prepares the hearts of His people to hear your testimony and to respond appropriately. It is no longer your words but His. It is no longer your will but His. It is no longer your reputation, but His. It is no longer your trial, but His. It is no longer your battle, but His. All He expects from you is to deliver the message or to share your testimony. If only we would stop worrying about how we will be received, how we will be listened to, how we will be treated, how we will be questioned. Then, God will begin to manifest His glory through us and we will always be amazed at the wondrous workings of our Lord. The good thing is that we don't have to defend God. All we need to do is to tell the world to come and see, come and taste of Him, come and experience Him, come and sit at His feet, come and touch the hem of His garment, come and let Him take your yoke in exchange for His. You cannot come and have a genuine encounter with Jesus and go back the same. The woman probably said: "He knew my past and He knew my present, but He spoke to me anyway." Isn't that amazing!

Walk down memory or imaginary lane a little bit with me. Think about what the Samaritan woman told the villagers who went with her to see Jesus at the well. Could it be that she started asking for forgiveness? Could it be that she started to explain how her life has been a mess since her first marriage? Could it be that she started to explain how she met Jesus? Could it be that she started to explain in detail their conversation and how He told her things that no one else knew about her? If one, some or all of the above mentioned is true, then imagine the expression on her face as she told her story. There was hope in her voice. There was a serene inexplicable attitude that she portrayed. Those who knew her started to look at each other and silently thought to themselves, "She looks different. It must be true! We know that she is the village 'bad girl' but if she is pulling our leg on this one, then she is the best con artist, liar, or lunatic this village has ever seen. But she can't be. She looks genuine! Look at her! See the excitement and enthusiasm with which she speaks." Based on all of these, their own excitement began to build. They also started having a sense of hope. Everything that is written in Scripture about the Messiah came back to their memory. Someone may have shouted from the crowd, "There is still hope for our village because God has not forgotten us. There is still hope for every one of us because Emmanuel (God with us) has entered this village to turn our mess into a message."

You need to know that there is hope also for you: hope for a fresh start, hope to turn your life around, hope to have your sins forgiven, hope to make you into a new person, hope to turn you into a messenger of Jesus, and hope to turn your mess into a message. Can you see that God has something wonderful in store for you? Can you see that He is working it out for your good? Don't be discouraged. God will see you through. There is hope for a fresh start no matter what your past has been and no matter what is going on right now. God gives hope to start afresh. If you are struggling to believe it or you know someone (whether a friend or a love one) who is having a difficult time believing that God wants to give him or her a second chance, remember the song written by Joel Hemphill entitled, "He's Still Working on Me." It says:

Chorus: He's still working on me to make me what I ought to be.
It took Him just a week to make the moon and stars,
The Sun and the Earth and Jupiter and Mars.
How loving and patient He must be, He's still working on me.

1ˢᵗ Stanza: There really ought to be a sign upon my heart:
Don't judge him yet, there's an unfinished part
But I'll be better just according to His plan
Fashioned by the Master's loving hands.

2ⁿᵈ Stanza: In the mirror of His word; reflections that I see
Makes me wonder why He never gave up on me.
But He loves me as I am and helps me when I pray.
Remember He's the potter; I'm the clay.

Can someone please be patient with me? He's still working on me. I know that it is going to take a long time and it might be a difficult hill to climb, but I know He is working with me. It might be a difficult battle to fight, but I know that He is helping me fight it and will not abandon me in the middle of the fight. I know that it might be a tough war to change my attitude, but I know that He has a plan and His Spirit will help in transforming my will and softening my heart. I know that it might require some cleansing, scrubbing, polishing, and shining, but He is working on me and won't give up on me. Please don't give up on me! Please give me another chance! That is my story; that is my message; that is my plea; that is my heart's desire! Please, I promise, it will be okay. Give me a second chance and I guarantee that things will be different.

What a testimony! This woman who did not fear God or man was now asking for a second chance. She was now talking about God and the Messiah. Something happened to this woman that they couldn't explain but that they were about to find out. If this Man (the one she claims is the Messiah) had this kind of impact on her in few minutes, He must come to our village. We need some soul cleansing, heart mending, mind relieving, and body healing in this village. So, John reports in verses 40-42, "When the Samaritans came to him, they urged Him to stay with them, and He stayed two days. And because of His words many more became believers." They said to the woman, "We no longer believe just because of what you said; now we have heard for ourselves, and we know that this man really is the Savior of the world."

Have you lived your life over the years with no regard for God and for your fellow man? Has your life been exactly like this Samaritan woman or even worse? Do you feel hopeless and sometimes think that life is not worth living? You need to know that there is hope. Jesus Christ is the same yesterday and today and forever (Hebrews 13:8). When Israel was in the midst of 70 years of captivity, they felt hopeless, but God, through the prophet Jeremiah, offered them hope. We read in Jeremiah 29:11-13, "'For I know the plans I have for you,' declares the LORD, 'plans to prosper you and not to harm you, plans to give you hope and a future. Then you will call upon me and come and pray to me, and I will listen to you. You will seek me and find me when you seek me with all your heart.'"

A second chance is found in a relationship with Jesus the Messiah, the Savior of the World (God in the flesh). He gives us a second chance by making us a new creation. Paul tells us in 2 Corinthians 5:17, "Therefore, if anyone is in Christ, he is a new creation; the old has gone, the new has come!" Now is the time for you to experience a new life and a new hope. Now is the time for you to experience salvation and forgiveness of sin. Now is the time for you to bow your knees and ask God to cleanse you from all your sins and give you His Spirit. Now is the time for you to forsake those ways that are not pleasing to Him and make Him your Lord and Master. Now is the time for Him to turn your mess into a message. Now is the time for you to begin to turn a new page in your life and allow God to have His will in your life. You have done things your own way for a long time. It is time you turn it over to Jesus. If you do, I can assure you

29

that you will smile for the rest of your days on earth. It doesn't mean that you won't have problems or challenges. It simply means that when they come, He will see you through. Those messy situations will be turned into messages of hope and a second chance. He is willing, ready, and able to change your situation, but the question is:

"WOULD YOU ALLOW HIM?"

Chapter II: Jabez (1 Chronicles 4:9-10)
God Turns a Mess of Pain into a Message of an Enlarged Territory

Jabez was more honorable than his brothers. His mother had named him Jabez, saying, "I gave birth to him in pain." Jabez cried out to the God of Israel, "Oh, that you would bless me and enlarge my territory! Let your hand be with me, and keep me from harm so that I will be free from pain." And God granted his request
(1 Chronicles 4:9-10).

As we begin this chapter it is important to keep in mind 1 Chronicles 4:9, "...and his mother called his name Jabez, saying, "Because I bore him in pain."

Mainly as a result of his prayer, the story of Jabez has become very familiar to many believers over the last few years. Little is actually known about him, but what catches our attention immediately upon reading the few verses mentioned above is the fact that he is named by his mother and she actually states the rationale behind the name. It is important to know that the naming of a child in biblical times was very crucial. For believers, it required divine insight, spiritual ingenuity, the spirit of discernment, and a vision of what the parents felt God would like to do in the life of that child. It meant, therefore, that the name given to a child often denoted the child's anticipated character, expected plights in life, or how he or she would be used by God.

For instance …

- *Jacob* (Genesis 25:26) in Hebrew means "held by the heel, supplanted, or protected." Figuratively it means, "He deceives." Jacob deceived his brother, Esau, of his birthright and his blessing as the older son.
- *Jeremiah* in Hebrew means "God will loosen (the bonds)" or "God will uplift." Jeremiah, best known as the "weeping prophet" had a harsh message but a sensitive and broken heart (Jeremiah 8:21-9:1). He was convinced that God would eventually forgive the sins of His people and set them free if only they would repent.
- *Ezekiel* means "God strengthens" and is appropriate in light of the difficulties Ezekiel would endure.
- *Amos* comes from the Hebrew, meaning "to be burdened, troubled." It is an appropriate name for one suddenly taken from his humble country roots and given the burden of serving as God's prophet.
- *Jesus* means "God saves." Through His life, death, and resurrection, He saves humanity.

Many of you may have heard of or listened to the legendary singer named Johnny Cash. The lyrics of one of his famous songs, (written by Shel Silverstein), *"The Boy Named Sue,"* [7] explain the emotional complexity of giving the wrong name to a child. Find the lyrics and read them, or listen to the song (if you haven't) and you will understand how giving a child the wrong name can be devastating.

In the case of Jabez, his name meant, *"to grieve, be sorrowful."* His mother, for whatever reason, chose to memorialize his birth experience by naming her son Jabez, *"because I bore him in pain."* It is not known if the "pain" being referred to by his mother was the pain associated with his birth or if it had to do with a relational pain that may have developed as a result of the pregnancy or for other unknown reasons.

I recall a few years ago I had the privilege of working with a couple who was on the verge of divorce. The wife had gotten pregnant with the fifth girl after several failed attempts to have a baby boy. It brought such

---

7 **"A Boy Named Sue"** is a country song, written by Shel Silverstein and sung by Johnny Cash. Johnny Cash was at the height of his popularity when he recorded this song live at San Quentin State Prison in California.

tension in the home that when the wife conceived for the fifth time, the couple decided not to find out the sex of the child until the child was born. Unfortunately, the dad had mentioned one day during a heated exchange of words with his wife that if she did not have a boy this time, their marriage was over. When the child was born and it was discovered that it was a girl, the wife decided to give her a name that meant in their local dialect, "because of you." God, by His supernatural intervention, prompted me to call the wife just when she was about to give the name to the nurses at the hospital. I asked her why she was giving the child that name and she said, "because of her my marriage is coming to an end." I couldn't believe what I was hearing and, by the grace of God, I was able to convince her not to give the child that name. I promised to counsel the couple and help them through their challenging situation. Today, they are still married and the child has a different name. Praise be to God!

We really do not know if that was the same situation with Jabez. However, one thing is sure. Jabez's messy situation began either before his birth or during his birth. His mother may have been so hurt that she was determined to remind herself and the child of the episode surrounding his birth. By giving the child the name Jabez, she was probably stating her experience or maybe she was trying to predict his future. The name signified pain! Maybe it was a pain that was uncomfortable, unwanted, unacceptable, and undesired! Yet, it appeared to be a pain that may have been unavoidable and left a scar in her life. A scar and a memory that probably meant, "If I had the option, I would not have chosen to give birth to you," or "if I had the choice, I would have given you up for adoption," or "if I had known, I wouldn't have done what I did to conceive you." "If I could get rid of you now, I would gladly do that." Or, maybe it was simply a name to remind herself that the pregnancy was a difficult one. Of course, like I already indicated, we don't know the exact reason why she named him Jabez, and we are not sure if these were the actual thoughts of Jabez's mother. But, if they were, wouldn't it have been a horrible way for Jabez to start his life, knowing that he was unwanted by the one who was expected to love, care for, and protect him?

What if it were you? What a way it would be for you to begin your life on earth, knowing that you are being blamed for something over which you had no control! How shocking it would be to you to discover as a teenager that life had dealt a severe blow to your mother and the enemy has made her believe that it was entirely your fault! You would probably be devastated when you found out that you were being blamed for something you did not cause, and sadly, you cannot undo what has already happened. Even worse is the fact that whenever you are called by that name, whether it is for something wrong you have done or something good, you are referred to as "pain." Wouldn't you finally feel like there is nothing you could do to make your parent(s) happy? Wouldn't you feel like there is no need to keep trying to do your best in life? That is indeed a messy situation, isn't it?

The good news is that God delights in rescuing us from those kinds of situations. Jabez's mother probably wanted the child to remember that his life resulted from pain and probably would continue as a pain-stricken life. But, I submit to you that it did not work. Whatever could have happened to him because of the name he was given, did not work because the God of the Heavens intervened. In 1 Chronicles 4:9 the Bible declares: "Now Jabez was more honorable than his brothers…." Notice that the description was given before Jabez prayed to the Lord. Something apparently had happened in his life that was different from what the enemy had desired. Instead of being an individual filled with hatred towards his mother or others, he was more honorable than his siblings. It is worth noting that I am not implying that being "honorable" means that one cannot sin or cause inadvertent pain and suffering for others. I am simply pointing out that Jabez became honorable more than his brothers because he refused to allow his today to determine his tomorrow. Instead of being sorrowful and living a pitiful life, he realized that God could turn his pain into honor. His life, therefore, became one of honor and admiration. The question is, what did he really do? What was the game plan that took him from pain to gain? What made him escape a life of pain to start living a life of honor? Better still, the question is: Can God do the same in your life today? I believe that He can!

Allow me to walk you through some indisputable facts. The first is that Jabez realized that his destiny was in the hands of Yahweh and not in the hands of his mother or those who constantly reminded him of the circumstances surrounding his birth. He understood that God had a plan and a purpose for his life that was greater than what others were saying regarding him. In Jeremiah 1:9-10, we read, "Then the LORD reached out his hand and touched my mouth and said to me, 'Now, I have put my words in your mouth. See, today I appoint you over nations and kingdoms to uproot and tear down, to destroy and overthrow, to build and to plant.'"

For God to change your mess into a message, you must realize that your destiny is in His hands. He made the world and everything therein.

In His infinite wisdom, He created you for a reason. The Psalmist says in Psalm 139:14, "I praise you because I am fearfully and wonderfully made; your works are wonderful, I know that full well." The fact that you have been carefully chosen and made by God illustrates the fact that you are not here on this earth by chance. In Psalm 8:3-4 we read, "When I consider your heavens, the work of your fingers, the moon and the stars, which you have set in place, what is man that you are mindful of him, the son of man that you care for him?"

God's love for us is immeasurable and undeserving. It does not depend on who we are, what we have done or who others say we are. Our destiny is in His hands, and He will bring to pass that which He has destined before the foundation of the earth.

Second, Jabez realized that there were "destiny vultures" determined to destroy his destiny and God did not want them to prevail over him. In order to avert their plans and frustrate their efforts, the first thing that Jabez had to do was to agree to a partnership with God. He had to realize that he could not withstand the "destiny vultures" all by himself. He needed the help of God Almighty. Secondly, he had to accept what God had destined for him, believe it, and act accordingly in spite of his past or what people were saying about him. The writer of Ecclesiastes had a supernatural insight into what happens many times in our lives when we allow "destiny vultures" to prevail. He declares in Ecclesiastes 10:7, "I have seen slaves on horseback, while princes go on foot like slaves." In other words, many of us (princes and princesses) are not in the places where we ought to be and enjoying the blessings that God has destined for us to enjoy. Servants are upon our horses (they have taken possession of what God has made available for us) while we (princes and princesses) are walking and working like slaves!

A study of the characteristics of vultures would reveal some shocking realities that might help us understand why "destiny vultures" could cause so much destruction to our future if we allow them. A vulture is a large bird that does not seize or tear its food. In fact, it is not likely to kill its food or other animals though it has the ability to do so if it chooses. It preys on animals that have been killed by other animals or by human beings and those that die naturally. In other words, it feeds on dead flesh. In terms of physical appearance, it is an ugly creature. Most of its head and neck is hairless. What is amazing about a vulture is that it has the ability to smell death from afar and it has a good sense of smell. In other words, a vulture can tell when something is about to die. It then waits patiently for the person or animal's death before it starts to consume its flesh. You see, there are spiritual vultures as well. They might not come against you directly but are anxiously waiting to see how you will react to a challenging situation in order to devour your flesh. They are waiting to see if you will give up and abandon your faith so that they can mount their attack on you. They are waiting to see if you will allow all that has been said about you to discourage you to the point where life will seem useless and God will appear to be powerless so that they can come to accompany you to the place of no return.

Third, Jabez realized that not only were there "destiny vultures" but that if he (Jabez) would experience what God had in store for him, he would have to step out into his destiny. That is to say, he had a part to play in stepping into his destiny, and God expected Jabez to cooperate with Him. The Bible declares that Jabez became honorable. The word honorable *(kabod)* means "to be heavy." In a positive sense, it means "abound more, great, magnitude and glory." Being honorable speaks to the character, responsibility, and respect of the person. Being considered honorable is not an attribute or characteristic that can be bought or demanded. It has to be earned over a period of time through one's comportment. Now, imagine Jabez being teased, insulted, castigated, belittled, and ostracized because of his name, Jabez (pain), yet he begins to develop a character that is honorable, admired, praised, and worth emulating. Honestly, in order to exhibit these characteristics, Jabez had to have a deep sense of knowing his purpose and destiny. It comes also from knowing the God you serve and that He is able to change your mess into a message. It comes from putting your trust in God and having the full assurance that He is Lord of all. Jabez went from being a pain to being more honorable. His life took a turn for the glory of God as he abounded into greatness not based on his own merit.

Finally, Jabez realized that even though he bore no responsibility for the pain that surrounded his birth, his mother still believed that he was somehow responsible. It is true that at times, things we have done in the past do cause problems for us later on in life. However, in this case, I do not believe that Jabez personally did anything wrong. Nevertheless, he did not excuse himself from the fact that his mother believed him to be part of the problem. He prayed in 1 Chronicles 4:10 "…and that you would keep me from evil, that I will not cause pain." From this we can deduce that for us to have our mess turned into a message, we need to acknowledge whatever wrong we may have done, or our action that may have led to the undesirable situation. For God to move us forward, we must examine ourselves and repent of known or unknown sin. The Bible declares in 1 John 1:8-9, "If we claim to be without sin, we deceive ourselves and the truth is not in us. If we confess our sins, He is faithful and just and will forgive us our sins and purify us from all unrighteousness." Jabez prayed that God would help him not to cause pain. Jabez's prayer meant one of two things: 1) he was acknowledging that he had caused pain and did not want it to be repeated and, therefore he was praying, "Lord, please don't allow me to continue to cause pain in the lives of others;" or 2) he was not agreeing to the fact that he had been the cause of pain in the lives of others (especially his mother), but that he did not want what had been said about him to come true. Therefore he was praying, "Lord please don't let what they said and continue to say about me ever come true!" What a powerful way to pray: "Lord, I may have caused this problem and I am sorry. But even if I didn't, please don't let it ever happen." You can't (for the most part) control what people say about you but you can control how you react. You might not be able to stop them from talking or calling you names, but may it not be true of you what they are saying. That is what Jabez realized and therefore prayed. For you to have your mess turned into a message, you must turn away from those things that are not pleasing to God and live a life that is without reproach.

Here is an interesting question. What made the difference in the life of this man, who was at one point characterized as causing pain, to become a man remembered as more honorable than his brothers? I think that the defining characteristic of Jabez's life and situation is that he was a man of prayer. If we are to have our mess turned into a message, we must pray. We must petition heaven to make known God's plan for our lives. We have to be ready to travail in prayer until something happens. Someone used the acronym PUSH (pray until something happens) to describe the persistence that is needed in prayer.

Jabez is distinctly remembered, not for what he did, but for what he prayed. His prayer became the casting distinction in his life to remove him from causing pain to being blessed by the hand of God. As you read the two main verses in the Bible about Jabez,[8] you'll quickly come to the realization that they do not give a complete background of Jabez's life. They do not tell us if he became a rich or poor man. Many biblical scholars have predicted that he became rich and that his territory was extended because 1 Chronicles 4:10 says that the Lord granted his request. However, we don't know with certainty what happened after that. Did the extended territory remain with him forever? Was it physical territory that he wanted expanded? In fact, we don't know how old Jabez was when he prayed this prayer. The Bible simply says that he prayed and his prayer was answered. The most important thing to remember is that in Jabez's mind, he realized that prayer could change his mess into a message. There is an old song that says,

> *Prayer is the key of heaven, but faith unlocks the door*
> *And if that is the way to the Kingdom*
> *I'm going to tell it wherever I go.*

In Jabez's mind, he may have thought: "If only I could pray and get the attention of the God of the heavens, my life would never be the same." He probably thought to himself, "I know that I shouldn't be anybody. I know my name says that my future is supposed to be full of sorrow, but if only I can pray, my life will be that of joy. For I don't want to live in sorrow; in fact, I refuse to live in sorrow." Maybe he said to himself, "I know that my circumstances don't want to permit me to make it, but I'm going to make it anyhow. I'm going to make it whether I'm supposed to make it or not. I am going to make it whether the strongest demon in hell wants me to make it or not. I am going to make it whether my family members want me to make it or not, because if God is for me who can be against me?" The Apostle Paul reminds us in Romans 8:28-31:

And we know that in all things God works for the good of those who love Him, who have been called according to His purpose. For those God foreknew He also predestined to be conformed to the likeness of His Son, that He might be the firstborn among many brothers. And those He predestined, He also called;

---

8   It is worth noting that in 1 Chronicles 2:55 we read, "And the clans of scribes who lived at Jabez: the Tirathites, Shimeathites and Sucathites. These are the Kenites who came from Hammath, the father of the house of Recab." Jabez is described as a town inhabited by scribes who were identified as Kenites attached to the tribe of Judah. Some scholars have speculated that the man, Jabez, became so prosperous that a town, where clans of scribes were trained, was named in his honor.

those He called, He also justified; those He justified, He also glorified. What, then, shall we say in response to this? If God is for us, who can be against us?

Someone reading this book needs to know that the Spirit of God could be saying that the fact you are down today does not mean you will be forever. The fact that your answer has been delayed does not mean it has been denied; because you disappointed God does not mean He does not love you anymore; because your life is a mess today, does not mean that He cannot transform it into a message that is powerful enough to shake the earth; because you left Him and walked away, does not mean that His hands are now folded and He is so angry that He does not want you to come back. I am simply trying to say, "Stop letting your past or current circumstances predict your future. Stop letting your past or current circumstances deter you from going back to the Father. Stop letting your past or current circumstances hinder you from praying to the Father for His forgiveness." Even if you have to be like the Prodigal Son who said, "I am no longer worthy to be called your son; make me like one of your hired men (Luke 15:19)," then say the prayer of the Prodigal Son and go back home.

I believe also that the Spirit of God is saying, "Don't let your circumstances predict your praise and your future." The fact that you grew up in a terrible situation where your dad was on drugs and your mother was a "call girl" doesn't mean that God doesn't have a plan for you. The fact that your daddy didn't do anything with his life doesn't mean that you can't do something with yours. The fact that people say you look funny doesn't mean that in God's eyes you look funny. The fact that people have said that you won't succeed in life, doesn't mean that it has to be realized. In fact, God is ready to make the enemy ashamed. He is ready to pour His anointing upon you and bless you by expanding your territory. What the enemy meant for evil, God is turning it around for your good. If you will only believe it and walk in faith, your territory will be larger than you can handle! Those years the "locusts" have eaten will be restored according to Joel 2:25.[9] If you read Joel 1:4, the Bible declares that what the cutting locust left, the swarming locust has eaten, what the swarming locust left the hopping locust has eaten. What the hopping locust left the destroying locust has eaten. This is a complete description of hopelessness! But the

---

9   "I will repay you for the years the locusts have eaten – the great locust and the young locust, the other locusts and the locust swarm - my great army that I sent among you."

good news is that God is ready and willing to turn your messy situation into a message of hope, trust, joy, and victory. This is demonstrated by the fact that in the text, God answered Jabez's prayer and He is willing, able, and ready to answer yours as well. The Bible says that Jabez knew what people said about him. His own mother had condemned him to be nothing, but Jabez went to someone else. He called on God! The Bible says he prayed to God, and I can imagine that Jabez prayed hard. He probably cried on his knees before the Lord and said, "Lord, don't let my enemies triumph. Bless me Lord. Enough negative things have been said about me. Change my life, change my situation, change my testimony, change my heart, change my environment, change my destiny, change my life, and let it be completely yours."

Thank God that He is still in the prayer answering business. In Luke 11:13, we read, "If you then, though you are evil, know how to give good gifts to your children, how much more will your Father in heaven give the Holy Spirit to those who ask Him!" He is still in the business of hearing His children when they call upon His name. God did it for Jabez, He can do it for you! Jabez's mess of pain was turned into a life of honor, enlarged territory, and influence. Yours can be the same!

Chapter III: Zacchaeus (Luke 19:1-10)
God Turns a Messy Life of Corruption into a Message of Honesty, Trust, Restitution, and Redemption

Jesus entered Jericho and was passing through. A man was there by the name of Zacchaeus; he was a chief tax collector and was wealthy. He wanted to see who Jesus was, but being a short man he could not, because of the crowd. So he ran ahead and climbed a sycamore-fig tree to see him, since Jesus was coming that way. When Jesus reached the spot, he looked up and said to him, "Zacchaeus, come down immediately. I must stay at your house today." So he came down at once and welcomed Him gladly. All the people saw this and began to mutter, "He has gone to be the guest of a 'sinner.'" But Zacchaeus stood up and said to the Lord, "Look, Lord! Here and now I give half of my possessions to the poor, and if I have cheated anybody out of anything, I will pay back four times the amount." Jesus said to him, "Today salvation has come to this house, because this man, too, is a son of Abraham. For the Son of Man came to seek and to save what was lost" (Luke 19:1-10).

There are certain things that happen in this life that are beyond our control. You begin to discover some of them while growing up and notice that there seems to be a problem: You are different from everyone else. Somehow everyone else seems to have a normal life but ours is abnormal. Everyone else has a mother, but yours is nowhere to be found. Everyone has a father who attends his or her baseball, basketball, or band rehearsals but yours can't be found. In fact, when you ask your mother about him, it is like all hell breaks loose. She, who was laughing with you before the question was asked, becomes angry to the point where you begin to wonder what was so horrible about the simple question: "Where is my daddy and why isn't he at home?" Or, maybe your situation is different in the sense that while other kids are happy when the bell rings and school is over, you are afraid because there is a drunk who you call "stepfather," who is waiting for you at home and has promised, for no apparent reason, to "beat the devil" out of you when you get back. How you wish you could change your life, be born into another family or have the Lord take one of your parents home earlier, but it is not happening. For others, it is not a dysfunctional family dynamic that they are dealing with; it is a situation that has to do with certain physical characteristics that they possess. It could be that they are not as beautiful as their friends, are a little overweight, have little or no hair, or are a little too short or too tall.

The story in Luke 19:1-10 has to do with a man called Zacchaeus who was dealing with a situation. He was a little too short. I was first exposed to Zacchaeus as a child in Sunday school. I can still remember the song we sang about him written by Elsie Leslie. It goes like this:

> *Zacchaeus was a wee little man,*
> *A wee little man was he,*
> *He climbed up in a sycamore tree*
> *For the Lord he wanted to see;*
>
> *And as the Savior passed that way,*
> *He looked up in the tree,*
> *And He said, Zacchaeus, you come down,*
> *For I'm going to your house today,*
> *For I'm going to your house today.*

There may not be a song about your messy situation, but that doesn't mean that it is less important than Zacchaeus' situation. As a matter of fact, yours is so bad that the best song composer might have difficulty putting the lyrics and rhythm together that could genuinely express your dilemma. You might be saying to yourself, "I wish I had Zacchaeus' problem because it is not that bad of a problem after all." I had a classmate in Cote d'Ivoire (West Africa) when I was studying at the University who always said,

"There are problems among problems." One day, I was explaining about the challenges I was having in getting a visa to go to Israel and he said, "I wish I had your problem, because where I am, I only need money to buy food to eat and going to Israel is my least concern or worry." The point that I am trying to make is that we all have messy situations that we deal with continuously. Though they might not be of the same magnitude, they are still messy situations. In fact, who determines the gravity or magnitude of a given situation? I think that it is the person who is going through it. It is for this reason that I bless the Lord because He does not downplay our situations or place them into categories of importance. He wants to address all of our headaches and challenges. He wants to be our friend in order to stand with us during our darkest hours and to save us. That is exactly what He wanted to do with Zacchaeus. Verse 10 of Luke 19 tells us, "For the Son of Man came to seek and to save what was lost."

The story of Zacchaeus has become popular because it resonates with us whether we are believers or not. Allow me to paint a picture of Zacchaeus' birth and early days for you. Hopefully, it will help you understand the story a little better. This is not intended to add to the account given in the Bible and I must add that it is just my imagination (but a powerful one that will hopefully bring the story to life).

Zacchaeus' mother started to scream one day after carrying the pregnancy for nine months and said that her stomach was hurting. It was an unusual pain – not a pain caused by indigestion or stomach cramps – but the one that only women can explain, the one that happens when a child is due. His dad becomes confused and not knowing what to do, starts to pace up and down the house. He wanted to go into the room to help his wife but he was afraid that he would start to cry with her. There was no doctor and the midwife was far away. What would he do? He heard his wife yelling from the room, "Get the midwife, I can't hold on much longer. The baby is coming!"

He started to run and pray, "Oh, God, please let her be there!" Upon arrival at the midwife's house, Zacchaeus' father saw the midwife who apparently was on her way to see his wife. Together, they quickly hurried to his house. As they approached the house, his heart sank. Was she okay? What happened? Then he heard his wife scream again. This time, the scream elated his heart. She is alive! "Please hurry, hurry." He gently pushed the midwife through the door. She entered their room and in a few minutes, the baby was born. The family had already decided on the name of the child. They had been praying for a boy and decided that if they did have a boy they would name him Zacchaeus, meaning "pure or untainted." He would be the purest thing that ever walked on this earth. He would not be tainted by corruption, bad judgment, jealousy, rudeness, anger, hatred, rage, or any form of sin that is condemned in the Torah. That was their wish and so they named him Zacchaeus.

When Zacchaeus' father heard the sound of the baby crying, he rushed into the room, and fell on his knees, picked up the baby and raised him to heaven. He asked that God would grant little Zacchaeus protection, guidance, and wisdom. Most especially he asked that God would allow him to live up to his name (pure and untainted). A huge celebration followed and the entire village came and rejoiced over the birth of Zacchaeus.

As Zacchaeus grew, it became noticeable that he had a defect. He was short and there was nothing that could be done to help him. The priest joined the parents to pray but it did not help. He tried playing basketball but that also did not help. After trying other methods like trying to pull his hands and legs, all to no avail, his parents left him alone and silently hoped that he would come to accept his height as a strength and not a weakness. They ended up trying to encourage him to see his God-given potential and see his height as a gift and not a curse. Zacchaeus loved his parents and tried very hard to listen to them as they shared their thoughts with him and encouraged him to be strong from within and not allow his height to limit what he could do and who he would become in the future. He also tried hard to believe what they said, but as he grew, he noticed that he was becoming the object of ridicule and laughter in the town. His height impeded him from climbing trees like many little boys did. His height made him a constant object of bullying by others. His height caused him to be overlooked even by those who were younger than he was.

All of this did not really bother Zacchaeus as much as when he heard some adults referring to him as a dwarf and an abnormal child. He couldn't understand why. He had done nothing wrong to them. These were adults who ought to know that some things happen to people that are beyond their control. His parents had been nice to everyone. How could they repay his family by calling him a dwarf? Now he started to understand why they didn't want their children to hang out with him. Now he started to understand why they stared at him when he passed their way. Now he started to understand why they whispered to each other and pointed their fingers at him when he came walking down the gravel road to the marketplace. But, what did he do wrong? Why did this happen to him? Why should he be ill-treated for something that was beyond his control? If

Zacchaeus was living in our times, he would have been bullied at school, teased by students in his class, beaten by older kids on the bus, and maybe would not have gotten a girl to attend the junior and senior prom with him. That was his situation! How do you explain to a teenager not to be angry with the world if he or she is treated this way because of his or her height? How Zacchaeus longed that people would get to know him and not judge him by his height! How he longed for people to give him a chance to prove himself and not reach conclusions about his ability because of his height! He did not have any mental, social, or psychological deformities. He had only one challenge – his height. He was short.

As time went by, Zacchaeus tried everything he knew to win the hearts and minds of those he loved in the villages and towns around Jericho, but all his efforts proved futile. No one wanted to be his friend. The ridiculing continued and life became miserable and undesirable. To his utter amazement, he started to secretly plot in his heart to get back at those who were ill-treating him. He started to plan how to make them pay for all those years that he was robbed of laughter and happiness that other young boys enjoyed in their village. He had developed an attitude and was bitter and angry because of how he had been treated by others. He started to say to himself, "As soon as I get the opportunity, they will pay and pay big, they will."

Somehow, the opportunity presented itself a few years later. A position opened up for a job that was hated by all true Israelites who loved their God and their people. It was the position of being a tax collector. That is exactly what Zacchaeus needed. Of course he knew that tax collectors were likened unto harlots (women who sold their virtue for money) and they were hated by the Jews. There are some biblical writers who have tried to compare tax collectors in those days to IRS agents in our days. I think that the comparison is not completely accurate simply because tax collectors were hated during Zacchaeus' days. Today, we don't like IRS agents but we certainly don't hate them because they are simply doing their jobs (collecting taxes that are necessary for the development and ongoing upkeep of the nation's infrastructure). In contrast to IRS agents, tax collectors were viewed as traitors and betrayers. They did not work for the nation of Israel. On the contrary, they worked for the Romans, a people group so hated by the Jews because they were occupiers and believed to be very arrogant and cruel. Zacchaeus knew all of this, but who were they to tell him about morals and ethics? Where were theirs when they ill-treated him and said all kinds of nasty things about him? Now the opportunity had presented itself and he was determined to make good use of it. Zacchaeus applied for and was accepted for the job. In a few months, he was doing so well on the job that he was promoted and became the Chief Tax Collector.

Let me explain a little more about how the tax system worked in those days. The Romans (the occupiers) would hire native Jews to be tax collectors and would require each tax collector to pay them a certain amount or percentage of the taxes collected. It meant that the tax collectors were not paid by the Roman government and therefore they did not have a fixed salary. The tax collectors were the ones required to pay the Roman government for the right to tax in the name of Rome. Each tax collector paid for a certain section or geographic location to tax and they would charge what the Romans wanted plus what the tax collector wanted. Hence, they were viewed by the Jews as thieves because they charged whatever they felt people were capable of paying or an amount based on their personal financial need. This system was hated by the Jews but they had to pay or risked being imprisoned. This system proved to be very effective but it was full of fraud and uncertainties. Taxes being levied were inconsistent and unstable. Zacchaeus became good at what he did. Had he been in the mafia he would be called the godfather, or had he been in the drug world, he would be called the kingpin. He became rich and nobody could play games with him. His words became "law and gospel." He liked his job and took comfort in it. It was in this system that Zacchaeus prospered.

I am sure you can identify a little bit with a system like that where there are corporate bonuses and compensations given to chief executive officers after shareholders have lost millions of dollars, or after corporations have received tax payers' dollars in order to be bailed out of the financial mess that the same chief executive officers have gotten them into. I am sure that you know of a system where there is no accountability and anyone can take the country's resources and divert them for personal use. I am sure you know of a system where you cannot question those in authority because if you do, your sleeping place would be changed without your approval (you could be jailed or killed without a trial). I am sure you know of a system where taxes fluctuate because of greed and poor governance. I am sure you know of a system where someone has gotten hold of power and is determined to make everyone pay for the miserable days he or she has had on earth. Such was the situation!

From a distance, anyone would have said that Zacchaeus was living a good life. He had prestige, power, security, political clout, money, and probably all the women that money could buy. The same town girls that did not want to hang out with him before were now at his mercy. All he had to do was to say the word and whatever he wanted would be given to him. He wasn't just a tax collector... he was a CHIEF tax collector. He was the "chief among the publicans." That basically means he was what we might refer to as "Commissioner of Taxes."[10] This phrase also indicates that he had other collectors working under his supervision. He was now a BIG man. People feared him. They may have loathed him and hated him, but they feared him. He was a man of power and influence. My little daughter would say, "This is the life!" Unfortunately, this is not all to life. He had a void within him. He knew that something was wrong but did not know how to fix it.

I am sure that Zacchaeus built walls around himself designed to insulate himself from the insults and indignities of his past. BUT, he was still a short man that nobody liked. He was still a lonely, isolated man who had everything ... except what he really wanted. He had tried in the past to correct this problem by being nice, by loving others, by caring for them and by trusting them. His kindness was repaid by insults only because of his height. Now the situation was hopeless. It was a real mess. He had no good relationship with his own people and because his job required him to be in constant contact with the Gentiles, who were considered unclean, he became ceremonially unclean himself. It meant that he couldn't go to the temple and offer sacrifices in worship to his God (Yahweh). What a situation to be in! He doesn't have a good relationship with his fellow man and now God too! The job had robbed him of his ability to worship God. So Zacchaeus was cut off from his people and alienated from his God. What could he do? Who could he talk to? No one listened or cared before, why would they care now? He was tired, but he couldn't let down his mask. He had to survive. This world is cruel and only the strongest can survive. He was determined to continue even though he knew that he was not happy. Are you in a messy situation like that? If you are, you need to realize that there is a solution!

It happened that Zacchaeus started to hear about this man everyone called "Jesus." People were saying some incredible things about him: He was the Son of God; He was God who had taken on human form and was dwelling among mankind; He was a mighty prophet of God; He

---

10   Charles F. Pfeiffer and Everett F. Harrison, Editors, *The Wycliffe Bible Commentary*. Chicago, Illinois: Moody Press, page 1059.

was Elijah; and He was the Son of David, the promised Messiah and Savior of the universe, according to the writings of the Old Testament, etc. Surprisingly for Zacchaeus, each time he heard a story or something being told about Jesus, there was something unexplainable about Jesus that touched a hidden chord in his soul. He had also heard rumors that Jesus made friends with everyone and that He didn't care who you were, what you looked like, or what you had done. Word on the street had it that this Jesus had even eaten with tax collectors. He had heard from a reliable source that one of Jesus' disciples had been a tax collector – Matthew or Levi, or something like that. It had also come to his attention that Jesus had told the Pharisees and Sadducees that He did not come for the righteous but for sinners (Matthew 9:9-13). All of the reports he heard about Jesus sounded too good to be true, but somehow he knew that they had to be.

Zacchaeus remembered how one day he went to work. It was a usual working day and nothing out of the ordinary took place on that day. Given the mode of transport and the nature of his work, he had to walk or ride a donkey from one home to another to collect taxes. While he was out collecting taxes, he came to the home of a blind man whose name was Bartimaeus (Mark 10:46-52). Zacchaeus demanded the taxes he owed, but Bartimaeus didn't have it!

He told Zacchaeus, "Please sir, I am just a poor old blind man, have mercy."

Zacchaeus, who cared less about Bartimaeus being blind or poor, threatened him that if he returned in 30 days and Bartimaeus didn't have his money, he would go to jail. Then Zacchaeus went to the next house and began to demand the taxes they owed.

The lady began to explain to Zacchaeus, "Sir, my husband is a demon possessed man, known as the Maniac of Gadara (Mark 5:1-20) and he lives among the tombs. Believe me sir," she begged, "I am telling you the truth. My husband runs crazy, screaming and hollering. Please give me more time. Please! I am deeply saddened by his condition but moreover, his behavior is causing a lot of problems for me because he continues to attack people and destroy their belongings. They keep coming and asking me to pay. I am in a lot of trouble. Please understand, Sir."

Reluctantly, Zacchaeus gave her 30 days also to come up with the money to pay the taxes. Then he went to the next house and he immediately noticed something strange: A wreath was on the door. A lady came to the door and identified herself as the widow of Nain (Luke 7:11-15). As usual,

Zacchaeus demanded the taxes that she owed. She explained to him that her son had just died, and she was preparing for his burial. The bills were high and she needed to bury him immediately before his body started to decompose. She begged Zacchaeus to give her more time. He reflected for a few seconds and said to himself that it is only fair to give her 30 days as he had done with the other two. So, he told her that he would be back in 30 days to collect his taxes and this time, no excuse would be accepted.

Time goes by really fast, especially when you are a chief tax collector and have a lot of clients to deal with. Before Zacchaeus realized it, the thirty days had gone by and it was time to revisit the three homes mentioned above to get his taxes. He went on his way and soon arrived at the first home. He knocked on the door and a bright-eyed man answered the door.

"This man seems familiar," Zacchaeus thought to himself. "This man looks a whole lot different than before! What happened?"

To appease his curiosity, Zacchaeus decided to inquire from the man what happened. With a surprised look on his face he said to the man, "I don't understand, I thought you were...."

Not sure if he should say the word, Zacchaeus hesitated. The man interrupted. "You mean, blind? It's okay, you can say it. Yes, I was. But, as you have already noticed, I can see again."

Bartimaeus invited Zacchaeus into his house and narrated the entire story of how he met Jesus and how Jesus healed him. After listening to what seemed to be an impossible, illogical, and a mystical testimony of a man who everyone knew to have been blind but could now see, Zacchaeus left Bartimaeus' home with the taxes he came to collect. However, as he left he started to scratch his head in bewilderment saying to himself, "What in the world did I just hear? This can't be true. He was definitely pulling my leg." Yet, the more he said it, the more he knew that it was true. Instantly his mind began to wonder, "If this is true, what kind of man is this Jesus?"

In what seemed to have been a few minutes, though it had taken him 35 minutes, Zacchaeus found himself at the door of the second person on his list. He had to quickly gather his thoughts and recompose himself in order to determine his course of action, just in case he did not get his taxes. The chief tax collector took a deep breath and knocked on the door. A few seconds elapsed and the door swung opened. Before him was a man who must have been at least seven feet tall with a weight of nothing less than 300 pounds. He was neatly dressed and had a calm, non-threatening look on his face. Surprised and a little frightened, Zacchaeus took a step back but quickly recovered from his shock and said in a professional and authoritative voice, "I'm Zacchaeus, the chief tax collector, and you are....?"

"Oh, nice to see you, Zacchaeus," the tall, well-built man responded with a smile on his face, apparently having noticed how surprised Zacchaeus had been to see him. "I used to be the Maniac of Gadara. My wife told me you came by."

"Who?" Zacchaeus said, thinking that his ears betrayed him. He quickly reminded himself that the last time he heard about a man with that name, he was told that the person was living among the dead and he was very dangerous to the point that the law enforcement agents couldn't contain him. How did he get here? Why does he look so calm and respectful? Why did his wife and the villagers lie to him about this man being so dangerous? Seeing how confused Zacchaeus looked, the man invited him to have a drink. Zacchaeus accepted simply because he didn't think he had a choice, given his curiosity, the man's size, and his gentle insistence that Zacchaeus listen to his story. The man explained to Zacchaeus how he had met Jesus a few weeks ago and how Jesus delivered him from the power of the demonic forces that controlled his life. He concluded by pointing out that he had been set free and now he had his life back in order and his family was happy.

Then the man reached into his pocket and took out the taxes. As he handed it to Zacchaeus, he said, "I am sorry for all the trouble you went through. It won't happen again. I now have a good job and I will do everything I can to stay on top of my bills."

Speechless, Zacchaeus placed the money in his bag, and arose. He thanked the man for the drink, and said that he had to leave immediately. As he walked away, the same thoughts that haunted him when he left the home of Bartimaeus came rushing back like floodwaters. "Who is this Jesus?" he asked himself again! "He not only opens the eyes of the blind but is able to set people free from demonic possession. Wow! I must meet him. This can't be true! Am I going mad?"

The chief of the tax collectors did not have much time again to continue to focus on trying to find answers to all his questions about Jesus because the next home was right around the corner. Before he knocked on the door, he promised himself that he would do everything he could to find out who this Jesus is and why he was changing the lives of so many people in a positive way. He also secretly wondered if this same Jesus could change his messy situation into a message in the same way he did for the two people he just encountered. The first person had said to him, "I had a messy situation of both physical and spiritual blindness, but now I have a message to tell the world that I cannot only see spiritually, but also my physical eyes have been opened by this man called Jesus." The second one had said, "I had a messy situation of demonic oppression, possession, and obsession, but now I have a message for the world and that message is that Jesus can set anyone free from any form of demonic attack."

"Wow! Can Jesus set me free also?" Zacchaeus thought to himself.

At the third house, he knocked on the door as usual and waited for someone to answer. A young man answered the door with a smile on his face. Zacchaeus introduced himself and asked: "Who are you?" This time, he did not want any other surprise about a blind father seeing or a demon possessed man being well dressed and telling him about this Jesus. The young man said, "Well sir, you should know me, but....it's a long story, I'll let my mother tell you. Please come on in."

He hurriedly got his mother and the both of them came into the living room to meet Zacchaeus. She greeted Zacchaeus with joy and asked him to sit. He refused because he wanted to get straight to the point and leave. All he wanted was his money, because he had so much on his mind and did not have time to sit around and talk. The lady said, "Oh sir, all is well. I've got your money."

She sent her son to get the money in her room from under her pillow and she started to explain. "You see, I experienced a miracle of divine proportion. You won't believe what happened!" She continued, "You remember the last time you were here and I told you that my son had died? What happened is that they were carrying my dead son in a casket to the graveyard. And as they approached the grave site, there was this man who met us on the way. His name was Jesus. He touched the casket and said, 'Young man, I say unto thee, Arise!' The next thing I knew was that my son sat straight up in the casket and began to talk!"

She continued after a brief pause. Looking as if she had received a revelation, she said: "Here is what I think happened. On that road, death met deity and when death met deity, there was a resurrection! And...here is the best part," she added. "When Jesus spoke to my son's body and he arose from the dead, it scared the undertaker so badly, he gave me all my money back for the funeral, and here is the money I owe you for taxes!"

Zacchaeus said to the woman, "Are you just pulling my leg? Who will raise a dead child by just speaking to his body? It doesn't make sense!"

The lady replied, "I know that it doesn't, but trust me, it is true. I was there, and it was my son! In fact, where do you think I would have gotten all this money to pay my taxes after burying my son? You know me…this is my only child and my husband is dead. Talk to others in the village and they will tell you that it is true. God is good, isn't He, Zacchaeus?"

Dumbfounded, the Chief Tax Collector was out of words to express himself. He just took the money from the lady's hands, put it in his bag, turned around, and left the house with the intention of not stopping at any other house. He had heard enough for the day. He needed time to digest all of the information he had received about this Jesus and try to find a way to get to meet him or at least see for himself some of the things that had been reported about Jesus.

As Zacchaeus went home, he could not help but wonder like the Samaritan woman at the well, "Could this be the Christ? He must be! These people were not lying. Maybe, just maybe – this Jesus could turn his mess into a message. But, how could he get to him?"

Zacchaeus continued to be preoccupied with his thoughts all the way home. About a mile to his house, he heard a woman shouting to her husband that she would be back in a few minutes to continue cooking but she had to go and meet Jesus. Jesus? Did he hear her right? Where is he?

Zacchaeus ran to the woman and asked, "Did you say that you are going to see Jesus? Where is he?"

The lady said, "I heard that he is on his way to Jericho."

"What a coincidence," he thought. "This must be my lucky day." Somehow he did not realize that it was all in God's plan and purpose for his life. He did not know that God saw his heart and knew that he needed to receive a touch from Jesus. He did not realize that God had seen his tears all these years and knew that it was time to wipe them away. He did not realize that God had seen how he had been rejected, despised, and abused, and knew that it was time for him to be recognized, comforted, and elevated. He did not know that there is nothing called "luck" for those whose steps are ordered by the Lord, that everything was being orchestrated by God, and this was a part of His divine plan for a divine encounter. All he knew was that Jesus was coming his way and he had to seize the opportunity.

He thought to himself, "This visit of Jesus to Jericho may be my one and only chance to find out if what they are saying about this man called Jesus is true because He might never come this way for a long time." Zacchaeus had an itch in his heart that all his wealth couldn't scratch. He probably didn't even know what he needed. He just knew he desperately needed something. When he heard this news about Jesus, he was hoping Jesus might have the solution to his problem. He didn't know it, but he was searching for God with everything in him.

So Zacchaeus started to run ahead of the lady. He saw the crowd and someone said that Jesus was there. He tried to push his way through but he couldn't. No one would let him. Nobody liked him and nobody wanted him there. They acted as if he was not there even when they saw him and knew he was trying to get through the crowd. He tried to jump to see Jesus and to see if he could get His attention, but he was too short. Then... he saw a tree – a sycamore tree. Sycamore trees of that region were fig trees with wide branches that sprouted out from the trunk very close to the ground. They were easy, even for children, to climb. Here was his chance. He would climb and even if all he achieved was getting a glimpse at Jesus, then it was worth his effort.

While the thought seems to be an excellent one, Zacchaeus realized that he couldn't just climb a tree. As desperately as he wanted to meet Jesus, he knew that he couldn't disregard certain things. Without any doubt, he wanted his messy situation to be turned into a message but it would cost him a lot. Could he afford to do it? What if it was not worth all this effort and the possible aftermath? He had to think fast because Jesus was coming. Here are a few of the challenges that he thought about:

1. **His social status.** What would people say about him when they realized that he was in the tree trying to see a religious man? Doctor Luke tells us in Luke 19:2 that he was rich (a man of great possession). Zacchaeus said to himself, "But having a high social status shouldn't stop me. Some religious people also have money....even though they got theirs by hard work and honesty." He was right, because quite often riches can be a source of hindrance to salvation. Jesus himself alluded to this truth when He said, "How hard it is for the rich to enter the kingdom of God" (Luke 18: 24)! There were some in Zacchaeus' day as there are in our day that are very rich and still love the Lord. Patrick Henry,[11] the man to

---

11   *"Give me Liberty, or give me Death!"* is a famous quotation attributed to Patrick Henry from a speech he made to the Virginia Convention. It was given March 23, 1775, at St. John's Church in Richmond, Virginia, and is credited with having swung the balance in convincing the Virginia House of Burgesses to pass a resolution delivering the Virginia troops to the Revolutionary War. Among the delegates to the convention were future US Presidents Thomas Jefferson and George Washington.

whom the famous quote, "Give me liberty, or give me death," is attributed, is also believed to have said the following: "I have now disposed of all my property to my family. There is one thing more I wish I could give them and that is faith in Jesus Christ. If they had that and I had not given them a single shilling, they would have been rich; and if they had not that, and I had given them all the world, they would be poor indeed."[12] True as it may be (having Jesus is worth more than all the riches in the world), Zacchaeus knew that if he was caught in a sycamore tree trying to get to Jesus, he might not be able to bear the shame and disgrace that could result from all the gossips in the village. But, he also knew that he couldn't continue like this. It is true that he was rich but he was equally unhappy. He knew that he had to climb into the sycamore tree. That was his only hope to see Jesus. He was desperate and desperate people do desperate things. They search for answers, they cry for help, they put aside dignity and pretenses in hope of finding a lasting solution to their dilemma. Zacchaeus knew that most adults don't climb trees to see someone coming. They only climb trees when they are being chased by a mean dog or their lives are in danger from a cruel animal trying to kill them or they are trying to escape from a flood. Climbing a tree is an act of desperation. But, he reminded himself that he was desperate. His happiness was at stake, his peace of mind depended on the decision he was about to make, his salvation was in the balance and he knew, without anyone saying it, that he had to climb. Yes, he had to climb! But…there was another problem.

2. **His physical status**. This was not a secret. Zacchaeus was short and he knew it and everyone else knew it. Just one look at him would make anyone wonder which planet he came from. But his shortness was not just physical. He remembered that some people had said that he was a dwarf and that he was an abnormal child. What does it mean? Did they think that there was a spiritual reason for his shortness? Was he connected to the underworld? Allow me to point out that

---

12   Independence Day: Immortal Words of the Founding Fathers. Infowars, July 4, 2007. Retrieved on March 14, 2010 from http://www.infowars.com/articles/us/july_4th_words_of_founding_fathers.htm

in many cultures where people don't know and understand the biological explanation of dwarfism, they usually think that dwarfs are cursed and they cause "bad luck." In other cultures, dwarfs are considered to have supernatural powers and deal with the unknown world. In the case of Zacchaeus, we have no reason to believe that he had supernatural power from another world, but what if that was the perception of the people concerning him? What if he is caught in the tree and people begin to spread the rumor that he was up there performing some kind of spiritual exercise? He actually did not know what to think. He knew that he had to climb the tree in order to see Jesus, but he was concerned about what others would say. He probably did not think about his shortness as being representative of his inability and insufficiency in approaching a holy God. He probably did not realize that the only way he could meet Jesus was by going to the tree, just as we do when we go to the cross on which He was crucified. It is what one of Jesus' disciples said, in 1 Peter 2: 24: "He himself bore our sins in His body on the tree, so that we might die to sins and live for righteousness; by His wounds you have been healed." He didn't realize that the tree is still the only place the lost sinner can meet the Savior. His mind was preoccupied with what people would say, even though he knew that he had to climb the tree to see Jesus. He just couldn't afford not to climb the sycamore tree. But, he thought again, there is a third problem, as if he didn't have enough to deal with already.

3. **His religious status**. Doctor Luke had mentioned in Luke 19:7 that Zacchaeus was a sinner. Zacchaeus knew that he had done a lot of unpleasant things in his life. He knew that he was an angry man. He knew that he had harbored hatred in his heart against the villagers. He knew that he had taxed people unjustly and forced them to pay taxes that they could not afford and did not owe. He knew that his action had probably been the primary cause of some families becoming homeless while others faced extreme difficult financial hardship. He knew that he had insulted others when they least deserved to be insulted. That was the real problem that he had to deal with each day of his life. As a result of his sin, he couldn't approach God. He realized instantly that it was not really

his shortness of stature that prevented him from being God's child, but his shortness of spirit – his inability to come to God on his own, and by his own merit. How could he now try to approach this man who is believed to be a holy man, the Messiah, the Christ, the Son of God, God in the flesh? Before your mind goes wandering or condemning, let me quickly remind you that all who have not turned from their sins and received Christ into their heart as Lord and Master is in the same condition as Zacchaeus was – they are "short." The Bible says, "For all have sinned and fall 'short' of the glory of God" (Romans 3: 23). Zacchaeus knew all these things and worried that his sinful state would prevent him from having a personal contact and relationship with Jesus. He quickly thought about everyone else he knew and how Jesus had touched and changed their lives. As he reflected on their situations, he felt that his was hopeless. These people had real visible issues: blindness, demonic possession, death, etc. His was different. Would Jesus understand that his problem was that of the heart? Would Jesus see and understand that he did not want to be this way but situations and circumstances had forced him over the years to become this monster that even he hated? In his confused state of mind, he remembered that it had been said that Jesus had mentioned that he had come to seek and to save the lost.[13] Though he knew it to be true and believed that Jesus would see him, he still had this inner battle going on. The devil wanted him to believe that he was not good enough, that his sins were so great that God would never forgive him, and that if he came into contact with Jesus, he could be ridiculed again and his deepest sins would be exposed. Since Zacchaeus had not had a personal encounter with Jesus, his judgment was only based on what he had heard. He didn't know that when it comes to God's standard, we are all wee little people – spiritually. He probably did not know or had forgotten what the Prophet Isaiah had written centuries ago, "Surely the arm of the LORD is not too short to save, nor his ear too dull to hear. But your iniquities have separated you

---

13   Luke 19:10

from your God; your sins have hidden His face from you, so that He will not hear."[14]

As much as Zacchaeus knew that his social, physical, and religious status had the potential of being major impediments to his encounter with Jesus, he surmised that this was his opportunity to meet the Messiah and nothing was going to stop him. Whatever the aftermath would be, he would deal with it later. Zacchaeus had learned about pride and how it could be man's greatest enemy to achieving his visions and goals in life. He therefore told himself that he would neither allow what people would say or think nor his past to stop him from seeing Jesus. Armed with this thought, Zacchaeus began to climb the Sycamore tree. He soon found a branch that was perfect for him. He had a good view of everyone below. He thought secretly in his heart that it would be nice if Jesus would just stop under the tree and start to teach or perform one of His miracles. This would be the experience of his life. He couldn't ask God for more. "Oh God, please let it happen," he silently prayed.

Zacchaeus sat on a branch of the Sycamore tree and waited patiently. In a few minutes, the crowd started to come closer. Jesus kept walking and talking with those who were with him. It was a large crowd and Zacchaeus could hardly see the one who was called Jesus. Zacchaeus guessed that He was the one in the middle. It must be Him because He was the center of attention. He looked ordinary, yet there was an air of intelligence, righteousness, and godliness surrounding Him. He looked "godly" while at the same time, loving, caring, friendly, innocent, and easy to talk to. How could it be? No one is like that. You either have to be a leader who commanded everyone and they obeyed, or you are a servant who is expected to serve without asking any question. He did not know that Jesus had come to institute a new leadership model called "Servant Leadership," hence, he was confused.

Another fact that Zacchaeus did not know in advance was that Jesus Christ was on the greatest search and rescue mission in history! Zacchaeus was lost, and Jesus came all the way from heaven to find and help him. In Luke 19, Jesus is on the way to Jerusalem to die for the sins of the world. He would be arrested and crucified just a few days after He visited Jericho. But on His way to the cross, He would stop in Jericho to seek him out. It was all in God's plan, just how it is in God's plan for you to be where you are today and for Him to come seeking you out.

Then came the moment of truth! Jesus stopped. The crowd stopped

---

14   Isaiah 59:1-2

with Him. He was right under the tree. It was as if He knew something was wrong, as if someone was missing from the crowd, as if someone had been busted, as if something had to be done, as if someone had to come down.

"No, no, no, please don't look up," Zacchaeus thought. "It is not looking good. He is going to look up. He is going to expose me!" Zacchaeus closed his eyes because he didn't want to see what would happen next. His stomach began to twinge, his head began to ache, the devil began to whisper in his ears that it was not a good idea in the first place and now he would be busted. He struggled to hold onto the branch in order not to fall. He knew that he wouldn't be able to hold on much longer.

Just then, he heard, "Zacchaeus, come down immediately. I must stay at your house today" (Luke 19:5).

Zacchaeus thought, "Who was calling his name? Why can't people mind their own business? Why can't they leave him alone? Why should they expose him in this manner?"

But, he was not being exposed. The voice was not a familiar voice of an acquaintance. Actually it was the voice of Jesus. Jesus just called him by his name. Zacchaeus, who had probably been called many unmentionable names must have thought, "He knows my name! How does He know me? What did he hear about me? Was it good? Was it bad? Does He know who I am really? But, how could He since I don't have on a name tag?"

Somehow the wee-little man did not know that Jesus knew his name for the same reason that He knows your name and mine – because He is God and He made us. He knows everybody's name. Jesus must have known that Zacchaeus' name meant pure and untainted and that he was not living up to his name, but he called him Zacchaeus anyway. By calling him by his name, Zacchaeus, was Jesus acknowledging that there was still the possibility that he could be pure and untainted as his parents had desired when they gave him that name?

Just the fact that his name had been called was a miracle to Zacchaeus. No matter what others said, he knew that the Messiah knew him by name. It was like the president of the United States calling me by my first name. How awesome is that! It can't get better! Yes, I am known by the One who is the center of attention! I am known by the One who created the universe and in whose hands lay the hearts of kings! The Prophet Isaiah had said, "Fear not for I have redeemed you; I have called you by name; you are mine."[15] You may think you are all alone in this world and nobody

---

15   Isaiah 43:1

knows you and nobody cares. But there is a loving God who created the universe and He knows you by name. The best thing about Him is that He knows, is willing, and able to provide for your needs according to His riches in glory. All He wants you to do is to seek first His kingdom and righteousness, as Zacchaeus was doing, and all other things will be added unto you.[16]

It is one thing to have your name called, but it is something else to know why your name has been called. After Jesus called his name, He beckoned Zacchaeus to come down from the tree. In the song mentioned above about Zacchaeus, many times when it comes to the place where Zacchaeus is told to come down, little kids are told to shake their finger as if they are angry or giving a stern warning and say, "Zacchaeus, you come down!" But the tone of Jesus' voice was one of tender compassion and friendliness. In a way, it was disappointing to many of those who were around Jesus, including His disciples. Some of them thought to themselves, "Where did He get to know this cheater, con man, barracuda, crook, deceiver, hustler, mountebank, scam artist, swindler?" Others expected Jesus to deliver an excoriating rebuke to Zacchaeus. They whispered to one another, "Oh boy, Zacchaeus is finally going to get what he deserves! This righteous teacher will let him have it with both barrels!"

When his name was called, Zacchaeus did not know what to expect. He knew that Jesus would be right if He chose to call him a sinner and were to ask him to repent. In fact, he was ready to do so. He was tired of running, hiding, and wearing a mask. He knew that he needed to have a relationship with God. He desperately needed God and needed his situation to change. He was ready for whatever the Messiah would say to him, even if it meant calling him a filthy, rotten sinner who needed to repent, pay back everything he had stolen or else God was going to get him really good.

He probably said to himself, "I am ready to do whatever it takes and whatever He asks me to do!"

To his surprise, Jesus said, "Zacchaeus, come down and let's go to your house."

Zacchaeus hurried down the tree, and with a smile on his face, he pointed the way to his house. He started to leap like a three year-old child who is about to be taken to McDonalds for his or her favorite meal with toys included in the package. He couldn't wait to reach home in order to sit with the Lord. He was filled with joy and did not have words to describe

---

16   Matthew 6:25-33

how he felt. As he skipped alongside Jesus, the religious crowd continued to grumble and murmur against Jesus. They criticized Him silently for going to the home of a sinner but did not dare speak up against Him. A few of them said to themselves, "We'll wait to see what He will do once we arrive at Zacchaeus' home."

Once they arrived at Zacchaeus' home, which was less than two miles down the road, Jesus was invited to sit in the seat of honor (the best seat in the house). It was a beautiful house filled with antiques and a very expensive décor. It was the first time for many of Jesus' disciples to enter such a well-decorated and expensive home. They looked around with awe and marveled at the beauty all around them. Some envied Zacchaeus' home but instantaneously reminded themselves to be 'au courant' of the fact that the monies used to purchase all these things were stolen.

As they sat, a servant came and washed the feet of Jesus and all the guests that were with Him, as was customary in the Jewish culture during those days. In spite of the beautiful décor, serenity, and quietness that were present in Zacchaeus' house, there was an unexplained tension in the air among the disciples and followers of Jesus who were present with him. Maybe it was because some of them expected Jesus to ask Zacchaeus to sit so that He could tell him about the need to be honest and stop treating others the way he had over the years. The more religious and perhaps self-proclaimed "Spirit-filled" followers expected Jesus to begin a prayer meeting so that He could cast out the demons in the house that had caused Zacchaeus to behave this way against his fellow citizens. Some of these could hear Jesus in their minds saying: "Demon of greed, come out, come out! You don't belong here, I say, come out!"

Unfortunately, they heard Zacchaeus offering Jesus a meal and He gladly accepted. What! Was He going to allow Zacchaeus to bribe Him with a meal? Can't He see that this is all intended to silence and prevent Him from telling Zacchaeus that he is the worst sinner there is? They may not have understood that even though Zacchaeus had stolen money constantly and that there may be some spiritual forces that may have influenced his actions, there is a always a place, a time, and a perfect condition under which issues of such magnitude and sensitivity must be addressed. Hence, Jesus began to sip some juice as He dipped pieces of pita bread in the humus sauce that had been placed before Him. After a few minutes, He calmly asked Zacchaeus about his day, his job, and where he was coming from. He also asked Zacchaeus what he was doing in the sycamore tree. In what seemed to be an unexpected twist of events,

Zacchaeus started to confess to the Lord. He poured out his heart and explained how his life was a mess and that he wanted it to change. He explained how he had tried to get back at others for what they did to him but he knows that it was wrong. With tears in his eyes, he unraveled the story of his complicated life and asked Jesus to have mercy on him. As if he wanted to demonstrate how sorry he was and how desperately he needed the Lord to forgive him, Zacchaeus stood and, to the surprise of everyone, said to Jesus, "Look, Lord! Here and now I give half of my possessions to the poor, and if I have cheated anybody out of anything, I will pay back four times the amount" (Luke 19:8).

Everyone was speechless. This is not what they expected. They had hoped that Zacchaeus would admit or acknowledge that he was corrupt and had robbed innocent people of their livelihood, but to say that he would give half of this wealth to the poor was not something they expected from him. They couldn't have been more pleased to hear him say something like that. He didn't have to give half of his wealth to the poor and repay everyone four times what he had robbed! Yet, it was a decision he had made and pronounced in the presence of everyone. Wow! A glance at the crowd showed mixed emotions on the faces of everyone. For some, it was an expression of shock and disbelief. For others, it was an expression of joy and relief. Yet for the rest, it was simply a pleasant smile as they gave God thanks for the miracle of salvation that had come to the home of Zacchaeus. His mess had been turned into a message of repentance, redemption, restitution, and restoration.

Jesus quietly placed his hand on Zacchaeus' shoulder and said to him, "Today salvation has come to this house, because this man, too, is a son of Abraham."

As I bring this chapter to a close, it is important that you understand that God sees you, not as you are, but as who He has destined you to become. People may see you and define you by your actions, but God sees you and defines you by what Jesus did for you and your willingness to accept His love and come into His fold. Everyone except Jesus defined Zacchaeus by his looks and actions. When they looked, they saw a mean, little, dirty rotten sinner who was a disgrace to his people and his nation. But when Jesus looked, He didn't see a short, crooked tax collector. Rather, He saw someone who had the potential of being pure, untainted, humble, generous, and lovable.

What have others said about you? How have they defined you? What have you done that seems to justify the way you are seen and or perceived by others? Has your life been a disgrace to your family? Have you made mistakes that you think are unforgivable?

If you answer yes to any of the above questions, there is good news. The Bible declares that Jesus is the same yesterday, today, and forever.[17] He loved Zacchaeus and accepted him just as he was and He is willing to do the same for you. The only thing that He expects is for you to come to Him and ask for forgiveness and cleansing. He wants to establish a relationship with you so that He can change your mess into a message.

Here is another important thing that took place in the life of Zacchaeus after his encounter with Jesus. He demonstrated that he was a changed man. He arose the next morning and went from home to home paying back everyone four times what he had stolen, and gave half his money to the poor. Think for a moment what he said when he approached someone whom he had robbed in the past. He probably said something like this: "I met Jesus and my life was changed. I have, therefore, come to give you back four times the money that I took from you unjustly. Can you please forgive me? I am really sorry!"

What a message! It was enough to turn the entire town of Jericho upside down! There might have been a mighty revival that took place. Not only was Zacchaeus paying back everyone whom he had robbed, but it also meant that he would not rob anyone again. By sharing his message, he was also implying that, "I cannot continue to do what I used to do before; I can't tax you the way I used to tax you before; I can't talk to you the way I used to talk to you before; I can't cheat you the way I used to cheat you before."

That was his message! It's easy for us to say, "I've met Jesus! I'm a Christian! I've been changed!" But the proof is in what we do. Has there been a change in the way you think, talk, and live? God will forgive your sin, but like Zacchaeus, we have to tell others about our commitment and newfound faith and even make restitution (when possible) to others in order to demonstrate our forgiveness.

Finally, some of you reading this book may not identify with Zacchaeus, because you are not living in sin and have already accepted Jesus as your Lord and Savior. You may have already made restitution for the things you did in the past and asked God for forgiveness. Here is one more thing that you can do: YOU CAN BE A SYCAMORE TREE! You might not know how to share the gospel with others or how to lead them to Christ, but you can share the message of how God transformed your messy life.

---

17   Hebrews 13:8

By so doing, you will be lifting people above the crowd so that they can see Jesus clearly.

In the same way, you might not have the authority to change the lives of others but you can share your story (your testimony) of how God changed yours. You then become a sycamore tree that lifts up others to see Jesus so that He can take over. Think for a moment with me about what would have happened to Zacchaeus if there hadn't been a tree there that day? Obviously we don't know and can only speculate, but I thank God that tree was there. God had planted a tree just in the right spot so Zacchaeus could see Jesus. Probably God has planted you somewhere and given you a message to simply lift someone up so they can see Jesus! Would you begin to share that message? If you feel too intimated to share the message, briefly pray this prayer:

> *Father, in Jesus' name, I thank you for saving me. I thank you for turning my mess into a message. I know that you desire for me to share my testimony with others. You saved me for a purpose and desire that I be a light to the world. Lord, please grant me the boldness I need to be able to share my testimony. I know that your Word says that you have not given me a spirit of fear but of power, love, and a sound mind.[18] I want to be that tree that you have planted in my family, among my friends and my acquaintances that will lift them up to see Jesus. Thank you for enabling me to be your ambassador. In Jesus' name, AMEN!"*

---

18   2 Timothy 1:7

Chapter IV: Ruth (Ruth 1:1-4:22).
God Turns a Messy Situation of Death and Hopelessness into a Message of God's Kinsman-Redeemer

Ruth, the eighth book of the Bible, was named after the heroine and main character in this story of redeeming love and grace. It begins with Elimelech, an Israelite who left Judah and relocated his family in Moab because of the famine that had struck his land. His wife, Naomi, along with their two sons, Mahlon and Kilion, went with him in search of "green pasture." The book of Ruth does not report if their economic situation improved, but one could easily conclude that life in Moab must have been better than the famine-stricken land of Judah. They must have been a happy family trying to raise their boys in the fear and admonition of the Lord until a messy situation struck the family. Elimelech suddenly died. With no account of what led to his death, readers of Ruth are brought to the harsh reality of some of life's unexpected potholes. Allow me to explain the magnitude of their "mess" using an illustration of a driver suddenly encountering a pothole while driving more than 45 miles per hour. The driver's chance of survival depends on several factors, namely, the depth of the pothole, the speed at which he is driving, the durability of the car, the flow of traffic, and the ability of the driver to maneuver the car in a way that could minimize the damage, etc.

Potholes are challenges you unexpectedly encounter in life irrespective of who you are and your relationship with God. Potholes present themselves as though they have the ability to hinder you from reaching your destiny and alter the course of your very existence when actually they have no power over you, if you are a believer. Don't get confused! As a believer, your destiny, which results from a predetermined course of events, is beyond the enemy's control. He may delay it but he can't stop it if we don't team up with him. Each of us has a destiny that has been preordained by God. God had a plan set up for you before you were born and it is incumbent upon you to seek His face in order to find out how to fulfill your destiny. If you don't, you could be misappropriated, misaligned, misused, and reassigned by others who think you should be this or that when they did not invent or make you. Potholes are, therefore, those unfortunate situations that life brings your way to hinder you from achieving God's plan and purpose.

There are certain things that you need to know about potholes:

- They seldom come with warning signs.
- They can be prevented, but not at all times.
- They can lead to bodily injury and property damage.
- They are not covered by most insurance companies because of their unpredictable nature.
- They can cause minor or major damage, thus hindering you from reaching your destination on time.
- Nothing can adequately prepare you for some of the potholes that await you.

The unfortunate thing is that many times when we encounter potholes on the road to our destiny, we react in ways that do not allow us to assess the situation and take the appropriate actions in order to minimize the damage and continue the journey. Some potholes are so little they may cause minimum or unnoticeable damage, whereas others are so huge that when we encounter them, we would need to pull aside and properly evaluate the damage in order to avoid further destruction or to be able to continue our journey. It is important to note that there are a number of things that could happen when you experience a small pothole. You could become nervous for a few minutes, recompose yourself, and continue your journey, or you could continue the journey without stopping to appraise the situation. However, for bigger potholes, you can't just keep on driving. They require that you stop in order to evaluate or take an inventory of the damages. An example of a bigger pothole encounter could be the passing of a loved one, especially if that loved one has played a major role in your life. Bigger potholes are difficult challenges that require honest assessment and implementation of appropriate measures. The death of Elimelech was a big "pothole" for Naomi on the road to her destiny. Besides being her husband, he represented her financial, social, moral, religious, cultural, and emotional security. Without any doubt in my mind, I believe that his death certainly left her devastated. She became a widow. In the Old and New Testaments, a widow is synonymous with being poor, not having legal standing or rights in the eyes of the law, and representing a depressed class of citizens.

In her desolation, Naomi may have turned to her sons or she was probably comforted by the fact that Elimelech had left her two sons who were of age to get married and take care of her. Though her sons could not replace her husband, they represented hope, comfort, and love. In other words, Naomi probably felt that all was not lost. She may have watched with great delight when they decided to marry Orpah and Ruth, two Moabite women. Maybe somewhere in her heart she remarked: "The Lord has seen my tears and granted me the honor to see my sons get married and start their families." Maybe she said, "The Lord will grant me many grandchildren through my two boys and all will be well."

Little did she know that there were still bigger potholes on the road to her destiny! The Bible declares that ten years later, her two sons, Mahlon and Kilion, died. Again, just like their father, the Bible gives no advance notice to its readers and it does not give any reason for their death. Another sudden and major pothole! It was a messy situation! Interestingly also, both men were married for ten years and neither of them had children by their wives. Words could not comfort Naomi. In fact, she was convinced that the God of the heavens had personally brought this disaster upon her. We read in verse 1:13 "Things are more bitter for me than for you, because the Lord's hand has gone out against me." I don't think anyone could have convinced her otherwise. How could anyone explain the sudden death of her husband and two sons? Today perhaps, given our level of education, advancement of technology, and medical science and the fact that we have the Word of God as our guide, we can safely say that we encounter calamities (potholes) because of several reasons and not necessarily because the "hand of God" is against us. It could be:

1. **Based on some personal decisions that we make (knowingly or unknowingly).** Even though we are not sure if Naomi's personal decision brought this calamity on her family, her statement, "Things are far more bitter for me than for you,

because the Lord himself has raised his fist against me," leaves one wondering why the Lord raised his fist against her if she was innocent (that is, if we could interpret her statement literally).

2. **Based on someone's decision that directly or indirectly affects us.** An excellent example is someone deciding to run a traffic light and in so doing, runs into your car. This was probably not the case here with Naomi.

3. **Based on God's chastisement.** The Bible declares in Hebrews 12:4-12 that we ought not to take lightly the discipline of the Lord because He disciplines the ones He loves and chastises every son whom He receives. I don't know for sure if God was chastising Naomi because the Bible does not say. This is in contrast to David's story when he slept with Uriah's wife, Bathsheba (2 Samuel 12), Nathan made it clear to David that the Lord would discipline him.

4. **Based on Satan's plan to destroy us.** Jesus declares in John 10:10, "The thief comes only to steal and kill and destroy; I have come that they may have life, and have it to the full." In other words, the enemy does place potholes before us with the intention of destroying us or hindering us from reaching our destiny. Maybe that is the case here with Naomi. Maybe the enemy wanted to destroy her, but I thank God for the fact that He does not allow the will of the enemy to prevail over His children. The Bible says, "Everything will work out for the good of those who love the Lord and for those who are called according to His purpose" (Romans 8:28). Thank God that He can turn whatever mess the enemy has brought my way into a message and a blessing.

5. **Based on the sinful world in which we live.** Paul writes to the church in Rome in Romans 8:19-22:

> *The creation waits in eager expectation for the sons of God to be revealed. For the creation was subjected to frustration, not by its own choice, but by the will of the one who subjected it, in hope that the creation itself will be liberated from its bondage to decay and brought into the glorious freedom of the children of God. We know that the whole creation has been groaning as in the pains of childbirth right up to the present time.*

Basically, the apostle acknowledged that the world in which we live has many challenges because of the sin of Adam and Eve. Hence, the inhabitants of this world encounter challenges – not because of what they did, what others have done, God's chastisement, or Satan's plan to destroy them – but simply because the world itself has issues. A good example is the eruption of volcanoes, earthquakes, etc. These are natural disasters that do not necessarily happen because of any of the above mentioned reasons. In Naomi's situation, we don't know how her husband and sons were killed. Therefore it would be difficult for us to say that their deaths resulted from a natural disaster.

6. **Based on God's testing**. Scripture reports that God does test believers. The problem we have with the concept of God testing us is that we view testing to have negative objectives. However, when God tests us, his objective is positive. Examine Judges 2:18-23. Verses 21 and 22 say, "I will no longer drive out before them any of the nations Joshua left when he died. I will use them to test Israel and see whether they will keep the way of the LORD and walk in it as their forefathers did."

There are a number of things we must know about God testing us. They are:

a. **When God tests us, His goal is to change our view of Him**. He is our friend and not our enemy. Hence a test involves changing our perception of who He is, what He is capable of doing, what He wants to do, and what He is going to do.

b. **When God tests us, it is for our benefit**. In other words, it provides us with an opportunity to examine our own hearts and to know where we stand.

c. **When God tests us, it is to prove His power and ability in our lives**. It is intended to make known to the host of darkness and those around us that we will not waiver in our faith and we will trust in the Lord.

In spite of all the reasons that cause calamities (potholes) as mentioned above, it is important to note that when they happen, we need to, depending on the depth of the pothole, assess the situation and take the appropriate action based on the leading of the Spirit of the Lord. When Naomi lost her husband and two sons, she evaluated her situation and decided that it was time for her to return home. She also decided that it was time to be realistic and fair with her daughters in law. I love Naomi! She did not live in her past or agonize about what she had or didn't have. Also, she recognized that she had to change her lifestyle, environment, associates, etc., if she wanted God to turn her mess into a message.

Many of us hold onto the past. We are not experiencing our breakthroughs because we continue to live in the past. We daydream of what life used to be, the kind of cars we drove, the husband or wife we had, the home we lived in, and the friends that we associated with. As good as daydreaming may feel, it is not reality! A daydreamer must awake to the realities of life. There is no need for me to sit and contemplate things of the past. As good as they may have been, they were for a season. I must realize that God wants me to enter into a new season, a new opportunity, a new focus, a new blessing, and a new life. Consequently, I have to tell myself that for God to turn my mess into a message, I must let those things that are dead, be dead; those things that ought to be buried, be buried; and I must let those doors that the Lord has closed, remain closed. God has a reason for allowing some things in my life to die. I must trust that He knows what is best and move on. You see, if a man or woman left you for someone else, don't keep daydreaming of the love that existed. The relationship is dead, bury it! He has left; let him go! God has better things in store. If he were good enough for you, he would have stayed. Don't limit God and what He wants to do. God will turn your mess into a message.

This is what Naomi realized and she decided to call her two daughters-in-law in order to tell them that they had to leave her because she was returning to Judah. She released them to go to their homes in Moab. Orpah accepted Naomi's proposal, kissed her mother-in-law good-bye and left, but the Bible says that Ruth clung to her.

A few years ago, I read an interesting story. I can't remember the source but it goes like this: A problem-plagued daughter complained to her father, who was a chef, about how things were so hard for her. She kept complaining and in spite of all the advice her father gave to her, she seemed not be able to find solutions to her challenges. Finally, her father decided one day to teach her about life using an object lesson. He took her to the kitchen, boiled three separate pots of water, and placed carrots, eggs, and coffee beans in each of the three pots. Twenty minutes later, he took them out and placed them in three separate bowls.

What do you see?" asked her father. "Carrots, eggs, and coffee," she replied.

The father asked her to feel the carrot, break the egg, and sip the coffee. The daughter felt the softness of the carrot, noted the hardness of the egg,

Turning Your Mess Into A Message

and tasted the richness of the coffee. Confused, she then asked her father to explain what it meant.

The father explained: "Each of them had faced the same adversity, boiling water, but each reacted differently. The carrot went in strong, hard, and unrelenting, but after being subjected to the boiling water, it softened and became weak. The egg had been fragile. Its thin outer shell had (always) protected its liquid interior. But after sitting through the boiling water, its contents became hardened. The ground coffee beans were unique however. They sat in the water like the carrot and the egg for the same amount of time and faced the same temperature, but instead of the water changing them, they changed the water."

The father then asked his daughter, "Which are you?"

Let me ask you the same question: "Are you a soft carrot, hard-boiled egg, or rich, strong, aromatic coffee?" After you have been tested and tried, do you allow God to shine in you and turn your mess into a message or do you turn your back on Him, the Church and His people?

Allow me to explain Ruth's situation a little more so that you can fully understand the gravity of the situation with which she was confronted. First, Ruth, Naomi's daughter-in-law, was faced with a sudden deep pothole that took away her husband. He was dead and left her childless. It meant that she had no one to console her, no one to take care of her, no one to serve as a remembrance of the wonderful love relationship that existed between her and her husband. She had nothing to show as a product of her marriage. Wow!

Second, she was confronted by her mother-in-law who was suggesting that she return to her parents' house because she, Naomi, could no longer have children. Even if she could have more children, Ruth should not have to wait until her (Naomi's) child is fully grown in order to remarry. Imagine with me for a second that the young woman may have turned down some other young men from her town/village that wanted to marry her. She may have rejected her parents' admonition to marry someone who was from her town or people. If that was the case, she disobeyed her parents and married this outsider who has now died, and she is being told to return to her town to confront those she may have hurt. How could she do that? How can she go back to a place she once rejected? How can she go back to a god she knew was false? How could she go back to her old ways of life after having tasted what it meant to serve the Living God, YAHWEH?

Third, were she to decide to follow Naomi, she would have to adjust to a new culture and people. Would she be accused of being the cause of her

71

husband's death? Would she be seen as being an ungodly person? Think about these questions for a minute and ask yourself, how would I respond in a situation like this? Finally, she would have to worship a different god, not the one that she knew and worshiped before she got married (even though we don't know at what point she became converted). Honestly, wouldn't it have been easier for Ruth to do as Orpah did? Sometimes, when we encounter a sudden deep pothole in life, isn't it easier for us to turn around and go back, especially when we haven't gone too far and when the road ahead is uncertain?

Ruth was a remarkable woman. She lost her husband of many years in Moab and her mother-in-law did not want her presence in Israel. Naomi urged Ruth to remain in Moab and remarry a local, but Ruth would not listen. She cheered, fed, and inspired Naomi. Having just lost her husband, Ruth understood how Naomi felt. Naomi thought of her past, but Ruth's thoughts were for Naomi's future. It was not that Ruth had nowhere to go, no one in Moab, or nothing to do, but Ruth always placed Naomi's feelings, interests, and well-being ahead of her own. How many daughters-in-law in their right frame of mind would give a blank check to their mother-in-law, saying, "I will do whatever you say" (Ruth 3:5)? Ruth said it and did it (Ruth 3:6). Doesn't it remind you of the love that Christ continues to display towards us? Aren't you reminded of how at times, when you want to have nothing to do with Him, He is still tugging on your heart and working on your behalf? Does it remind you of how, when you reject Him, He is still standing at the door of your heart and calling you to Himself and softly whispering in your ears about how much He loves you? Oh, what a God we serve! One who will never leave us nor forsake us! This is the kind of love that Ruth exemplifies towards Naomi.

When Naomi asked Ruth to leave, she did everything else but leave! She displayed a stubborn streak of toughness and a high tolerance of pain when tragedy struck. She had lost her husband, and there was no question about that. However, she had some precious things left: her life, her health, her sanity, and her mother-in-law. The Gentile widow apparently did not believe in fate, omens, and curses. She did not and would not yield, bow, or surrender to doom and gloom. Her grief, pain, and loneliness were unspeakable, but to throw in the towel, wallow in self-pity, and to rail at God were unimaginable. I love her spirit!

Naomi said to her daughter-in-law in Ruth 1:15-18: "Look, your sister-in-law is going back to her people and her gods. Go back with her." But Ruth replied, "Don't urge me to leave you or to turn back from you. Where you go I will go, and where you stay I will stay. Your people will be my people and your God my God. Where you die I will die, and there I will be buried. May the LORD deal with me, be it ever so severely, if anything but death separates you and me." When Naomi realized that Ruth was determined to go with her, she stopped urging her.

It is important to understand that a Gentile woman married to a Jewish man was obligated to convert, but a Gentile widow of a dead Jewish husband was free to choose if she would remain committed to her newfound faith or return to her former religion of idolatrous worship. Ruth's declaration of embracing Yahweh was perhaps her first solo break from idolatrous worship and the declaration of choosing mother-in-law over parents. Leaving Moab for Israel would be the final break from idolatry. Ruth, as a single, Gentile woman, would rather suffer discrimination, receive rebuke (Ruth 2:15-16), encounter harassment, experience hindrances, and even tolerate harm (Ruth 2:22) in the new land than return to Moabite religion and worship.

The first solo action of Ruth in the book described the character of Ruth. When the other daughter-in-law, Orpah, kissed her mother-in-law goodbye, Ruth clung to Naomi (Ruth 1:14). She was a clinger, a hugger, and a sticker. She was tenacious, steadfast, and feisty. The feisty daughter-in-law stuck to Naomi like glue, Velcro, and gum. That's who she was and who she chose to be. She was Naomi's shadow, twin, and angel. She fastened to her mother-in-law before Naomi could turn, look, or walk away. The Hebrew word for "cling" occurs four times in the book, all related to Ruth (1:14; 2:8, 21, 23). Ruth literally owned, defined, and glorified the word in the Bible. The Hebrew words for cling (or the Hebrew word for cleave) and leave (Ruth 1:16) were similar words to the vow of marriage in Genesis 2:24: "For this reason a man will leave his father and mother and be united (or cleave) to his wife, and they will become one flesh." In another instance, upon arrival in Israel Ruth stayed, kept or stuck close to the servant girls of Boaz to glean until the barley and wheat harvests were finished (Ruth 2:23). She never strayed or departed from that way of thinking in her life or in her job, with Naomi or with others, for an entire day or a full season. What a testimony to her tenacity, fortitude, and resolve. She never gave up on life, herself, or others. She resolved in her heart that God was going to change her situation. Had she been around when the Apostle Paul wrote in Philippians 4:19, "And my God will meet all your needs according to his glorious riches in Christ Jesus," Ruth would have said, "Amen" or, "I am a witness!"

Ruth was not afraid of working hard, starting a new career, entering a new land, or adjusting to a new status. She worked at a back-breaking and feet-hurting job in heat-sweltering conditions for mere leftovers, the minimum, odds and ends. She did not consider it lowly to pick food from the floor, to depend on people's good graces, and to live on grains and nuts. She would rather work for the minimum than stay at home, wait for handouts, or stare at the wall, ceiling, or Naomi. Except for a short rest in the shelter (Ruth 2:7), Ruth worked non-stop on her feet, in the sun, as a picker, the whole day and the whole season (Ruth 2:23), to make enough for the two widows to have food to eat the whole year.

Many of us would give up if we found ourselves in a situation similar to Ruth's. Many times we give up on our situation before God can give the final word. It is good to be able to analyze, rationalize, and theologize. However, the final word rests with God. He should have the final say in every situation that concerns you. Your situation is not done until God says it is! Your marriage is not done, until God says it is! Your life is not done until God says it is! You are not dying until God says it is time. He should have the final word in every matter that concerns us! Stop listening and believing everything others are saying concerning you, whether they are your doctors, lawyers, or even pastors. If what they are saying contradicts God's Word and plan for your life, be respectful and listen, but quietly remind yourself that God has the final say in all matters concerning your life. I hope you get this revelation in Jesus' name. If you have to repeat it a hundred times a day until you begin to believe it and begin to act upon it, then say it a hundred times. Remember that faith comes from hearing the Word of God. He declared to the children of Israel in Psalm 40:5, "Many, O Lord my God, are the wonders you have done. The things you planned for us no one can recount to you; were I to speak and tell of them, they would be too many to declare."

God has a plan to turn our messes into messages. Naomi had a mess, but God had a message. She understood that her God was still in the providing business. He was still in the healing business. He was still in the comforting business. He was still in the helping business! I don't care what others say about you or your God, you need to know and believe that He does not change. He did it before for others like Ruth. He can do it for you and me! Our major problem is that we sometimes focus too much on the problem and not on what God has done or is doing.

I read an email a while ago that I kept in my inbox. As I wrote this book, the Holy Spirit brought it to my mind and I looked it up again.

This is how it reads: "An Everyday Survival Kit." However, this survival kit does not have a flashlight, a blanket, food, or the normal emergency-preparedness stuff. Here are its contents:

a) Toothpick - to remind you to pick out the good qualities in others (Matthew 7:1);

b) Rubber band - to remind you to be flexible. Things might not always go the way you want, but it will work out (Romans 8:28);

c) Band Aid - to remind you to heal hurting feelings, yours or someone else's (Colossians 3:12-14);

d) Pencil - to remind you to list your blessings every day (Ephesians 1:3);

e) Eraser - to remind you that everyone makes mistakes, and it is okay (Genesis 50:15-21);

f) Chewing gum - to remind you to stick with it and you can accomplish anything (Philippians 4:13);

g) Mint - to remind you that you are worth a mint to your God (John 3:16-17);

h) Candy kiss - to remind you that everyone needs a kiss or a hug every day (1 John 4:7);

i) Tea bag - to remind you to relax daily and go over that list of God's blessings (1 Thessalonians 5:18).

Allow me to conclude this chapter with a few things that I would like to bring to your attention. The first thing is that life will always have potholes. Sometimes the potholes are big and sometimes they are strong. However, one thing is certain! There is no pothole too large to destroy God's plan and purpose for your life. The pothole might slow you down, injure you, take tears from your eyes, leave you feeling sad and lonely for a while, but God will always be there to turn that situation around for your good. He will always be there to lift you up from the miry clay and set your feet upon the rock to stay! He will always be there to clean you up and set you on the path in order for you to complete your race. You need to submit the situation into His hands and leave the result to Him. I can assure you that you will not be disappointed. King David once said, "I was young and now I am old, yet I have never seen the righteous forsaken or their children begging bread."[19]

Second, we can learn from the situation that Ruth went through that

---

19   Psalm 37:25

when we are dealt an ugly hand by life, we should be gentle with others around us and not blame them for our situation. When you read the story of Ruth, it's easy to see that she was tender to others even when she was wounded and hurting on the inside. She saw the shock, suffering, and struggles of Naomi and tended to her in a compassionate way. Ruth could have blamed Naomi for her misfortune and even say that staying with Naomi would have reminded her of her husband; therefore, she was going to move on. Fortunately, she did not do any of that. She clung to Naomi (Ruth 1:14), stating her point loud and clear, "Don't urge me to leave you or to turn back from you. Where you go I will go, and where you stay I will stay. Your people will be my people and your God will be my God" (Ruth 1:16).

The commandment given in Genesis[20] and reiterated by Jesus in Mark 10:7 was for men to leave their parents and to cleave to their wives and not for daughters-in-law to cleave to their parents-in-law, but Ruth made cleaving to Naomi her choice, her business, and her destiny. Additionally, the vow was meant for potential spouses, and not former daughters-in-law. Now that Ruth's husband was dead, the covenant she made to him was no longer binding. Also, given the fact that Ruth's brother-in-law was also dead, her obligations to Naomi were minimal. In spite of all of the above mentioned, Ruth decided to keep the vow she made to her husband, volunteered her commitment, and bound herself to her mother-in-law, Naomi. Ruth was worth more than seven sons to Naomi. Ruth's support for her mother-in-law was compared to a man's provision for his wife, and more: "Where you die I will die, and there I will be buried. May the LORD deal with me, be it ever so severely, if anything but death separates you and me" (Ruth1:17). Ruth chose the role of being an attending and abiding daughter-in-law.

When we don't blame others for our misfortunes and don't even blame God, we set the stage for God to turn our mess into a message that has the potential to bring glory and honor to His name. Additionally, when we try to meet the needs of others even while we ourselves are struggling, God has a way of taking care of our needs as well. Paul wrote to the Corinthian church in 1 Corinthians 15:58 saying, "Therefore, my dear brothers, stand firm. Let nothing move you. Always give yourselves fully to the work of the Lord, because you know that your labor in the Lord is not in vain."

Third, Ruth, the widow, trusted in the Lord God. More specifically,

---

20   Genesis 2:24 "For this reason a man will leave his father and mother and be united to his wife, and they will become one flesh."

she trusted in His sovereignty, wisdom, and ability to provide. Her faith in God was real. The first words out of Ruth's mouth were a testament to her unmistakable faith, trust, and belief in God. Like Rahab (Joshua 2:11) and the Gibeonites (Joshua 9:9), all of which were Gentile believers who were integral to Israel's history, Ruth called on the name of God (verse 16 of chapter one) and more specifically, Yahweh, the distinctive Hebrew deity (Ruth 1: 17). Naomi asserted that Orpah had returned to her gods (Ruth 1:15), but Ruth insisted on following Naomi's God and called Yahweh (Ruth 1:17) her God. Naomi may have thought that Ruth was a convert or believer by way of marriage, for the sake of love, her husband, marital bliss, out of personal convenience, social sensibilities, and domestic harmony. If that was part of her thought process, Naomi certainly was wrong. Ruth, single and untied, freely decided to make Yahweh her own God and destiny. Her husband was dead, but her faith was alive. Nobody could force her to accept a God in whom she did not believe. No one could push her around or try to make her do anything with which she was not comfortable. Ruth had made up her mind to serve God, obey Him, and love her dead husband's family until death. She was even ready to be buried in Israel when the Lord called her home.

The same can be true of you. No one has the right to force you to accept Jesus as Lord or to trust Him to change your mess into a message. It is a decision that you must make alone. God can't force you to accept Him as your personal Lord and Savior. Jesus states emphatically in Revelation 3:20, "Here I am! I stand at the door and knock. If anyone hears my voice and opens the door, I will come in and eat with him, and he with me." He will remain standing until you make the decision to allow Him into the secret places of your life. It could be the place of disappointment, hurt, sorrow, frustration, etc. You have to invite Him in order for Him to come. The decision is yours to make. He is waiting!

Fourth, in any situation where you find yourself as a Christian, God already has a plan to get you out. The Bible declares in 1 Corinthians 10:13, "No temptation has seized you except what is common to man. And God is faithful; He will not let you be tempted beyond what you can bear. But when you are tempted, He will also provide a way out so that you can stand up under it." Many times when we read or hear this verse, we think about temptation as in "sin," that is, disobeying God's commandments. It is true that it concerns sin as we normally define the word, but the word really has to do with missing God's mark. In other words, it has to do with any and every situation which has the potential to lead us away from

God, doubt His word, miss His perfect plan for our lives, or take matters into our own hands. It is important to understand that in every perplexing circumstance, God has a plan and He has a "kinsman-redeemer" that He has prepared to help you out of that situation. In the case of Ruth, God had supernaturally prepared Boaz, the kinsman-redeemer to help Ruth.

Let me explain a little more about the "kinsman-redeemer" so that you can fully appreciate how God turned Ruth's mess of death and hopelessness into a message of redemption. A "kinsman-redeemer" is what is referred to as a *Goel*. It simply means to redeem, buy back, or receive. This concept is taken from the Law of Moses where provision was made for the nearest of kin to intervene or buy back a poor person who was forced into slavery or forced to sell some property to pay off debts (Leviticus 25:25). What is also very interesting is that a "kinsman-redeemer" had the responsibility of redeeming his kinsman's lost opportunities. In the case of homicide, the kinsman-redeemer acts as the avenger of blood and pursues the killer, and in the case where debt threatens a poor man's existence the "kinsman-redeemer" steps in to redeem his homestead, thus allowing him and his family to live in peace. Now, in order to be a kinsman-redeemer, there are several conditions that must be met: he had to be the nearest of kin (Leviticus 25:25, 48); he had to be able financially to redeem (Ruth 4:4-6); and he had to be willing to redeem (Ruth 4:6). The last point is very important: Someone can be the nearest of kin and have the means but might not be willing to redeem the situation.

In the case of Ruth, the brother of Boaz ought to have been the kinsman-redeemer but we don't know why he didn't. He was probably afraid that it could have endangered his own estate though we don't know that for sure. However, the point is that, there are people in our lives who by virtue of their relationship with us ought to be our "kinsman-redeemer." They are our closest relatives and have the financial ability to be our "kinsman-redeemer." The problem is that some of them are not willing. Some fear that if they play the role of a kinsman-redeemer in our lives, their financial assets may diminish, their credibility will be ruined, their credit history may be jeopardized, their plans may have to be altered, and their future may be called into question. Hence, they become afraid or apprehensive. Yet for others, it is not the issue of being afraid or uncertain of the financial, social or moral implications if they were to decide to become your "kinsman-redeemer." They simply find pleasure in wanting you to remain in trouble and eventually be ruined for life. Redeeming you might grant you the possibility of having a second chance and who knows, you just might eventually get to their level. This is an uncomfortable thought for many. They want to retain their position of power and superiority in the family and be the ones to whom you run for handouts. But you need to know that in every situation, God has a kinsman-redeemer prepared to meet you at the point of your need. It may be a relative, a friend, or a total stranger. God can use anyone. God's concern is that we receive His divine help, and He often uses our human relationships, but He has not limited Himself only to those who are our closest relatives or friends. He could also use the natural resources He has made available to us to redeem us as well. But, if those two (human and natural resources) don't work, He won't hesitate to use supernatural means to meet our needs.

When you read the story of Elijah in 1 Kings 17:2-6, you will notice that God chose to work outside of natural circumstances. As Elijah camped beside the Cherith brook, God sent ravens twice a day to supply Elijah with meat and bread. God decided to use what we call "supernatural means." God can use anything or anyone at anytime to redeem and get you out of your mess in order for His name to be praised in all the earth.

In the story of Ruth, when Naomi and her family voluntarily left their home and lands in Israel to live in Moab, their actions, on the one hand, serve as a picture of Israel's departure from God. On the other hand, Ruth's action is a picture of the Gentiles joining themselves to and claiming allegiance to the God of Israel. Boaz's brother is a picture of how the law of the Old Covenant is inadequate to truly redeem us. Though it is exciting to know that the story of Ruth forecasts our (Gentiles) acceptance of the One and Only True God, I am more excited by the fact that Boaz is, in my mind, a picture of Christ, the ultimate Kinsman-Redeemer. You may be wondering why I am making such a declaration. You may think that I am stretching the truth, but I am not. Jesus does meet the three requirements mentioned above for a "kinsman-redeemer."

First, Jesus is your nearest kinsman to God through the incarnation. Romans 8:3 says, "For what the law was powerless to do in that it was weakened by the sinful nature, God did by sending His own Son in the likeness of sinful man to be a sin offering. And so He condemned sin in sinful man." Second, He has the power to redeem you. 2 Corinthians 8:9 states, "For you know the grace of our Lord Jesus Christ, that though He was rich, yet for your sakes He became poor, so that you through His poverty might become rich." Finally, He also is willing to redeem you. In Titus 2:14 we learn that He gave Himself for us. By doing that, He set us free from all evil. He wanted to make us pure. He wanted us to be His very own people. He wanted us to long to do what is good. He serves as our "Kinsman-Redeemer," taking away our bondages, sins, and death. He gives us a second chance to make things right. The Apostle Paul writes to the church in Ephesians 1:7 that it is through Christ that we have redemption through His blood, the forgiveness of sins, according to the riches of His grace. The means of our redemption is through the substitutionary death of Christ as a sacrifice for our sin. His blood became the ransom payment (cf. Ephesians 2:13 and 1 Peter 1:18-19). What is more enlightening is the fact that Christ did not just perform the role of a kinsman-redeemer and leave us to figure things out for ourselves; He is involved in our everyday lives helping along the way. To do this, He places people in our lives to be that physical, visible, tangible, believable, kinsman-redeemer. He does all of that just to change our mess of hopelessness and death into a message that there is a "Kinsman-Redeemer" and to remind us that we have not been left hopeless in our situation.

Finally, don't allow one ugly life experience to negatively impact you for the rest of your existence on earth. Don't allow any situation, relationship, or disaster to destroy you. God can use any situation in your life to take you to another level of growth in Him. He can use those bad situations to shape your character and propel you to a higher level, whether at your place of work, at church, in your relationships with others, or even in your marriage.

Over the years that I have served as a pastor, I have seen people who are still bitter with God because of an ugly situation that occurred in their lives many years ago. They are disgruntled, mean, unfriendly, uninterested, cynical, unapproachable, and sometimes even hateful because of what someone did to them in the past, or an unfortunate situation that occurred. It might have been an ugly relationship where someone you loved "dumped you" for a friend, or following a contentious, bitter divorce. For some of you, it might have been a pastor (unfortunately) that caused you to be in this situation. Yet, for others, it is life itself and there is actually no one to blame for your misfortune.

Whatever the situation, it is important for you to know that no one or no situation is powerful enough to destroy your life or even change your positive disposition towards life. The only person who wants to destroy you is Satan and he is not powerful enough, and even if he were, God will not allow him to put his hands on you. God, who has the power to destroy you, will not because He loves you too much. Therefore, why are you allowing a situation that happened years ago affect your future? Why are you giving the devil or others the attention they don't really deserve? They are losers and want you to be like them. Alright, you made a mistake, and so what? You are not the first and will not be the last person to make mistakes in life. Even if they won a battle, that is not the end of life. Move on! There are more important battles to be fought and with God on your side, you will win. Shake off those situations and disappointments. Go to God in prayer and leave them at the Cross. Then begin to believe God's Word that says He has a plan and a purpose for your life and that everything, including disappointments, will work out for your good (cf. Jeremiah 29:11; Romans 8:28). That is what happened to Ruth. She did not allow one ugly situation to stop her from enjoying life. I believe that the key is in your ability to understand God and His ability to turn your mess into a message. The Bible asserts in Ephesians 2:10, "For we are God's masterpiece. He has created us anew in Christ Jesus, so we can do the good things he planned for us long ago" (NLT).

You might say, "Yeah right, me, I am God's masterpiece?" Yes, that is right! You might not feel like it, look like it, smell like it, dream like it, speak like it, or even walk like God's masterpiece, but you are! It is easy to say, "If we are talking about X, then I understand, but not me." Beloved, believe it! You are God's masterpiece. God does not lie. If He says that you are His masterpiece, then you are. According to *Merriam-Webster's* online thesaurus, synonyms of masterpiece are: "showpiece, blockbuster, success, gem, jewel, prize, treasure, and piece of the master." Insert any of these words into Ephesians 2:10, in place of masterpiece and you will begin to fully appreciate what God is saying about you. All that I can say is, WOW! This is the concept that the Psalmist understood when he wrote, "I praise you because I am fearfully and wonderfully made; your works are wonderful, I know that full well. My frame was not hidden from you when I was made in the secret place. When I was woven together in the depths of the earth, your eyes saw my unformed body. All the days ordained for me were written in your book before one of them came to be."[21] Doesn't it just take your breath away to know that the Master of this universe thinks and feels that way about you? That is why He wants to turn your mess into a message.

It's been said, "Tough times never last, but tough people do." The Bible says, "For His anger lasts only a moment, but His favor lasts a lifetime; weeping may remain for a night, but rejoicing comes in the morning."[22]

---

21   Psalm 139:14-16 (cf. Job 5:9, Psalm 71:15).
22   Psalm 30:5

Tragedy strikes when we least expect it. Some trip over suffering while others triumph over tragedy. Those who know their God do exploits in the midst of adversities. They become better, not bitter. They live triumphant and not troubled lives. They recover faster than others, and praise their God for turning their mess into a message.

Why not submit the issue that you are going through to the Lord? Allow Him, the One who is able to still the troubled waters, speak to the storm to be still, and cause the rain to fall again, to turn your mess into a message. Is your problem bigger than what Ruth went through? Is your situation harder for God to solve than the situation that Ruth presented to the Lord? If so, read on and see for yourself how He turned other situations around in the lives of ordinary people like you. If it is not, then pause, present your situation unto the Lord and leave it at the foot of the cross. Trust that He has what it takes to solve the problem. I can assure you that you won't be disappointed.

Chapter V: The Thief on the Cross (Luke 23:39-43)
God Turns a Messy Situation of Eternal Separation into a Message of Abiding Presence

One of the criminals who hung there hurled insults at him: "Aren't you the Christ? Save yourself and us!" But the other criminal rebuked him. "Don't you fear God," he said, "since you are under the same sentence? We are punished justly, for we are getting what our deeds deserve. But this man has done nothing wrong." Then he said, "Jesus, remember me when you come into your kingdom." Jesus answered him, "I tell you the truth, today you will be with me in paradise" (Luke 23:39-43).

There are several powerful and life-transforming stories in the Bible. These stories are intended to first of all help us to understand God, His character, and His handiwork. Second, they are intended to help us understand and appreciate His love, compassion, justice, and fairness. Third, they help us understand His plan and purpose for our lives. Finally, they help us understand the mistakes (sins) that people in the days of old made so that we do not repeat them and thereby disappoint God.

For a number of reasons, the story of the thief on the cross found in Luke 23:39-43 is one of the most powerful stories in the Gospels. The narration is about Jesus, the Son of God (God incarnate). Jesus was a righteous, godly, and innocent man, having done nothing but good deeds, yet He was being crucified between two thieves (sinners) who by their own admission deserved to die on that day. In addition, this story is the fulfillment of an Old Testament prophecy from Isaiah 53:12, "…He poured out His life unto death, and was numbered with the transgressors. For He bore the sin of many, and made intercession for the transgressors." But, most importantly, this story is powerful because it explains how during Jesus' last agonizing moments before His death on the cross for sins that He did not commit, He was able to grant forgiveness to one of the criminals who repented, while the other died mocking God's plan of redemption for humanity. In other words, this story explains how one of the thieves died with curses on his lips and without hope for redemption because of his cynicism, unbelief, hatred, hardened heart, and doubt, whereas, the other thief died with the promise of hope in his heart and the assurance of being with the Lord in Heaven immediately after his spirit left his body.

There are a number of questions that come to mind as one reflects and tries to comprehend the story. How did it happen? What went wrong? How did one of them get it and the other one didn't? Why did God turn one thief's situation around and not the other? What can we learn from this story to apply to our lives so that God can turn our mess of being separated from Him into a message of being in His abiding presence?

The story has to do with three individuals condemned to be crucified on three crosses that stood on Golgotha. Of the three, one was about to die IN sin and to be lost forever. On the other cross was another thief who was about to die TO sin and be transported to the right hand of the Father. On the final cross, there was the Lamb, the Son of God, who was about to die FOR sin, and accomplish the mission for which He was sent to earth.

Without any doubt, like I mentioned previously, this is a powerful story of forgiveness and redemption that is extended to the worst of sinners at a time when all hope may have been lost – on his deathbed, if you will. But, before proceeding, let me point out that there is a tendency for people to misunderstand the "moral" or "underlying principle" embedded in this story. It is also very easy for people to develop wrong impressions when they read the story.

Allow me to use a story to illustrate the point that I am trying to make. It has to do with a conversation that took place between a man who claimed to be a Christian and wanted to join a certain church and the pastor of the church in question. The pastor asked the aspiring member an unexpected question, "Have you been baptized?"

The man replied, "No, but the thief on the cross was not baptized and he went to Heaven."

The pastor asked him another question, "Have you ever been a member of a church or active in a local church?"

To that question the self-professed Christian replied, "No, but the thief on the cross was not a member of a local church, neither was he active."

Finally, the pastor asked: "Do you partake in the Lord's Supper with other believers?"

Again the man replied, "No but the thief on the cross did not partake in the Lord's Supper and he still went to heaven."

The pastor looked at the self-professed Christian and said, "Do you know the difference between the thief on the cross and you?"

The man replied, "I'm listening."

The pastor said, "The difference is that the thief died in belief and you are living in disbelief."

Given the above story, let me point out two of the most common misconceptions or misinterpretations that I have heard and read from some who have preached, written, or taught from this passage of scripture. This might help us redirect our focus, eliminate some false exegetical interpretations we have read or heard, and comprehend Christ's message as it was meant to be understood.

The first misconception that has been drawn from this story is that you will be given the opportunity to repent on your "deathbed." This assumption is misleading and deceptive simply because, given the nature of death, it is hard, if not impossible, to know when someone is going to die. Hence, no one can count on a "deathbed conversion" because all of us might not have the privilege of knowing when we are going to die and, thereby, be able to repent on our "deathbed." That is why the Bible says in Hebrews 9:27, "Just as man is destined to die once, and after that to face judgment." We know one thing for a fact: We all will die one day. However, what we don't know is the precise time death will come knocking at our door. When Jesus was questioned by His disciples about His return, He explained that even He did not know the day or the hour.[23] There are some things that the Lord, in His divine wisdom, has chosen to hide from us. Deuteronomy 29:29 says that, "The secret things belong to the LORD our God, but the things revealed belong to us and to our children forever, that we may follow all the words of this law."

Having established that we can't count on a "deathbed conversion,"

---

23   Matthew 24:36

we can't deny that this is exactly what the thief on the cross experienced. He was literally minutes or hours away from dying. He had been judged, condemned, nailed to the cross, and there was no way humanly possible for the sentence or his situation to be reversed. It appears that before his conversation with Christ, his destination was hell. He apparently knew it, and so did the crowd and Jesus. He himself had said, "We are punished justly, for we are getting what our deeds deserve. But this man has done nothing wrong" (Luke 23:41).

He was a condemned man but God, in His mercy, elected to save his soul though his body was paying the price for the crime that he had committed. It was indeed a true and miraculous deathbed conversion. It is my ardent prayer that if you are on your deathbed reading this book, you will stop reading and pray to accept the Lord as your personal Lord and Savior. Pray that He will remember you and forgive your sins, like He did for the thief on the cross. Please do! He is able and willing to forgive you of all of your sins and cleanse you from all unrighteousness! He is able to take your mess and turn it into a message like He did with the thief on the cross. However, if you are not on your deathbed and you love to procrastinate, please remember that God has given us ONE EXAMPLE of a deathbed conversion to prove it could be done. But, note that there is ONLY ONE example recorded in all of Scriptures. For me, the fact that there is only one example should be a caution that I should not assume that it will happen for me, nor can I can continue to put off making the decision to get my life right with the Lord.

The second misconception or conclusion that could be easily drawn from this story (which is more of a doctrinal issue) is that the thief is an example of New Testament salvation and since the thief was not baptized, believers don't need to be baptized or be active in a church. Inasmuch as this sounds good and could probably make life easier for most pastors and converts alike, we need to remember that the thief died as an Old Testament Jew and NOT a New Testament Christian. Notice that the promise was made to the thief before the death of Jesus. It was only after Christ's death that the New Testament Covenant came into effect. This concept can be fully understood by reading Hebrews 9:16-17. It states, "Now when someone dies and leaves a will, no one gets anything until it is proved that the person who wrote the will is dead. The will goes into effect only after the death of the person who wrote it. While the person is still alive, no one can use the will to get any of the things promised to them" (NLT).

In the New Covenant, Christ calls for repentance and then baptism. He also calls for us to serve and not to forsake the assembly of the brethren (Hebrews 10:25). For us to use this story of the thief on the cross to conclude that Christians don't need to participate in the sacraments established by Christ Himself and His Church is far from the truth. The argument can even be made that Jesus Himself was baptized and when John the Baptist hesitated to baptize Him, Jesus replied, "'Let it be so now; it is proper for us to do this to fulfill all righteousness.' Then John consented" (Matthew 3:15).

Having taken the time to dispel two of the most frequent misconceptions and misinterpretations associated with this story, let us examine the situation as it relates to God turning our mess into a message of His abiding presence. There are a few things that I would like to help us see in this story, namely, the thief's condition (sinfulness), his confession (repentance), and his commitment (Lordship of Christ).

The thief's condition is one that is hard to determine or analyze because of the small amount of information we have about it. It would be unfair to read a whole lot into the story when the Bible has not said much about his social, physical, emotional, or even psychological state of mind. Unfortunately, the Scriptures have not given us the name of the thief, his place of birth, religious belief, level of education, or his upbringing. However, a critical analysis of the various passages in the Bible where the story is recorded can help us draw some very important conclusions that might help us fully understand the condition, confession, and commitment of the thief.

First and foremost, it is indisputable that the man in question was a thief. Matthew and Mark describe him as a robber or bandit. In Luke, however, he is described as a criminal. The discrepancy or use of other terminology could simply be attributed to it being a semantic issue or it could be that he was more than a thief. For the sake of doing justice to the text, let's assume that he was only a thief. Based on that assumption, we could assume that becoming a thief was most likely a matter of choice. He had basically adopted a lifestyle that was inconsistent with the moral laws governing the lives of those who lived in that area. As a thief, he had ignored and deliberately broken the laws of the land and violated the trust, confidence, and privacy of the people with whom he lived. The fact that he was being hung (which was severe treatment for a simple thief) lends to the idea that this was not a mistake or a first, second, or third offense. In addition, given the severity of the penalty being imposed (the death sentence) it is easy to conclude that this was not a *"petty thief,"* meaning he did not steal little or inexpensive things. His crime would be compared to that of a web wizard hacking into a secured internal banking system and stealing millions of dollars, or perhaps a thief using a deadly weapon to rob a bank. Possibly some would even compare him to disgraced financier Bernard Madoff. The thief on the cross had intentionally broken the laws of the land and inadvertently, the laws of God.

The second thing worth noting is the fact that this man's sin was not simply a crime against society or against cultural mores. It was not simply committing acts of degradation. Though all of the above mentioned are true, his crime can be further viewed as a willful ignorance of God's laws. It was not simply that this man ignored God; he willfully ignored Him. Probably God had been perceived by the thief as being an inconvenience, an obstruction, a roadblock to achieving his dream. In his lifestyle, the thief may have simply put God out of his mind as many of us do as we go about trying to achieve our desired goals. If he knew the Word of God, he may have purposely chosen to ignore it and categorized it as being irrelevant. He had defied the laws and had broken them. The central principle of his life was that he was self-centered and did not take into consideration how his actions might eventually affect those he loved and those who loved him dearly. Basically, he must have had an "I don't care!" attitude about God and those around him. Could it be that his parents had not brought him up the right way? Could it be that his parents abandoned him at a young age? Could it be that at a young age he was exploited by others and he eventually decided to retaliate against society? We don't know that for sure, but I do acknowledge that we live in an evil world and therefore, anything is possible! He may have been raised in a very tough society amongst gangsters and hooligans. He may have been molested, abused, indoctrinated, etc., but it does not change the fact that he was responsible for his actions just as we are equally responsible for ours. Just as we can't claim, "the devil made me do it," he can't claim the same either. In other words, this man was guilty! He had done the crime and needed to pay! This is an indisputable fact.

However, I think that beyond the fact that he had committed the crime and needed to bear the consequences for his actions, was the fact that the thief's condition is a portrait of mankind's condition before God. We steal from God the very thing that is most precious to Him – our lives. We may not break society's laws but we break God's greatest law: "Love the Lord your God with all your heart and with all your soul and with all your mind and with all your strength" (Mark 12:30). It means that when we hold back from the Lord in our commitment to doing what He has called us to do or wants us to do we become thieves, denying Him His rightful place in our lives. That is what being selfish is all about! We must become Christ-centered instead of self-centered!

Let's assume for a minute that the thief found himself in a compromising situation and that this was not really his lifestyle. Let's also assume for a minute that he tried to stop himself or get rid of this habit but failed (because he had been caught, tried, and is about to be executed). Wouldn't it be fair to say that he did not only break the law, but the law had or was about to break him? Sadly, that is the condition we constantly find ourselves in as believers. No matter how hard we try to break certain sinful habits that are contrary to God's word, we fail continuously and the "law" breaks us down to the point where many times we resolve to just continue sinning because there appears to be no other viable alternative. The thief is, therefore, an excellent illustration of our inadequacies, emptiness, powerlessness, and brokenness without God when we are faced with sin's brutal grip on our lives. This was the man's condition and may be ours as well.

Now, let's look at the thief's confession that led to his repentance. Hopefully we can learn a few lessons from there as well.

Again, given the fact that we know very little about the thief, one could argue that this could have been the thief's first and only contact with Jesus. We don't know that for sure, but it is possible since we don't know where he lived or the proximity of his location to where Jesus ministered. Let me quickly add that though this seems likely, I would be hard pressed to say with certainty that the thief didn't know anything about Jesus given the impact of Jesus' ministry in Galilee, Judah, Samaria, and other areas around Jerusalem and the controversies that surrounded some of the miracles Jesus performed. I believe that he knew about Jesus or had possibly listened to Jesus preach or teach. Didn't he attest on the cross that Jesus had done nothing wrong (Luke 23:41)? However, prior to his arrest, condemnation and soon to be execution, he probably had dismissed Jesus. The thief may have labeled Jesus as being a fanatic, a loser, a God-freak, a liar, or a lunatic. Whatever his thoughts may have been regarding Jesus and His ministry, he certainly did not submit to the Lordship of Christ. Jesus' teaching did not seem to have the desired effect at the time. Maybe the "Word" had simply been planted and God was waiting for the appropriate time to bring about conviction.

When one takes a critical look at the story, it is evident that Jesus was crucified before this thief on the cross. Undoubtedly this man witnessed with fear what was being done to Jesus. He saw the nails driven into the legs and hands. He heard the insults coming from the lips of the soldiers and those who were either standing or passing by. I believe, to his greatest bewilderment, he noticed that in spite of all that was being done to Jesus, there were no complaints, insults, curses, or words of regret coming from Jesus' lips. Just like the Prophet Isaiah had prophesied, "He was oppressed and afflicted, yet He did not open His mouth; He was led like a lamb to the slaughter, and as a sheep before her shearers is silent, so He did not open His mouth" (Isaiah 53:7). Rather, this thief heard (and could not believe what he was hearing) Jesus declare, "Father, forgive them for they know not what they do" (Luke 23:34)! Wow! What a statement to make when you are being beaten, insulted, mishandled, and crucified for something you did not do!

Let me help you further understand what was happening and why it might have been mindboggling to the thief. Jesus was hanging on the cross, and while on the cross He spoke seven times. Among the first words He uttered were, "Father, forgive them for they do not know what they are doing."[24] Remember that Jesus is on the cross and by uttering those words He was doing a number of things. Let me share only two with you. First, He was praying. Like my kids would say, "It does not take a rocket scientist to know that you don't pray while hanging on a cross." A cross is a place of excruciating pain, disgrace, and humiliation. Therefore, it is not a place to pray. If you want to pray, you go to the church, the synagogue, the garden, a place of tranquility, but not to the cross. In other words, you don't pray on the cross. The cross is a place where you complain, beg for forgiveness, express innocence, yell, cry, and then start cursing. Even if you don't do all of that, it is still not the place where you find people praying for those who perpetrated the crime for which they are being innocently accused.

Second, Jesus is asking the Father to *"forgive"* them. Was Jesus praying for a *"blanket pardon?"* In other words, can we say based on this prayer that Jesus was saying that God should forgive all those who were participating in his crucifixion whether they repented or not? I am not convinced that this was the kind of prayer that Jesus was offering to the Father, simply because God does not force His forgiveness on people. Forgiveness is always linked to repentance in Scriptures. Don't misunderstand me. Christ paid the price and because of what He did, God offers forgiveness freely. However, that forgiveness is free to those who want it. It is a free gift that

---

24   Luke 23:34

has to be accepted! Additionally, Jesus is not excusing ignorance when He says, "They don't know what they are doing," therefore, forgive them. If you read part of Simon Peter's sermon in Acts 3:17-19, regarding the crucifixion of Jesus, he admitted that the people might have acted out of ignorance and that it was part of God's plan in order for Scriptures to be fulfilled. Nevertheless, Peter called on them to repent in order to be forgiven.

He stated: "Now brothers, I know that you acted in ignorance, as did your leaders. But this is how God fulfilled what He had foretold through all the prophets, saying that His Christ would suffer. Repent, then, and turn to God, so that your sins may be wiped out." If Jesus had offered a *"blanket pardon"* when He prayed on the cross, then logically, Peter should have said, "Now, Jesus prayed to the Father on the cross for your forgiveness, therefore you all are forgiven; go and sin no more." Instead he said, "Now repent and turn to God so that your sins may be wiped out."

I know that what I stated above may sound radical for some readers. However, if you have another biblical explanation, I would be willing to listen. I don't think that a careful study of the passage would give any biblical scholar the right to think or teach that Jesus gave a *"blanket pardon"* on the cross and therefore we are to do the same. In any case, the question still remains that if Jesus was not praying for a *"blanket pardon"* and He was not excusing ignorance without repentance, what was He praying for?

Understanding the meaning of the word *"forgive"* can help explain exactly what Jesus meant when He prayed this prayer. In the New Testament, there are a number of words used for *"forgive."* The meaning that is commonly referred to is, *"to forget, wipe out completely, release, or cancel."* That is to say, God wipes away our sins and remembers them no more (Isaiah 43:25; Hebrews 8:12; 10:17; and 1 John 1:8-9). But there is another word that is used in the New Testament that denotes the concept of forgiving. It is translated in English as *"hinder, or interfere."* It is found in Matthew 19:14 where the little children are brought to Jesus and the disciples try to keep them from coming to Him. Jesus said, "Let the little children come to me, and do not hinder them for the kingdom of heaven belongs to such as these."

The word that is translated *"let"* in the statement, "Let the little children come..." is the same word translated *"forgive"* when Jesus said, "Forgive them" on the cross. So what was Jesus saying? He was not saying, *"Forgive the little children,"* is He? I don't think so! He was basically saying, *"Let them* come. *Don't stop them. Don't hinder them from coming. Don't stand in their way. Don't interfere."* That same word is used again in Matthew 27:48-49, when the soldiers reached up with a sponge filled with vinegar to wet the lips of Jesus. It says, "Immediately one of them ran and got a sponge. He filled it with wine vinegar, put it on a stick and offered it to Jesus to drink. But the rest said, 'Leave Him alone. Let's see if Elijah comes to save Him.'" The expression there is, *"Leave him alone, or, don't interfere!"*

Combining the two we get, *"Don't stop the children from coming and don't wet his lips with a sponge."* Hence Jesus was praying on the cross to the Father, "Father, leave them alone. Father, don't rush to inflict your wrath upon these people. Father, hold back your wrath please, don't interfere."

You see, Jesus was pleading with the Father to give them a chance to come to the full realization concerning the gravity of their sins. Again, He was praying, "Father, please give these Roman soldiers who are driving these nails into my hands a chance to repent. Give this angry crowd a chance to get right with you. Give all of the sinning and evil people a chance to be redeemed. I'm paying the price, Father. Hold back your wrath. Give them the chance to be forgiven, cleansed, and made new."

What a prayer! What a Savior! Even now, as Jesus sits at the right hand of the Father making intercession on our behalf, He is still praying, "Father, forgive them. Hold back your wrath. Please don't interfere because I want to turn their mess into a message. Give them one more chance because I am sure my Spirit will bring conviction to their hearts. I have a plan for them that is unfolding! I love them so dearly and that is why I paid the ultimate price of death to save them. Please, please, Father, don't do that!"

Thanks to Jesus' prayer, the Father is holding back His wrath today from falling upon us. In spite of the fact that we willfully sin daily, Jesus is seated at the right hand of the Father pleading with Him to withhold His wrath.

His prayer is, "Please Father, just give them one more chance simply because of the blood that I shed on the cross on their behalf."

This prayer must have had a bearing on the thief's attitude toward Jesus. He could not understand how someone could exhibit such an attitude toward those who were persecuting him (even if that person were guilty of the crime of which he was being accused). I believe that as he watched, as he listened, and as he processed what was happening, he finally got a revelation of who Christ is. He got a revelation of His mission. He got a revelation of His plan of salvation. He got a revelation of the purpose of

Christ's death. It all became clear! There must be a divine reason! Maybe all that he had heard Jesus say or teach came back to his mind. Maybe everything he had heard people say about the Lordship of Christ finally became real to him. Maybe all that he had done finally began to weigh on him as he realized that life is unfair and he had treated others unfairly! Maybe, he finally realized that he had to make it right with his Maker and Redeemer, because his minutes were numbered. I believe that he got a glance into the kingdom of God like Stephen did when he was being stoned. In Acts 7:55-60 we read:

> *But Stephen, full of the Holy Spirit, looked up to heaven and saw the glory of God, and Jesus standing at the right hand of God. "Look," he said, "I see heaven open and the Son of Man standing at the right hand of God. At this they covered their ears and, yelling at the top of their voices, they all rushed at him, dragged him out of the city and began to stone him. Meanwhile, the witnesses laid their clothes at the feet of a young man named Saul. While they were stoning him, Stephen prayed, "Lord Jesus, receive my spirit." Then he fell on his knees and cried out, "Lord, do not hold this sin against them." When he had said this, he fell asleep.*

Probably, the thief did not "see heaven open and the Son of Man standing at the right hand of God" simply because the Son of Man was right next to him on the cross, but he "saw" something that made him recognize what was happening. Consequently, he could not just remain silent. He had to speak up and not only confess with his lips that Jesus is Lord, but he felt obliged to "defend Jesus." When everyone else could not see who was being crucified, he saw; when everyone else failed to recognize who was being crucified, he recognized. When everyone else failed to take a stand against injustice, insult, cruelty, and abuse, he stood because of the revelation that he had received about the Son of God. That is why when the other thief started to ridicule and reject Jesus, this man who had seen Jesus in a new light quickly responded to the other thief, "Don't you fear God, since you are under the same sentence? We are punished justly, for we are getting what our deeds deserve. But this man has done nothing wrong."

How many times have we stood up for Christ, His Word, or the Church? Many of us claim to be Christians (Christ-like), but we refuse to defend what we know about Christ and His Church. We allow others to blaspheme the name of Christ and we comfort ourselves by saying, "Each one is entitled to his/her personal opinion." If God is going to change our mess into a message, we must be willing to take a stand for what we know is true, for what we know is right, for what we know to be the will of God, for what we know to be the mind of God, and for what we know to be the plan of God. We can't afford to just stand by, passively listen, and silently walk away.

Recently, one of my spiritual daughters was asked by someone to give him some money. She was considering the request and then he started to say some negative things about me. She immediately told him to keep quiet or he would not get what he had asked for. In her rebuke, she reminded him that I am her spiritual father and if he wanted to be favored by her, he had to not only be mindful of what he says about me, but he had to guard his heart and attitude.

When we have a relationship or a revelation of who someone is and that person becomes dear to us, the least we can do when that person is being falsely accused is to speak up, and defend the person. The words spoken by the thief were not spoken to Jesus but about Him. They reveal to us a change in the outlook and attitude of this man. The thief may have ignored God for a long time, but it was time to put things into perspective. It was time to right the wrong! It was time to defend the innocent. It was time to acknowledge the lordship of the One who made him and who holds the universe in His hands. Without Him (Christ), there was nothing made that has been made. It was time for the thief to remember! He had wronged others, caused many to suffer, but now he admitted that they were both receiving the just reward for their sins. But about Jesus, he responded, "This man has done nothing wrong."

What is important to underline at this point is the fact that for our situation to be changed and for God to turn our mess into a message, we must first and foremost recognize our sinfulness. The Bible declares that we are all sinners (Romans 3:23).

There are basically three types of sin. The one being referred to here is called personal sin. It is the kind of sin that is committed every day by every human being. Because we have inherited a sin nature from Adam, we commit individual or personal sins, everything from seemingly innocent untruths to murder. You may not have committed a heinous crime such as murder which could have caused you to be incarcerated, but that does not mean that you are not a sinner. The Greek word *"hamartia"* (ἁμαρτία) is usually translated as *"sin"* in the New Testament. In classical Greek, it means *"to miss the mark"* or *"to miss the target."* Please don't tell me that you have never missed the mark before in regards to moral laws!

The second type of sin is known as inherited sin. The human race inherited the sinful nature from Adam and Eve. When they sinned against God in the Garden of Eden, their inner nature was transferred to us. In Romans 5:14 we read: "Nevertheless, death reigned from the time of Adam to the time of Moses, even over those who did not sin by breaking a command, as did Adam, who was a pattern of the one to come." Hence, we are sinners, not because we sin; rather, we sin because we are sinners. Just as we inherit physical characteristics from our parents, we inherit our sinful natures from Adam. King David lamented this condition of a fallen human nature in Psalm 51:5. He said, "Surely I was sinful at birth, sinful from the time my mother conceived me."

The third type of sin is known as imputed sin. The Greek word translated *"imputed"* means *"to take something that belongs to someone and credit it to another's account."* Before the Law of Moses was given, sin was not imputed to mankind, although we were still sinners because of inherited sin and we were subjected to death. However, after the Law was given, sins committed in violation of the Law were imputed (accounted) to them. Romans 5:13 declares, "For before the law was given, sin was in the world. But sin is not taken into account when there is no law." This means then, after the Law was introduced by Moses, humans were subject to death both because of inherited sin from Adam and imputed sin from violating the laws of God. It is very easy for us to argue that this type of sin (imputed sin) is unfair, but when we consider the fact that God used the principle of imputation to benefit mankind when He imputed our sins to the account of Jesus Christ, we might fully understand and come to accept its importance and implications. When God imputed our sins to Christ's account, He (Christ) had to pay the full penalty for the sin (death) on the cross. Imputing our sin to Jesus, God treated Him as if He were a sinner, though He was not, and had Him die for the sins of the entire world (1 John 2:2). It is important to understand that sin was imputed to Him, but He did not inherit it from Adam. He bore the penalty for sin, but He never became a sinner. His pure and perfect nature was untouched by sin. He was treated as though He were guilty of all the sins ever committed by the human race, even though He committed none. In exchange, God imputed the righteousness of Christ to believers and credited our accounts with His righteousness, just as He had credited our sins to Christ's account. We read in 2 Corinthians 5:21, "God made Him who had no sin to be sin for us, so that in Him we might become the righteousness of God." There is a song known to have been written by G. McSpadden entitled, "He Paid a Price He Did Not Owe." McSpadden writes, "He paid a debt He did not owe, I owed a debt I could not pay. I needed someone to wash my sins away. And now I sing a brand new song, 'Amazing Grace.' Christ Jesus paid a debt that I could never pay!"

Those who have not placed their faith in Jesus Christ must pay the penalty for these personal sins as well as their inherited and imputed sin. However, believers have been freed from the eternal penalty of sin – hell and spiritual death – because Christ paid the debt that we owed. Additionally, through this resurrection and victory over death, He gave us power to resist sin. That is, we can say NO to sin and YES to righteousness. Consequently, we can choose whether or not to commit personal sins, in accordance to Romans 8:9-11, because we have the power to resist sin through the Holy Spirit who dwells within us. The Holy Spirit also convicts us of our sins when we do commit them. Thankfully, once we confess our personal sins to God and ask the Lord to forgive us of them, we are restored to perfect fellowship and communion with Him (1 John 1:9).

That is what the thief on the cross recognized and did. He basically repented of his sin: "Please Lord, remember me when you enter into your kingdom. I may not have lived a wonderful life, but please Lord, remember me. I stole, insulted, cheated, killed, but please, Lord, don't hold it against me, remember me. I know that I deserve your judgment, but please forgive me and remember me."

Beloved, that is the beginning point of having your mess changed into a message. It all starts with repentance. Repentance is infinitely more than feeling sorry for one's sins. Repentance is a changed mind. This is exactly what happened with this man. He changed his mind concerning his attitude toward God, and concerning his attitude toward his fellowmen. It is noticeable that the other thief did not repent. Both had received the same information (both saw how Jesus responded to his crucifixion). Yet one repented, the other did not. What a pity! It tells me that everyone could be exposed to the same gospel, experience the same miracle, and be given the same opportunity – and yet some will decide not to repent of their sins.

Having dealt with the thief's condition (sinfulness) and his confession (repentance), let us focus on the thief's commitment (accepting the Lordship of Jesus Christ) which is the key that turned his mess into a message. The thief said, "Jesus, remember me when you come into your kingdom."

Think about those words for a minute without trying to do an exegesis or word analysis of the sentence. It appears, and I think that you will agree, that the thief's words were an acknowledgment that, though Jesus was being crucified, numbered with thieves and labeled as a criminal, He was nevertheless the King. You are aware that there are different forms of governments around the world. Each is designed to be governed by a ruler or a set of rulers. For example, a monarchy is a form of government in which supreme power is absolutely or nominally lodged with an individual, who is the head of state, often for life or until abdication. An oligarchy, which is the Greek word for *"few,"* is a form of government in which power effectively rests with a small elite segment of society distinguished by royalty, wealth, intellectual capability, family, military or religious hegemony. Similarly, a kingdom is a nation being ruled by a king or a queen. *"Kingdom"* implies that there is a king or queen who governs. The thief's choice of words is quite noticeable. He said, "When you enter into your kingdom." The word, *"your"* is an adjective (of or relating to oneself, especially as possessor). The kingdom, therefore (in the mind of the thief), belongs to Jesus. He is King of the Kingdom!

Let me draw your attention to another fact that is embedded in the thief's remark that I should have mentioned initially. He said, "Remember me when you enter into your kingdom." Doesn't it appear from this statement that the thief was asking to be a part of the kingdom? To be a part of a kingdom is to become a subject and submit to the authority of the king. Hence, the thief was not only acknowledging Jesus as Lord and King but he was also submitting himself to the Kingship of Jesus. Additionally, the expression, *"remember me"* doesn't appear to simply mean, *"keep me in mind."* It was a plea for mercy, forgiveness, and pardon. It was an acknowledgement of guilt and recognition that a wrong had been committed that deserved to be punished. But what is intriguing is the fact that the thief was not asking for God's intervention so that he could be released from the cross. Many of us, when we have an encounter with the Divine, ask not only for our sins to be forgiven, but for the impending consequences or punishment to be dropped. It is true that Christ has the authority not just to forgive sin but to also grant us favor with the judicial system for the litigation to be dropped or sentences reduced. Yes, He can turn your mess into a message, but the thief saw more in Jesus. He saw something that we miss many times in our crisis situation. He caught a glimpse of eternity. Oh, how pleasant it is to see and know that you have been forgiven and that in spite of your sins, you will be spending eternity with Christ! The thief probably had taken a few minutes to reflect on his life and what brought him to this point. He probably had reflected on how hard he had tried to live a respectful, sinless and holy life in his own strength. He probably had thought about his once held desire to please God and live in peace with his neighbors. He probably reflected on how he had asked others in his own community to help him break his uncontrollable stealing habit, but they failed to come to his rescue. He probably reflected on how he had asked for advice from others and made himself vulnerable thinking that someone was going to come to his rescue, but all he got was bad advice and further into trouble with the law. Just a glimpse into heaven was all he needed to realize that he was just passing through this earthly realm and that his final destination was a place beyond this world. Sooner or later, his life here would come to an end and whether the sentence was dropped and he was taken down from the cross was not what was important. All that would change is the day he would die, for it was certain that he would die one day. What a difference just a glimpse into heaven could make!

Pray that the Lord will open your eyes and give you a glimpse into Heaven! It would change your perspective in life. Those things that appear to be so important will become less important and attractive. Your goals in life will change, your friends will change, your day planner will change, your faith will change, and Jesus will become your focus and heaven your destination. Your mind will be heaven-focused and your constant desire will be to be with Him. I have had the opportunity to hear testimonies of people who had an encounter with heaven either through a vision or dream. One such person is Gabriel Hope. She writes in her book, *Royal Steps: Destined for Dignity*, after one of her visits with Jesus in heaven, "Immediately, I missed him! I missed my Heavenly Father, and my best friend Jesus. I lived each day after that in hopes I would return to heaven again. In exasperation of missing Him, I began to share my experience with a handful of people."[25]

When we get a glimpse of heaven and of the One who sits on the throne being worshiped day and night by angelic beings and the twenty-four elders, our entire being is consumed by the desire to be with Him, to please Him, to love Him, to be like Him and to worship Him. Don Moen writes this in his song: *I Want to be Where You Are.*

---

25   Hope, Gabriel. Royal Steps: Destined for Dignity. Kentwood, MI: Hope Harvest Book, 2008, page 204.

I just want to be where You are,
Dwelling daily in Your presence
I don't want to worship from afar,
Draw me near to where You are.

I just want to be where You are,
In Your dwelling place forever
Take me to the place where You are,
I just want to be with You.

I want to be where You are,
Dwelling in Your presence
Feasting at Your table,
And surrounded by Your glory.

In Your presence,
That's where I always want to be
I just want to be,
I just want to be with You.

With such a desire, Jesus is very likely to say to you, "Welcome my child, sit at the table and feast with me."

To the thief he said, "I tell you the truth, today you will be with me in paradise." What a promise! The One who had said, "I am the way, the truth, and the life," spoke the truth into this man's life. Just when he needed a NOW word from the Lord, he got it! Do you need a NOW word from God? Do you feel like the world is falling apart on you and God needs to speak a word into your situation? Remember, He is able. He is the same yesterday, today, and forever. He spoke a NOW word to a dying criminal and He can do the same for you. The key is to ask.

The thief said, "Lord, remember me."

You need to say, "Lord, remember me....not because I am holy, not because I am special, not because of the color of my skin or my origin, not because of my works of righteousness, but because of Your blood and the cross. Lord, remember me because of what You did on the cross! Remember me and change my mess into a message."

Beloved, there is not a demon in hell that can hold back God's blessing when He remembers you! I am not saying that it won't get rough. It could get rough and challenging and at times it may seem like God is nowhere to be found. But, don't give up! It will never be over, until it is over. Jeremiah wrote in Lamentations 3:19-23, "I will remember my affliction and my wandering, the bitterness and the gall. I well remember them, and my soul is downcast within me. Yet this I call to mind and therefore I have hope: because of the Lord's great love we are not consumed, for His compassions never fail. They are new every morning; great is your faithfulness."

Like the thief, you have the opportunity to evaluate your condition. How have you hurt others? How have you disobeyed God's laws? How has your life negatively impacted those who love you and the society in which you live? Please take a retrospective look at your life and allow God to show you some deep things about yourself. It may not be a comfortable exercise but I can assure you that it will eventually be worth your effort. Second, the fact that you are reading this book means that you are alive and still have the opportunity to confess your sins unto the Lord. Ask Jesus to forgive you of things you have done whether intentionally or unintentionally. Finally, submit your life to the leading and lordship of Christ. Tell Him that you want to follow Him all the days of your life. God can't turn your mess of eternal separation from Him into a message of abiding presence if you refuse to follow these simple but very important steps. Please do that, would you?

Chapter VI: Jephthah (Judges 11:1-40)
God Turns a Messy Life of Being an Outcast into a Message of Being a Hero, but...

Every day we make decisions. Some of the decisions we make are done consciously while others are made unconsciously. To not make decisions everyday is not an option or a luxury of life. Making decisions daily does not depend on our age, social, political, humanitarian, or religious status. As long as there is life within a human being, he or she will have to make decisions daily. Many of us use different techniques to help us in our decision making process. Some of the methods include:

A. Analyzing the advantages and disadvantages of each option;
B. Choosing the alternative with the highest probability;
C. Accepting the first option on our list that seems like it might achieve the desired result;
D. Speaking to a person in authority or an expert on the issue;
E. Using random or coincidence methods (flipping a coin);
F. Prayer and other spiritual methods.

It is important to note that, on the one hand, some of these daily decisions we make are big and have long-lasting consequences. They may relate to immediate life and death or have consequences which linger until the individual who made the decision dies and sometimes, even beyond this life. For example, the decision to accept Christ as your Lord and Savior is a decision that affects your life here on earth and your life when you leave this earth. Another example of a decision that could have a long-lasting consequence is the decision to get married. On the other hand, some of the daily decisions we make are so minute that we are not even aware that we are making them and their consequences may not even be noticed.

One fact about the results of decisions we make is that sometimes the physical consequences cannot be reversed even after we get saved and ask God and those we have offended to forgive us. A classic example is when a young lady becomes pregnant outside of marriage and is unprepared for the child. Asking God's forgiveness and even becoming a Christian does not remove the fact that she has had a child for whom she will be responsible the rest of her life.

The story of Jephthah that we will be studying in this chapter is very similar. Decisions were made and the domino effects were very devastating. Though it seems like Israel repented, that Jephthah's siblings may have regretted their actions, and Jephthah certainly would have loved to have another chance to change some of the decisions he made in life, the consequences nevertheless remained.

It is for some of the reasons already mentioned that everyone ought to be mindful when making decisions, especially those decisions that have the potential to dramatically alter one's life, have devastating aftereffects, or a chain reaction. Each and everyone needs to have a set of standards, morals, ethics, customs, norms, etc., that guide him or her when faced with making a "big decision." For Christians, the Bible ought to be our standard. I believe that Christians need to be more mindful and prayerful about making major decisions in life simply because our decisions have to be in the will of God. I once heard it said that for a Christian to make major life decisions without referring to the illuminating Word of God is almost like trying to set up newly purchased electronic equipment without referring to its manual of operation (although few people are able to do it with relative success). For a Christian who wants to make a decision that pleases the Lord and remain in the center of His will, he or she must ask several key questions and be willing to allow God to speak to him/her. A few of these questions are:

1. Will this decision violate God's teaching in the Bible? If you know that the answer to this question is yes, then don't do it. No amount of justification could suffice (Psalm 119:105; 2 Timothy 3:16).

2. Will this decision cause my brother or sister to stumble in his

or her faith? Again, if the answer is yes, don't do it. You have a testimony to protect and a brother or sister to help in his or her faith journey. If you decide to ignore His Word, God will hold you responsible for the possible spiritual effects your decision would have on a brother or sister who is looking up to you as their "Christ" on earth (1 Corinthians 8).

3. Will this decision, cause me to violate my body as the temple of the Holy Spirit (1 Corinthians 6:19; Romans 12:1)? It is clear from the Bible that God wants us to remain holy because our bodies are His temple.

4. Will this decision violate the expressed will of my superior, especially in the case where it is not legally, morally, and ethically wrong (Ephesians 5-6)? An excellent example is the fact that we are told in the Bible that children are to obey their parents and employees are to obey their employers. If you are a child or an employee, the question is: Would the decision you want to make violate the expressed will of your parents or employer? For some people, and depending on the situation, this could be a gray area.

5. Will this decision bring glory to God (1 Corinthians 10:13)? This question is very important. In other words, will God be praised as a result of this decision that I am about to make. The question is not, "Will I be happy?"

6. Will I be able to honestly ask God to bless my decision (Romans 14)? Some decisions we make are so terrible and morally wrong that we can't even pray for the Lord to bless us or the decision. If you think that you would be uneasy about praying to God regarding a decision you are about to make, then it is probably not a good one. Now, I understand that some people have no morals or are bold to go to God to pray for something that is just outright wrong. I recall a story of someone going to a pastor and asking him to pray for her boyfriend, a married man, to leave his wife so that he could finish the construction of the house that he had started for her. We all know that it is wrong! My wife would say, "Don't even go there..."

7. Will I be at ease with this decision (1 Corinthians 4:4)? In other words, after having made this decision, would I be able to sleep at night in peace? Better still, will I be able to stand in my church and give my testimony about the goodness of God

in this situation? If not, then you probably need to reconsider the decision.

8. Will I be able to live with the consequences and still glorify God (Proverbs 22:3)? Maybe another way to ask the question is, "Will I still love God the way I do now after I have made this decision? Will this decision improve my relationship with God or would it serve as a major distraction?"

> After these questions have been asked, and of course, if a Christian feels that he or she can answer yes to all of them, then the decision can be made in a prayerful manner. In other words, no one should hastily make decisions that could have long-lasting effects, because to every decision there is a ramification (whether little or large). Some outcomes may be experienced immediately while others may be experienced in the future. In fact, some of the repercussions of our decisions may not even be experienced by us. Rather, our children or grandchildren may be the ones to reap what we have sown. Unfortunately, it could be too late for us to reverse the consequences or there might be little or nothing our descendents might be able to do about it. Even for those who are saved or would be saved by the blood of Christ, depending on the nature of the circumstances, it might become difficult, if not impossible, for them to have the consequences reversed.

The story we are dealing with in this chapter concerns a man named Jephthah and can be found in Judges 11:1-31. It is a story about decisions made that had messy consequences that affected three generations (Jephthah's parents, Jephthah himself and his relationship with his siblings, and Jephthah's daughter). Some of the decisions made (though innocently) even affected Israel as a nation.

In the book of Judges, we are constantly reminded by the phrase, "In those days Israel had no king; everyone did as he saw fit" (Judges 17:6). A quick glance at Judges 17 and 18 will reveal how the children of Israel committed blatant sin, rape, violence, and bloodshed simply because everyone was doing as he saw fit. God's laws and precepts were ignored and everyone felt he or she knew what was good for him, his neighbors, and the world at large. As we would say today: "Everyone did his or her own thing." There was no authority to impose the laws of the land and the Laws of God. This led Israel, as a nation and a people called and set apart by God, to drift away from Him. They worshiped other gods, violated the commands of Yahweh, and did what seemed right in their own eyes. What happened to them spiritually can be summed up into three categories: rebellion, retribution, and repentance.

The children of Israel rebelled against God, His Word, and His laws. Lawlessness became the order of the day, and the unspoken understanding that existed was that the society had turned into one in which only the strongest could survive. Not only was this true socially, politically, and economically, it also became true religiously. In their quest for survival, many Israelites had placed their trust in idols and ignored Yahweh, the God of their ancestors Abraham, Isaac, and Jacob, who had brought them out of the land of slavery and proven Himself to be their shield and their great reward.[26] They worshiped, admired, or interacted with the Canaanite gods of Baal and Ashtaroth; the gods of Syria, Hadad, Baal, Mot, and Anath; the gods of Sidon, Baal and Astarte; the gods of Moab, Chemosh; and the gods of the Philistines, Dagon, etc. These false religions and gods included some of the most perverted and depraved practices ever known to man. The children of Israel had no excuse for their behaviour and God's anger and wrath burned against them. In previous chapters in the book of Judges we read, for example, how God miraculously intervened in the Israelites' lives and situations and brought deliverance to them through Gideon. Additionally, they had seen the disaster of apostasy in the life of Abimelech. Also, they had known the leadership of two minor judges named Tola and Jair, and in spite of experiencing God's love, mercy, protection, and forgiveness, they turned away from Him and did what seemed to be right in their own eyes.

The Israelites thought that ignoring Yahweh, worshiping idols, and rebelling against the Torah would grant them the freedom to sin without being held accountable by their conscience and God. One important truth that evaded their thought process was the fact that these idols did not and could not provide for them any means of salvation. Consequently, in Judges 10:7-8 we read that "God became angry with them and He sold them into the hands of the Philistines and the Ammonites, who that year shattered and crushed them." The Ammonites were a people group who lived on the eastern side of the Dead Sea. They had initially fought and conquered

---

26   Genesis 15:1, "After this, the word of the LORD came to Abram in a vision: 'Do not be afraid, Abram. I am your shield, your very great reward.'"

the tribes of Reuben and Gad and half of the tribe of Manasseh, who had settled on the east side of the Jordan River, at a place called Gilead. For eighteen years, these tribes were oppressed and crushed on the east side of the Jordan. In verse 9 of Chapter 10, we read that the Ammonites decided to cross the Jordan to attack the tribes of Judah, Benjamin, and Ephraim, the central tribes of Israel. It was a time for retribution that had been sanctioned by God. These tribes had sinned and in a sense, it was "payday." God had pulled back His blessings and probably His angels that were protecting the Israelites. The hedge of protection that God had supernaturally built around them had been removed and they were now vulnerable to their enemies.

The Israelites soon realized that God had withdrawn His protection because of their disobedience and sinful nature. Consequently, they started to cry out to God for His mercy, forgiveness, and protection because they knew that only the Lord could deliver them from the hands of their enemies. Initially, it appears as if their appeal for mercy and compassion was not because they were sorry for their sins and wanted to return to God. Rather, it was simply a matter of convenience and not of commitment. They regretted the consequences of their behavior but did not have repentant hearts.

It is important to understand the difference between regret and repentance, because these two words can be easily confused. In the New Testament, when we read certain passages regarding regret and repentance, it is possible that we come away confused as well because in some instances we see the word "sorry" in place of regret or repent. This happens because there are three words used in the New Testament to describe *"repent"* or *"repentance."* The first word is *"metamelmai"* (see Matthew 14:9 and Matthew 27:3). It is a term that is used to describe remorse with no change of heart. In the case of Judas Iscariot, he regretted his action but did not go to God to repent. The same is true of King Herod, because even though he regretted the promise he had made to the daughter of Herodias (to grant her whatever she wanted) when she asked for the head of John the Baptist, the Bible says that because of his oaths and his dinner guests (saving his face), he granted her request. The second word, *"metanoeo,"* is a combination of two words, *"meta"* and *"noeo."* On the one hand, *"meta"* means, *"after, with, around."* On the other hand, *"noeo"* literally means *"to direct one's mind to a subject."* However, in classical Greek, *"noeo"* means, *"to perceive,"* or, *"to notice."* When combined, *"metanoeo"* literally means *"after directing one's mind to a subject."* To the Greeks this word meant, *"to change one's mind or adopt another view after recognizing an error."* It is a term that was used to describe regret because of the fact that one has been caught. In other words, you are sorry, or have a change of mind after a sinful act has been committed, not because of the act itself but because you were not careful enough and you have been caught. You therefore are sorry for yourself because you were not smart enough in the execution of your plans. The third word is *Metanoia*. It is what is described in 2 Corinthians 7:10 and Psalm 51:17.[27] This word means a real change of heart, mind, and attitude. It also means to hate sin and to admit one's own guilt with no excuse. The word, *"metanoia,"* comprehends the terribleness of sin, but also quickly recognizes the great mercy and compassion of God. In the case of the children of Israel in Judges 10:10, it is safe to say that they initially experienced *"metamelmai"* and *"Metanoeo"* (regret or remorse with no change of heart and for having been caught).

Their regret was simply remorse over the consequences of their actions but not for having done or allowed the act itself to occur. Their regret touched their emotions but did little or nothing to their conscience or new man (spirit man). I think that it is for this reason that God responded in a way that could be considered to be "sarcastic" when He said to them: "Go and cry out to the gods you have chosen. Let them save you when you are in trouble!"[28] In verse 15 however, we see a shift to *"metanoia"* (true repentance – a change of heart, mind, and attitude). True repentance, therefore, involves asking God for forgiveness and deciding not to ever repeat the act. What I love most about His Excellency, our Lord God, is when we come to Him and ask for forgiveness, He not only forgives us but also gives us the ability we need not to sin again.[29]

Sometimes I wonder, though, if my obedience to God is based on convenience instead of commitment, on blessings instead of the fear of being cursed, on riches because of the fear of not wanting to be poor, on healing because I don't want to experience sickness, on heaven because I don't want to go to hell. Have you ever thought about that? I have also wondered at times if my "repentance" is because I am experiencing the consequences of my action and would like God to intervene instead of my being truly sorry for having committed an ungodly act in the first

27   (2 Corinthians 7:10) "Godly sorrow brings repentance that leads to salvation and leaves no regret, but worldly sorrow brings death" (Psalm 51:17). "The sacrifices of God are a broken spirit; a broken and contrite heart, O God, you will not despise."

28   Judges 10:14

29   Romans 6:12-14

place. I sincerely hope that my act of repentance is genuine and honest and not based on what God can do for me or on how He can get me out of a tough situation that I have gotten myself into as a result of my sin. I hope that my repentance is because I am truly sorry and would like to restore my relationship with Him, while at the same time, being willing and ready to bear the consequences of my action. When that happens, God is ready to change my mess, no matter how bad it is, into a message. That is what He did again for the Israelites. When they cried to him in genuine repentance, He decided to send them a leader. In my opinion, this is someone that no one would have turned to under normal circumstances to be their leader. Fortunately, God uses abnormal circumstances to raise up abnormal leaders in order for Him to receive abnormal praises. He always has a plan and a strange way of redeeming us even when we are walking in rebellion. He always wants to turn our mess into a message. This is why He chose a man (in this case) whose life was a mess from birth and turned it around for His glory but….

The man chosen by God to deliver the children of Israel was called Jephthah. His name in Hebrew means, *"God opens."* I'd like to call him, "the loser who became a winner and went back to being a loser." He did not go to the best of schools like Moses. He did not have the strength of Sampson. He did not have the wisdom of Solomon, nor did he have the political clout, tenacity, leadership ability, and craftsmanship like Nehemiah, and he certainly did not have the anointing of God like Elijah. Anyone reading the story for the first time might start scratching the back of his or her head in an effort to figure out what is going on and why Jephthah was selected as a judge and military leader of Israel. I think his less-than-stellar qualifications perhaps reflect the infidelity of Israel and the love of God that is poured upon us irrespective of who we are. Inasmuch as Jephthah may not have been the man I would have chosen for the job (and I am sure that he might not have been yours as well), I thank God that He is no respecter of persons. You may recall that Peter, one of the disciples of our Lord Jesus Christ, was a simple fisherman with a mouth that was sometimes difficult to control. He had little or no education and a reputation for being so talkative that he sometimes said things that he later regretted. In spite of his poor track record with Jesus and the other disciples and the fact that he had denied the Lord three times, God nevertheless chose him to preach the inaugural sermon when the Church was first launched in the book of Acts. On the first day when he preached, approximately 3,000 persons came to the saving knowledge of our Lord. It is, therefore, evident that God's desire to use us is not dependent on our education, social upbringing, political affiliation, sex, marital status, or country of origin. It is based on our willingness to yield to His Lordship and to be used as vessels of honor. It is for this reason that we have Jephthah, a loser who became a winner and ...

In life, some people become "losers" because of a simple mistake or an opportunity that was missed. Other times, people become losers as a result of a series of misfortunes or mishaps that lead one down the road to "loser's street." Many Americans would agree that the late Senator Ted Kennedy would have been an excellent President of the United States. He was called the "Finest and best US Senator in modern history" by world leaders when he died. His love for his country coupled with his leadership skills, abilities, and vision to work across the aisle to pass legislation on health care reform, equal rights for minorities, immigration reform, etc., and to carry out the legacy of his brother, John F. Kennedy, may have made him the best president that America never had. His failure to ascend to the presidency, I believe like many Americans do, was based on one simple mistake that he made earlier in his life and political career. In the Commonwealth vs Edward M. Kennedy trial, we read:

"This complaint charges that Edward M. Kennedy of Boston, Mass., on the 19th day of July, 1969, at Edgartown, did operate a certain motor vehicle upon a public way in said Edgartown and did go away after knowingly causing injury to Mary Jo Kopechne without stopping and making known his name, residence and the number of his motor vehicle.[30]

> That incident changed his life for the better or worse (depending on your view). However, one thing is indisputable: It destroyed his chances of leading this nation and he regretted it until his death. One unfortunate mistake, one error, and....

That was not the case with Jephthah. He did not have just one strike against him. He had many things against him that made him an unfit candidate (some he probably brought upon himself while others were caused by his parents). In many of our lives, there are things we or our parents did that caused others to believe we couldn't be trusted with certain responsibilities or positions, whether in society or the church. Thank God that He does not look at things the way humans do. In 1 Samuel 16:7 we

30   "Grief, Fear, Doubt, Panic – And Guilt," *NEWSWEEK*, from the magazine issue dated Aug 4, 1969.

read, "But the LORD said to Samuel, 'Do not consider his appearance or his height, for I have rejected him. The LORD does not look at the things man looks at. Man looks at the outward appearance, but the LORD looks at the heart.'"

There are a few things that made Jephthah an unfit candidate in man's eyes for the job that he had to perform. This was indeed the highest office in the land and therefore, the best candidate was required to fill this position. It doesn't appear as if Jephthah was the best candidate and yet, he got the job. We will certainly find out why later, but before then, let's examine a few reasons why he was not the best candidate for such a high office.

The first reason was that Jepthah was an illegitimate son of Gilead. In Judges 11:1, we read that Jephthah, the Gileadite, was a mighty warrior. His father was Gilead and his mother was a prostitute (a harlot) whose name was not even mentioned in Scripture. Notice that Gilead was also the name of the city or district in which Jephthah was born. Let me ask a question that you have probably already thought about. Given the fact that his mother was a prostitute, is it possible that Jephthah's father was unknown and that is the reason he was referred to as "the son of Gilead"? In other words, any male of Gilead who visited that prostitute could have been his father. This was quite possible since she had slept with many men in Gilead. If this is true, think about the shame, embarrassment, and mockery that Jephthah had to endure daily as he grew up.

I must admit that there is a problem with the theory mentioned above because the Bible describes his brothers as sons of the same man by his lawful wife, driving him from home because they did not want him to share in their inheritance. Some biblical scholars may still argue that there is a possibility that an elder of Gilead took him in and adopted him as a son and tried to raise him as his own son in order to cover his shame. I cannot quantify enough biblical evidence to support this rationale; therefore let's operate under the assumption that his actual father was called Gilead. It still does not change his situation, because there is no other way to explain who his mother was except that the Bible says that she was a harlot. If we want to be generous, we could try to beautify her lifestyle by saying that Jephthah's mother was an innkeeper, but that generosity, interpretation, or translation cannot be easily reconciled with the harsh reality of his rejection and ostracism by his half-brothers who called his mother "that other woman." She was more likely a Canaanite prostitute who had an extramarital affair with Gilead. It was probably an affair that surprised and angered the entire family. It brought disgrace and reproach to the family and perhaps brought into question their reputation in the community. When the child was conceived, it is possible that Gilead tried to hide it from his family for a long time, but news broke within the community and he had to admit that he had hurt his family and had to ask for forgiveness. As was expected, the child was brought into the home but to the dislike of the other children and their mother. He was an illegitimate son, and his siblings were determined to remind him of who he was and to ensure that he did not participate in their family's inheritance. Thank God that though we, as Gentiles, were once considered "illegitimate" by the Jews, God, in His wisdom, still had a plan and a purpose for our lives. The fact that anyone is born in or out of wedlock does not influence God's love for him or her. His love is unconditional!

The second reason that made Jephthah unfit to occupy this high office was that he was *"a child of shame."* His father had chosen to break his marital vow and defile the marriage bed. He was a disgrace to his family, had shown a lack of respect and decency for his marriage, and demonstrated an unholy attitude, not just against God's Word, but against his own body. Jephthah's mother was no better. She was a professional outcast who was considered ceremonially unclean, spiritually bankrupt, emotionally unbalanced, and socially inept. Consequently, as Jephthah grew he started to notice the strange ways people treated him, the names he was being called and the anger expressed toward him from members of his own family. He could not understand why ugly names were flung at him before he was old enough to know their dark and sinister meanings. Later he realized that because he was a child of shame, no one wanted to be associated with him!

The concept of *"shame"* might be difficult for some of us to understand because many of the cultures in the Western World are based on guilt and the concept of *"being innocent until proven guilty."* A *"guilt culture"* gives the one being accused an opportunity to protest his or her innocence and fight the accusation leveled against him or her. But, in a *"shame culture,"* the rules of the game are different. If someone is being accused of an act or crime, whether he is guilty or not, he is shamed and dishonored because of the belief of others. Proving that you are not guilty is not a huge deal. The fact that you were accused and others believed that you directly or indirectly contributed to the act is what matters, and you are, therefore, dishonored. Because shame is about who you are (the perception you have about yourself and how others feel about you) it is much more intolerable than guilt, which is about what you have done. In the case of Jephthah, he was not guilty of any wrongdoing, but his parents' act had brought disgrace on him and the family and, therefore, he was unworthy, unholy, unfit, and ultimately condemned. Isn't it mindboggling how Yahweh is able to wash away our ancestors' sins and set us loose from our past if we come to Him and ask Him to do that for us?

The third reason why Jephthah was probably not the right candidate to fill this position was because he was a man with an improper pedigree. A pedigree is a chart of an individual's ancestors used in human genetics to analyze Mendelian inheritance of certain traits, especially of familial diseases.[31] In order for Jephthah to become a judge in Israel, he was expected to meet certain qualifications. A judge in Israel was not simply someone who led the people of God during times of war or chaos. A judge was also expected to be spiritually sound, intellectually balanced, and endowed with good moral values and judgments. These virtues were expected to be passed on primarily from parents to children in accordance to the *"Shema"* found in Deuteronomy 6:4-9. The child of a prostitute certainly did not fit the description of someone whose life was without moral flaws and who could receive the right teachings and training from his parents based on the Holy Scripture. He was conceived out of wedlock and in sin. His pedigree was stained. From a moral standpoint, one could easily argue that if a child of a prostitute is permitted to lead Israel, sooner or later, it would lend a level of respectability to this "profession" that was spiritually and morally wrong. Some may have feared that if he had been permitted to lead Israel, the stigma placed on prostitution or soliciting prostitutes might be lost, because it would appear that if the son of a prostitute can become judge, then it is not a bad profession after all. Isn't it interesting how God can ignore all the criteria others use to devalue us and by the "stroke of His pen," erase our past and give us hope for a better tomorrow?

Maybe you feel that your background disqualifies you from God turning your mess into a message. Whenever the enemy brings this lie to your mind, please remind him about Jephthah and even the Apostle Paul. For the Apostle, whose original name was Saul, his mess was turned into a message on the road to Damascus while traveling between engagements as an agent of Satan, persecuting and imprisoning Christians. If God would do it for someone who was persecuting Christians, he can do it for you!

---

31   Pedigree. (n.d.). *The American Heritage® Dictionary of the English Language, Fourth Edition*. Retrieved November 02, 2009, from Dictionary.com website: http://dictionary.reference.com/browse/pedigree

The fourth and final reason for which I think that Jephthah was not the right man for the job was because he had not received sufficient preparation. In Judges 11:3 we read, "So Jephthah fled from his brothers and settled in the land of Tob, where a group of adventurers gathered around him and followed him." We previously explained that in verse 2, Jephthah was shunned by his siblings and had to leave his house so young. Consequently, he probably didn't have the opportunity to acquire the skills, training, and techniques needed to move up in social circles and eventually position himself as a leader of his people. He apparently didn't have any genuine military experience. Rather, he seemed to have acquired his training from the street. Using today's terms, we would probably say that he had learned to be "street smart."

Here then we have a man who was least fit to become judge of Israel during this time of great turmoil because he was an illegitimate son of Gilead, a child of shame, a man with an improper pedigree, and a man with insufficient preparation. In spite of all these flaws, God looked at him and said, "That's the guy I pick," and in verse 29 it says that the Spirit of the Lord came upon Jephthah.

It may interest you to know when the Spirit of God came over someone in the Old Testament, it was to empower that individual to perform a specific task usually associated with battle. Examples can be found in 1 Samuel 11:6; 2 Chronicles 24:20; 1 Chronicles 12:18; 1 Samuel 10:10; and Judges 14:6, 19, etc., and when that happened, the Spirit of God usually removed his or her personal inadequacies in order for that individual to be able to fulfill God's plan.

Think with me for a moment! Many people, including you yourself, might be unlikely candidates to become heroes in the Lord's army, unlikely people that God would use to militarily defeat other nations. In fact, your improper pedigree might confirm that you are not from the lineage of military warriors. Or, your family might not be a "ministerial family." Worse still, you may not come from a Christian family at all. Perhaps you're a new Christian who came from another religion. You might be thinking that the Lord couldn't or wouldn't want to use you, not when there are so many more obvious choices. How wrong that perception is! God chooses people like the Prophet Amos who said, "I was neither a prophet nor a prophet's son, but I was a shepherd and I also took care of sycamore-fig trees."[32] Amos continues, "The LORD took me from tending the flock and said to me, 'Go, prophesy to my people Israel.'" This is exactly

---

32   Amos 7:14

what Amos did and his message touched the hearts of God's people. The point that I am making is that having an excellent résumé can be very helpful in many instances, but God does not need one in order to use you for His purposes and turn your mess into a message. Jephthah is not the only one whose life God supernaturally transformed and turned into a warrior for His glory. He did the same for Gideon in the book of Judges. God found Gideon in a hole in the ground, hiding his wheat from the enemy, and the angel of the Lord addressed him (the apparent coward) as "mighty warrior." The heart of the matter is that God uses whoever He wishes for whatever He wishes to accomplish. He is not concerned about our inadequacies, because as the Scripture says, "His power is made complete in our weakness."[33] The only reason why God wouldn't use you is if you don't want to be used by Him.

Jephthah had all odds against him. He was rejected by his siblings, despised by the elders of Gilead, and had to find a place where he felt safe. Sometimes in life, when things are against us, and people despise us, we need to get away and find a safe place. We might not necessarily be running away from the problem, but there comes a time when we need to find a safe place to sort things out, to ask ourselves some hard questions, to wrestle with God, to refocus and put things in perspective. Hence, Jephthah ran to live in the land of Tob (east of the Jordan). What is interesting and probably ironic about the word, Tob, is that it meant *"good."* In spite of the meaning of its name, this place was inhabited by bandits, hooligans, and worthless men who banded together with Jephthah and went raiding with him. Though the name of the place meant *"good,"* its name did not guarantee the character of those who lived there. This means that living in a *"good place"* may not necessarily ensure that you will become a good person or that you will be successful in life. More is expected or required in order for you to achieve your God-given vision and goals.

Personally, I believe that Jephthah had to evaluate his situation and his environment and make the best out of it. He had some hard decisions to make. One of the many questions he probably asked himself was, "What do I do when all odds are against me?"

In life, there are usually three groups of people. There are the accusers, the excusers, and the choosers. The first group of people (the accusers), are those who accuse us of something wrong that we might or might not have done. The Bible describes Satan as the accuser of the brothers.[34]

33   2 Corinthians 12:9
34   Revelation 12:10

Unfortunately, Satan is not the only one accusing us before the throne of God. Believers and non-believers constantly accuse us whether we have committed a wrongful act or not. They don't accuse us before the throne of God, but rather accuse us daily to others here on earth. The second group (the excusers), are those who excuse themselves from anything and everything that has gone wrong. They simply refuse to take responsibility for their mistakes or the role they played in bringing about an unfortunate situation. They prefer to blame the world for all of their challenges and behave as if they could not have averted the unfortunate situation. Finally, the third group of people (the choosers), are those who see their situation, the role that they and others have played, and yet choose to take control of their situation so that with the help of God, they will implement the necessary changes in order to alter their destiny. Jephthah refused to be an accuser who excused himself and only blamed others for his misfortune. He knew that if God would intervene in his situation and change his mess into a message, he would have to become a chooser, one who sees what others have done and still believes that with God's help, he has the potential to change the course of his life.

After serious contemplation he counseled himself, "I have a few options: I can give up or get up; get an attitude or get some altitude; isolate myself or associate with others; feel like a victim or become a victor." It became clear to him that he had to decide to become a chooser because his destiny was on the line. He could either sit and enter into deep depression and blame the world for his problem, or seek the help of those around him to do what he felt was good for himself, those associated with him and for the people that had rejected them (Israel). As he continued to analyze his situation, perhaps the Spirit of God reminded him of some positive things he had in his favor. I can hear him singing, "Count your blessings, name them one by one…" He remembered someone saying to him that he would make an excellent leader one day because of the leadership skills that he had exhibited. He also remembered that he was a very persuasive individual and commanded the respect of his peers. Finally, he remembered that he was strong and could fight like a gallant soldier. As if a light bulb was turned on in his head, he said to himself, "I can organize, direct, empower, persuade, and command this little group of hooligans and redirect their energy for our greater good and survival." Wow! This would become his new mission and vision.

Kicked out of home, separated from family and from his countrymen, Jephthah had to fend for himself. Other roughnecks, probably outcasts as well, heard about him and his small group of men and sauntered out to the wilderness, to the land of Tob, to hang out with them. As the group grew larger, Jephthah immediately embarked on the task of organizing the men and helping these men in the land of Tob to understand that Israel was not their real enemy even though they had been rejected by Israel. Gradually, his skills, persuasion, tactics, strength, endurance, and dedication began to pay off. A kind of gang developed and Jephthah became the leader of this band of hoodlums. The Hebrew word that is used is *"qyr"* (rake). It means *"poor, or someone without property."* Most scholars have treated them as plunderers who raided the territory of Israel's enemies and carried off their stolen goods. Interestingly, this is the same thing that David did when he was driven away by Saul who sought to kill him. Though he had been rebuffed by his people, Jephthah surprisingly defended and averted attacks on Gilead by attacking their enemies. This was not an honorable thing to do, but at least one could argue that it was a means of survival and the children of Israel were not being attacked by their own countrymen. In other words, Jephthah led a group of raiders and his adventures could be compared to Robin Hood who lived in Greenwood with Little John, Maid Marian and the Sheriff of Nottingham.[35] Jephthah and his men were basically land-based pirates, traveling around stealing, bullying people and making life miserable for the rich, like Robin Hood and his merry men except that they were probably not giving things to the poor as Robin Hood did. You would agree that this was not the type of military training needed to head a country's army and it certainly made Jephthah an unlikely candidate (in the eyes of man) to become a judge of Israel. He wouldn't have received a security clearance under normal circumstances because, as a roving plunderer, he had broken all the laws in the book. Therefore, the issue of becoming the head of the country's army and leading the entire nation was out of the question. Here is evidence that God uses abnormal situations to develop abnormal individuals for abnormal missions. God can use our worst and weakest attributes to develop us into the individuals that will bring Him glory!

Allow me to add one more comment which will help you to view Jephthah in a more favorable light. Jephthah was convinced the territories he was raiding actually belonged to Israel but had been occupied by intruders and invaders. Thus, he was only taking possession of what rightfully belonged to Israel in the first place but had been seized by their

---

35   Marshall, Henrietta Elizabeth. *Stories of Robin Hood Told to the Children.* Chapel Hill, North Carolina: Yesterday's Classics, 2005.

enemies because of a lack of strong leadership in Israel. Jephthah knew that he couldn't just sit and give up when he was faced with this challenge. He made himself resourceful and made the best of his situation. It means that while I wait for the Lord to turn my mess into a message, I need to find something that my hands can do and then do it to the best of my ability. Don't get me wrong! I am not advocating that you do anything illegal or destructive. I am simply saying that while I await my miracle, I need to direct my energy into accomplishing something positive and useful. In other words, I need to occupy my time constructively. I need to ask God for direction to do something meaningful with my life while I await His promise and redemption. It also means that I need to realize that whenever my back is pressed against the wall, God will always have another route of escape for me to use. There is always another door that is opened or will be opened by the Lord. My job is to prayerfully find that door that leads to my redemption. Jephthah, as already mentioned, means, *"God opens", "an opening",* or *"an opportunity."* Jephthah looked for an opportunity to make his life better and basically said, "If they will sit and fight over whether I am a legitimate child or over a few pieces of furniture, then I will possess the goods of the lands that rightfully belong to Israel and partake of it."

He therefore decided to become Gilead's daring mountaineer who had nothing to lose but all to gain. He basically rediscovered himself and found a reason to live, a way to make money, an opportunity to provide for himself and his compatriots. Jephthah became so successful that no one could ignore him and his group. At first, I am sure that the inhabitants of Gilead tried to dismiss the stories of successful raids that they heard about from foreigners who managed to escape the assault of Jephthah and his men. However, as the stories became more and more frequent and the victories and bravery of his men became legendary, the elders of Gilead could no longer ignore them. As a result, the very elders who caused Jephthah to be displaced decided to call upon him to come to their rescue. When they were threatened with total annihilation they considered Jephthah to be a legitimate son of Gilead after all, and they formed a delegation to seek his help.

When we listen to God and submit to His plan for our lives, He has a way of lifting us up. No one can destroy what God has placed in you. You may be relocated, resigned, mistreated, insulted, overlooked, and redirected, but what God has placed in you will resurface at the appropriate time to His glory. Joseph, the dreamer, was placed in the pit and then in prison but none of those places could hold him down. He was a dreamer.

He was destined for greatness. It had been written by the hands of God Almighty and nothing could change his destiny. The same is true about you. The enemy could try to delay your future but he is simply wasting his time. He is late! God has already deposited the seed in you and nothing can stop you! Not even the greatest demon in the pit of hell. It happened to Jephthah and it will happen to you!

It is quite interesting how God can transform a hopeless individual into someone others trust for guidance, direction and protection. Jephthah's fame had grown as a result of his skill, expertise, and leadership in organizing a band of warriors (fellow outcasts and misfits), and now he had became the only hope of Israel to stop the Ammonites' invasion. In their desperation, the elders of Gilead decided to look for and negotiate with Jephthah.

When God is ready to turn your mess into a message, people who have neglected, despised, spoken against, insulted, mistreated, and sought your downfall will come to look for you to ask for your help. They will come to you to seek counsel, guidance, advice, and consolation. You, the rejected stone, will become the cornerstone. You need to know that and prepare yourself for what the Lord is about to do in your life. The time will come when those who have walked on you will come running to you, and bow before you. They will see the manifestation of God's glory in your life and will want to be associated with you. They will want to be your friend and will expect you to respond favorably to their requests. I hope that when you find yourself in that situation, you will be able to reach out to them and say like Joseph, "You intended to harm me, but God intended it for good to accomplish what is now being done, the saving of many lives."[36]

As the elders of Gilead entered the woods to find Jephthah, he saw them from a distance and wondered why they were looking for him. It goes without saying that the elders of Gilead were fearful that Jephthah's men would attack them, so in anticipation of a conflict or battle, they might have raised white cloths as a symbol of peace and reconciliation as they approached Jephthah's men. As they drew closer and Jephthah was able to recognize them, he probably thought to himself, "What in the world do they want?"

He became even more perplexed when they raised their hands in a gesture of peace and pleading. "Please, come help us! Please be our commander! The Ammonites are unbearable! They have destroyed our towns! Please, can you help us?"

---

36   Genesis 50:20

Jephthah probably could not believe his ears. He might have felt his ears were playing tricks on him or that this was the Israelites' trap to capture him after all of their earlier failed attempts. However, something within him caused him to believe that this was a genuine plea. There may have been rumors circulating that an attack from the Ammonites was imminent. What should he do? How should he respond? Should he kill the elders of Gilead for having caused him to live a miserable life all these years? Were they not the same ones who drove him from his father's house and took away his inheritance?

How would you have reacted? Have you been hurt by someone who later came to ask forgiveness? Did you give that individual a second chance to redeem himself and be restored to trust and friendship? How did you receive him when he came back to ask for forgiveness? Jephthah had a choice to make just as we have a choice to make regarding those who have hurt us. He could have decided to release his anger and attack them or sit with them to listen and find a way out of the predicament. Thankfully he chose the latter. If you were in his situation, what would you have done? What do you do when those who have hurt you come to ask for your forgiveness? Do you listen and forgive or do you turn them away, refusing to talk to them?

It is worth noting as well that Jephthah found himself in a situation where he could not run away from his past. Running away is not always the best option. Some issues have to be confronted in order for a solution to be found. He needed to resolve this conflict that had haunted him for years. In fact, I would say that he had to confront this issue in order for his mess to be turned into a message. Many times we run away from our past. We make excuses not to confront it because we are afraid, do not want the situation to become worse, or simply don't want to be reminded of the past frustration, disappointment, hurt, and heartache we experienced. Whether we like it or not, there are some situations we need to confront in order to be propelled into our destiny. Some conversations are difficult to have but have them we must.

Jephthah was forced to confront the elders, remind them of the treatment he had received, and be assured that they would not bring up his past ever again after he led them to victory. It was a tough discussion but one that was necessary. If you refuse to confront key issues in your past, your destiny could be severely hindered or you could be used as a "spare tire" for the one who thinks you are not the real thing but will only suffice until the "real thing" becomes available. In other words, others, on the one hand, will not recognize the potential and high calling God has placed in you if you, on the other hand, have not acknowledged and appreciated God's gifts and abilities He has given to you. What you need to do is to first ask God to open your eyes to see what He has placed in you. Second, ask Him for wisdom to deal with issues of importance that have the propensity to slow down, derail, obstruct, impede or thwart your destiny.

What is crucial to understand is that there will always be misunderstanding, disappointments, and hurt. Conflict is a part of life and can't be always avoided. There are certain things that cannot be totally eradicated because we live in a fallen world. Conflict is certainly one of them. That is why the goal of conflict resolution is to try to manage conflict when it arises in order to minimize the impact or negative consequences it could possibly have on the parties concerned. This means that all conflicts cannot simply be ignored. Some must be faced and a solution sought. It is for this reason that experts on conflict resolution usually encourage communication and dialogue as key components in resolving conflict.

There are two major roadblocks to conflict resolution. These can become powerful obstructions in our lives and severely hinder us from reaching across the aisle to seek resolution, no matter how little or big the problem is that needs to be reconciled. You may be asking yourself if it is necessary to seek reconciliation in every situation. I am not sure if I can honestly say yes. However, when faced with that question as a Christian, always remember Romans 12:18, "If it is possible, as far as it depends on you, live at peace with everyone."

If you are wrestling with what has been stated above, it would help you to know the first roadblock to conflict resolution is our attitude. In order to effectively resolve a conflict, we need to have a Christ-like attitude of humility and servanthood. Paul, in his writing to the church in Philippi, says, "Do nothing out of selfish ambition or vain conceit, but in humility consider others better than yourselves."[37] Those are very strong words. Wouldn't you agree? Our attitudes can be severely affected if we're holding onto unresolved anger and resentment. If we have not forgiven others or even ourselves for what happened in our lives, we might find it difficult to have an open, caring attitude that is needed for genuine conflict resolution to take place. Additionally, when we have a negative attitude, we become susceptible to the enemy who could influence us and hinder our desire to reconcile with a brother or sister in accordance to the will of God.

The second roadblock to conflict resolution is the lack of communication

---

37   Philippians 2:3

skills. Possessing good communication skills permits the expression of one's thoughts and feelings in a way that is clear, precise, and respectful. The goal in conflict resolution is to know the thoughts, feelings, and desires of the sister or brother with whom you are having a challenge and communicate yours with the aim of finding a suitable compromise. As is usually said, "It is okay to agree that you disagree." Disagreeing doesn't warrant fighting or killing each other.

Usually when the issue of conflict resolution is being discussed, one of the first questions that is asked is, "Can I forgive and not forget?" Some believers even ask, "Can I forgive and move on but not want the relationship to be the same way it was in the past?" I believe the answer can be in the affirmative for those two questions. However, without any doubt in my heart, I must say you are the only one who could genuinely answer those questions for yourself based on your relationship with Christ, your willingness to submit to the leading of the Holy Spirit, and your desire to live at peace with others. I certainly don't want to belittle the matter being discussed, but the simple, yet profound answer would be for you to ask yourself, "If Christ was in this situation, what would He do?" Give some serious prayerful thought to it and then act based on the leading of the Holy Spirit.

Jephthah had to remove those two roadblocks in conflict resolution in order to deal with the situation with which he was confronted. He had to make sure that he possessed the right attitude and he needed to communicate effectively in order to resolve the conflict. He probably knew the elders had tried to find someone else to lead Gilead into battle against the Ammonites but did not succeed. The Bible says (before they headed into the woods to find Jephthah), "The leaders of the people of Gilead said to each other, 'whoever will launch the attack against the Ammonites will be the head of all those living in Gilead.'"[38] Apparently no one came forward to lead them in battle. Hence, the elders had to humble themselves and come to ask Jephthah to take over, or at least to try and drive out the Ammonites. As they approached, we read in Judges 11:7, "And Jephthah said unto the elders of Gilead, 'Didn't you hate me, and drive me out of my father's house? Why are you coming to me now when you are in trouble?'" Jephthah was simply using some of the tools in effective conflict resolution. His goal was to first know their thoughts, feelings, and desires. However, when you listen to the question he asks, don't you hear some kind of cynicism in his voice?

---

38   Judges 10:18

He might have been thinking, "Why have you come to a boy you once rejected? Why did you come to someone you labeled as an outcast? Why did you come to be rescued when you refused to rescue me at the time I needed you most? You look so pathetic with your heads covered with shame and disgrace!"

If you were in that situation, wouldn't you have thought the same way? That would be our natural reaction, wouldn't it? The elders seemed to deserve what was being said about them, right?

Before we go off passing more judgment on the elders of Gilead, let's examine ourselves a little bit. Have you ever done something like that to anyone or to the church? Don't we sometimes go off on our own when things are going well, when we feel that we don't need them or the church again? But when we encountered a roadblock, didn't some of us come back to God and His Church with lame excuses while others returned to Him and His Church with repentant hearts? Have any of us abandoned our children or friends during their most vulnerable hours and later, when we were going through a trial expected them to show us the mercy we did not show them? You have probably never treated anyone that unfairly, but perhaps someone acted this way toward you or to another person you care about deeply.

Jephthah had the choice to forgive and move forward or to hold a grudge. The elders had acknowledged their mistakes, probably asked for forgiveness, and were pleading for his help. I am sure that one of the elders in the crowd pleaded when Jephthah started to question and to remind them of the ill-treatment he had received, "Mercy, son, Mercy!" Jephthah might have swallowed slowly, suppressing a smirk. Old memories probably flooded through his brain. He had to choke that flood of emotion and to quickly get his feelings under control. After all, a commander cannot be a weakling. He couldn't afford to laugh at them, for it would be disrespectful. At the same time, he couldn't afford to cry now as it would be interpreted that he is weak and thus unfit for the job. He would have sufficient time to express his emotion but now was a time to negotiate and set the rules of the game! He had heard their thoughts, feeling, and desires. Now it was time for him to communicate his thoughts, feeling, and desires to them in a respectful yet, clear and precise manner.

God had finally given Jephthah the opportunity to express himself to those who had hurt him. He never thought this day would ever come. As he looked on, he couldn't help but say, "This is the Lord's doing and it is marvelous!" Deep inside, he could feel the stir of joy, peace, vindication, pride, and restoration. When the Lord restores and vindicates, He does it without any strings attached. In fact, He has a way of putting you in the "driver's seat," thus enabling and empowering you to dictate the terms of the conflict resolution and or negotiation. Jephthah the Hopeless had now become the hope of Gilead. Jephthah the Castaway had now become the desired. Jephthah the Outlaw was now being asked to become the judge and keeper of the law. Jephthah, the one who could not partake in the possession of his father's household because he was the son of a harlot, was now being asked to be the chief steward of all of Israel's possessions.

According to Judges 11:11, the negotiation ended with the elders covenanting with Jephthah in the name of the LORD. Jephthah and the elders walked from Tob back to Gilead where a meeting was arranged in Mizpeh. Before an entire assembly called out to witness this occasion, the elders confirmed that Jephthah was Chief Governor over the tribes east of the Jordan. They stood in a solemn assembly before the Lord as Jephthah took the oath of office before the Lord.

Notice how God unfolded this story and gave it a wonderful conclusion: Jephthah regained the respect of his family, his mother's past life of sin and disgrace was redeemed, and his "slate was wiped clean." God had turned his mess into a message. Imagine what was being said by his siblings. Imagine the surprise on the faces of those who were his most vocal critics.

They were probably saying, "This must be a mistake! We can't believe what we are hearing and seeing!"

Some of them may have thought of fleeing into the forest for their lives, thinking that he would have killed them for the pain they had caused him. But that was not his intention. God had used their evil plan to prepare him for such a time and had anointed him to be the battle axe against the Ammonites.

What is important to underline at this point is that even though God had placed Jephthah in the driver's seat, he had to learn to heal the pain of the past. He had to confront it by talking about it. He had to release those who had hated him. He had to love them and talk with them. He had to allow God to work in and through him for His glory. It is extremely necessary for us to understand that we don't have to let our past weigh us down. The author of Hebrews encourages believers saying, "Therefore, since we are surrounded by such a great cloud of witnesses, let us throw off everything that hinders and the sin that so easily entangles, and let us run with perseverance the race marked out for us" (12:1). God will not turn your mess into a message if you have an unforgiving heart, if you refuse to let go and let God take over, if you refuse to pray for your enemies, or if you refuse to throw off everything that hinders or entangles you. You might be saying, "But you don't understand what was done to me." Indeed, you are right. I don't, and probably would never understand, not because I don't care but simply because there are some things that others will never understand about us. However, I must submit to you that if you believe in the Bible, then you must also believe that some things that the devil meant for your destruction, God has a way of turning around for your good as in the case of Joseph and his brothers. God turned Joseph's mess into a message only after he was willing to forgive and love his brothers who sold him into slavery. Have you been sold? Think for a minute about what it means to be sold? Have you been rejected? Have you been disgraced? Have you been falsely accused and maligned by those who claim to love you? God is able to heal the wound if you will only allow him! Yes, He can do it!

Jephthah's first task as Commander of the Army and Judge of Israel was to resolve the military quandary between the Gileadites and Ammonites. Indeed that was the primary reason for which he had been selected as the leader of Gilead, wasn't it? It would have, therefore, been expected that Jephthah would quickly begin to gather his men for battle in order to prove that he was able to meet the challenge at hand and successfully defeat the enemy. What is odd is that he does not immediately storm into battle. He first and foremost attempts to find a diplomatic solution by negotiating with the Ammonite king. To his credit, he tries to resolve the conflict without bloodshed. His line of reasoning is recorded in Judges 11:14-27. The inhabitants of Canaan regarded the Jews as invaders, and Jephthah uses this opportunity to explain the legitimate claim and divine right of Israel to possess the land. By trying to negotiate with the Ammonite king, Jephthah extends to him an opportunity to yield to God's will before force is used. I don't think that Jephthah was afraid to confront the enemy militarily, but he sought to avoid an unnecessary war and bloodshed.

Do you think that the way Jephthah had been treated had anything to do with the method he employed? Is it possible that he felt that he was never given a fair chance to be heard? Perhaps if the elders of Gilead had treated him in a more reasonable and respectful way, he would not have been driven out of Gilead in the first place, and consequently, would not have had to endure such hardship. I am not sure why but somehow, it is interesting to see that Jephthah decided to reason with the Ammonites before going to war. It showed his strength, leadership skill, and how God had prepared him to lead. Unfortunately, the Ammonite king rejected Jephthah's reasoning, so both sides prepared for battle.

We're told in Judges 11:29 that, "The Spirit of the Lord came upon Jephthah." He had been anointed and empowered by God for the task before him. It is evident that the battle had already been won by Yahweh and Jephthah was simply a tool that God was going to use to manifest His glory as a "God of War." It is, therefore, puzzling to read in verses 30-31 that he makes a vow to God saying, "If you give the Ammonites into my hands, whatever comes out of the door of my house to meet me when I return in triumph from the Ammonites will be the Lord's and I will sacrifice it as a burnt offering." Oh, my, why did he say that? Was he so eager for victory, or was he afraid that God wouldn't come through for him? Everything seemed to have been going so well for him until he made that unwise vow, and centuries later, it is the main thing by which he is remembered. Isn't it sad?

Vows in the Bible are not mere bargains or cheap talk without real consequences or commitment attached thereto as they are regarded in some cultures today. On the contrary, vows in Biblical times were binding obligations not to be taken lightly. They are very serious matters in Scripture. Ecclesiastes 5:5 warns, "It is better not to vow, than to make a vow and not fulfill it." Vows are oaths, pledges, obligations, even prayerful transactions between God and individuals. In the Bible, vows are not commanded, but they were tightly regulated. Once made, they were binding. As already mentioned, Jephthah didn't rashly go to war. He tried to negotiate in order to avert the destruction of innocent lives. He appeared to be someone who calculated his moves and wisely chose his words. It is precisely for this reason that his vow is puzzling and leaves one wondering why he felt that he had to make a vow of this magnitude.

Up to this point, Jephthah had trusted the Lord and exhibited excellent characteristics worth emulating. It appears that he forgave those who had mistreated him while at the same time praying for the blessing of the Lord in his endeavors. He received a special anointing of the Spirit that came only upon special people anointed by God to carry out specific tasks. Additionally, he was not eager to shed blood. Remember, he tried to resolve the dispute by sending ambassadors to Ammon. But in a moment of desperation he forgot who he was and who had called, appointed, and anointed him for the task at hand. He was probably afraid and wanted an assured victory.

It certainly would be very easy for us to condemn Jephthah and say that he made an irrational, solemn, and tragic vow. Think about it, but while you are at it allow me to ask you another question. How many times have we done the same thing? Maybe not committing yourself to sacrificing a human being or an animal, of course, but how many times have you said, "Lord, if you do this, I swear, I will….." or, "Lord if you allow this to happen, I vow, I will….."

Unfortunately for Jephthah, when he returned home from defeating the Ammonites, his daughter, who was also his only child, was the first "thing" that came running out of his house to meet him. Obviously, this was not what he expected and he was devastated. Had he known, he would not have made that vow. However, it was too late and there was nothing he could do but to carry out his vow and have his daughter sacrificed.

Most church fathers and Biblical scholars up until the middle ages that I referenced while writing this book agreed that Jephthah did offer his daughter up as burnt offering. There are some modern scholars who believe that Jephthah gave his daughter to the Leviticus priests to serve in a religious vocation. There isn't much evidence from the text to support that claim though it sounds good and appealing to our culture, theology, norms, and beliefs in light of what we consider to be morally right and wrong. Let's assume for a minute that this interpretation is accurate and that Jephthah committed his daughter to a life of celibacy and of course, never to bear children. You would probably agree that this still does not make the vow any better or easier. It was still a rather tragic and illogical vow. Here are a few reasons why.

First, if he committed her to a life of celibacy, it was without her consent and certainly not his initial plan for her life. In fact, it appears from the passage that she was actually looking forward to being married because she said in Judges 11:37, "Give me two months to roam the hills and weep with my friends, because I will never marry."

Second, if she was committed to a life of celibacy, it meant that Jephthah's family would be cut off from Israel and his inheritance would eventually go to someone else since she was his only child. This is the same situation that Abraham struggled with when God told him that He would bless him. Abraham responded in Genesis 15:2, "Oh Sovereign Lord, what can you give me since I remain childless and the one who will inherit my estate is Eliezer of Damascus?" Without an heir from one's lineage, a man during the Old Testament days (and still in some cultures today) feels incomplete. Jephthah must have felt incomplete. Even worse, as evident in some cultures (especially in male dominating cultures), when a man only has female children, he feels incomplete or uncertain about his family line until he has a boy.

My culture of origin is somehow the same and I also experienced the same thing in my family. My father had nine siblings and he was the oldest. All of his sisters (which total five) gave birth to boys but he and his brothers could not give birth to boys. It became a concern in the family until my dad had me when he was 48 years old. It was for this reason that though my father's name was Joseph Howard, he named me Josef Howard. Josef in Hebrew means, *"May the Lord add another son."* Having another son was important to them in order to continue the "Howard family line." Certainly, Jepthah may have felt incomplete and knew that his name would now be wiped out of the history of Israel even after his victory in battle against the Ammonites, simply because of the fact that he did not have a son and now his only daughter would not be able to get married.

Third, if indeed Jephthah's daughter was committed to a life of celibacy, it also meant that there was no hope of the Messiah being born through his family. All of Israel looked forward to having the Christ come through their family line. Hence, this too was a huge tragedy for Jephthah.

Even if Jephthah only committed his daughter to a life of celibacy (and not imminent death), it was still a big deal. He had to live with that painful decision for the rest of his life. However, I would like to say that I don't believe this is what happened. The Bible seems to point to the fact that she was indeed offered up as a burnt sacrifice.

I am aware of the fact that saying Jephthah did sacrifice his daughter as a burnt offering sounds cruel, very primitive, inhumane, and barbaric. However, there are several things I would like for us to consider.

The first is that Jephthah had grown up in exile among the same Ammonites whose worship of Moloch regularly required human sacrifice. Hence, though he could not have imagined that it would be his daughter (only child) that would come running towards him after the victory, killing a human being in order to fulfill a religious vow was not something strange to him and the children of Israel. You may recall that though the situation and circumstances were different, Abraham, the father of our faith, was prepared to sacrifice Isaac (his only son and the son of promise) in obedience to Yahweh. God intervened through an angel and provided a sacrificial lamb.

Second, Jephthah understood the importance of keeping a vow. We read in verse 35, "When he saw her, he tore his clothes and cried, 'Oh! My daughter! You have made me miserable and wretched; because I have made a vow to the Lord that I cannot break.'" It is obvious that he was deeply sorry and regretted the vow made but he also realized that he had to fulfill the vow he made to God, even though this was his only child. He valued the sacredness of his vow more than he dreaded the deep, emotional pain of losing his daughter.

Third, we read in verse 36 of chapter 11, of his daughter's noble submission and plea for him to respect the vow he made to the Lord. She said, "...you have given your word to the Lord. Do to me just as you promised, now that the Lord has avenged you of your enemies, the Ammonites."

Fourth, verses 38-40 seem to confirm that she was sacrificed after her period of mourning when she returned from the hills. We read that "He did to her as he had vowed. And she was a virgin. From this comes the Israelite custom that each year the young women of Israel go out for four days to commemorate the daughter of Jephthah the Gileadite."

Let me quickly add that Jephthah's sacrifice of his daughter did not necessarily please the Lord. In the Book of Deuteronomy, we read of God's admonition to the children of Israel not to follow the religious practices and worship of their heathen neighbors. In Deuteronomy 12:31, God expressly forbids human sacrifice.[39] Somehow, Jephthah missed that in his desire to experience victory. Please don't get me wrong. There is nothing wrong with making a special vow unto the Lord in a crisis situation. However, to make a vow impulsively and rashly without fully evaluating the consequences is foolish and ungodly. In other words, before a vow is made, it must be fully understood and a determination made that it will be honored. In fact, I think that it is prudent for a vow to be made out of thanksgiving to the Lord and not because we want to get God to do something for us. Because "bargain vows" can be extremely dangerous Jesus gave a new command concerning vows, by saying:

> *Again, you have heard that it was said to the people long ago, "Do not break your oath, but keep the oaths you have made to the Lord." But I tell you, do not swear at all: either by heaven, for it is God's throne; or by the earth, for it is his footstool; or by Jerusalem, for it is the city of the Great King. And do not swear by your head, for you cannot make*

---

39   Deuteronomy 12:31 "You must not worship the Lord your God in their way, because in worshiping their gods, they do all kinds of detestable things the Lord hates. They even burn their sons and daughters in the fire as sacrifices to their gods."

*even one hair white or black. Simply let your "Yes" be
"Yes," and your "No," "No;" anything beyond this comes
from the evil one.*[40]

Based on the command of Christ regarding vows, we are instructed
not to make them either to the Lord or to one another. There are several
reasons why I believe the Lord gave this instruction. In the first place, we
cannot know for sure if we will be able to keep our vows or not. Some vows
are foolishly made either out of immaturity or the lack of proper guidance
while others are based on poor judgments which in part can be attributed
to our fallen nature. The second reason why we need to avoid making vows
is because we don't know the future – only God does.[41] It means that we
are not in control of our lives as we think we are. It is God Almighty who
is in control, not us, and it is He who has the ability to work everything
out for the good of those who love Him and are called according to His
purpose (Romans 8:28). Third, and finally, Jesus seems to imply that vows
are unnecessary because our words should be sufficient if we are honest and
sincere. When we say "yes" or "no," that's exactly what we should mean
and people should be able to trust us based on our testimony as children of
God who are using the Word of God and His divine principles established
therein as our standard.

It is true that we live in an era of the dispensation of God's grace,
yet we should not take His grace for granted and think that we can go
on making vows and not keeping them. God expects our "yes" to be
"yes," and our "no" to be "no." Hence, if for any reason, especially out of
ignorance, you have made a "bargain vow" that you know that you can't
keep, please take the time to confess to the Lord that you will not be able
to keep the vow you made. Ask for His forgiveness and move on. Don't
live in bondage or try to keep an unlawful vow even if it was made with
the purest motive. God is merciful and does not need our vows to turn our
mess into a message. He will do it whether we make a vow or not. In other
words, God will not hold us to vows made imprudently if we take the time
to honestly confess them and ask for His forgiveness, but He expects us to
obey Jesus and refrain from making vows in the future.

I believe also that if Jephthah had gone to God and repented of his sin,
he would not have had to keep the vow that he made to the Lord. God is
merciful and His compassion is renewed each day in our lives. Each day is

---

40   Matthew 5:33-37
41   James 4:14, "Why, you do not even know what will happen tomorrow.
What is your life? You are a mist that appears for a little while and then vanishes."

an opportunity for a fresh start. He finds no delight in seeing His children suffer in trying to keep a vow that should not have been made in the first place. I remember a story of a little boy and his sister who were living with their grandmother. One day while they were playing outside, the boy mistakenly broke their grandmother's flower vase. He was so terrified because it was very expensive and it was Grandmother's favorite flower vase. He begged his sister not to tell their grandmother. She agreed but from that point, he had to do whatever she wanted (clean her room, do her dishes, etc). Basically, she kept blackmailing him until he could not take it any more. He finally decided one day to tell Grandma what had happened. This he did and he also explained how he was truly sorry.

To his utmost astonishment his grandmother said, "I was standing at the window when you broke the vase. I saw everything. I have also been watching how your sister has been blackmailing you. I was simply waiting for you to realize that mistakes do happen and I love you more than a flower vase."

Indeed, God loves us dearly and He knows everything about us. What matters to Him most is the relationship we develop and maintain with Him. Even though He has commanded us not to make vows, He does not want a vow, foolishly made, that He knows we can't fulfill, to keep us away from His presence.

What is crucial and worth remembering is the fact that when our mess becomes a message, we need to guard it so that it doesn't become a mess again. Jephthah had trusted the Lord and God had shown Himself to be faithful. He had been restored to his family, clan, and nation and given a position that he never imagined that he could one day have. His mess of being an illegitimate child, a child of shame with improper pedigree, and insufficient preparation had been turned around by God. His messy life of rejection, hatred, anger, hopelessness, and vagrancy had been changed into a life of hope and a bright future. He now had a message! His very life was a miracle! He was an inspiration to the homeless, the unfortunate, the sinful, the disgraced, the helpless, the outcasts, the sick, the downtrodden, and the good-for-nothing. His message was that "God can make something out of nothing. God can set the captives free. God can do miracles. God can smile on you again. God can turn your mourning into laughter. God can make you want to live again. God can set your feet upon the solid rock to stay. God can do it in spite of what you or your parents have done, because He is the God of a second chance." What a message! I see him saying through my eyes of faith, "Look at me. If He could do it for me,

He can do it for you." If I were preaching a sermon, I would have added, "Can I get a witness in the house?"

What is it that you are going through that the enemy has said can't be resolved? If you put your trust in the Lord, He will see you through in spite of what others have said or what statistics have proven. Your God is a miracle-working God who will never fail and will never change. He is known to be immutable. In Malachi 3:6, we read, "I the LORD do not change. So you, O descendants of Jacob, are not destroyed." Let Him manifest Himself in your life and transform your entire life into a message of praise!

After He has done that, please don't fall into the trap of the enemy like Jephthah did. After your situation has been changed, you will become a target of the enemy. He will try to destroy your testimony like he did with Jephthah's. He will try to make you question the ability of God to do another miracle, but remember what God has done.

Do you remember the story of Jesus feeding the five thousand in Mark 6:30-44? The Bible teaches that after feeding the five thousand men, He told his disciples to go on the other side of the lake. Later that evening, after praying, He went for a "stroll on the lake." As He passed them, they thought He was a ghost. Instantly, they panicked and were terrified. Jesus immediately spoke to them and identified Himself. After entering the boat, the wind died down and they became amazed (Mark 6:45-51). What is interesting is that Mark mentions in verse 52, "For they had not understood about the loaves, their hearts were hardened." Each of the disciples had a reminder with them on the boat (a basket of leftovers) from the miracle of five loaves and two fish. After feeding the crowd, Jesus had instructed the disciples to gather the leftovers and there were 12 baskets (one for each of them to have) in order to remember the miraculous power of Jesus, but they forgot. If He had wanted them to perish, He wouldn't have fed them earlier. If He did not care about them, He wouldn't have fed them. If He did not love them, He wouldn't have met their physical needs. Now the question is: Why would He do that and then turn His back on them now? Why would He bring you this far and abandon you? Why would He give you hope and cause that very hope to be dashed in a few days or months? This is what Jephthah failed to understand. The best things in his life were yet to be experienced. God was just beginning to set him up for bigger miracles. He is about to do the same with you. A little miracle is a gateway to a bigger miracle. Capitalize on the little things that God has done. Trust Him and He will do bigger things. When your mess has been turned into a message, guard that message. Share it, praise God for it, tell the enemy what God has done and remind him that his days of pushing you around are over. That is how you keep your message from returning to a mess!

CONCLUSION

I have taken the time to write this book because I believe that it is what God wanted me to do. It has been a long, but rewarding experience. You probably have already realized that I tried to put my best into this book. I believe it will touch lives in ways that I can least imagine. However, I must confess that the biggest fear that kept coming to my mind as I wrote this book is that people will not believe that God is able to turn their mess into a message like He did for the six characters discussed in this book. This is the lie that the enemy will try to put in your mind. I, therefore, feel that this book would be incomplete were I not to address this fear.

The first fundamental issue that you will have to deal with in regards to this lie of the devil is whether you are worthy of God's love and attention. In other words, the devil will have you question the authenticity of God's love for you and whether He cares enough to turn your mess into a message. His question might be, "Who do you think you are for God to take His time and change your mess into a message like He did for the woman at the well, Jabez, Zacchaeus, Ruth, the thief on the cross, and Jephthah?"

A few years ago, one of my favorite Christian music groups, Casting Crowns, produced a hit song titled. "Who Am I?" In the opening verse the lead singer, Mark Hall, asks:

Who am I that the Lord of all the Earth would care to know my name, would care to feel my hurt? Who am I that the Bright and Morning Star, would choose to light the way for my ever-wondering heart?

As one reads Psalm 8:1-9, it appears as though the Psalmist David, after considering the majesty and greatness of God, felt insignificant. He logically analyzed the splendor, glory, majesty, and magnificence of God and could come to no other conclusion in his bewildered state of mind, but to ask the question, "Who am I that You would notice me – a mere mortal man?"

It is crucial for you to understand that from a secular view you could be considered as insignificant. From a materialistic perspective, you are but a portion of matter, a collection of molecules. In other words, you are what you eat. From a psychological perspective, you are a creature formed by heredity and environment – basically who conceived you and where you were conceived determine who you are. From a sociological perspective, everything is determined by a group of collective rules. Using another expression, you are who you hang around with. From a philosophical perspective, you are an animal and it is only your mind that makes you unique from the other animals. Hence, you are what you think. From the existential perspective, you are what you make yourself to be. An existentialist would therefore say, you are what you do. I thank God that even though I know these views, I do not allow them to define who I really am. I know beyond any shadow of doubt that I am who God's Word says I am. I am not important because I have done something great. On the contrary, I am important because God has said that I am, and because He has an important task for me to accomplish that will bring glory and honor to His name.

David, the Psalmist, through his writing of Psalm 8:1-9, shows us how God opened his eyes to three wonderful and life-transforming truths that explain both the intrinsic value of humanity and the awesome majesty of God.

First, David understood that you were specifically created by God. Even though God had set in place a magnificent universe, He took the time to create you. You are God's most marvelous creation. That is why He bothered to create you. This means that you are not an accident. You're not a fluke of nature or a by-product of irresponsible parents. You were handmade by God Himself. God prescribed every single detail of your body. He deliberately chose your race, the color of your skin, your hair, and every other feature. He custom-made you the way He wanted you. That is why when you are in a messy situation, He can't afford to let you remain there and rot. His name, glory, honor, and the well-being of His church are at stake when you are in a messy situation. After all, it was He who created you for His glory, wasn't it? Why should He not be willing to rescue the one He created in His image and likeness and upon whom He has placed His mark of ownership?

The second truth that David discovered concerning you is that God not only created you, He cares about you. He writes in Psalm 8:4, "What is man that you are mindful of him, the son of man that you care for him?" In *The Purpose Driven Life*, Pastor Rick Warren writes, "Why did God do all this? Why did he bother to go to all the trouble of creating a universe for us? Because He is a God of love. This kind of love is difficult to fathom, but it's fundamentally reliable. You were created as a special object of God's love! God made you so He could love you. This is a truth upon which to build your life."[42] The Lord spoke through the Prophet Isaiah to the children of Israel saying, "Listen to me, O house of Jacob, all you who remain of the house of Israel, you whom I have upheld since you were conceived and have carried since your birth. Even to your old age and gray hairs, I am He, I am He who will sustain you. I have made you and I will carry you; I will sustain you and I will rescue you" (Isaiah 46:3-4).

Allow me to break this down even further. Did you know that before you came into this world God cared so much for you that He made this world inhabitable? Before you needed salvation, Jesus was sent to die for you. Before we needed instruction and guidance, He wrote the Bible. Before we walked through the valley of the shadow of death, He offered eternal life. Before your mess could lead to your destruction, He already made a plan to rescue you. As insignificant as the devil may want you to feel, you need to remind him that the God of the universe had only one Son (Jesus Christ) and He sent Him to die for you. He did not die to save the Empire State Building or the most beautiful animal on the earth. He died to save you simply because He wants to turn your mess into a message!

The third and final truth that the Psalmist David discovered was that you have been crowned by God. He wrote in Psalm 8:5-8, "You made him a little lower than the heavenly beings and crowned him with glory and honor. You made him ruler over the works of your hands; you put everything under his feet: all flocks and herds, and the beasts of the field, the birds of the air, and the fish of the sea, all that swim the paths of the seas."

In order to be theologically accurate, I have to point out that this Psalm is first and foremost referring to God's crowning of Adam and Eve

---

42   Warren, Rick. *The Purpose Driven Life*. Zondervan Publishing Company, 2004. p.24

and, by extension, all of humanity (Genesis 1:26). Additionally, Psalm 8 is considered Messianic in nature. In other words, it is specifically speaking about the Son of Man's authority over all the earth (see Hebrews 2:9). But, more than what has already been mentioned, this Psalm speaks to our intrinsic worth as human beings in the eyes of God, how we discover who we really are, and what we are expected to do in light of our value. You need to know that in all of creation, from the microscopic amebas to the mega-ton Apatosaurus, only human beings were created in God's image. While all of creation declares God's glory, only humanity can reflect God's glory. It means that you have been designed by God to reflect His glory. Think about it! If you are in a messy situation, how would you reflect that glory? It is simply by turning your mess into a message that His glory is made known and His praise is sung to the uttermost parts of the earth.

When you find yourself in a messy situation or you are simply struggling in your faith, sit back and reflect like David did. When the enemy comes to bring doubt and you begin to ask yourself, "Who am I that God would think of me?" or, "Who am I that the Lord of all the earth would care to know my name?" When you feel worthless and think that there is no way out, think about the woman at the well in John 4; Jabez in 1 Chronicles 4; Zacchaeus in Luke 19; Ruth; the thief on the cross in Luke 23; and Jephthah in Judges 11. Consider also the words of Psalm 8 when you begin to feel worthless because of the burden of sin, the lies of the devil, or the ridicule of others. Then shake yourself out of that situation. If you can pray, then start praying. If you can sing, start praising God. If you can laugh, start laughing at the devil. If you can shout, start shouting at the devil and remind him that he is a liar and the father of lies. Remind him that God loves you. Remind him that you will not die, but live to declare the glory of the Lord. When you start to do that, your spirit man will arise in you. All of heaven will break loose on your behalf. Angels will start to do battle on your behalf. God the Father will stand up for you and the enemy will have no other option but to flee. It is about time that you realize that you are valuable to God. He will turn your mess into a message simply because He created you in His own glorious image, cares for you with an unrelenting love, and is ready to crown you with glory and honor in the presence of your enemies. It is because of these reasons that your mess is bound to turn into a message if you would only turn it over to Jesus.

BIBLIOGRAPHY

Arndt, William F., and Wilbur, Gingrich F. *A Greek-English Lexicon of the New Testament and Other Early Christian Literature*, 2nd Edition. Chicago, Illinois: The University of Chicago Press, 1979.

Blaiklock, E.M. *Today's Handbook of Bible Characters: A Panorama of Valuable Information on All the Major Men and Women of the Bible, Combining Historical Data with Spiritual Insight.* Minneapolis, Minnesota: Bethany House Publishers, 1979.

Coleman, William L. *Today's Handbook of Bible Times and Customs: Cultural, Social and Political Background on the Land and People of the Bible, Based on all the Recent Archaeological Discoveries.* Minneapolis, Minnesota: Bethany House Publishers, 1984.

'Grief, Fear, Doubt, Panic'—And Guilt, NEWSWEEK, from the magazine issue dated Aug 4, 1969.

Hope, Gabriel. *Royal Steps: Destined for Dignity.* Kentwood, Michigan: Hope Harvest Books, 2008.

Hunter, Charles and Frances. *Don't Limit God: The Story of Gene Lilly.* Houston, Texas: Hunter Ministries Publishing Company, 1976.

Kelley, Earthquake and Stone, Diana. *Bound to Lose Destined to Win.* Cleveland, Tennessee: CopperScroll Publishers, LLC., 2007.

Marshall, Henrietta Elizabeth. *Stories of Robin Hood Told to the Children*. Chapel Hill, North Carolina: Yesterday's Classics, 2005.

Swindoll, Charles R. *Living Above the Level of Mediocrity: A Commitment to Excellence*. Dallas, Texas: Word Publishing, 1987.

Taylor, Ellen Gunderson. *Ruth: A Love Story*. Wheaton, Illinois: Tyndale House Publishers, Inc., 1986.

The Collegeville Pastoral Dictionary of Biblical Theology. Stuhlmeuller, Carroll, General Editor, etc. Collegeville, Minnesota: The Liturgical Press, 1996.

The New Bible Dictionary. Douglas, James Dixon, Organizing Editor. Grand Rapids, Michigan: William B. Eerdmans Publishing Company, 1962.

The NIV Study Bible: New International Version. Barker, Kenneth, General Editor. Grand Rapids, Michigan: Zondervan Bible Publishers, 1985.

The Wycliffe Bible Commentary, Pfeiffer, Charles F. and Harrison, Everett F., Editors. 16th edition. Chicago, Illinois: Moody Press, 1990.

Tyndale New Testament Commentaries, LUKE, Revised Edition. Morris, Canon Leon, General Editor. Grand Rapids, Michigan: William B. Eerdmans Publishing Company, 1988.

Vine, William Edwin. *The Expanded Vine's Expository Dictionary of New Testament Words*. Kohlenberger, John R. III, Editor. Minneapolis, Minnesota: Bethany House Publishers, 1984.

Warren, Rick. *The Purpose Driven Life*. Grand Rapids, Michigan: Zondervan Publishing Company, 2004.

Whitburn, Joel. *The Billboard Book of Top 40 Hits*. 6th edition. New York, N.Y.: Billboard Book, 1996.

Zerwick, Max, S.J. *A Grammatical Analysis of the Greek New Testament*, Unabridged, 3rd Revised Edition. Translated, revised, and adapted by

Mary Grosvenor, in collaboration with the author. Roma: Editrice Pontificio Instituto Biblico, 1988.

Pedigree. (n.d.). *The American Heritage® Dictionary of the English Language, Fourth Edition*. Retrieved November 02, 2009, from Dictionary.com website: http://dictionary.reference.com/browse/pedigree.

Independence Day: Immortal Words of the Founding Fathers. Infowars, July 4, 2007.
Retrieved March 14, 2010 from http://www.infowars.com/articles/us/july_4th_words_of_founding_fathers.htm.
Give me Liberty, or give me Death! From Wikipedia, the free encyclopedia. Retrieved, December 3, 2009 from http://en.wikipedia.org/wiki/Give_me_Liberty,_or_give_me_Death!

ABOUT THE AUTHOR

 Dr. Josef A. Howard is an Ordained Minister of Bethel World Outreach Ministries International who currently serves as Resident Pastor of Bethel World Outreach Church, Robbinsdale, Minnesota. He heads the credential committee of Bethel World Outreach Ministries International (BWOMI). His primarily responsibility is to ensure that ministers of BWOMI receive the necessary training and preparation required to serve God's people and, as such, supervises the process for licensing and ordination. Dr. Howard is also the Executive Director of the Liberian Ministers Association, a religious, non-profit organization that serves Liberian pastors in Minnesota. He has been privileged to work for the last five years as a chaplain at Regions Hospital in Saint Paul, Minnesota.

Rev. Josef A. Howard earned a Doctor of Philosophy (PhD) in Missiology with emphasis in Leadership Development from Concordia Theological Seminary in Fort Wayne, Indiana, a Master of Divinity in Pastoral Care from Bethel Theological Seminary in Arden Hills, Minnesota, and an advanced certificate in Biblical studies and preaching from the Monrovia Bible Training Center in Liberia, an affiliate of Living Word Missions, Massachusetts. He also holds a diploma in Cross Culture Ministry from Bethany College of Missions in Bloomington, Minnesota.

Additionally, Dr. Howard studied Business Administration and Economics at the University of Liberia, West Africa, and holds a Bachelor of Arts degree in French Studies from Universite Nationale de Cote d'Ivoire.

The author feels called by God as a West African missionary to the United States to help churches understand the richness found in multiculturalism and to explain how churches can overcome the challenges found therein. It is in this regard that he wrote his PhD dissertation on: "Challenges a non-Westerner faces in establishing a multicultural church in the United States." He intends to publish his dissertation into a book to help non-Western missionaries to the United States understand the challenges of planting a multicultural church and to be armed by the Spirit of God with the necessary tools needed to overcome them.

A teacher, preacher, musician, author, conference speaker, chaplain, and trainer on church leadership, church ushering, multiculturalism, church growth, spiritual care-giving and spiritual warfare, Dr. Howard loves the Lord and has dedicated his life to help in the establishment of God's plan and will in the lives of His people and His church. He is of the opinion that nothing is impossible with God. If God has said it, He will surely bring it to pass. It is this message that forms the core of his ministry.

Dr. Howard is married to his lovely and charming wife, Lees Howard, and they have been blessed with three children: Cecil, Caleb, and Marylyn.